THE CONSCIENCE OF
THE KING

Robert Cecil summons the gentleman spy, Henry Gresham, to his deathbed, to give his archenemy one final, deadly case. A bookseller has obtained devastating correspondence between King James I, Robert Carr and Viscount Rochester, Gresham is the one man who can return the letters, saving the monarch from potential scandal. Also in the bookseller's possession are two stolen manuscripts by Shakespeare. Gresham has no cause to realise that he is being used as live bait to draw out a murderous madman, or that he is set to unravel the truth behind the authorship of the greatest plays the world would ever see.

THE CONSCIENCE OF THE KING

The Conscience Of The King

by

Martin Stephen

Magna Large Print Books
Long Preston, North Yorkshire,
BD23 4ND, England.

British Library Cataloguing in Publication Data.

Stephen, Martin
    The conscience of the king.

    A catalogue record of this book is
    available from the British Library

    ISBN   978-0-7505-2678-4

First published in Great Britain in 2003 by Little, Brown

Copyright © Martin Stephen 2003

Cover illustration © Larry Rostant by arrangement with
Little, Brown Book Group Ltd.

The moral right of the author has been asserted

Published in Large Print 2007 by arrangement with
Little, Brown Book Group Limited

Magna Large Print is an imprint of Library Magna Books Ltd.

Printed and bound in Great Britain by
T.J. (International) Ltd., Cornwall, PL28 8RW

The play's the thing
Wherein I'll catch the conscience of the King

Hamlet by William Shakespeare
1601 version, Act 3, Scene 1, 1.47.

For Jenny

ACKNOWLEDGEMENTS

I am extremely grateful to Sonia Land, Ursula Mackenzie and Tara Lawrence for the faith they have placed in Henry Gresham, and in me. Thanks to Lawrence James, Philip Franks, Val McDermid, Jenni Murray, Simon Russell Beale, Graham Seel and Len Rix for all their help and advice, and for Jenny, Neill, Simon and Henry for putting up with me and Henry Gresham. I am grateful to Dr Andrew Stephen for advice on matters medical. I also owe a great deal to Cambridge University Library, the Bodleian Library, Oxford, the John Rylands Library, the University of Manchester, Chetham's Library, Manchester, and Fitzwilliam College, Cambridge. For access to the rarer parts of King's College Chapel, Cambridge, I am indebted to the Provost and Fellows of King's, the Domus Bursar and Mr John Boulter.

AUTHOR'S NOTE

Historical notes on the characters mentioned in this work of fiction can be found at the end of the book.

Sir Francis Walsingham created what was arguably the largest and most sophisticated espionage network in all of Europe for Queen Elizabeth I, funded largely out of his own pocket. He recruited a number of poets and dramatists to act as couriers or spies, most notably Christopher Marlowe and Anthony Munday. Walsingham's spies frequently used aliases: Anthony Munday, for example, used the name George Grimes. 'William Hall' is mentioned several times as an agent, but nothing is known about him except his name and that many of the people he is known to have been involved with were acquaintances of William Shakespeare. Thomas Thorpe published an edition of Shakespeare's sonnets in 1609 in which he states that 'Mr W.H.' is the 'only begetter of these ensuing sonnets'. The word which follows 'Mr W.H.', with an extended space, is 'All'.

'A significant feature of Shakespeare's life history ... is that virtually all the records that would have referred to him have mysteriously vanished... The suspicion is that someone or some agency, backed by the resources of Government, has at some early period 'weeded' the archives and suppressed documents with any bearing on William Shakespeare...'

John Mitchell, *Who Wrote Shakespeare?*

'The mystery of William Shakespeare is thus exacerbated. If the Stratford Shakespeare *was* the great playwright, how did no one in his home town appear to know? No one writes about him or speaks of him as a dramatist, his tomb honours him merely as a grain dealer, and his epitaph reads simply 'gent'. Why is there no indication of his learning? There is no record of his education, he apparently buys no books, nor does he leave any in his will... Why does he leave no writings? There are no letters, diaries or mere jottings that survive... What of his poems, plays or manuscripts? None have surfaced, nor are they ever mentioned in Elizabethan Stratford... He only signs his name to documents drawn up by others...'

Graham Phillips and Martin Keatman,
The Shakespeare Conspiracy

'Shakespeare as a person seems to have left no literary impression on anyone... In his will Shakespeare left detailed instructions but he mentioned no manuscripts, no books owned or borrowed, no rights to published plays or poems... Geniuses such as Mozart or Michelangelo arouse great feelings during their lives and at their deaths. The man from Stratford aroused none. An inferior playwright Francis Beaumont, who also died in 1616, was buried at Westminster Abbey, but no such public honour was accorded William of Stratford until 1740'

Kevin Gilvary, '*Twelfth Night*', '*A Midsummer Night's Dream*' and the '*Earl of Oxford*'

PROLOGUE

30th May, 1593
Deptford, South London

'A great reckoning in a little room...'
    SHAKESPEARE, *As You Like It*

'Time for you to die.' Poley's voice was quiet, menacing.

The river by Deptford was stained a dark red-brown. The slaughterhouses were at work. They cut channels in the hard floors to take the blood of the slaughtered animals and feed it out to the waiting Thames. The river was foul enough anyway, carrying all London's sludge with it, and on killing days the blood, shit and piss of the terrified beasts stained it an even deeper brown. The noise of the animals, sensing their own death and the death of their kind, was terrible, shrieks and roars that could have come from the mouth of Hell. However deep they dug the channels, the blood seemed to splash against the timbers of the walls and rot them quicker than the wettest winter.

'*I* will decide when it is time.' Marlowe flung himself on the window seat. Christopher Marlowe. Kit Marlowe. The greatest, the first and the finest dramatist in England. His extravagantly slashed black velvet doublet was stained, elbows rubbed to a matt sheen where they had rested on

19

tables in so many taverns.

'You no longer decide things. We do. You lost the power to decide anything when you became unsafe.' Poley spoke as calmly as ever, but with the slightest edge to his voice. 'You had a bargain. You did as you were told and you kept silent. As all of us do. But you had to speak out, didn't you? You had to make a noise, draw attention to yourself.' There was hatred in Poley's eyes, in his voice. A hatred of weakness. A hatred of men who let their emotions take control.

'Sweet Jesus!' said Marlowe, grinning stupidly. 'Is even the great Master Poley showing signs of strain?' But to die in Deptford, he thought to himself. The heroes and villains he had created in his plays had bestrode heaven and hell, and all that lay between. The poet who had given them life was to die in London's arse-end.

'It's time.' The control in Poley's voice was more frightening than any anger. 'It's time *now*.'

He was right. The agreement was that Marlowe would die in a dispute over the bill for the meal they had shared. The meal had been eaten. It was time for the reckoning.

Marlowe jumped up steady enough. Poley remained seated, watching him, outwardly calm, as emotional as drawn steel. Frizer and Skeres, the hired help, edged back, nervous, eyes flicking between Marlowe and Poley, waiting for orders. Marlowe looked at them and let a thin sneer curl his upper lip. He started to strip off, first the doublet, then the lace collar he had always preferred over the ruff. The poor clothes lay on the table waiting for him, the jerkin stained and

20

stinking of sweat.

They had supposed they would find a young sailor to kill for the body that a simple local Justice would accept as being that of Christopher Marlowe. Bodies of all sorts were cheap in Deptford, and souls even cheaper. Then providence had intervened. They had decided to hang a mad Puritan, the writer of the infamous Marprelate tracts, four miles up the road at St Thomas-a-Watering only yesterday evening. John Penry was a year older than Marlowe and, ironically, also a Cambridge man. Some money to a sexton who cared little where a hanged man was buried had emptied the cheap coffin, and a ruff in place of Marlowe's lace collar would hide the rope marks well enough. It was better than the sailor. They would have had to have got him drunk, which would have been easy, and then separate him from his friends, which would have been harder. True no one would miss another dead seaman. But they would miss someone already dead even less, and a body whose fingers had the dark stains of ink on them and were untroubled by hauling ropes for a living was an unexpected bonus.

The act of putting on the filthy clothes sobered Marlowe. The purse was heavy, and he half waited for an attack from Poley and the two other men. It did not come. They would try to kill him, of course, despite their agreement and the bond struck with Henry Gresham. Poley had not lived and prospered as long as he had in England's dark underworld by being stupid. He wouldn't risk doing it in the house. There would be one or two men waiting on Deptford Strand, Marlowe thought, or, even better, one of the sailors on board the brig Poley knew he was to sail on with the tide. Well, sweet Robin Poley was in for some shocks of his own.

Marlowe nodded to the men. Poley stepped out of the door, and returned a minute or so later.

'It's clear,' was all he said. The less Poley spoke, the more dangerous he was.

Marlowe felt stupid in his stained working-man's clothes. He wanted to make a grand exit, like one of the characters in his plays, or speak an epilogue to his own life. What were the lines he had written for Faustus?

Cut the branch that might have grown full straight,
And burned is Apollo's laurel bough

Instead, all he could think of was a line from the same play:

Why, this is Hell, nor am I out of it

The three watchers saw nothing of Marlowe's inner turmoil. One moment he was standing by the low wooden door, silent, unmoving, the next he was gone into the deepening light of the evening. It was the last any of them would see of him. In a few moments they would start the ruckus that would lead to the supposed death of Christopher Marlowe, and poor John Penry's body, already suitably mutilated, would be laid out and buried in an unmarked grave in Marlowe's name.

1

May, 1612
The Globe Theatre, Bankside, London

'Murder most foul'
SHAKESPEARE, *Hamlet*

The blue of the sky was almost painful to the eyes. The thin pall of smoke hanging over Bankside was pungent, the smell of unseasoned wood, the sap bubbling and boiling and snapping at the nose, mingling with the heavier, earthier stench of sea coal. The smoke had given up trying to dampen the warmth of the sun, roasting the men and women still for the most part dressed in heavy, winterish woollens that exuded the thick, musty smell of a long winter.

Five hundred years ago, the Norman conquerors had set down the forbidding bulk of the Tower of London to control men's bodies and the mass of St Paul's Cathedral to control their minds. Both still squatted over London's citizens, a raw glare of power. Yet now there was a new power afoot, uncontrolled, anarchic, threatening. The theatre had come to London.

They came to the play in their thousands. Shipwrights and sailors from St Dunstan's; weavers and cobblers from St Giles Cripplegate; the silk weavers from Allhallows Honey Lane. From the

23

fine, high-timbered merchant's houses to the acrid stench of the hatmakers' workshop, through the narrow streets where the shrieks and cries of the vendors seemed to overwhelm the ears, they flocked over London Bridge or called out from the landing stages – *'Westward Ho!'* *'Eastward Ho!'* – to be ferried across the Thames. The boats buzzed and flicked around the jetties like flies to horse dung.

The flag flew above The Globe theatre, its sides high to wind and weather. It was a packed house. The timbers cracked and spat like an old man roused from slumber by his family.

'Like an old woman, isn't she?' John Hemminge was one of the founders of the company. 'All the paint and gilt in the world can't cover up her cracks!'

The Actor listened and smiled despite his sickness. He loved The Globe. He had been there on that famous night eleven years ago when the players had taken down the timbers of The Theatre plank by plank and seen them off in a string of wagons and then boats across the river to build The Globe. The Lord Chamberlain's Men, the finest troupe of actors in the realm, had not owned the land on which The Theatre sat, but they had ownership of its timbers. The bastard Alleyn, who owned the site, had threatened to foreclose on them. So they had taken what was their own and moved it piece by piece over the river to make their new home: The Globe.

'Don't watch too long, old friend.' Hemminge spoke softly to the Actor. 'Watch too long and you might start to think we have any real importance.'

Thousands flocked to see them play. They had kings and admirals as their patrons. They stood in the sunshine of public adoration and fame. Yet, thought the Actor, the players were little more than piss and shit in the eyes of the power brokers. At best they were seen as popinjays with no breeding. At worst they were considered seditious, riotous drunkards. Those in power detested most of all their capacity to arouse deep emotions in their audiences. What had a noble lord said recently of them? 'Of no more worth than a common beggar.'

The newer, younger members of the company groaned and grumbled, affecting a distaste for the cramped and crammed hordes filling the playhouse. 'Oh God!' one of them murmured as he wafted by, scented handkerchief held to costumed lips, 'so very many of the poorer sort! This is so *vulgar.*'

Hemminge exploded, rounding on the new recruit. 'And what's *vulgar* about good people wanting to see us perform? Stick your vulgarity up your arse! This *vulgarity* is what we exist for. *Two and a half thousand people* out there, two and a half thousand people who've paid to see us perform! D'you hear, young 'un? There's fewer people at a king's funeral!'

The handkerchief wondered whether to have a tantrum, remembered who he was talking to and bowed instead. He felt the excitement. The Actor could see it in the boy's face and in his body as he walked away. They all did.

'We've spoilt them, haven't we, these young fops?' John Hemminge grabbed a cheap stool, a long-forgotten prop from a play, and sat opposite the Actor. 'Let them forget their meat and drink, forget where they really come from. They've had it on a plate; never had to fight, as we did.'

Too many indoor performances, the older ones said, either at Court or in the new theatre at Blackfriars.

'What about this new play?' asked Hemminge after a moment's pause, patting the pocket specially put into his doublet to hold his pipe. 'This lost manuscript. By Marlowe.'

The Actor felt the band of pain tighten across his brow. 'Steer clear of it, John,' he said. 'Well clear of it. Marlowe was trouble when he was alive, and people like him are trouble when they're dead. God knows what he knew. If he's put half of it into this damned play no one appears to have seen, I dread to think what the consequences will be. The last thing this company needs is the government down their throats after a riot. Can you imagine? They say this mysterious manuscript has the King as a sodomite and his favourite as Satan.'

'Strange, isn't it?' mused Hemminge, contentedly drawing the foul smoke down into his lungs and making a small 'o' of his mouth as he gently exhaled it, 'how Marlowe could be so prescient as to write a play about a sodomite king and an anti-Christ favourite? With Queen Elizabeth still on the throne when he died and six years – was it six? – to go before good King James took over? Remarkable.' The smoke rose slowly until the air, agitated by the vast crowd, caught and dispersed it. The two men's eyes locked for a moment. 'They do say it's very, very powerful. A masterpiece, they say, those few as are meant to have seen it. Better than anything anyone else has done...' A thin smile crossed Hemminge's face as he mused, outwardly at peace with the world and his pipe.

The sweeping tide of nausea came on the Actor again, as if his lips and nose had been sealed. The thin, bitter vomit rose in his throat, burning as it cascaded on to his tongue. Thank God he had not thrown up, in front of them all.

'Are you ... well?' asked John, always sensitive despite his bluster, always his friend.

'No,' the Actor said simply, 'not well. Not well at all.' Neither in body nor in mind, he added silently. Not for some months now. He paused, swallowed, felt the beads of sweat break out across his forehead. 'It's this same sickness, the one I told you about before. It doesn't go away.'

'Can you play?'

'There's no option. I have to.'

'Perhaps not. I think one of your parts turned up an hour ago, pleading for work. Old Ben Thomas, remember him? We sacked him for drunkenness – two years ago, was it? A bit player, but good enough when he works at it. Well, he's out there, sober for once, and he knows the play.' John Hemminge looked down at the Actor, more worried than he tried to show. 'Take a rest. You look as if you need it. And Ben certainly needs the work.'

'Will you ask him? And thank you,' the Actor replied.

'Yes, of course,' said John, throwing the words back over his shoulder as he strode purposefully away. 'Provided *you* pay him!'

Hemminge went off to the back room where the actors were gathering, and where Old Ben had gone to scrounge whatever food, coin and drink his old companions might give him. The parts were easy, undemanding, thought the Actor. Rather demeaning, actually. What they revealed was that the Actor was not really a very good actor at all. Well, he had made Ben's day at least.

The boy came round, pasting up details of the plot backstage along with a list of scenes and who was required in each one.

From where he sat the Actor could see out into the Pit and the galleries. The merchants, the doctors, the lawyers and the incessant flood of foreign visitors crammed the galleries, their ladies giggling as they tried to keep decorum while forcing their way up the narrow stairs to the seats. The vendors were moving among the crowd, cheerfully breaking the law by selling their nuts, apples, gingerbread, pears and bottled ale. It was the noise and smell he would always remember. Two thousand and more bodies crammed together: the sweating excitement; the rustle of silks and taffetas from the ladies in the galleries; the shouts of the vendors; the cracking of the nut shells and the clink of glass on glass; the conversations in roars and the conversations in secret whispers; the raw smell of dock tobacco mingling with the stale smell of beer and the tang of garlic. The half hour before a performance to a packed house was better than being drunk, better than sex – it was all life's excitement rolled up into one ball and flung in the face of time. Caught up in it, the Actor even forgot the pain in his gut.

The tension in the air now was palpable. One of the younger players looked as if he were about to be sick. Stage-fright, the Actor thought, and understandable. Where else since Roman times had a man been able to speak in the voice of a poet to thousands of souls gathered before him? It was the power of the gods, the power of kings.

The Actor realised Henry Condell was sitting by him. He had not heard him come, realised it must have been a result of Hemminge tipping his other old friend off that there was something wrong. He and Condell gazed for a moment on the seething mass of humanity waiting to hear their play. Old friends do not always need to speak in order to communicate.

'A bad business, the other night.' It was Henry who broke the silence.

'Bad for us,' the Actor answered, 'and even worse for Tom.' Tom was the porter at The Globe, given his bed and keep there in order to guard it overnight and in the few hours when it was not occupied. He had been found by his young apprentice, his throat slit, two nights previously.

'Why steal two manuscripts only? Why not take the whole lot?' Henry spoke in a musing tone.

Two manuscripts had been found missing from the store where they kept the precious paper. The real text of a play was the most valuable thing a company held, after its costumes. They had paid Tom to protect both.

'Why indeed?' the Actor responded as his heart jolted. He knew why. And not even one of his oldest friends could be allowed to share in the

29

secret. He had brought death to old Tom. Was he to murder his oldest friends as well by telling them a truth they did not need to know?

'And then all this fuss about Marlowe's lost play... When ever has there been such fuss about manuscripts?' Henry looked into the Actor's eyes. There was no response.

The trumpet blew for the last time. As much of a hush as ever fell over an audience at The Globe dropped down on them. They opened.

'Who's there?'

'Nay, answer me. Stand and unfold yourself!'

Hamlet was still one of the great attractions, old as it was. And even greater with Burbage in the lead. The audience were moved in a moment from an English summer to the freezing battlements of Elsinore, moved by words alone. Two frightened men on guard, terrified by a ghost. It shut the crowd up like a finger snap. They were off and away.

The Actor had fallen asleep for a while, something he noted he often did after the sickness came upon him, and woke with a start. In the play-within-the-play Old Hamlet, played by Ben in place of the Actor, was about to have poison poured in his ear. Lucianus, the poisoner, flourished the bottle with much evil gesturing and grimaces. Strange, the Actor thought, it was a different bottle. His usual prop was a nasty green thing, its colour screaming something wicked. This time Lucianus had an expensive blue bottle, rather elegant in fact. He poured the poison into Old Hamlet's ear.

The Actor had always hated this part. Whatever

30

he did, the fluid in the bottle was cold, and he could never persuade the others to leave the bottle empty and mime it. It had become something of a joke within the company. When the cold water hit his inner ear he always jerked convulsively with the shock. It was no bad thing, of course. As the stuff was meant to kill him he would have to jerk up and down anyway.

'Ben's going overboard on this one, isn't he?' Condell had drifted back to the Actor's side. Old Hamlet was throwing huge spasms, hurling himself around on the bed with gasps and muffled shrieks of heart-breaking proportions.

What a pity, thought the Actor. All that effort from Ben for no reward. The play was broken up in chaos just after the moment of the poisoning, the real King rising in guilt and anger and storming out. With Hamlet mouthing off and the King just about to ruin the party, no one would have time to look at an old actor going way over the top in a death scene no one was interested in anyway. Ben was wasting his energies, even to the white froth he had managed to make come from his lips.

Something was wrong.

The Actor could sense it, even on the sidelines. The actors on stage had picked up a signal, the tremor that goes round live performers when things start to go wrong. Horatio's eyes were flickering backwards and forwards, Hamlet ill at ease and muffing some of his lines. The King, Claudius, had risen to his feet in uncontrollable anger. The whole assembly – courtiers, actors – should have splintered from the stage in apparent chaos.

Old Ben's body was still on the stage.

'Bloody hell!' said Condell. 'Sodding bloody buggering fucking hell! *Why doesn't he get up and go?*'

You never left a body on the stage. It was the golden rule. It spoilt it if the audience saw a character they had just been told was dead suddenly get up and walk off before the next scene. It wasn't as if they could draw a curtain over the stage. Yet this was different. The audience knew that the body in the play-within-the-play was an actor's, had not really died. He was expected to run off with his tail between his legs, realising the actors had caused offence. Yet Ben lay there, stiff, unmoving.

They were seconds away from the audience realising something had gone tragically wrong. Ben lay flat out on the bed, eyes agape and mouth open, a thin line of dribble from his lips over his chin.

'I do believe,' said Condell, in a tone of hushed disbelief, 'that the stupid old bastard has gone and died on us.'

The Actor turned to Condell. He had only half-heard. 'It's all over,' he said sadly.

The great Burbage, playing Hamlet, had gone glassy-eyed and had lost the plot completely. The line should have been: *'O good Horatio, I'll take the Ghost's word for a thousand pound!'* Instead, Burbage started to gabble complete nonsense, *'For thou dost know, O Damon dear...'*

'Damon? *Damon!* Who the fuck's Damon when he's at home?' Condell was incandescent.

This realm dismantled was
Of Jove himself; and now reigns here
A very, very...

There was an appalling pause...
'*Paiock!*'
'Oh sweet Jesus!' moaned Condell, wringing his hair. 'What's he doing?'
'He's regressed,' said the Actor. 'Don't you remember? He's mangling lines from that monstrous load of old garbage we did years ago – *Gorboduck*, wasn't it? – and it was bad enough then.'
On stage, Horatio turned to Hamlet, a look of total scorn on his face. '*You might have rhymed...*' he said tersely.
Horatio saved the day, with no help at all from Hamlet. He motioned firmly to one of the actors off stage and together they draped Old Ben over their shoulders. Never explain. Never apologise. If you make it look as if you meant it, the audience will believe you. It was a basic rule.
They dumped the body by the Actor's feet. He gazed into the staring eyes of Old Ben and a pain like an icicle in his chest clutched his heart. Vaguely he was aware of Hamlet's voice: '*O good Horatio, I'll take the Ghost's word for a thousand pound...*'
Burbage had got it together again. They were back on track. It hardly seemed to matter to the Actor. Old Ben was dead, clearly. Condell bent down to feel in his neck for a pulse, for form's sake. There was nothing.
The Actor smelled something. His hand shot

out, stopping Condell just as his bony fingers were to touch the corpse's flesh.

'Hold it! Don't touch him!'

The smell, that metallic, vinegary stench with an acidic burn to it. He had researched poisons, knew their reality. This was not water that had been poured into Old Ben's ear. Someone had substituted the green bottle with its harmless contents for a sophisticated and expensive poison, the ingredients known to only two or three men in London at most. Someone, carefully and methodically, had sought to murder the actor taking the part of the Player King. Only at the last minute had a different man taken on the role for that one performance. Ben's death was no accident.

Which meant that someone had tried to murder the Actor. Or to be more precise, actor, poet and playwright. Shakespeare. William Shakespeare, the author of this very play, *Hamlet*. William Shakespeare, the actor who had always taken the role of the Player King, the actor who should have been playing it this afternoon except for a last-minute change because he felt sick.

The sickness came upon him again, wave after wave, and did not go away. Cecil, he thought to himself, I must tell Cecil. It had gone too far, gone on far too long.

One moment he was there. The next moment he had gone. In his tension and sickness he failed to take note of the small, cloaked and hooded figure, following him with burning eyes and a strange, high-prancing step.

2

May, 1612
The Merchant's House,
Trumpington, near Cambridge

'There was given me a thorn in the flesh, the messenger of Satan to buffet me.'
                    THE KING JAMES BIBLE

Henry Gresham sat in the great high-backed chair, looking out through the tall mullioned window over the East Anglian meadows. For a few moments he was at peace, the sardonic smile gone from his face, features relaxed, the book lying almost unnoticed in his lap. The smells of early summer wafted across the Great Hall, grass and turned earth mingling with the faint smell of smoke from garden fires.

He felt extraordinarily calm. He had risen early that morning, noting the still-warm other half of the bed. For years Jane, now his wife, had always managed by some alchemy to rise before he did, and grant him the space to re-enter the world in private.

In private, that is, except for the figure of Mannion. If the one certainty in Gresham's life was that Jane's slim, warm body would be gone from his bed when he awoke, the other was that Mannion, that immense hulk of a man, would drift in silently to the room almost as soon as Gresham's feet touched the floor, towel in hand, ready to guide his master to the adjoining room where the bath had already been filled. This morning he had rejected the ritual, putting on instead a rough country jerkin and trews over his clean linen, stuffing a simple cap on his head and walking out past the startled servants wiping the sleep from their eyes as they came to terms with their own world. He had strode out of the house, lungs taking in great gasps of the still, chill morning air. Mannion, with a wistful eye back at the house and breakfast, had followed him in silence. He knew where Gresham would be going. It had to be Excalibur's pool.

Gresham had called it that when he bought the house. If ever there was a pool from which an enchanted hand might bring Excalibur, this was it; a bend in the river channelled out by the years into almost the size of a small lake, the water deep in history, cool and pure.

Mannion sniffed as Gresham stripped off and prepared to dive into the pool. Gresham heard it, as he was meant to. He turned to his body-servant, grinning, stark naked in the still-cold morning air.

'This is a magical place! An enchanted place! Can't you feel it, old man?'

'Funny how you can miss these things,' Mannion replied in a tone that did not imply any great respect for magic or enchantment. 'I thought it was just cold and damp.'

'Have you no imagination?' Gresham half shouted as he prepared to dive in to the darkness of the pool, thin strands of early morning mist still clinging to its luminous surface.

'No,' said Mannion, at least able to close that one up without further discussion. 'And if I did have, you can be sure neither of us'd be standing here catching our deaths this morning!'

Gresham pulled back, aborting his dive, interested.

'And how do you reckon that?'

'Because it's your so-called imagination that's got you into most of the scrapes that my lack of it has helped pull you out of. Now are you going to dive in, or are we both going to die of your imagination?'

Not for the first time, Gresham reflected that it was usually a bad thing to engage the servants in conversation before breakfast. He gasped as the cold river water bit benignly into his flesh. Mannion was waiting with the towel as he climbed out, dripping, on to the grassy bank. Mannion noted with approval, as he always did, the firmness of Gresham's body, the muscle under just the right layer of flesh. In the cold, patches of Gresham's skin, all down his right side, had turned just the slightest shade paler than the rest of his flesh. If Mannion remembered holding Gresham in his arms for weeks on end, or Gresham his screaming for release from his agony when the powder had burned all that side of his body, then neither said anything. They did not need words in order to communicate.

They walked back in companionable silence to The Merchant's House. Medieval in its origins, it had once been little more than a Great Hall with a kitchen attached. Extended and added to over two hundred years, Gresham could feel the heat of the house extend towards him like outstretched arms. He found it difficult to explain its magic, but he knew it was centred in the Great Hall. Once, in a different age, whole families and their retainers had lived, squabbled and loved in this Hall, with only the kitchens, store houses and rooms for the master and mistress separated off. Now, with its tapestries and fantastic gilded and beamed roof, the Great Hall was simply the largest room at the centre of a complex of corridors, levels and parlours, a positive industry of a house, the noises of which Gresham could perpetually hear faintly in the background. Summer was truly in the air, and there was a sense of reawakening in all the subdued sounds around him, a stirring of limbs aching from the winter. Yet the Great Hall seemed almost impervious to this tumult. In its time it had seen and hosted all that human life could offer. It was called The Merchant's House, but Gresham guessed some rich merchant had bought it from the nobility who had first built it and then fallen on hard times, or perhaps even fallen on the executioner's block. No merchant would have built that Hall. Its confidence was the confidence of a blood-line, not of earned money.

His children had come in through the door at the other end of the Hall, talking quietly to each other. The room gleamed, rich with the shine and smell of polish. Gresham felt an irritation, and half rose to banish them from the formal room of the great house, the room that was his to be alone in whenever and howsoever he required it. This was an adult room, not a nursery. Then he fell back, unseen, as he caught the words of their conversation.

'Sssh!' It was Walter, six this year and the older of the two, who happened to be making the most noise. 'If they hear us they'll make us leave!'

'Why will they make us leave?' That was the small, piping voice of Anna, rising five. Learning to speak extraordinarily early, she had always done so with perfect clarity.

'Because adults do that sort of thing.'

'Then are adults not very clever?'

'I ... I ... I don't know!' said an exasperated Walter. 'Let's get on with the game.'

Gresham relaxed back into his chair, grinning, still hidden from his two children. Now there was the subject of his next academic work, he thought. Man, the dominant species, brought to a grinding halt by the seventh rib asking a sensible question. And what was Man's answer? 'I don't know! Let's get on with the game!' How many men had Gresham known who treated the deadly serious business of life as simply a game? The only difference between Gresham and other men was that he had learned long ago that there was no answer, that life was indeed a game and survival its only victory.

The game in this instance, or so it appeared, consisted of skipping the length of the vast table centred in the Hall and placing something a few feet past its end, itself only a few feet from the back of Gresham's chair. Feeling increasingly like a naughty child himself, Gresham looked round to catch sight of what his daughter had laid on the floor.

Good God. It was a bum roll. Or two bum rolls, to be precise. These were the padded half-hoops that a woman wore resting on her bottom to exaggerate the size of her hips and the narrowness of her waist, and to put a barrier between the flesh and the steel wires that extended her skirt out to the ludicrous lengths required by Court fashion. There would be hell to pay when their loss was discovered.

The game quickly became clear. Walter and Anna each had a packed leather ball. Underneath the table was a narrow tunnel formed by the extravagantly backed oak chairs tucked under it. Bowling the ball under the entire length of the table so that it emerged to rest in the centre of one of the bum rolls acquired top points. Bowling the ball so that it hit the end of the bum roll meant no points. A few points were scored for clearing the table but not reaching the embrace of the bum roll.

The temptation was too much.

'Can I play?' asked Gresham, standing up.

Children were meant to doff their caps to their father after his breakfast, ask him to pray for them and invite his formal blessing. Formal. Restrained. Fathers did not romp with their children on the floor.

But it was a good game, and he did want to play.

His two children, ludicrously small now that he was upright, jumped back as he spoke but calmed

40

immediately as they recognised their father.

'Do you ... do you ... do you mind us being here, Father?'

It was Walter, the brave little soldier standing in front of his officer, always unsure of what erratic authority would decree yet wanting so much to get it right.

'Of course I do!' said Gresham firmly. 'You've disturbed my peace and quiet and you've no right to be here.'

Interesting, he thought, most children's faces would have fallen at that. His children were too young to control all their muscles. Both flickered, and blinked, but their control at what must have seemed disaster in their tiny lives was remarkable. Both stood straight before him. Unwilling to demand more of their courage, he spoke again.

'But then again, this looks a good game, and the least you can do if you've disturbed me is let me play it too.'

They smiled then, shy little smiles. Trust and fear, thought Gresham, and some affection. Three of the ingredients that make a fine commander. Am I treating my children like soldiers under my command?

If he was, one soldier kept a lawyer in the barracks.

'Your arms are bigger than ours,' said Gresham's daughter. 'You must have a forfeit!'

Where had she learned to speak like that at her tender age? Those huge, dark eyes; the thin, wiry little body; the intensity and the control in the voice. In a moment Gresham was rushed back to his first meeting with her mother, Jane. A bastard

41

girl in a godforsaken village, beaten to perdition by a vicious stepfather, demanding that the gentleman pay a forfeit because he had blinked before she did.

He blinked now, and saw his daughter before him again. Yet as it had always been with her mother, he felt a strange, defenceless feeling overwhelm him. She was very like Jane.

He became businesslike. Fathers should be formal, precise and definite with their children. In a very short space of time it was agreed that he should have a five-point handicap on a match of six throws. He had argued for three points, his children for ten, and they had compromised at five. His children forgot who he was as he totally threw away the first ball, hitting the leg of the third chair along.

'Damn!' he said, engrossed, then looked round with a guilty start. Walter and Anna pretended they had not heard him. Walter landed his neatly within the circumference of the bum roll and Anna lodged her ball just outside of it.

When Lady Jane Gresham entered the Hall, with Mannion beside her, it was to find her husband, Sir Henry Gresham, kneeling on the floor in peasant's jerkin and trews, beating it with his fists and yelling in mock horror that he had lost to devilry and witchcraft. Walter and Anna were dancing round him, alternately shrieking, 'We won! We won!' and trying to hug him to say thank you for the fact that he could be so silly.

Jane had seen Gresham kill a man by cleaving his head in half with a boat axe, an exultant grin on his face as his teeth drew back over his lips.

He had consigned men to torture, had himself been strapped to the rack. She knew he could be without pity or remorse for those who threatened him, or her. And here he was, treating his children as if they were the most fragile alabaster.

The children saw their mother and rushed towards her, all decorum forgotten. In a trice they were wrapped round her.

'Mummy, Mummy, Father came and we thought he was angry but he played with us and we won...'

Jane was dressed plainly, to manage the house and her children rather than to impress at Court. Nonetheless, every lady painting and corseting at Court would have given their souls to look as she did. The body was straight as an arrow, the complexion clear, the legs as long as heaven and the breasts the reward for having made the journey. Her head was chiselled and her face extraordinary. Its classical beauty was simplicity itself, yet it flickered and changed and flashed a different reality every second. The eyes. It was always the eyes with her, almost black but with a strange sparkle to them and the same primeval depth as the pool that Henry Gresham had dived into this morning.

'Good morning, my lord,' said Jane, managing to manifest total control, exasperation and a mild, irritated affection all at the same time. 'I thought I had only two children in my care. Now it seems I have three.'

Gresham stood up. 'Madam,' he announced, standing to his full height, 'I must make formal complaint regarding your motherhood.'

The two children disengaged from their mother and stood back, alarmed.

'Sir Henry!' replied Jane, sweeping to her full dignity, 'I am appalled. How may I have failed in my sacred duty to your heirs?'

'You have failed, my lady,' replied Gresham in the most sonorous tones he could muster, 'in that you have had the temerity to bring into this world two young striplings,' he glowered at his children with such severity that they fell back, 'who have managed to beat me fair and square at bowling!'

With that, he flung out his arms and his children ran in glee to their embrace.

'Take these young hounds outside,' Gresham said to Mannion after a moment, gazing swiftly at Jane who nodded imperceptibly, 'and give them some exercise, so they learn to leave their father undisturbed and, of course, to let him win.'

Mannion, like a vast and ragged hen, gathered the two chickens under his arms and led them off, chattering happily. He would walk them for an hour or more through the woods, as he had done with Gresham when he was a child, pointing out to them the different notes of the birds and the names of the wild flowers. They would know how the other birds fell silent when a hawk was in the wood, spot the patches of water where the fish were to be found in the river and learn which leaf to rub on a nettle sting.

'They're good children,' Gresham said when they were alone.

'Well, I'm glad,' said Jane. 'It'd be a little difficult to put them back from whence they came if you didn't like them.' They talked for a while, the tittle-

44

tattle of houses and servants. There was no mention of the sadness that joined them, the memory of the baby who had been born dead. The baby who had broken the fragile cycle of Jane's fertility. There would be no more children born to Sir Henry and Lady Gresham.

Was he finally calming down, this husband of hers? Jane wondered. With a king secure on his throne, a brilliant heir to the Crown and the Catholics vanquished, would he cease to be Henry Gresham the soldier and spy she had always known? Would he increasingly be taken over by the College he had refounded, and become Sir Henry Gresham the gentleman and the academic? A part of her soul yearned for it to be so. The other, stronger part told her the truth. Yet for a moment she allowed herself to gaze on Gresham, slightly dishevelled, seemingly at peace with himself.

It did not, could not last. It was late in the afternoon, the rooks and the men in the fields starting to head home, when they heard the sound of a tired horse, and a beating at their door.

Cecil's messenger. Robert Cecil, First Earl of Salisbury. Lord Treasurer and Chief Secretary to His Royal Highness King James I of England and Scotland. Cecil hated Gresham with the malice of acid on steel. It was a feeling returned with interest by Gresham. Yet each needed the other, a poisoned symbiosis that grappled both to its breast. Cecil's messengers had summoned Gresham countless times, always the harbinger of potential death and destruction, always the guarantor of trouble, and always, for some reason, coming just before or after nightfall.

'Perhaps,' said Jane caustically, cynicism the first cover she could find for her growing fear, 'he lies waiting outside for the last two or three hours of daylight, so as to make an entrance?'

Cecil was dying, they both knew. Those who had seen him said he stank and was rotting from within, his thin limbs no longer able to support him and racking him with pain. Jane had not expected this last summons. The fact of its coming from a man so nearly dead chilled her to her bones, made this last call from Gresham's old enemy the most terrifying of them all.

The messenger's name was Nicholas Heaton. Gresham took care to know these things. He was muddied enough, almost as big as Mannion, sweat-stained and stinking from his ride. His hair was thinning on top, though he tried to cover it with long, lank strands plastered down over the bald patch on his pate. As if to compensate for the lack of hair on his head, he wore a huge, florid moustache that extended in two luxuriant curls beyond the side of his face. It would have been ludicrous were it not for the almost palpable sense of threat the man emanated.

Heaton managed the merest nod of a bow to Gresham.

'My master is dying. He requests that you might spare time from your academic pursuits to visit him on his way to Bath. He has urgent need of speech with you.'

A man soon to be out of a job might be expected to show more respect. Gresham had too much self-respect of his own to allow Heaton's

46

insubordination to get beneath his skin, yet he was intrigued.

'And after his death, what fate befalls you, Master Heaton?'

'My master has arranged for me to transfer my service. To the King.' There was pride in his voice, and arrogance.

'I'm delighted for the both of you,' said Gresham with an unctuous sincerity that only a liar could muster. Suddenly his tone cut the air as a razor through soft flesh: 'Take care. Those who rise to greater heights have far further to fall.' Only much later was Gresham to realise the appalling irony of his words. 'As for your present and still-living master, I'll come. I've always come, haven't I? Tell him so. Where do we meet?'

'He's left Theobalds to go to Bath. Some of his physicians believe there'll be a relief from his pain there, in the waters. The pain is constant, and agonising. You should be warned, Sir Henry. My master is not as he was.'

'Well, that's good news at least,' said Gresham briskly. 'He couldn't be any worse, and perhaps he's improved.'

They did not offer Master Nicholas Heaton lodging, and he did not ask.

'Will you ride tonight?' Jane asked, seeing the nervous energy beginning to flow through Gresham.

'It might be wise. If Cecil's as ill as his messenger says he is—'

'Please. We know what this summons means. Cecil's never invited you into anything other than mortal danger. Tonight, stay with me. Let's

47

remember who we are.'

Gresham half turned towards the door. Mannion was standing there, blocking it. No words were spoken.

Gresham drew himself up to his full height, arms akimbo.

'Am I the lord and master of this house? Do I have authority over my wife and my servants?'

Jane dropped her eyes, her shoulders sagging slightly. Her normal spirit seemed to have been sucked out of her by the messenger and all that he stood for. She could cope with Gresham. Sometimes it was his life that overwhelmed her. She gave a slight curtsey, an almost involuntary reversion to a childish state. His heart went out to her in a fierce bite of love. So strong. So vulnerable.

'You know that I'm yours,' she replied softly.

Good God, thought Gresham, what must it have cost her fiery spirit to say that? A pang of guilt hit him like a blow to the stomach. Who was he to march like a peacock over those whose only fault was to give him their love? None of it showed on his face. Impassive, he turned to Mannion, who had folded his arms and was stood before the door like Leviathan. 'And you?'

'Yes to the first. You're lord and master of this house. And you've certainly got authority over one of the other two, though I'm damned if I know which one...'

'Do you defy me?' Gresham stuck his chin in the air, glaring at Mannion.

'Only when it matters,' he replied.

'And you?' Gresham turned to Jane.

'I just want you to spend the night with me.'

None of the haughtiness, the icy distance she could muster with a king and the frightening authority she could exert over the servants, was there now. He loved her, he thought, more than he had ever thought he could love anyone.

Gresham looked from one to the other, Jane now looking directly into his eyes. He grinned.

'We ride at dawn for Bath. I sleep the night here. *I* have decided.'

Mannion refrained from winking at Jane. Of course he had decided. Yet not without a little help from his friends.

They were holding hands as they left the room, Mannion noticed. Babies. Babies. And the two people for whom he would cheerfully lay down his life.

3

May, 1612
Bath

'Are all thy conquests, glories, triumphs, spoils,
Shrunk to this little measure?'
SHAKESPEARE, *Julius Caesar*

The sun was hidden behind a grey haze as he mounted his horse at dawn. The mist that had been but thin wisps yesterday was now a blanket, waist high, converting the flat landscape to a world of ghosts.

Was this the last summons to Cecil that Gresham would ever answer? In farewell to his ancient enemy, Gresham rode as never before. The hooves of his horse hit the ground with such force that it was like a hammer to his spine, the mud and earth they flung away from their impact flying up with the force of cannon balls. The wind tugged at his hat and as the leaping, shaking, shattering world ran by his watering eyes he urged the horse on, faster and faster. It was as if his mount knew that summer had come, and felt its strong legs stretch to three times their length, the fine muscle tightening like steel and releasing again with every movement of the insane gallop. For some wild minutes man and horse were as one, invincible, immortal in their speed and shared madness.

It had to end, of course. Gresham was not a man to take pleasure in riding a fine horse to the ground. He allowed the beast to slow down, praised it for its strength and beauty, timing it superbly so that before too long his once fiery mount was ambling along like any farmer's hack. He waited for Mannion, cursing under his breath, to catch up, and grinned at him. Mannion stayed on a horse and with a good seat, but no one in the kingdom could catch a well-mounted Henry Gresham with the devil in him.

Gresham was wealthy enough to have his own horses stabled at stages along the road to London from Cambridge. Each horse was ridden like the one before, so that when Gresham reached London the fine leather of his boots was in tatters, every muscle ached as if a hot iron had been passed over them and he was near dead with exhaustion. He slept for three hours. There were none of his own horses between London and Bath. Rather than trust to those he might find to hire or purchase along the way he took a string of his own animals, knowing that from there on his pace would have to be more seemly. He spurned the coaches that increasingly clogged the muddied roads and brought London traffic to a halt. He was not that old, not yet.

The waters of Bath had been used, so they said, in Roman times and ever after to cure the elderly and the infirm. Some of the Romans seemed never to have left, judging by the presence of the elderly and infirm. The old Abbey dwarfed the town, almost as if by squatting over it its dead hulk took life away from the miserable place. There was an air of decay everywhere. Gresham was used to the stink of towns, but this stench had the tinge of rotting flesh in it. They brushed bugs from their sweating faces as they rode. Even this early in summer, everything in Bath was fly-blown.

Mannion had taken a drumstick from one of the birds they had been served at the last inn and was now devouring it, on horseback. 'Do you want to know what I think? he asked now, a small piece of desiccated meat shooting from his mouth past Gresham's left ear as he spoke.

'You mean you *can* think? I'm not sure I want to go anywhere near your mind if your physical actions in any way reflect its contents. But,' Gresham sighed, 'I expect you'll tell me anyway.'

'In the past he wanted to use you, and didn't mind if you died in the process. Now he's dying, he'll want to use you *provided* you get killed in the process. He'll want to take you along with him to hell. You're the only one who's ever got the best of him.'

Gresham did not challenge the conclusion. Instead, he looked at the population of Bath. 'Do people ever walk in Bath?' he asked, looking round. 'Or do they only hobble, or be carried by servants?'

He was surprised at the address he had been given by Nicholas Heaton. It was grand enough for a successful provincial lawyer but too poor by half for the King's Chief Secretary. He said as much as his knock on the door was answered by an obsequious servant dressed in Cecil's livery.

52

'I wonder at my lord of Salisbury taking such lodgings. Aren't they beneath his usual style?'

'My lord has great pain in any movement. It's necessary for him to be as near to the baths as possible.'

They waited in a dingy room. Its panelling had been brightly painted quite recently, in the current fashion, but the job had been badly done and paint was flaking off already. The hangings had faded almost completely into drab greyness, and only a few vague figures could be discerned among the overwhelming pattern of dust that was all that held them together. The glass in the windows was of poor quality and had a sickly yellow tinge. Everything was coated with filth, and the smell of damp in the room made it stink like something unwashed. Another servant brought in wine. He was fresh-faced, little more than a boy, with eyes wide open to the wonder of the world and his luck in being servant to such a great man.

'Thank you,' said Gresham, whose life had been saved on more than one occasion by a servant who had noticed that Gresham called him by name and treated him as a human being. 'Your name is...?'

The servant halted, on his way out of the room, surprised to be addressed. 'Me, sir? I'm Arthur, sir...' Arthur gazed at Gresham in total awe, unaware that his mouth was hanging open. 'Sir ... sir, forgive me, I...' Arthur was clearly bursting to say something.

'Spit it out, lad,' said Mannion.

Arthur saw a tall, muscled figure dressed from

top to toe in black except for a white collar worked with breathtaking and exquisite skill. The clothes breathed money, despite being almost ostentatious in their lack of ostentation. The body they covered seemed as if it were a coiled spring, ready at any moment to break out. Yet it was the face that Arthur could not take his eyes from, a face of arrogance, of immense strength, of flickering humour yet strange vulnerability – a face that seemed to have all the humours of the world in its angularity.

'Sir ... sir...' Arthur was stuttering. 'What I wanted to know, know more than anything else was ... did you meet Guy Fawkes, as they say you did?'

Gresham looked Arthur straight in the eye. 'Yes, Arthur, I did meet Guy Fawkes. As they say I did.'

Yes, thought Gresham, I did meet Guy Fawkes, a rather decent and honourable man in many respects, certainly more honourable than many of those who hounded him to his death. And I was responsible for stopping his escape, springing a trap upon him and delivering him to a death no animal should endure, administered by your master, Robert Cecil. And by failing to tell the truth about Guy Fawkes, quite deliberately, I helped keep your master in power and a dribbling Scottish homosexual as king. All in all, I did a brilliant job.

'And, sir,' said Arthur, so intent and intense that he forgot to splutter, 'was he as they say? Was he the devil incarnate?'

'Yes, Arthur,' said Gresham solemnly. He felt

54

the mischief in his soul bubble and start to rise. 'He was the devil incarnate. And I tell you what very few other people know, a secret you must vow at all costs to keep to yourself. Do you vow, on your soul and all that you hold holy?'

'I do, sir, I do, I do...' Arthur was transformed by a paroxysm of yearning.

'When he was examined, it was proven that he had a cloven foot!'

There was a moment of extraordinary silence.

'Sir!' said Arthur, standing to attention, real tears in his eyes. 'I shall never tell a soul! And ... thank you!' He rushed from the room.

'Well,' said Mannion, 'that'll be round the servant's hall in five minutes flat. Still, at least you made him leave the jug.' Mannion helped himself. Cecil's wine had always been cat's piss, served in golden goblets, a strange emblem for the man. Mannion would have drunk real cat's piss quite cheerfully if it had been proven to be alcoholic.

There was a noise of carriages outside, in surprisingly short time, and much shouting and apparent confusion. The Earl of Salisbury had made haste back from the baths. He was bustled in to the room in a chair carried by four men, another man by his side.

There was a moment of stunned silence. Cecil was shrouded in blankets, a thin, emaciated version of his former self, shrunken, wizened and dried out. The skin on his face was drawn tight over his skull like a death's head, only the hard, dark eyes recognisably the same as ever. One hand protruded slightly from the blankets, shaking uncontrollably. This was a wreck of a man,

55

thought Gresham, a pitiful caricature of what had once been. A stench of something foul and rotten came from within the blankets. There was scant dignity in death, and what little that there was had been taken away from Robert Cecil. And what good to you is it now, thought Gresham, that you are the First Earl of Salisbury, that you have held power beyond the desire of monarchs? You have no power over this ignominy, this humiliation that leaves the vision of a demented cripple as your memorial.

'Good day, Sir Henry,' said Cecil. The voice was thin, wavering, but still recognisably the same. It reeked with the same insincerity. 'As ever, it is a pleasure to see you.'

'My Lord Salisbury,' said Gresham urbanely. 'And Sir Edward Coke.' He nodded to the figure beside Cecil. 'Not only the normal pleasure, but a pleasure almost doubled.'

Cecil's companion was a surprise. After Cecil himself, Sir Edward Coke was the man Henry Gresham most loathed above all others. Old now – he must be sixty – Coke exuded a youthful energy, a magnetism that all near him felt. Setting himself up as England's leading legal expert, and of ferocious, icy intelligence and application, Coke had been chief prosecutor at the trial of Sir Walter Raleigh. A charade, the trial had turned Raleigh from one of the most hated men in England into a folk hero, by virtue of its palpable unfairness and the dignity with which Raleigh had defended himself. Denying Raleigh any legal representation, Coke had not even allowed him to call his chief accuser as a witness, and had made a mockery out of justice. Every reason for hating lawyers, and for hating men with no principles except their own vainglory, was summed up for Henry Gresham in the figure of Sir Edward Coke. And now both he and Cecil were facing him.

'Have you both had a pleasant day?' asked Gresham solicitously. Cecil was dying in agony. Coke's idea of a pleasant day was finding yet more reason to hate papists, sodomites and his own daughter, not to mention anyone the King needed convicting at short notice. In Gresham's experience, being nice to such people caused them more agonies than anything else.

'I am lowered into the baths, Sir Henry,' said Cecil in a parody of his former voice, but still with a practical, factual tone to it. 'They do it in a strange contraption of a chair they have built specially for me. The ropes snag on occasion, which is not pleasant. My numerous physicians tell me it is important I go no deeper than waist height.'

'Indeed, my lord,' replied Gresham easily. 'I must attempt to be present the next time they hoist you over the watery void, and see if I can cut the rope–'

'My lord. Is this ... impertinence necessary?' Coke spoke with chilling calm.

Cecil turned to Sir Edward Coke with an effort that cost him dear. The lawyer held Cecil's gaze, then only reluctantly dropped his eyes. A tall, forbidding man with a long, oval face, Coke was ill at ease, unhappy and uncertain with this fencing between the two men. He lusted for control, for power, and hated any situation where power

57

seemed to be ceded to others. Coke had become too used to being both judge and jury, Gresham thought.

Cecil produced something that might almost have been a chuckle, with a strange, dry rattle to it.

'Ah, Sir Henry! So droll, as ever. How much I have enjoyed your sense of humour over the years I have known you.'

'Yes,' said Gresham, 'much as the body enjoys the dagger that enters it, or the hare enjoys the hounds.'

'I wonder if it is not time...' Coke's voice was gravelly, sharp, though not pitched at the roar he used in court against those he had decided to condemn. They said he was charming to prisoners in interrogation, turning into a frothing fiend when later he had them in the dock. Cecil held up his hand, the blanket dropping away. Coke swallowed his words, waiting. Gresham looked in horror at Cecil's arm. The skin was discoloured, the flesh almost all wasted away. His lips drawn back over rotten teeth, the gums retreating as if the outgoing tide on a beach, it was clear that even the gesture of holding up a hand for silence had caused Cecil acute pain.

'You think, perhaps, Sir Edward, that if I do not make haste to stop this small talk then I may be dead before we can reach an outcome?'

Coke's self control was enough to resist the sally. 'Of course, such were not my thoughts, my lord.' Outwardly servile, the phrase 'of course' made Coke's comment shiver on the edge of impertinence.

'But you would be wrong to deny it!' Something of the old spirit came back into Cecil's voice. 'You would be right to urge me to make haste, Sir Edward. I command all England, but even I cannot command death.'

No, thought Gresham, though you have commanded enough men to their deaths.

Cecil turned to Gresham, in obvious pain at the exertion. 'Sir Edward is here because he will live on after me. He is a man of power...' Coke drew back, and gave a short bow towards Cecil. His face and posture gave nothing away. 'His power will be necessary to see a certain business through. It is this business that will need your help.'

Now it comes, thought Gresham. The muscles in his face did not move, the colour neither rose nor fell in his skin, the pulse in his neck remained constant. Those outward tricks he knew. Yet inside it was as if a slow-burning fire had burst into full riot of flame.

'Sir Edward, you will please leave us for a short while. And, Sir Henry, perhaps that great ox of a man you carry with you might leave as well.'

Gresham nodded at Mannion, and he slipped out of the room, moving quietly and silently in a manner that belied his bulk. Coke was less happy. He drew himself to his full height, chin jutting forward, hand posed on the hilt of his sword.

'Is this wise, my lord?' The thinly veiled arrogance in Coke's voice was like the flick of a whip across Cecil's words. Yet Cecil's authority held, just.

'We agreed that I would approach Sir Henry with a certain proposal. I wish to do so, in these

59

my last few days on this earth, in private. You will lose no information that you need to know. And you will gratify the whims of an old man to whom you have some cause to be grateful.'

Coke stood for a moment, as if wondering whether to challenge Cecil. Finally he gave a curt nod to Gresham, ruder than no bow at all, and clattered towards the door. He was wearing a sword, probably for no other reason than to show off to the citizens of Bath. Yet he was clearly no swordsman, and like all men who did not understand the weapon they wore he had no knack of controlling it when he moved suddenly. The scabbard swung as Coke wheeled round, and as he reached the door the sword and scabbard jammed across the entrance, bringing him to a sudden halt. The leather of his belt was too strong to tear, but Coke's boots skittered out from under him and he fell forwards to scrabble on the floor. His sword landed at his feet, the hilt towards Gresham.

'I accept your surrender, Sir Edward,' Gresham murmured, 'though I am accustomed to rather more of a fight beforehand...'

Coke's eyes blazed pure hatred. He still favoured the huge ornate ruffs that had been fashionable in Queen Elizabeth's time, and his fall had skewed one side of it so that it hung by his ear, ludicrous. He flung himself to his feet, picked up his sword and thrust it back into his scabbard, and left, slamming the door behind him. Dust shot from the hangings and danced in the putrid light that came through the windows.

'Well, Sir Henry,' said Cecil, voice almost back

to its old strength, 'you have a quite extra-ordinary capacity to make men hate you.'

'Thank you, my lord. We share that at least. To be hated by certain people is a privilege. And is there any man who Sir Edward likes except himself?'

Cecil started what might have been a laugh but turned instantly into a cough, a tearing, searing cough that seemed to pour acid from the depths of his belly to his lungs and out through his thin lips. Gresham moved to help him, but he was waved feebly away until the fit ceased.

'Ring the bell, for the servant. He has medicine...' For a moment Gresham thought Cecil was going to die there and then. He rang the bell and the servant who had been waiting outside the door entered quickly. From a pocket in the side of the chair he brought a stoppered bottle, and forced some of it down his master's lips. It settled Cecil. At the merest nod, the servant left.

'I will be ready to speak in a few moments,' Cecil gasped, and paused. God knows what this is costing him, thought Gresham. He is shortening his life by every sentence he speaks.

'You are aware of my lord the King's affections towards young men?' Cecil's voice was clear again.

'The whole country could hardly be unaware of them.'

'And do you know Viscount Rochester?'

'My lord, I am in Court on occasion. Who does not know of Robert Carr, Viscount Rochester? I believe also that the good lord was given some property belonging to a friend of mine.' Carr had a special place in Gresham's catalogue of sinners. King James had taken away Raleigh's beloved estate at Sherborne to give to his lover, on whom it was wasted.

Robert Carr, a lowlands Scot with the body of an angel and the brain of a sheep, had been King James's favourite for several years, dominating his company and, it was said, his bed. With Cecil's impending death there would be no barrier to Carr becoming the sole source of favour at Court.

'I understand Viscount Rochester was recently made a privy councillor?' Gresham said, as if it were a point of no real consequence. It was known that Cecil had bitterly opposed the appointment. As his illness had grown, so Cecil's power over the King had been slipping. King James had a morbid fear of death, and the smell of death was all over Cecil.

Cecil ignored the jibe. Gresham knew him too well to believe that he had not noticed it.

'I will be blunt with you. It appears that letters exist between my lord the King and Robert Carr – or Viscount Rochester, as he now is – that are of a compromising nature.'

'How so?' Gresham's interest quickened.

Cecil coughed again and Gresham waited for the spasm to pass.

'I have not seen these letters. I am given to believe they are ... specific ... perhaps even ... highly coloured ... concerning relationships between men. The physical nature of relationships between men. And between two men in particular.'

'Ah,' said Gresham. There was silence for a few

moments. 'I take it that in effect these are love letters between the King of England and his male lover. *Specific* love letters.' Cecil said nothing. 'And,' Gresham continued, 'that were these letters to become public it would not help the status of the monarchy?'

Cecil's eyes turned up towards Gresham. There was more in them than the pain of a terminal illness.

'*Help?* It would destroy all I have worked for in these years of trial! The Church would condemn the King instantly. The Puritans in Parliament would call out the hunt of the self-righteous upon him. The saner element in Parliament would look at the uncontrolled expenditure they are increasingly asked to fund and call foul on a sodomite king. And England would laugh at its monarch! Do you hear me? *The country would laugh at its monarch.* Monarchy can withstand many things – corruption, abuse of power, immorality. Ridicule it finds hardest to survive.'

Cecil had feared ridicule more than anything else in his life. A cripple, the runt of the litter yet brought up as a great man's heir, he had more to fear than many in an age which mocked deformity. Gresham thought for a moment. He settled on a poor stool, one of four by the scarred and battered table in the room.

'There must be more,' Gresham said. 'No monarch has been laughed out of power. The executioner's axe cuts short laughter alongside life.'

This time it was Cecil's time to pause.

'Yes, there is more. The King increasingly

63

withdraws from political life, seeking only to hunt obsessively and spend time with his young men, Robert Carr in particular. Yet this is not the time of Queen Elizabeth, when the only alternative to her was rule by Spain or Civil War.'

'Prince Henry?' Gresham interrupted.

'Yes. Prince Henry.' Cecil's voice was so dry and wasted that Gresham had to lean forward to hear it, like a rustle of dead leaves on the earth. 'We have a brilliant young prince, an heir to the throne who promises more than any other in living memory. A statesman, a man of faith, a man of intelligence and skill – and still only a child! O dear God in heaven! Had I had such material to work with! What a world we might have made!'

The intensity in the whispered voice was all the more frightening because of its fragility, the impression of a man clinging on by willpower alone.

'Well, it is not to be. But there are those, not least of all the Prince himself, who see the way things are going with King James in charge, and who seek a change now, before the monarchy rots beyond redemption. These letters could be just the cause they need – not to kill the King or rise up in rebellion but to force him to step aside for his eldest son and heir.'

'"Had I had such material to work with." My lord Cecil,' said Gresham, 'if the disclosure of these letters would bring about such events, why should you or I oppose them? You yourself have praised the heir. Why not King Henry IX? Why should he not take over?'

'Because they must not learn how to depose a king

and replace him with another! Do you not see? Parliament, the Puritans, the country ... once they are given the right to choose a king, they will never lose it.'

'Would it be such a bad thing?' mused Gresham.

'It would be a terrible thing!' hissed Cecil. 'Politics can never look at the man. It must always look at the principle. They rid themselves of a king they do not like, justifying it on the basis that the heir is different. Then what follows? What if the heir turns rotten? If he dies? If he offends one of the great noble families, who then turn to one of their own nominees? Then turn to the next best, or the most promising, and do so time and time again. This way is madness. It must not be allowed to happen!'

'And do you think these letters could depose a king?'

'I think a king can depose a king, if the king is a sensual fool whose instinct for survival lessens with every month that goes by. King James is indolent, and confident. It is a dangerous, dangerous mixture. The letters could be the push that topples him over the edge of his own making. *I do not know what will come to pass!* I would know, if God had only allowed me to live, and I had been able to advise and perhaps even influence the outcome for the better. Now others must do it for me.'

'What role does Sir Edward Coke play in all this?'

'It was reported to him that the letters had been stolen, from Sir Thomas Overbury. I suspect

Overbury sees Coke as powerful enough to take action, lawyer enough to relish the intrigue and self-serving enough to realise how much credit the safe recovery – and destruction – of the letters would bring him with the old King. In any event, Overbury will work with Coke to regain the letters, which is more than that most impossible of men will do with any other.'

Sir Thomas Overbury was Robert Carr's dark angel. They were inseparable. Intelligent, ruthless, determined and arrogant almost beyond belief, Overbury was seen by many as Carr's manager, providing him with the intelligence he himself lacked. If any incriminating letters existed, Overbury would want their power and be most aware of what the loss of it would mean.

'However, these letters are not all. You are a playgoer, I believe, Sir Henry?'

'I frequent the playhouses when I am in town, yes.'

'Two manuscripts were stolen recently from The Globe theatre. Both were plays, both written by the man they call Shakespeare. You know Master Shakespeare.' It was a statement, not a question.

The air thickened between the two men. There was a long pause. Finally Gresham spoke.

'I know him, though I knew him first by another name. William Hall, was he not? Or at least that was the name he used when he travelled abroad on state business and claimed his thirty pieces of silver.'

'You overestimate Hall's part in your friend Raleigh's downfall. As does Raleigh himself.'

'I doubt it,' Gresham replied. 'But what I do accept as truth is that Mr William Hall – whose company of players, I seem to recall, suddenly became The King's Men and the most favoured actors in the land very shortly after Sir Walter Raleigh's conviction and imprisonment – has hung up his spying boots and become Master William Shakespeare. Actor, poet and play-maker, no less. He's done very well since Raleigh was imprisoned on a false charge. Very well indeed. Was that the reward you chose for him? To make his disorderly crew The King's Men? And, yes, I know his plays. They are very good, unfortunately. Outstanding, even, better perhaps than any others. Surprisingly so for those of us who knew him when he was doing a different job.'

'You will know what price is placed on these manuscripts, and what security surrounds them.'

There was an insatiable demand for plays for the theatre as companies were putting on sixteen or seventeen shows a season. Any company with a hit on its hands kept the manuscript as secure as a prized daughter's maidenhead. It did not stop rival companies from putting shorthand writers in the audience to scribble down the text of a hit, or bribing leading actors in a company to dictate a verbatim account of their parts – and what they could remember of other people's parts. To lose a manuscript was to give your play to your rivals. Apart from reasons of security, the expense of copying out whole texts meant that full versions of a play often only existed in at most three copies. Actors were given their own

67

lines and cues on separate sheets for rehearsal and learning, and these were counted out and counted in as if the paper they were written on was twenty-four-carat gold.

'Difficult for the players if a manuscript is stolen,' mused Gresham, 'but hardly life-threatening for the King, I would have thought?'

'Life-threatening for the porter who was murdered to gain the manuscripts,' croaked Cecil. 'Yet the players are The King's Men, are they not? They see this theft as an insult to the King himself – or so they say, in asking for his help. But the importance is that our information suggests the same person who stole the manuscripts may also have stolen the letters. A Cambridge bookseller, we think – another reason to call on you and your local knowledge. Identify the man who stole the manuscripts and we believe you will identify the man who stole the letters.'

'So what is my role in all of this?' asked Gresham, frantically working to process the information he had received.

'Sir Edward Coke is a lawyer, not a spy or a diplomat. Whoever has these letters needs to be found, then killed or bought off. Coke would kill readily enough, but he only knows how to do so by means of the law. He lacks the skill to find a secret package, and lacks the experience of dealing with its owner once found. Skills you have in plenty, Sir Henry. And you, of course, know Cambridge very well.'

Gresham's use of his father's wealth to refound Granville College in Cambridge was widely known.

'I am to mind Sir Edward? One of the people I despise most on earth?'

'You have worked with me plenty of times. In comparison, your hatred of Sir Edward is mere flash-frying, while mine has lingered long in the oven.'

'And why should I help?'

'Firstly, because for all your oft-expressed selfishness and lack of faith in anything, you know that peace, continuity and stability are the most important things for this country. These letters threaten all three. Secondly, because Sir Edward needs watching. He is a man of over-weening self-importance and ambition. In his heart he does not believe in the absolute power of the king, but in the absolute power of the law – the law as defined and exercised by himself, of course. As things stand, he wishes to find these letters and destroy them. It would take little for him to use them instead to destroy the King. I think you would not wish your enemy to have such power.'

'So I am to find some letters that could blow the present King into hell, but do so while allowing a man I hate above all others to think that it is he who has found the letters. Then I am to watch him, and if needs be kill one of the country's leading lawyers in order to allow a sodomite king uninterrupted access to his pleasures for the remainder of his natural life. And at the same time I am to find stolen manu-scripts of plays written by a man who betrayed the one man I truly love.'

'An admirable summary, Sir Henry,' muttered

69

Cecil. 'You miss the final point, however. And by so doing, preserve peace and the reputation of the monarchy.'

'And do you trust me to do all this?'

'I trust you to do the right thing for all the wrong reasons. I trust you to take this whole sorry mess on board because it has the raw smell of danger, and for no other reason. I trust you to think it through after you have taken the decision, and to discuss it with your beauty of a wife and your clod of a servant, and then through the red haze of your excitement see some sense to it. And I trust you to survive, Henry Gresham. For that is your code, is it not? Survival as the prime virtue? For as long, that is, as God decides to spare you an illness such as mine.'

The raw hatred of Gresham, and of his own plight, that burned out of Cecil's eyes would have heated an ocean to beyond boiling.

Gresham took the decision that Cecil had known he would.

'I'll assist Sir Edward. It will be amusing to see how long he can cope with help from someone he loathes.'

'Sir Edward loathes everybody. And he would work with Satan if he thought Satan would help him win his case.'

'Well,' said Gresham lightly, 'you'll soon have the edge on us all. You'll be able to ask Satan yourself, face to face.'

'At least I believe in God, Sir Henry,' grated Cecil. 'At least I may intercede with Him. You, who have no belief, will surely go to hell.'

'If there is a God, He and not you will decide

70

that. As for death, I prefer Master Shakespeare's vision of an "undiscovered country". Perhaps I'll be able to present the record of my life to an unbiased judge when I die. Perhaps, and God forbid, I'll meet the reincarnation of Sir Edward Coke. Perhaps I'll sense nothing except sweet oblivion. You're right, I've no certainty. I echo a line from *Hamlet*: "The readiness is all." There, you see, I do know Master Shakespeare's work.' He paused for a moment. 'I'm ready for whatever I meet, Robert Cecil. Are you?'

For a long moment Gresham thought he had killed Cecil. His head had slumped forward, his breathing had become inaudible. Just as Gresham was about to test to see if there was a pulse in Cecil's neck, Cecil raised his head.

'"The readiness is all"? We are ready in our different ways, I think, and I am certainly ready for what I will meet after death.' Cecil's voice seemed increasingly to be coming from a pile of stinking blankets and not a human being.

Gresham rose to his feet. 'I'll arrange to meet Sir Edward in London,' he said lightly. 'Goodbye, my lord. We shan't meet again, I fear. I could pretend regret. You'd see it as a lie. I wish you well on the journey you're about to take.'

'There is only one certainty, Henry Gresham. It is that you will take that same journey, sooner or later.'

'That's why I wished you well,' said Gresham as he left the room. 'And I intend, my lord, to make it later.'

He did not turn round to take a last look at Robert Cecil, First Earl of Salisbury. He wondered, as he slammed the door, whether the dust from the hangings would settle on Cecil, and how long it would be before someone thought to brush it off.

4

May, 1612
Sir Francis Bacon's Residence, London

'No man can serve two masters... Ye cannot serve God and Mammon.'
THE KING JAMES BIBLE

Sir Francis Bacon and Bishop Lancelot Andrewes sat on opposite sides of the fire, outwardly companionable enough. Sir Francis, author of some of the greatest works of natural science ever written; Bishop Andrewes, prime component in the greatest translation of the Holy Bible ever published. The two men had waved the servants away, and brought two chairs closer to the blazing hearth. It was summer, but the old stone of the building kept the chill that was so welcome on a hot day but which could bite into the bones at night.

There was a wariness between the two men, something admitted by Bacon.

'We're old friends, my lord Bishop,' said Bacon, gazing into the fire, his hand loosely clasping the goblet of wine. 'Yet it shouldn't be so.'

A thin smile crossed the face of Lancelot Andrewes, Bishop of Ely.

'And why shouldn't the King's Solicitor General and his Bishop of Ely be the best friends in the world?' Andrewes replied lightly. 'We've known each other for many years now. You certainly need someone to safeguard your soul, and at times I need someone to tell me about the way of the real world. We face a common threat, after all. We're both deemed by others to be men of wit. And we've both been disappointed, I think...'

It had been a year since King James had made another, weaker man Archbishop of Canterbury, when all the world and its priests thought Andrewes was the only candidate. As for Bacon, his lifelong battle for preferment seemed to have stalled on the rock of Sir Edward Coke, apparently the lawyer more trusted by King James.

'All of which is true,' said Bacon, not turning to look at his companion. 'But the real reason's elsewhere. You see...' And now he turned to look Andrewes full in the face. 'You, for all your ambition, are a man of morals. I, for all my ambition, have none.'

'All men have morals,' replied Andrewes mildly, his eyes amused despite himself.

'Perhaps. But mine appear to have been lost by the wayside at an early age. It doesn't make me an evil man, you understand.' Bacon spoke as if lecturing a child. 'Indeed, the fact that I've placed self-interest above morality, and made it my substitute, means I'm actually very predictable. Far more so than many who've been bitten by the illness of religion. For example, I'm quite likely to spare someone because they amuse me, rather than kill them because they have a different religion.'

'There's a difference between religion and faith,'

answered Andrewes. 'Religion is the institution man erects around faith, and because it comes from man it must be fallible. Faith is what we're given from God. It's pure.'

'Well preached!' said Bacon, without malice. Andrewes was renowned as the best preacher in the country. His sermons were a potent blend of intelligence and wit, but the driving force that drove his congregation to tears was the combination of humanity and sincerity. 'But we really do need to move off spiritual matters and on to Mammon. Or Cecil, to be precise. You've heard he's about to die?'

Andrewes crossed himself instinctively. 'How certain are you?'

'As certain as one can be in these matters.'

'And are you pleased?' Andrewes spoke with no hint of accusation.

'Yes, I think so. He's blocked me all these years, been the main reason for my lack of preferment despite our family links. His death will certainly open up new opportunities for me. But that's not why we needed to meet; Cecil sent a summons out from Bath yesterday.'

'A summons? To whom?'

'To Sir Henry Gresham.'

There was silence.

Andrewes spoke first, hesitantly. 'And what do you think was the purpose of this ... summons?'

'I can only guess that it's the business that joins us. As far as Cecil's concerned, it's perhaps the greatest loose end in his life. Started by his father, watched over by him but never ended. Now threatening to blow up in the face of the country he thinks he's ruled for all these years past, damaging – perhaps even destroying – the stability he thinks is the inheritance he's left to the future. Gresham is the obvious man to bring it all to an end.'

'Is Gresham as dangerous a man as his reputation allows?'

'In some respects, my old friend,' said Bacon, sipping his wine thoughtfully, 'he's very like you. He has more wit and intelligence than he knows how to handle, a brain as powerful as any I've ever known and as sardonic a sense of humour. He's as restless as you. In the room he occupies, time seems to go just a little faster, as it does in any church where you preach. Oh, and at times he's crippled by a sense of duty. Far too much of this dreadful morality; just like you.'

'And the differences, assuming I accept your rather wild description as holding any truth at all as far as I'm concerned?'

'Well now, there's the problem,' mused Bacon. 'Gresham's fabulously rich, so he needs bow his knee to no man, and he's utterly ruthless, sometimes even cruel. He really doesn't care about his own life. He's probably the best fighter – and I do mean fighter, not just swordsman – in the country. He and Cecil loathe each other with a venom I've rarely seen anywhere else, yet they seem to have an understanding between them that no outsider comprehends. If Cecil sets him on the trail of the truth, the odds are more than even that he'll find at least some of it.'

'Are the consequences for us and the others as bad as we've persuaded ourselves they are?'

asked Andrewes.

'They vary for each of us, I think,' said Bacon. 'For you and me, there's the fact of us having been involved in a deceit, telling the great public a lie for so long. It's not good for lawyers or for clergymen to be seen as deceivers. Then there's what it is we've been doing. Given the ferment in my Parliament and your Church, we're not clever to be seen as active in that particular field. In your case, the risk is greater. There are things the man responsible for the greatest edition of the Holy Bible ever written can't be seen to be involved with. As you've been so involved. Finally, for both of us, there's the humiliation of the real truth. More so in my case than yours.'

'And for the King?'

'The same. With the complication of these letters. A great complication, I fear. And the madman who has them now.'

The silence hung heavy.

'I won't have him killed.' Andrewes' tone was peremptory.

'Who?' said Bacon, startled out of his reverie for a moment.

'Shakespeare. I won't have him killed.'

'Yet if he's stopped, much of the danger goes away,' Bacon stated factually. The part of his mind that from his earliest days had been distanced from him, an eavesdropper perched over his ear listening and reporting, wondered how this sight would look to an outsider. The Solicitor General and the Bishop of Ely quietly discussing the merits of murdering a man.

'As you've said, I have my morals.'

'I take the point. Yet there must be a chance that Gresham will kill him. There's no love lost between them. Gresham won't be constricted by your morality,' said Bacon.

'I've no control over Gresham,' replied Andrewes, aware of how thin the theological and moral ground was over which he skated.

'Well,' said Bacon, a sigh accompanying his words, 'the job may be done for us, without our lifting a finger. It seems they're queuing up to do away with Master Shakespeare.'

5

Late May, 1612
The Anchor Inn, Bank Street, London

'The evil that men do lives after them,
The good is oft interred with their bones.'
SHAKESPEARE, *Julius Caesar*

The disease was affecting him now, Marlowe
knew. He was starting to lose feeling in his hands
and feet, could not always sense the hardness of
the ground under him as his feet landed and so
had the prancing, high-stepping gait of the pox
sufferer. The doctor had said the growths would
come eventually – hard little carbuncles on his
flesh that first blackened and then fell out, leaving a gaping hole behind them. They would be
active around his penis, the doctor had said. He
would piss like a watering can. The cures could
stave off the end, but that it would end in death
was inevitable. So little time. So much revenge.

The Anchor Inn was by the Clink Prison and
there was little to choose between the clientele of
both places. They were all lost souls. The river
pirates used the Anchor as their base, as did
several highwaymen. A warren of passageways
allowed escape down to the river. This was a
sump, a noisome gathering place where many of
the conversations were in grunts, where men

79

came to become seriously drunk in the shortest possible time and where nameless deals were struck in dark corners. Occasionally a flash of light from one of those darkest corners would reveal a jewel or a necklace being covertly shown, before being stuffed back into the stinking cloth in which it was wrapped. The women here were old before their time, cackling hags at twenty-five years. Marlowe had no pity for them. It was one of their kind that had launched the acid of the pox into his body and into his mind.

He had paid one of the boys to keep filling his tankard. A thin, small-faced creature with a great lump and a bruise on the side of his head, he seemed incapable of moving forward, favouring instead a crab-like sideways walk, his chin permanently held down into his puny chest as if to avoid a blow from any of the roaring mob that frequented the inn. His face was quite beautiful, Marlowe noted, if you cut through the grime and the swelling, the big green eyes and the high cheekbones set off surprisingly well by a mop of auburn hair. His innocence was pathetic. Well, innocence did not last, thought Kit Marlowe.

As his hand caressed the letters he remembered his failure. The porter they paid to guard The Globe theatre had been old, and sleeping off his drink. It had been easy to slit his throat while he slept – who would have thought the old man had so much blood in him? – and pleasurable to watch as he writhed and twisted down the slippery road to hell, trying vainly to scream his fear as the air whistled out through the bloody slice in his air passage. Marlowe had broken into the room as easily as he had slit the throat of the porter, leafed frantically through the hundreds of papers. These were fair copies! Not the original manuscripts he craved! Only one scabby piece worth stealing, and that in the writing of a man long dead!

Marlowe took his grief, as he had learned to do over the years, and folded it over and over until it was a small package. Then he dropped it in the furnace of his hatred and watched it catch light and burn, renewing its strength.

With hindsight, his failure to kill Shakespeare had saved him. The man he had known as William Hall must know where the papers are, must have lied to Marlowe's spy when he said in his cups that they were stored at The Globe. His revenge would have been wonderfully byzantine, but the devil must be guarding him so that Shakespeare was still living. He would talk, again. And this time Marlowe would make sure it was the truth.

In the meantime, there were other debts to be paid. It would be too simple to kill Henry Gresham. Gresham must suffer, as Marlowe had suffered over the years. There was a most enjoyable way of achieving that end, he thought, as a grin seemed to tear his scarred face even further.

6

Late May, 1612
The Merchant's House,
Trumpington, near Cambridge

'O cunning enemy, that, to catch a saint,
With saints doth bait thy hook...'
  SHAKESPEARE, *Measure for Measure*

'It stinks!' said Mannion. 'As usual, he hasn't told
you half of it, and the half he hasn't told you is
what'll get you killed.'

They were in the library. Gresham had had it
built on when he had first bought The Merchant's
House, with long windows set almost from ceiling
to floor and a gallery. It was less splendid than the
library at his London home, known simply as The
House, but somehow it felt more like home. He
loved the smoke-free sky of East Anglia and the
glorious cacophony of light in its sunsets and
sunrise. He loved the mist over the meadows in
the morning, and the thrusting turrets of King's
College Chapel, forcing themselves to dominate
the Fenland on the ride from Trumpington to
Cambridge. He loved his relationship with Granville College of the University of Cambridge. His
college. His contribution to history. His only contribution until the arrival of Walter and Anna, his
children after a lifetime when he had thought

himself barren.

'Of course it stinks. Do you think I'm fool enough to believe that what Robert Cecil chooses to tell me is even half the truth?' Gresham was pacing the room. In front of him were Mannion and Jane, his council of war.

Gresham had been a bastard son. He had never known his mother. The whispers had been there as long as he could remember. The fabulously wealthy but elderly banker widowed, his only child dead. The enforced guardianship of Lady Mary Keys, sister of Lady Jane Grey and victim of an imprudent marriage. There was no one left now to confirm or deny Sir Thomas Gresham's secret, the name of Henry Gresham's mother. At least the distant, cold figure of his father had taken the boy in, clothed and fed him, let him roam like a wild young puppy through the house. He was left to drag himself up in its entrails, adopted in a strange father and son relationship by Mannion, himself a boy just turned man. Mannion had been the only servant Gresham's father had trusted near him in his final days. Gresham had been a non-person, a boy with no real status, a servant yet not a servant, gentry yet not gentry. A bastard, but with noble blood. He had inherited the fabulous Gresham wealth when he was nine years old. The servants who had been there remembered the thin, wire-straight boy with round eyes gazing steadily into those of the ancient lawyer, eyes that did not flicker as the nine-year-old was told he was now one of the richest men in the country. Henry Gresham had learned very young how to withdraw into himself.

He had first learned how to fight when, on his rambling through the night streets of London, street urchins had sensed the smell of money and set upon him. He had learned at times of crisis to force all other thoughts from his head, to develop a concentration of almost unnatural power and ferocity. He was showing it now, pacing like a wild beast up and down the room, almost unaware of the others in it.

'What do we actually know?' he asked, punching out the words.

It was Jane who answered. She could not keep the tension out of her voice, nor, to her regret, the fear. She knew fear was weakness, prayed that her weakness might not in some way reduce his respect for her.

'We know that whenever Cecil's entered our lives in the past, your life's been put at risk. The man's like some evil daemon, a harbinger of death, pain and suffering. He asked you to get involved in two things: these letters and the manuscripts.'

The tiny part of Gresham's brain that was always distanced from him, watching, waiting, picked up the tension and the fear in Jane's voice. A sharp pang cut across his heart. Fool! How easy for him to turn his agony of worry into the exquisite release of action. How terrible for her, condemned by the way men and women lived to be the passive recipient of his actions. His step did not falter. His eyes did not flicker. He would act, and speak to that fear. Later.

'Let's start with the incriminating letters. Would James be fool enough to write in explicit terms to his lover?' Gresham was acting as devil's advocate.

'Yes,' said Jane firmly. 'The ladies at Court say he kisses this Robert Carr full on the lips in public. They also say he fingers his codpiece as he walks along with him. Quite openly. That's not just a man taking his pleasure. It's someone who wants to fling what he's doing in people's faces, or who's simply forgotten to be discreet. Either way, it's hardly more of a risk writing letters. It's like when he fingers his codpiece, only he's getting pleasure from his pen.'

'Did you say his pen?' asked Mannion, confused.

'Yes,' said Jane with a look that would have frozen hell. 'Pen.'

'Ah...' said Gresham thoughtfully. 'Well, let's concede that King James could be so ... blown away by passion as to put his experiences into writing.' He grinned at Jane, which annoyed her. As this had been his aim, he carried on with renewed vigour.

'But how damaging would such letters be?'

'Very damaging,' said Jane. She was in her stride now, given a role, certain of herself. She knew she was Gresham's eyes and ears, knew his total trust of her judgement. 'The Puritans get louder and louder as the Court gets more and more openly sinful. The Puritans are increasingly powerful in Parliament, and James needs Parliament to approve the money to fund his goings-on.' Jane listened to all the Court gossip and reported back to Gresham. Just as importantly, she listened to the gossip among the booksellers at St Paul's, with whom she had long been a favourite and was almost a mascot. 'The Puritans are looking to

Prince Henry to bring a new age of goodness and purity to Court. I suppose they could always try to speed things up and get James to abdicate.'

'So where does that leave us?'

'The manuscripts.' Jane was away now, allowing her mind free rein. 'The stolen play scripts. They have to be more important than Cecil's owning up to, however damaging these letters might be. That's how Cecil's mind has always worked. Always give a dog a bone, and hide the butcher's shop from him.'

'You know how crucial these manuscripts are to the players.' Gresham was unconvinced. 'It's not unreasonable for The King's Men to put in a plea to the King's Chief Secretary to get them back, particularly if the thief is linked to the letters. Yet their value only holds good for other players or rival companies – and the actors might get drunk and brawl but they've never killed each other before for a stolen manuscript. What's so important about these plays? I know there's a power in the theatres Cecil's scared of, something he can't control for once, something that could challenge his law and order.'

'We don't know,' said Jane. 'But Cecil did, and that's what matters. There has to be something we're not being told. They're always is with Cecil.'

'There's something else that bothers me. Why steal only two manuscripts? If you're going to go as far as to murder an old man for them, you may as well take the whole lot.'

'Perhaps the thief was disturbed,' said Jane. 'You can't base anything substantial on the number of plays they took.'

Gresham stopped his pacing and sat down abruptly. The library had a view out on to the river and its peaceful, meandering summer mood, a band of blue winding its quiet way through the green of the pastures. 'And Shakespeare is a traitor. As well as a genius.'

'Are you sure?'

'Shakespeare was as rough as they come when he first arrived in town, and ready for anything. He was a natural recruit for Cecil. The players get everywhere, into Court and into the taverns. They travel the country – Europe even. And they drink and womanise too much and'll do anything for ready cash. Many took different names when they were paid. Shakespeare was always William Hall. Some Stratford link, I think. Raleigh believes it was Shakespeare – in the days when he was William Hall – who hit lucky and betrayed him in the Bye Plot. I've no proof, but straight afterwards Shakespeare's crew were made into The King's Men, and Shakespeare bailed out of the game. Raleigh's sworn to kill Hall, or Shakespeare. By his own hand. He was most insistent it should be by his own hand.'

'Was?'

Gresham turned to his wife, his hand resting lovingly in her hair for a brief moment, running it through his fingers. 'I was on my way to do it myself. Raleigh stopped me. I've his order to kill the man if Raleigh dies in the Tower. If he's ever released, Raleigh will do it as his first act.'

'That much hatred...' mused Jane, considering the brave, tragic, foolhardy figure of Raleigh, his heart being eaten out every day by hatreds from his lurid past. Raleigh frightened her, not for what he was but for what he was allowing himself to become.

'That much betrayal. Raleigh'd helped the man get a place with the actors in the first place.'

'The theatre's always been trouble, hasn't it?' said Jane.

'It's a new art form,' said Gresham, 'come screaming and yelling into the world. Come to London to be born. Sometimes I think it was conceived by God, like poetry and music. Cecil thinks it was conceived by Satan. He could never see its beauty. Only its power.' Gresham's own sonnets had been published anonymously to wide acclaim.

'What's an art form?' asked Mannion, finger in mouth and digging in his tooth for something dead.

'It's when you paint a bottle of wine instead of drinking it,' said Gresham.

'Doesn't sound much fun to me,' said Mannion, adding, with gross illogicality, 'I like the theatre.'

'The Puritans think it's Satan's doing,' said Jane. 'They frighten me, much more than Catholics ever have.'

'We took away the Puritans' natural enemy when the Gunpowder Plot blew the Catholics into limbo,' said Gresham. 'They've no one to hate now, except people who like cakes and ale, and the theatre. Or anyone who has fun!'

'The last time I was at the bookstalls,' said Jane, 'I saw a man with one of those stupid black hats they wear come and let loose a tirade against a bookseller who had play texts on his shelves. It was frightening. His eyes were rolling and half the time all you could see was the whites. He was shrieking, and there was white stuff round his mouth. The bookseller kept having to clean the man's spit off his precious covers. He was scared. So was I. I thought the man was going to do a clearing out of the Temple, and scatter all the books.'

'Men who think God's on their side often have trouble realising they're not God.'

'There's one other bit of stage gossip,' said Jane.

'Yes?' said Gresham, part intrigued and part wanting no more complications.

'They say there's a lost play by Marlowe that surfaced recently. *The Fall of Lucifer*. Apparently it's too dangerous to perform, so wild and heretical that it could shake governments. No one's seen it, though there's lots of talk.'

A strange, unfathomable expression flitted across Gresham's face at the mention of Marlowe's name. Jane carried on. 'If this lost play is so dangerous, and the sort of thing that causes a riot, could it have been this manuscript that the murderer was looking for? On Cecil's orders? You know how frightened he is of the theatre and its power over the common people.'

'So you think Cecil's real wish might be for me to find this lost play? Hide from me what it is? It's tempting, but it doesn't really work. If whoever murdered to steal these two manuscripts was in Cecil's pay, Cecil doesn't need me to hunt them out. I can't see a link between the letters and

89

these two stolen manuscripts, never mind a play written by a dead man that no one's seen.'

A young serving lad must have pinched a maid laden with bedding as they walked past the door. An outraged but part-pleased shriek was muffled in to silence as the pair realised their master and mistress lay behind the door.

'What do we know about Shakespeare?' asked Gresham. 'What's the gossip about him?'

'No one really seems to know him. He keeps a very low profile in town, and they say that back in Stratford, where he spends most of his time now – he owns half the town, apparently – they think of him as a grain dealer and hardly anyone knows about his plays! He's stopped writing, they say, and wants to sell his share in the company.'

'Well,' said Gresham, 'I suppose I'd better re-new my acquaintance with him, as the new man he is rather than the person I knew. I see Sir Edward Coke in London four days from now and I'm not feeling as if I'm going there knowing much more than I did when 1 left Cecil.'

'I'd be happier steering clear of this Sir Edward Poke,' interrupted Mannion.

'Sir Edward Coke,' said Gresham patiently. Mannion had taken an instant dislike to the man.

'Whatever,' said Mannion dismissively. 'He's trouble. I've got a nose for these things.'

'Be thankful your nose can't smell your own breath, old man,' said Gresham. 'As for Coke, you know I'm no friend of his.'

'No. But you ain't had to fight him before. Not direct. And I bet Sir Edward Joke can stop being funny right quick.'

'Coke...' Gresham started to say limply, and then gave up. He turned to Jane.

'Be careful,' said Jane in a sombre voice, before he could speak. Why waste her words? Henry Gresham could act almost all things except being careful. 'You've a weakness. This is the man who gave Raleigh a show trial, who preaches the law and then suspends justice when a king wants a man condemned. You hate him before you know him. Your hatred could blind you.'

'Well, we know more about Coke than we do about Shakespeare.' Gresham was pacing the room again, head down, hardly seeing the others.

'Top lawyer,' said Jane, 'but...'

'Go on?' said Gresham.

'The legal booksellers say that he trades on that reputation, and sometimes gives outrageous judgements which no one else dares challenge because of his reputation with the other lawyers.'

'What about the clash with Bacon?' Gresham asked. Sir Francis Bacon had brushed across Gresham's life as an academic author but never as a political opponent. There were very many who disliked Bacon intensely. Gresham had always found him human, amusing and able. He had a brain the size of a Spanish galleon, but much nimbler and faster. Of course he had no morality at all, except to his own self interest, but had freely confessed as much to Gresham with an engaging wit and honesty that somehow robbed his amorality of its venom.

'You know more than I do,' said Jane. Bacon was homosexual, tied to a wealth-generating but loveless marriage.

'I know he's locked into bitter battle with Coke over who'll be the next Attorney General. The popular bet has to be Coke. He's got himself the image of a legal god, he's done James's dirty work for him in court time after time and Bacon can be his own worst enemy.'

Jane prepared to reply, then noticed Mannion looking with excessive interest out of the window. Alice was the newest and youngest of the servants recruited to The Merchant's House, sent to work in the kitchens. A rather bewitching, fair-haired girl, she had been ordered into the kitchen garden to beg herbs for the cook from the gardener. Did she know how her hips swung as she walked into the garden, basket clutched before her? Or was it mere innocence?

'Do I have to warn you again?' Jane's voice was low and so threatening that it stopped even Gresham in his tracks. Fascinated, he watched a rare insight into the hidden relationship between two of the four most important people in his life. 'That girl is in my charge. I talked to her mother, I gave my word she would be looked after. *You will not touch her.*'

Mannion looked direct into her eyes.

'She's simple,' said Jane. 'She doesn't appear so. You might be forgiven for thinking her normal. And she's very beautiful. Her mother was in despair because no one would take her into service and all the men wanted to take her into bed. I said I'd help her. And if she finds her John the Ostler, who'll love her because she's the most beautiful thing he's ever seen, and who'll forgive her a simple mind, then so be it. That will be her choice, and his. But I'll not have her spoiled by a careless and powerful man, in breach of my word to her mother.'

'Well then, mistress,' said Mannion, grinning at her. *Grinning at her?* Gresham was part amused, part outraged. Would he have dared grin at Jane in such circumstances? 'You're lucky to have me on your side, aren't you? There's only one real man who could put her in harm in this place, and only one real man as could protect her. And I'm both.' He ambled over to Jane, as if to put his cup down on the table at which she sat. 'You see, I'm happy to go for the willing. I've never gone for the weak.'

'I know,' said Jane.

'You want her wed to John the Ostler?'

'He needs to love someone other than a horse, and her simple nature won't stop her being a good wife to him.'

'Leave it to me,' said Mannion.

And they both smiled.

'Excuse me!' said Gresham, 'and hello. Is there any possibility of my being allowed back into this conversation?'

It was rare for Jane to flush, but she did so. It was left to Mannion to resurrect the conversation.

'We were talkin' about Sir Edward Bloke, weren't we?' asked Mannion innocently.

'Sir Edward *Coke*, you blunt-wit ignorant peasant!' shouted Gresham, his patience at an end.

There was so much he did not know, the clinical part of Gresham's brain was telling him. Well, inaction would find nothing out. That sense of total concentration that Jane and Mannion

93

knew so well came over his whole body.

'London. All of us. To meet Sir Edward. And to visit the theatre.'

7

26th May, 1612
Sir Edward Coke's Home, London

'The first thing we do, let's kill all the lawyers.'
SHAKESPEARE, *Henry VI*, Part 2

Sir Edward Coke had let it be known that he rose at three o'clock every morning in order to extend his working day. It was an easy story to circulate and, thought Gresham, easy to maintain once it was established, without actually having to get out of bed.

They set out at noon. It was only a relatively short walk from The House, with its favoured position on The Strand, to Chancery Lane. Gresham and Mannion could have taken a boat, ridden or taken the vast coach that Gresham's father had had built when those cumbersome contrivances had been fashionable. Today Gresham felt the need to walk, to get back in touch with London's ebb and flow, feel its pulse.

It had been dry for weeks and within seconds a thin layer of dust covered Gresham's boots. The clouds hanging loose in the sky threatened rain, had done so for days. At least they were spared the sucking, clinging mud, but not the steaming piles of horse shit littering the road or the stained yellow and brown earth where night soil had been thrown carelessly into the street. The smell of grass still blew in from the green fields visible past the houses on the northern side of The Strand, to mingle with the stench of the river and the open sewer that occasionally the street was allowed to become. Then there was the endless, richest smell of all: the smell of humanity. The perfumes and scents worn by the wealthy men and occasional lady; the nosegays of sweet orange or apple designed to ward off evil vapours; the sudden, intrusive, raw stench of sweat from the carters or porters carrying huge loads on their bending backs; the stale, warm, sickly sweet smell of the men and women who could neither afford clean linen nor to have what linen they owned washed every day.

The nearer they came to the old City walls, the closer together the houses grew, the more cramped and crammed the streets. The steep-pitched roofs almost touched their opposite neighbours. When it rained an avalanche of water poured from the roofs on to a few yards of street below, digging a trench with sheer force of water. You could sink deeper than your knees into the mud of a London street, and leave your boots in the sucking mire when your friends dragged you out. The noise was incessant. The cries of the street traders were everywhere, raucous, yelling, insistent.

Coke may or may not have stinted on his sleep but he certainly did not stint on the furnishings he allowed himself. Mannion had been left in an ante room with a sniffing and disapproving clerk. Coke's study was vast, with crimson taffeta curtains and a turkey foot carpet laid over polished boards. The wall hangings on three walls were particularly fine. Coke must have had them commissioned. One showed Solomon giving judgement, another Moses damning the Jews for their worship of a golden idol, with a smoking mountain in the background. Very judicious. At a guess, Sir Edward Coke wanted to be Solomon and thought he might be Moses. It was only a short step for him to believe that he was God.

'Good morning, Sir Henry.' Coke spoke as if to a rather poor and badly behaved Ward of Court. He gave Gresham the merest glance and continued to inscribe a careful signature on the document in front of him. 'I am, as you see, most busy, most busy indeed...' The table at which Coke sat was littered with papers and bound volumes. He had not risen as Gresham entered, an act of extraordinary rudeness. Gresham adopted a solicitous expression and sat down on one of the ornately backed and armed chairs on the other side of the table, without being asked. From the slight stiffening of Coke's body Gresham knew he sensed the return discourtesy. *Touché.* One all. Gresham's eye was caught by not one but two fine portraits of Sir Edward, posing magisterially, adorning the wall over the vast fireplace, and a third showing him with what Gresham assumed was his first wife and vast brood of children.

'It's a pleasure to come and meet you, Sir Edward,' said. Gresham in his most understanding and sympathetic voice. 'Unlike your busy self, I've nothing at all to do with my time.' Coke did not look up. He was too much in control for that. But he had, Gresham noticed, managed to ruin one of the letters by the jerk his hand had given in response to Gresham's remark. He had done it just as he was forming the 'o' in his name, so that one missive was now apparently signed 'Ed. Cqke'. Gresham carried on. 'It's also always a pleasure to meet someone so exalted who is yet so ... humble, so ... well-mannered and lacking in vanity.'

Coke put down his quill, measured, making sure Gresham knew he was not hurrying. This was not a man to be underestimated, Gresham reminded himself. Coke had survived and flourished too long in the bitter, adversarial world of the law for that.

'You should know, Sir Henry, that the Earl of Salisbury is dead. He died yesterday at Marlborough.' Coke spoke solemnly, playing the part.

Cecil dead?

'Oh, good,' said Gresham, that same infuriating bland smile on his face. 'I'm so glad.'

That did get through to Coke. He had too much self control to rise from his chair but his colour roared up the scale towards red and Gresham saw his scrawny Adam's apple bobbing up and down several times as he swallowed. The skin was leathery, wrinkled, that of an old man.

'You are ... *glad?*' asked Coke, voice barely under control, rasping as if from a dry throat.

'Delighted,' said Gresham.

This man was an amateur! thought Gresham. He almost found himself missing Cecil. At least Cecil would never have let his true emotions show under such simple goading.

'How typical, Sir Henry, that you should go for a *theatrical* effect rather than deal with a serious matter with any degree of substance.' Coke put a special measure of loathing into the word 'theatrical'. Was he a Puritan? Gresham wondered. Or just someone who hated the thought of people letting their hair down and enjoying themselves.

Coke paused, and sipped from a king's ransom of a glass goblet. 'Quite frankly, Sir Henry, I was never able to see why the Earl wished you to become involved in this business.'

Coke's overwhelming sense of his own value and significance would never let him see why he could not be trusted with all and everything. Sharing a job was to Sir Edward Coke as much of an anathema as sharing a prosecution.

'No, Sir Edward, you would not be able to see why the Earl wished me to become involved in this business. I suspect my late Lord of the Flies recognised your weakness, which is that you think you know so much. Such people are a risk to themselves. They need to be placed with those who are willing to admit their ignorance.'

'You claim to know too little?' asked Coke, flat-voiced, his lawyer's brain leaping like a ferret at a rabbit's throat. He was almost visibly working to categorise and pin-point the nature of his opponent.

'I claim to have been *told* too little by my lord Cecil, and to recognise all the dangers to myself that lie therein. But then again, I'm more than used to working to Cecil's half-orders. You, I think, are a novice.'

'You are so little concerned for your own life

99

that you would risk it, by your own admission, for you know not what?' asked Coke, his fish-eyes giving nothing away this time.

'Good, Sir Edward, very good,' replied Gresham. 'Our language is starting to reverse. Your questions are becoming shorter and shorter, my answers longer and longer. If this carries on I shall start to reveal more and more about who I am to your lawyer's brain. Is this always how you trap witnesses?'

'I do not trap witnesses.' There was acid in Coke's voice. Gresham said nothing. The silence between the two men lengthened. It was Coke who broke first. 'I care more for the law, and for justice, than you can ever imagine,' he said.

'How can you know what I imagine?' asked Gresham.

'Do not play with words with me!'

'Isn't that what lawyers do?'

'How can such as you presume to be a man of law?'

'I don't presume. I have too much self respect,' Gresham replied self-deprecatingly.

Cut. Thrust. Parry. Cut. Thrust. Parry. Gresham was starting to enjoy himself. Coke was energised now, the power almost visibly flowing through his ageing body. He spoke with scorn, hurling his words at Gresham.

'Self respect for yourself! Self! It is all you know, all you can speak of! The law speaks of respect for all people and their rights. Your self respect is little more than glorified selfishness!'

'True,' said Gresham. The best way of disarming an opponent was always to recognise when he

100

spoke the truth. 'Yet my adoption of selfish survival as my creed is a response to those such as you who plead the law and justice as your creed, using it as a cloak for your greed and vanity.'

'A feeble defence!' grated Coke.

'Honesty is no defence against corruption, and never has been. Honesty merely makes men weak.'

'The honesty of the law is its strength!' said Coke, as if stating a truth that could not be denied.

'It would be, if it were honest.'

'A feeble plea!' said Coke, voice full of scorn.

'True again,' said Gresham. 'As feeble and as frail as the humans you tear to pieces in your courts. Yet the difference is that you claim to be honest to all people while seeking power and wealth through your sycophancy. I know only how to be true to myself.'

That seemed to halt Coke in his assault. Had there once been a decent man buried among that arrogance, and had Gresham somehow reminded him of the betrayal of his soul?

'So what is it that you live for, Sir Henry?' asked Coke, part scornful, part in fear.

'*For my honour*, Sir Edward.' Gresham said it simply, with a dignity that undercut the crowing of Coke's legal brain. 'So that when death comes to me, I will be able to say that for all the stupidity of this life, at least while I lived I made things happen. To say that I survived. To say that I kept my honour, my self respect and my pride.'

Coke was trying to answer, Gresham could see. Half-formed words seemed to launch up into his

101

throat and work the muscles there, but somehow died before they reached his mouth. Finally, his words emerged.

'So you will die happy, Sir Henry?' Coke tried to put a world of sarcasm into his words but somehow the sting was lost.

'No man dies happy. I hope to die at peace with my honour, Sir Edward. You? You pretend to serve the law yet serve yourself. I hope you die with honour. I suspect you will die merely with possessions.'

There was a long pause.

'It doesn't matter, really, does it?' said Gresham, his voice almost kind. 'You see, we only need to work with each other.'

'*Can* you work with me on this matter?' Coke's voice had regained its composure. The previous conversation had been inconvenient. It had provoked thoughts of the wrong kind, therefore it had been dismissed. Not forgotten, but placed somewhere in a file where it could be coldly remembered without impacting on present day reality. Good, thought Gresham, very good. Not as good as Robert Cecil, not yet, but getting there.

'I can work with Satan if I have to,' said Gresham. 'After all, I came near to doing so when I worked with Robert Cecil. As I was saying, shall we get down to business?'

The two men looked at each other. Again, Coke broke first. He glanced away, down to his long-forgotten papers.

'Then, as you said, we should get down to business. These letters that were stolen. Cecil had spies.' Coke raised an eyebrow in Gresham's direction. 'Spies other than yourself. They reported that a Cambridge bookseller had been involved in the theft. Rumour, you understand, only rumour, based on one single instance where a man who *might* have claimed to be a Cambridge bookseller *might* have tried to sell letters to one of Cecil's agents which *might* have been the ones we are seeking to find. That was one reason why the Earl thought of you to help us out, with your knowledge of Cambridge.'

'Does this bookseller have a name?'

'It is here, somewhere...' Coke rummaged among his papers. 'Ah, yes! "Cornelius Wagner". How very elaborate...'

A sudden, vague chill took Gresham's heart. Cornelius Wagner. There was no bookseller called Cornelius Wagner in Cambridge. Gresham knew them all. Yet he also knew of a Cornelius, and of a Wagner. Where had he heard the name?

'I had hoped to meet you with Sir Thomas Overbury,' Coke said, 'but it appears he must have been delayed...'

There was a ruckus outside the door then, shouting and a heavy thud. The door impacted inwards with a sharp crack and the servant whose head had appeared round the door earlier was flung into the room by what was clearly a hearty kick from the man standing in the doorway. The servant's head was bloodied from a cut that ran across his forehead. He was crying with a mixture of shame and anger, his hand wiping away tears and blood until they mingled and ran down his wrist to stain his shirt with a pink wetness.

103

'Sir!' The servant tried to speak. 'I am so sorry, I...' Coke raised a hand to silence him. The boy rose clumsily to his feet, a tear ripping half the leg of his hose. He bowed his head.

'You may go now,' said Coke, gazing at the figure in the doorway.

'Insolent pig!' said Sir Thomas Overbury as the servant scuttled past him, hand raised to ward off further blows.

As a consequence of his close relationship with James I, the vast majority of the King's correspondence was passed on to Robert Carr, unopened, for him to deal with. Carr, whose brain was small as if to compensate for his magnificent body, passed it on unopened to his oldest friend, Sir Thomas Overbury, who then dictated the answers. Overbury had brains enough for both of them. A tall, handsome figure capable of biting wit, his power as the *eminence noir* behind the King's favourite had added to his natural vanity and arrogance, until he was frequently described as insufferable by even the mildest men at Court. The King tolerated him because he was in love with Carr, but in truth, he both distrusted and disliked Overbury. Queen Anna, otherwise a feather-brained and overblown lapsed beauty, hated Overbury with unequalled venom. In a rare display of power, Queen Anna had forced Overbury to flee to Paris the year before. He had been allowed to return simply because without him Robert Carr had floundered under the duties imposed on him by the King. It was a very tender and fragile truce.

Overbury advanced into the room. He ignored

104

Gresham completely. 'Your servant is insolent, Sir Edward,' said Overbury, peeling off his fine-fitting gloves and flinging them carelessly upon the table. 'He presumed to question the time of my arrival. I've been deep in matters of state. I disciplined him, as you saw. It were better, of course, to come from his master.'

Well, well, well, thought Gresham. This one is very special. He looked with amusement to Sir Edward Coke.

It must have been Overbury who supplied details of the theft of the compromising letters to Coke. Why else was he here? The loss of these letters must be truly embarrassing. For all that he had made a show of his entry, and been deliberately late to make a point, the fact remained that Overbury *was* here, and at Coke's bidding. Rescuing the letters would therefore give Coke huge credit in Overbury's eyes and, in all probability, the eyes of Robert Carr and King James himself. It would also give Coke a huge moral advantage in his dealings with the King should he choose to act as saviour, and, the cynic in Gresham noted, an equally huge opportunity for blackmail.

Were the letters in King James's own hand? wondered Gresham. If they were, and Coke recovered them, he held the whip-hand over James. If they were in Carr's hand they could be more easily dismissed as forgeries. Either way, Carr could lose huge favour with the King if he was responsible for the permanent loss of such damaging letters. If Carr's reputation was at stake, then Overbury would be involved.

Yet how on earth was Sir Edward Coke, a man

of no small vanity himself, going to rein in his tongue in the face of this wholly offensive, reeking apology of a man? This is going to be more fun that it first seemed, thought Gresham.

Overbury sat down without invitation and knocked a few papers aside to show his superiority. His gaze wandering round the room, he finally allowed it to fall on Gresham.

'Gresham,' he said flatly, with a raised lip, an expression of total scorn and without so much as the merest nod of his head. It was extraordinarily ill-mannered. Duels had been fought and lives lost on the basis of lesser insults. Good manners were not simply outward courtesy. They were the measure of the respect in which a man was held.

Overbury swivelled his eyes round the room once more, then brought them back to rest on Gresham. Just at that moment Gresham's pupils seemed to enlarge. It was as if Gresham's gaze had decided Overbury was of no importance and looked through him in search of something of significance. Along with the eyes that did not seem to see him, Overbury was aware of the queer, sardonic half-smile on Gresham's face. It was as if he was being mocked and ignored at the same time.

'Gresham!' Overbury's venom reinforced the insult. 'Why do we need a ... *spy* to help us in this matter?' Overbury spoke to Coke. His tone was scornful, dismissive.

Gresham did the one thing Overbury found it hardest to cope with. He ignored him completely. His eyes turned from the window at which he had been gazing, through Overbury without register-

106

ing his presence and on to Coke's own eyes.

'As I was saying, shall we get down to business?' Gresham asked of Coke, outwardly thoroughly relaxed.

Overbury's mouth dropped. 'Cease your petty games, Gresham!' he announced, 'or I'll have to break your pate as I broke the servant's!'

Do I let it take its course now, or do I back down? This man would never bend, thought Gresham. So let it take its course.

Gresham waited politely for Overbury to finish, then carried on as if Overbury's words had never been spoken. So strong was the impression given by Gresham that there was only he and Coke in the room that Overbury almost had to shake himself to confirm he was actually there.

'Cecil was of the opinion that these incriminating and embarrassing letters must have been stolen from Carr or Overbury. If we're to do business, we really do need to stop playing games. I'm assuming that the letters were stolen from Overbury.' Gresham's tone made for no recognition whatsoever that Overbury was in the room with them. 'Overbury's clever enough to know how potentially explosive and destructive such letters would be. He's treacherous enough to keep them for future use against either his friend Carr or the King. He's arrogant enough and fool enough to lose them, and hated enough for any of his servants to risk stealing them if they thought that by doing so they could harm their master.'

There was a moment's silence while the enormity of what Gresham had said sank into Overbury's mind. He exploded. He leaped to his feet with a roar.

'You cur! You dog! You whore's whelp!' His sword was half out of its scabbard and he was rushing to fall upon Gresham ...

...and suddenly he was flying through the air, landing to the sound of a sickening crunch followed by the sharpest stab of pain and then blissful unconsciousness.

The pain was the first thing he remembered as he came to, the sharp, red-hot pain and the bubbling noise as air tried to pass to and fro between the blood from his nose and mouth. Dimly he heard a voice. It was Gresham.

'...so all in all there's little likely to result from our investigating the point at which the letters were taken. Whoever did it will cover their tracks. Equally, whoever took them will want to make either political or financial advantage out of them. They'll have to make themselves known. This Cambridge bookseller might do just that. Cecil's spies will have prided themselves on the fact they found this man out as having some involvement. It's more likely he made sure they knew what was going on. It has to be this bookseller. Here's where we'll have our chance to retrieve the letters. The real question is whether we do it on his terms, or invent terms of our own.'

Sir Edward Coke was frozen to his chair, eyes passing rapidly between Gresham speaking fluently and clearly to him and the tumbled heap of Overbury lying on the floor. It was not so much the fact that Sir Thomas Overbury had been knocked out and bloodied while launching an assault on Gresham. It was the sheer clinical speed with which it had been accomplished that had silenced Sir Edward, and provoked real fear in him for the first time he could remember in many years. He had almost forgotten the taste of fear. Things had happened in a blur of movement. Overbury, goaded, had embarked on a mad rush towards Gresham. Gresham had hardly seemed to move, merely sway to one side. The momentum of Overbury's forward rush was such that it carried him onto Gresham's outstretched foot, tumbling him over and forward across the floor to crash into the far wall, head and nose first. In a blur of movement, Gresham had resumed his seat almost before Overbury had ceased moving – surely it could not have been so? – and carried on talking to Coke as though nothing had happened. The servants had rushed through the door. Gresham had ignored them. Even the one with the broken head who might just have been smiling as he saw the mess that was Overbury on the floor. Coke had motioned them away.

They both became aware that Overbury was stirring back into a painful consciousness in the corner.

'You must interview Overbury's and Carr's servants to find out as much as you can about how the letters went missing. I will interview Master Shakespeare. It's almost certainly a waste of time. Yet it has to be done.'

Coke spoke sharply. 'The manuscripts are secondary. Plays are not our concern. Letters are.' Coke was showing that phenomenal capacity to take unpleasant facts and sideline them, lock them away so that they did not interfere with his management of the moment's business. Yet was the tone just a little too urgent in dismissing these plays? Gresham immediately racked them up to a higher priority.

Sir Edward Coke glared balefully at Gresham. He had thought Gresham an irritant and an inconvenience when Cecil had insisted on informing him of the missing letters and manuscript, but necessary if the one thing that Cecil and Coke needed to happen was to take place. He had agreed to Gresham's involvement because he had believed that Gresham was being used as livebait. Now the bait had revealed himself to be an extraordinarily dangerous figure. A dreadful fear crossed Coke's heart. Was he using Gresham? Or was Gresham using him?

'Do I have your attention, Sir Edward?' Gresham's tone was solicitous. Coke had done something he had spent a lifetime training himself not to do, drifted away from a conversation. Cursing inwardly, he dragged himself back. 'We must understand one thing, Sir Edward.'

'And what exactly is that "one thing"?' asked Coke, his voice almost a hiss.

'I don't for a minute believe that I've been told the whole truth. But as Robert Cecil might have found time to tell you before he died, I usually do find the truth eventually.'

'What do you believe?' snapped Coke.

'I believe I've been told some of the truth. I believe in these letters, and I believe both they and some play scripts have been stolen. I believe both items have the capacity to get someone important into deep trouble. I believe there is a

110

hidden agenda which means you need me to flush out the thief because you can't or daren't do it yourself.'

This was so close to the truth that even Coke could not stop a tiny tremor from crossing his face.

'Quite,' said Gresham, noting the tremor. 'I repeat: I do usually find the truth. You and Cecil believed I was an arrow that you could shoot in the direction you wanted. Your arrow has become a hawk, a lethal weapon with a mind of its own.'

Coke had always hated hawks. The total, unflinching, single-mindedness of their eyes, their utter focus on the prey, their inability to be distracted or diverted both undermined and angered him in a way he did not understand and could not therefore control.

Overbury groaned, rubbed his face and threw up as he felt and saw the blood on his hand. He tried to get to his feet, but fell on all fours.

'But don't worry too much,' Gresham said to Coke, almost sympathetically. 'Hawks get killed too. Who knows? Perhaps this is when my luck will run out.'

Coke tried not to show on his face just how very much he hoped that Gresham's luck would truly run out.

'By the way, Sir Edward,' Gresham said as he rose to leave, 'there's a foul stench in this room.' By the merest movement of his head he seemed to gesture towards Overbury. 'A stench of something rotten. Perhaps one of your hounds is so old or ill that it can't stop itself from breaking wind.'

There were no hounds in the room. Coke viewed them as unhygienic and anarchic.

'Such animals are dangerous. For all that they're useful, they can infect their masters with their own corruption.' Gresham flicked a speck of dust off the arm of his glorious velvet and silk doublet. 'If for pity's sake you can't have them put down, then you're well advised to keep them at a distance.'

Two sets of eyes directed glares of undiluted hatred at Sir Henry Gresham as he left the room.

Overbury dragged himself to the table. 'I...' he began to bluster.

'*Will you be silent for once?*' hissed Coke. And, for once, Sir Thomas Overbury remained silent. 'Gresham is dangerous. Above all, he's dangerous. You saw how dangerous. God knows why you seek to taunt and antagonise everyone you meet.'

Overbury flushed, and lowered his bloodied head. 'Why do we need Gresham?' he mumbled through bloodied lips. 'If he is so ... dangerous, why welcome this viper to our bosom?'

Do you ever listen, Sir Thomas Overbury? thought Coke. Have you ever listened in your life?

'We need Gresham,' Coke explained patiently, as if to a child, 'because the Cambridge bookseller is Christopher Marlowe. Kit Marlowe. Diseased, syphilitic. Returned from the grave with homicidal mania for all those who wanted him dead, and for all those who conspired in his exile.'

Sir Thomas Overbury vomited over the table, the thin yellow spume staining a multitude of papers on Coke's desk. It seemed to make him feel better. He sat up, ready to speak through his battered lips. Coke decided to get in before he did so. The acid, sweet smell of the vomit filled his nostrils.

'Marlowe simply wants to destroy: the King, the monarchy, you, me. He came back into the country with enough information from his past to do very, very serious damage. He stole those damned letters – from you, Sir Thomas! – so now he has even more powder in his gun. And he has the manuscripts. He wants to see his damned play–'

'The Fall of Lucifer,' croaked Sir Thomas. For some reason he had remembered that.

'Yes,' said Sir Edward, looking at his own fallen and bloodied Lucifer, *'The Fall of Lucifer.* He wants to see his damned play performed, and is convinced it will provoke a revolution.'

'Nonsense!' said Sir Thomas, learning how to speak again and fingering his lips. 'Plays don't provoke rebellion!'

'No?' said Coke, stung to a response. 'And when my good, and very dead, Lord Essex mounted his rebellion, didn't he inspire it by commanding a performance of *Richard II* by that upstart crow Shakespeare? The rebellion failed. The provocation worked very well.'

'Oh God!' said Overbury, 'I'm sick at heart.' He sank down in his seat.

'I think, Sir Thomas,' said Coke, 'that you're sick everywhere. We need Gresham because *we can't find Marlowe.* Cecil believed that if we set Gresham on to Marlowe, Marlowe will rush at him like an old man at a whore.'

Overbury raised his head again. 'And kill him?'

113

His tone was almost lascivious.

'Possibly,' said Coke. Good God! he thought. Overbury was now tracing patterns on the wood of the table with the yellow fluid of his own vomit. 'But more likely draw him out and be killed himself. Safely killed, with no direct government involvement.'

'So we hope that Marlowe goes at Gresham like an old man at a second, young wife?'

Coke had recently married again, to a young girl who was leading him a merry dance. Suddenly Coke knew why so many people wanted to kill Sir Thomas Overbury. I will ignore this, he thought. That foul fiend Gresham has shown me the way. *Ignore him.*

Overbury's finger paused in the middle of an intricate pattern. Most of the patterns had arrow-point heads, Coke noted. Overbury lifted his head once more. The effect was spoiled by the blood that smeared his whole face and had dried into his beard. Yet it was not spoiled for Overbury. For he had not just been bloodied and beaten by an opponent. It had never happened. It had been wiped out of his mind. Perhaps he even had the power to force his mind to cut off the signals of pain. All the old arrogance returned, his beating dismissed. It was a pity Gresham was not there. He would have noted the short-term effect of hitting someone and pointed it out to Mannion. Mannion believed in things that could be eaten, drunk and slept with. In addition, he believed anything that did not work properly, particularly human beings, responded to a careful, cautious and judicious thumping.

'Who can guarantee that any man will kill another? Gresham? Scum. A spy. A double-dealer.'

'How easily could he have killed you, Sir Thomas?' said Coke in words of ice.

For another moment at least, Sir Thomas Overbury was silent. God help them all, thought Coke. They had released an uncontrollable force of nature on to the hunt for Kit Marlowe. They had placed all their money on one bet, that these two very different forces of nature would neutralise each other. Gresham would find Marlowe and kill him. Then a source would be closed off, permanently. Or Marlowe would find Gresham and kill him. Then the only person who could find the truth would be dead, and the only dangerous person who knew the truth would have revealed himself, and so made it easier for him to be murdered.

It had to be the right policy. Yet why did Gresham's presence in it fill him with such dread?

8

26th May, 1612
The Globe Theatre, Bankside

'...within this wooden O...'
SHAKESPEARE, *Henry V*

Rain had fallen, perhaps only for a few minutes, while Gresham and Mannion had been inside Coke's house. Slight though it had been, it had calmed the dust and placed little diamonds of light on the crazy, leaning rooftops.

Mannion looked enquiringly at Gresham, who had halted and was gazing abstractedly up at the sky. Then, to Mannion's surprise, he turned on his heels and started to walk. In the wrong direction. Mannion swung his eyes around instinctively. No one was watching them, or no one doing so obviously. No sudden interest in the fine gentleman and his purse walking down the street, no nods between two or three men with one setting off to bump into Gresham while another cut his purse from his belt. Reassured, Mannion set off after his master.

They were going to The Globe, the round 'o' of a building with its centre open to the elements. It was late afternoon when they reached their destination, that afternoon's performance finished, the crowd long gone and evening already starting

116

to set in.

'What are we doing here?' muttered Mannion. He could see the reason for their long walk if there was a play to see, but no reason at all to visit an empty shell of a building.

'Looking,' said Gresham absent-mindedly. 'Just looking.' A theatre was naturally easy to defend, he was thinking. Entrances were kept down to a minimum so that everyone who went through one had to pay, and the high, outside walls of the building had little need for windows.

It was that time of day when no lantern was strictly needed to guide the way, but its warmth would still have glowed in the failing light. Gresham went to one of the narrow ground level entrances. The wood was thick but scarred and dry, leached with age. Gresham tried the iron handle, rattled the door. The great white curtain wall of the theatre was cross-hatched with the squares of its timber beams, standing out more and more as the gloom deepened. There was give between the latch and its lock, enough for a crowbar to wrench it open, but it was secure against anything except a direct and brutal assault. It was quiet now, especially after the noise and yelling bustle of the great city on the other side of the river, and Gresham waited while the echoes of iron on iron could be heard to ricochet around the vast empty space of The Globe. Nothing moved. No one stirred.

Gresham looked enquiringly at Mannion.

'Someone killed the porter here not so long ago?' Mannion asked. 'Glad they've tightened up their security.' He spat thoughtfully into the

117

damp earth at his feet, looking carefully to see that his spittle was clear. Satisfied, he hitched his belt up round his tunic and waited for Gresham to decide what to do next.

They started to walk round the girth of The Globe. Others would have looked for a lantern, for servants to guard them. There was a casual ease to Gresham's walk, his hand carelessly on the hilt of his sword, and clear menace in the bulk of Mannion. An onlooker would have sensed why these men needed no extra guard.

The theatre seemed deserted, silent. Like all great buildings that come alive when thousands throng into them, there was an almost death-like concentration to its stillness when empty, a sense of artificiality and yet of a great beast sleeping. Why did some buildings have a sense of history being made in them, thought Gresham, while others, outwardly more important, seem bland and inert?

They reached full circle. No sign of a new porter. Was he safely locked away inside, too terrified by recent events to explore the noise by the door? What had happened on the night of the murder? Had a door been left unlocked, by accident or on purpose? Had the porter been called to the door or had he known the person who had summoned him? Had it been someone already inside the theatre who had turned on the old man?

Too many questions, sighed Gresham. There always were too many questions. He had learned to stop the rampaging flow of his mind, haul himself back, restrict his questioning to one answer at a time. Well, there were no answers at The Globe, not yet. Except perhaps one. The King's Men were clearly not expecting a second break-in at their theatre or security would have been positively hanging off the walls. There was no shortage of ruffians and ex-soldiers to stand guard for those who had enough coin to pay them. Was that an answer in itself? Did it mean that those who ran the company had some reason to know that there would be no repetition of the break-in?

'Boat?' asked Mannion hopefully. It was their quickest way home, and Mannion hated walking nearly as much as he hated washing. There was not an ounce of excess fat on his great frame but how he kept himself as fit as a twenty-year-old was a mystery to Gresham, who had never seen him voluntarily work up a sweat.

'Boat,' agreed Gresham, his mind still wrestling with what he had seen and the realisation of just how much he did not know.

Behind them, the white mass of The Globe dominated the skyline, enigmatic, silent and empty.

9

25th June, 1612
Granville College, Cambridge

'The middle of humanity thou never knewest, but the extremity of both ends.'
SHAKESPEARE, *Timon of Athens*

In winter it was cold and damp in Cambridge. The chill winds blew in from Siberia. The low mists that breathed out from the river in the early morning gave a sense of mystery to everything they touched, as the snow gave a sense of magic. At night, with a clear sky, the moon picked out the stone and buttresses of the colleges with cold clarity, bathing them in white light. With snow on them they became monuments of stunning beauty.

In summer, even on the brightest day, the air was often thick and heavy, as if infected by the Fens. The flies were everywhere, even staying on meat as it was speared by the eater's knife and lifted to his or her mouth. The river flowed like a dark sludge, stinking, its water seeming to thicken as it slapped against the hulls of the boats plying their trade, staining the painted wood. When the air and the smell became particularly thick Gresham had seen people freeze in their tracks in the muddied street when a man sneezed. The plague

120

looked over Cambridge's shoulder at all times, the sneeze one of its first symptoms.

Gresham was back in his rooms at Granville College, the rooms in the medieval court he had claimed from the first days when his wealth had started to reinvigorate and refound the college. The shelves were country carpentry, rough-hewn but solid and not bending beneath the weight of books and papers Gresham had loaded on them over the years. Gresham doubted his guest for the evening had noted the books. He doubted he could read.

Candlelight usually hid a multitude of sins. In LongLankin's case it exposed them. The gentle light of the wicks flickered across LongLankin's face, revealing it for the battleground it was. Two or three huge boils disfigured his face, crusted volcanoes, enough to throw long shadows across it when the light glanced in a certain direction. The few teeth in his face reinforced the black, gaping holes where the others had been, emphasising the empty space rather than compensating for it.

'I dunno,' he said, 'I just dunno.' He swilled the remnants of his small ale round the tankard Gresham had filled for him. LongLankin never drank wine. Maybe he thought it might make him middle class.

'Let's try again,' said Gresham. *'Remember.* What did this bookseller look like?'

'I told yer. I were drunk. I was rubbished. I wouldn't 'ave recognised me own mother if she'd shoved her tit in me mouth.'

'LongLankin,' said Gresham with evident

distaste, 'please: spare me the details of your weaning.' No one ever called him 'Long' or 'Lankin'. For some reason, he was LongLankin. One word. Indivisible. And he was very drunk, with the memory of an alcoholic colander.

'Look,' said LongLankin, 'it's as easy as this.' He spoke with the certainty of someone who has completed the drunk's progress. Sober. Mellowed and softened. Drunk. Very drunk. Trashed. Unconscious. Awake and in agony. Nearly mellowed and softened again. 'He were ... a man. Shrunk. Warped. Dwarfed.'

'LongLankin,' said Gresham with a patience he did not feel. 'That doesn't help me find him. To be frank, Cambridge isn't agog with news of shrunken dwarves claiming to be booksellers–'

'Plays!' LongLankin had remembered something. It was a new experience, and he was clearly pleased with it. A smile appeared on the linked crevasses of his face. One of the boils on his neck, Gresham noticed, had a single tuft of thick hair sticking out of it.

'Plays?'

'He said he ... said he did things with plays.'

'What did he do with plays?' asked Gresham, intrigued, his boredom forgotten.

'Said ... said...' LongLankin's memory was fading again, like a candle guttering out its last few moment of light. 'Said he wanted the students to put one on, like. Y'know, like they do.'

Gresham knew. There had been riots lasting two days last year when the John's men, coming to see a Trinity comedy, had been locked out for shortage of seats. The John's men had tried to

122

break into the college, and the Trinity men had taken to hurling the heaviest objects they could find from the rooftops and gatehouse. Plays were hot material in Cambridge.

It was no good. LongLankin could tell him no more, and all he had confirmed was the existence of a man masquerading as bookseller, and the link to the theatre. Gresham bundled the semi-comatose man out of the room, and sat back in the high-backed oak chair. It was at a moment such as this that he savoured his loneliness. It was a huge luxury, another privilege of his vast wealth. Most of the other Fellows would board three or four students in their rooms, the Fellow taking the main bed, the students on truckle beds.

So there was a man who called himself a book-seller, appearing suddenly in Cambridge. Yet the few people this man had introduced himself to had heard nothing about stolen letters from the King to his lover. Plays. It was all he had talked about.

Plays. Theatre, Was this about politics? Or was it about plays? The only certain thing was that it would be about power. It was always about power. Gresham needed to regain his feel for the theatre. He and his family would go to the play.

10

July, 1612
The Globe Theatre, Bankside

'King: "What do you call the play?"
Hamlet: "The Mousetrap."
                    SHAKESPEARE, *Hamlet*

Summer was the best and the worst of times for the players. The best was when the weather allowed the old theatres to be packed to the hilt, with a roof open to the heavens. The worst was the plague, which could close the theatres and take the actors from roaring profit to catastrophic loss and god forsaken tours of the sticks. So far in 1612 their luck had held.

Going to the play was a ritual in the Gresham household, and huge fun. Soon they would consider bringing the children, but as things stood it was an outing for Gresham and Jane only. And, of course, the servants. Mannion considered it his divine right to accompany his master and mistress everywhere they went. Gresham also paid for some of the more senior servants to go with them, as well as some of the young ones. In return, the servants had to row the great eight-oared boat that was the pride of The House to deliver themselves and the couple from The House's own jetty across the bustling river to

124

within a few hundred yards of The Globe.

'So which idle varlets do we take to the play today?' asked Gresham, squaring his bonnet and straightening the sleeve of his doublet.

'Well,' said Jane, ticking them off on her fingers, 'there's Harry, of course, as boat captain. And I think we ought to reward the younger Harry, the one who joined us two years ago. He's put himself out to be pleasant, and he works like a horse. Then there's Jack in the stables–'

'Can any one of them *row?*' interrupted Gresham.

'Well,' said Jane, smiling sweetly, 'we'll all of us know the answer to that very shortly.' Jane commanded intense loyalty from the servants, despite an occasional fierce temper and on very rare occasions an ability to revert to her peasant upbringing and adopt a very forthright and robust style of conversation with a servant thought to have pocketed the occasional item, or bought two chickens but magically only delivered one to Cook. At such moments a dread hush descended over The House and people walked on tip-toe.

There were a few low clouds scudding across the blue and a brisk wind lifted their faces as they came out of the Water Gate and advanced down the stone jetty. The lapping of the water was music to them, alongside the creaking of the wood and the shouts vaguely heard from the river. Coming up to midday, the river was at its busiest. Every type of boat, from the gilded splendour of a king's barge down to the tiny, rotting tub with only one oar carrying what looked like a beggar erratically cross-stream, was scurrying up and

125

down the length of London's main street. With a brisk wind, those that had it put up sail, the stark white of a brand new set contrasting with the faded and yellowing canvas of the commercial traffic. Ropes snapped across the wooden pile of the masts, sails cracked in and out as the wind blustered, and everywhere was the lap of the tiny wavelets on the wooden hulls.

Their boat was for eight oarsmen, four to each side, with room at the prow and stern for easily that many passengers. Gresham and Jane took their seats at the stern, covered by a sumptuous awning. Jane had never favoured the pearly white complexion of the court lady and Gresham loved the subtle tinge of bronze her perfect skin always carried. She seemed impervious to sunlight, her upbringing having given her an immunity denied to other Court ladies. Gresham had questioned the need for the awning, designed to keep the sun off a lady's skin as much as to keep off the rain.

'Surety you don't need that great waste of money flapping over your head?' he had asked.

'My lord!' she had exclaimed. 'What would the world be coming to if Court ladies only demanded what they strictly needed?'

The motley collection of servants grinned at them in delight as they climbed on board, doffing their caps, not hiding their excitement and pleasure. What better day could it be? They served the handsomest man and the most beautiful lady in London, and were viewed with awe by other great men's servants because of their master's dark reputation. They had good food in their bellies and good cloth on their backs. They were to ride in style on the best boat on the Thames. The sun was shining, there was a snap in the air and they were off to the playhouse. It was good to be alive on that fine July morning.

'Well,' said Gresham, standing and looking down at his men as they pushed off, 'can you sorry-looking collection of apologies for men find the strength to hold an oar? Or have we wined and dined you and kept you in such luxury that with one pull you'll be moaning that you can do no more?'

The response was eight oars hitting the water in unison, and a massive surge out into the river that would have had Gresham off his feet had he not known exactly what was coming.

'Feeble!' he said mightily, gazing down on them with the half-smile that his face fell into in repose. 'Well, keep trying. At this rate we might make it for the third act.'

Gresham sat down again and raised an eyebrow at Jane, who was gazing out across the river with fascinated concentration. Mannion, behind them, had a firm grasp of the tiller.

The river here was fast-moving, muddy brown even in summer and with a blue sky. Unlike the Fleet river, which was little more than a stinking ditch of sewage, there was a semblance of health if one did not look too closely into the brown water. Yet only the crassest of fools would drink from it. Neither Jane nor Gresham had ever washed in it.

The flag was flying bravely from the thatched roof of The Globe, a many-sided brick and timber construction dominating the skyline. They landed the boat at a private jetty whose owner guaranteed secure berthing, and whose collection of thugs (most of them his own children) would have frightened off Attila the Hun and all his hordes had they come a-thieving.

The men held the boat while first of all Jane and then Gresham crossed on to the shore. Gresham looked down on the head of the younger Harry.

'Ready for the play, then, Harry?' Gresham took care to know all his servants by name. It was, he thought, one of the basic gestures of respect to the people with whom one lived and on whom one depended.

'That right I am, sir!' grinned Harry, tousled hair ruffed up by the brisk wind.

The roads leading to The Globe were narrow, and the vast coaches that some of the audience insisted on using could block whole streets, as had happened today. Gresham, Jane and his men marched through the throng and on to the gate that they and some of the more select of the audience used to gain access to their seats. The doorkeeper nodded them through. Gresham was well known. More and more mutton dressed as lamb going to the old theatres, thought Gresham, with each year that went by, despite divine visitations from the likes of whoever was in the coach. Further sign that the richer and better bred went to the indoor theatres, leaving the old amphitheatres such as The Globe for riff-raff. Oh, there was quality enough still, if one looked. The lawyers and MPs who had always supported The Globe were still there, but fewer, and there were more young men in cheap shoe buckles and rosettes, with extravagant embroidered waist-coats in appalling taste and bursting their seams because of cheap thread almost as soon as they were worn.

'Sir Thomas! How delightful to see you again!' Gresham spoke easily as the figure of Overbury clambered up the narrow stairs to the first tier. Overbury started, and turned around. His face was a mess, Gresham noted happily, a riot of black and blue bruising around his mouth and nose, ascending to a massive black eye. Over-bury's lip curled as best it could.

'The bastard and his whore!' he sneered at Gresham, daring him to fight, hand on his sword.

It was beginning again, thought Jane. Her stomach turned cold. The hatred. The violence. Men pitted against men. At least in the village that had spawned her you could predict the relationships, awful though they might be. Here, in the world of a Court lady, bitter hatred could be revealed in a glance from those who knelt together at the communion rail, vicious enmity enflamed by a chance meeting at the theatre.

'Why, Sir Thomas,' said Gresham, 'there's no need to refer to yourself in those terms. We all know you've no breeding and that your mother was a whore. But those of us who frequent high society know that the best sort are always liars.'

Sir Thomas made to draw his sword. Some-thing in Gresham's easy smile, and the men who moved to his side, stopped him. He gazed at Gresham, scorn enough in his voice to blister paint.

'You will pay for that. Not here. Not now. But in some other place.'

He turned, and with his servant brushed aside the bodies crowding up the stairs as they strode purposefully down them.

They took their seats, their servants in front of them. Gresham watched the audience, as much a show as the play itself. For many of the young blades the theatre was somewhere not to watch but to be seen. Preening and pandering, they were so tightly corseted they could not bend, and their vast collars or ruffs seized their heads and necks as if in a vice. Their hats rose like steeples into the sky, marking them out. Forced by the clutch of starch and lace to gaze down stiffly on everyone they saw, they could only look at a person by swinging their whole body round to face them. The apprentice boys were out in force in the Pit, brawling, scuffling and swearing to impress the schoolboys who would pay twice over for their place, once by their precious penny and another by the thrashing they would endure, bent over the block, as a result of their truancy.

The tier was full, unusually so, apart from the benches Gresham's money had reserved. Gresham was relaxed, happy. The momentary stain of Overbury's presence had rippled but not dented his composure. It seemed to have upset Jane more, but now she was gazing happily around her, nodding to an acquaintance, sharing as they all did in the excitement of so many people gathered in one such small place, feeding off the raw human energy the sheer intensity of contact generated.

There was what the players would call a fanfare of trumpets and what Gresham would call an unholy blast of noise. It was the traditional start to a play.

The audience called it *Beatrice and Benedick*, after the hero and heroine who were deeply in love but whose bickering and witty battling for position had caused audiences to howl with laughter and cry with sympathy for years. It was one of the plays that had made Shakespeare's name, a play loved by both the Court ladies and the groundlings in the Pit. The actors called it *Much Ado About Nothing*.

The play was beginning. A duke-like figure, gorgeously costumed, was speaking to two girls. The boy actors playing the girls were breathtakingly convincing.

'I learn in this letter that Don Pedro of Arragon comes this night to Messina...'
'How many gentlemen have you lost in this action?'

The first gallery usually housed the men of substance. There were other, more private boxes in the tiers, but the first gallery was a favoured and expensive spot. Gresham's mind had already engaged with the play, the extraordinary way in which a few words from a painted actor could take two or three thousand souls instantly into a strange court in a foreign land, and make them believe they were there. A distant, detached part of his mind noted that among the wealthy audience who patronised the tier were an unusually large number of heavy, thick-set men. Which

131

other gentry had brought their servants to the play? he wondered idly, without sufficient interest to look around and trace the man.

'I pray you, is Signior Mountanto returned from the wars or no?'
'He hath done good service, lady, in these wars.'
'He is most in the company of the right noble Claudio.'
'I will hold friends with you, lady.'

The house was restless. Sometimes in a play the noise would lower itself to a gentle hum, the nuts be consumed early on. Those selling their produce or their bodies in the Pit would be drawn into the play themselves. At other times the house spun and buzzed like an angry wasps' nest, the actors clinging on to every word and holding on for their lives. For no apparent reason, this was such a day.

'Good Signior Leonato, are you come to meet your trouble?'
'I wonder that you will still be talking, Signior Benedick. Nobody marks you...'

Something extraordinary happened. Three rather beautiful, pure amber lines of liquid arched from the very top gallery and splashed gently on to the crowd below. Confused, thinking it raining on a sunny day, men and women looked up, open-mouthed, and caught the liquid on their upturned faces and in their lips.

It was piss. Human piss. An appalling, humiliating, unbelievable insult to the honour of those soiled in the mess. Three louts had stood on the edge of the top gallery and pissed on the groundlings in the Pit.

There was an almost soundless roar as those desecrated in the Pit caught sight of the men who had dared to do this. As a single, heaving mass, the men among them, and a few of the commoner women, made for the stairs to confront their attackers.

Oh God, thought Gresham, as realisation of the truth banged down inside his mind like portcullis after portcullis smashing down on stone. There was chaos in the Pit, uproar as those dirtied by the act were ignited by it in a riotous desire for revenge. Panic spread through the two and half thousand souls in the audience, the play forgotten, reality smashing through the play's carefully wrought fantasy. Those not set on revenge rose to their feet, drew their loved ones to them, looked around in confusion.

Under cover of this total chaos, unseen by the audience blinded by fear, Gresham noted with horror the fourteen or fifteen men dressed as servants rise to their feet as one, reach inside their tunics and rough jerkins and draw out hardened wooden cudgels or wickedly edged cheap knives. Their target was clear.

Gresham.

Jane.

For a single, terrible, bleak moment, Henry Gresham gazed full into the face of his own death. In less than a second the appalled realisation of what he had done thudded into his brain. Lulled into false security. Seduced into relaxation by pleasure, like the man knifed at climax by his lover. His servants, his eight men, were here to enjoy. They were not armed. He started to draw his weapon out from the scabbard, as if in slow motion. It would be there fully two or three steps ahead of the man fixedly charging at him, club already upraised. He would, he could kill that man. *But what of the horde of others that followed him?*

He was too much of a fighter to take his eye off the man who would either be killed or who would kill him: the first in the mad rush of his attackers, the one with the brute strength to have hurled himself to the forefront of the charge on Gresham. Yet part of him disengaged from his main self, almost as if it floated above him.

Something extraordinary was happening.

His men were standing on their seats, drawing weapons from their tunics and jerkins. There was panic in their eyes, fear, confusion. The look of soldiers. The glint of metal. Boat axes! A heavy, short wooden shaft. A glinting, razor-sharp cutting and chopping edge on one side, a vicious sharp point on the other.

Mannion. Shouting orders at them. Not shrieking, nor yelling. Shouting – clearly, firmly, almost calmly. Mannion, who had risen to his feet a split-second before the attackers, a crucial, life-saving split second, to warn their men of danger. Mannion, who, for no reason he nor any other human would ever know, had quietly ordered the boat crew, as he usually did, to take the boat axes out of the locker, and a knife or two if they wished.

Just in case.

Gresham used his other arm to fling Jane viciously to the ground. Never taking his eyes off his attacker, he waited until the man had drawn back his cudgel for the blow that would have smashed in Gresham's skull. At that precise moment he flicked the blade of his sword across the man's face. He caught one eye, missed the second by a hair's breadth. The shock was terrible. Even though Gresham's flick had not caught a single muscle controlling his arms, the man's hand suddenly flexed open as his eye exploded and the club flew out of its grasp. Caught by his own momentum, lunging forward, Gresham stepped up on to the bench as his assailant, his face a bloody mess, flopped by him to crash senseless to the floor.

Someone screamed. Jane. Some primeval communication made him look not at her sprawled body on the floor but to his left. He had chosen the right assailant. The man rushing at him from the right had been the nearest, the most dangerous. Yet the man rushing down on him from the left had been only a second behind. Gresham's brain had mathematically computed the threat and turned instinctively to the right as the greater risk. It left him with no time to deal with the man charging in from the left.

The man had a short, flat forehead and thick, bushy eyebrows. For a moment Gresham's sword felt as if it weighed several tons, as if the act of dragging it round to meet his second assailant would take a whole lifetime.

Would his sword have met the man from the

left before his cudgel or his knife met Gresham's flesh? He was never to know.

Suddenly, unexpectedly, a hole opened up in the forehead of the second attacker. A flicker of light, and a boat axe was embedded there, between the bushy eyebrows.

As of a moment the light of life was expunged from the man's eyes. His sightless, mindless body flung past Gresham as had the other man's. Mannion had flung the axe. Mannion, hauling a second boat axe from his jerkin even as he yelled encouragement to Gresham's men.

One or two seconds, that was all it seemed. One or two seconds for the first of the attackers to be halted by Gresham, the second to be killed by Mannion. One or two seconds to cause the mass of men to falter, shocked at the sudden loss of two of their fellows. One or two seconds enough for Gresham's men to hurl themselves to their feet and gather round their master.

The attackers wavered. For another second it looked as if they might halt, turn and run, but their momentum as much as anything else carried them forward. They broke on the curtain wall of Gresham's servants, the strong keep of Gresham and Mannion, a double line before the prone body of Jane.

There was a sickening thud as body met body, club met flesh and muscle and sinew fought against muscle and sinew. The men grunted as they landed their blows, grunted as they took a blow and felt the pain searing up their limbs.

One of Gresham's men was lifted half off his feet by a blow from a cudgel, flung back into the

136

benching. Another man, scarred face, missing teeth, broke through a gap and lunged at Gresham. Off balance, Gresham lunged back, using the extra length of his blade, knowing that a swordsman against a club had only one chance. His sword pierced the man's shoulder. He screamed and fell, hand clutching the wound. Gresham's blade was stuck, in flesh or ensnared in the rough woollen cloth. With a final sobbing heave he yanked it clear.

They had to reach the back wall of the theatre. They had to position themselves so that they were only dealing with an enemy coming at them from the front. Thank God Jane was wearing a skirt more like a countrywoman's, without the huge hoops and farthingales a more vain person would have chosen.

The three men who had pissed on the Pit had vanished, the surge of men and women hunting for them dissipated in the long haul up the stairs and the fruitless search of the top gallery. There was chaos, men and women looking fearfully up at the roar of battle coming from the first tier. They were streaming out of the theatre as fast as the cramped exits and their legs would allow.

Three attackers had come leaping at four of Gresham's men.

'Get to the back wall!' Gresham yelled, his voice cutting through the shouts and screams. Clambering, clambering all the while for that damned wall. Thrusting as the pack closed in. Feeling their hot breath, the stink of garlic from one, the dreadful stench of rotting teeth from another. Keeping that grip on Jane's wrist. The grunts, sharp, spasmodic explosions of breath from both sets of men. Muttered curses, shouts, a scream as a blow landed. Feeling with his feet the broken benches beneath him. Only able to risk the quickest of glances backwards.

Young Harry had tripped over a bench and exposed himself to a blow from a swinging club. It hit his ribs, blowing the breath out of him. Just as his assailant was about to land a final blow on his pate, Harry turned aside, dodged. The club intended for his head smashed on to a bench. Splinters flew, the bench cracked near in half.

A rough, hard surface bit into Gresham's back. The wall! Now they could point outwards, a sharp-tipped semi-circle daring someone to break it. Jane suddenly dropped down behind a broken bench. Wounded? No, thank God. Sensible. Gresham was dimly aware of something lightly flitting past his face, a thud following on a short moment later. A fly? A bird? He had no time to ponder it. Was this Overbury's doing? Revenge for his humiliation? So where was he?

Some of the attackers were losing heart. This length of battle was not what they had been paid for. Yet by now the theatre was almost empty. The thugs decided to make a last throw of it.

They had guts, he would give them that, thought Gresham. That, or they were being extraordinarily well paid for their thuggery. The attackers hurled themselves at the line of Gresham's men. With Jane secure behind the upturned bench, Gresham leaped forward, sword in hand.

Two of Gresham's men went down, but several of their assailants grunted, screamed or dropped

138

like stones. Gresham's line swayed, seemed to buckle but then flexed out again. Knocked back, the man who was the leader of their attackers turned and swore at the rest for being cowards, and then leaped forward, flinging himself at the line with immense courage from the height of a bench. Whatever else he may have been, he was no coward.

He was a thin, wiry figure, with a goatee beard and small, close-set eyes. As well as a club, he brandished a long knife. Screaming, he leaped forward with his club arm upraised.

Suddenly, his hand was no longer attached to his arm. The severed body part, with the club still clenched in it, dropped to the floor while a jet of bright red blood shot from the stump. The man looked on in disbelief at his own hand falling to the ground. The blow Gresham had delivered with his sword was almost impossible. Bone needs an axe to slice through it, not a sword blade. A sharp edge helped, of course, but the real trick was a flick of the wrists – it could only be done two-handed – at the point of impact that delivered all the strength not just of the swords-man's arm but of his whole body. There was a sickening thud as Mannion delivered what must have been a death blow, breaking soft brain tissue as well as bone.

The attackers looked at the severed hand, the smashed head of their leader, the stump of his arm. Without a word, to a man they turned and ran. They were disciplined, still, after a fashion. There was a scream from one of them, and they turned to pick up their own. Eight or nine were grievously wounded, but still able to walk or be supported. Two of them dead? Three? Gresham reckoned it could not be less. Four with their leader. Two of the attackers, one heavy built, the other a light weight, made to grab their leader, legs stuck ungainly over a bench. Gresham's men growled, moved forward.

'Hold!' said Gresham. It was a croak, no more. His throat was dry beyond belief. It was enough. His own men held back. 'Take him,' said Gresham to the mob. His sword pointed at them, menacing, all-powerful.

The two men looked at him. His authority was complete. They darted in, grabbing the body, the bloodied head bumping pathetically as it dragged over the bench and floor. Gresham's men did not move. The heavy-set man flung the body of his leader over his shoulder. The stump of the arm was still losing blood, a thin stream now, almost in droplets. The pale, pathetic thing that had once been a human hand lay on the planks, still.

Gresham reached back to grasp Jane's wrist.

It was not there.

Then he heard a scream. Jane. Jane's voice. 'THERE!' it said.

He turned, and his heart froze in his ribs. Jane, his beautiful girl, the thing he loved more than life itself, was smeared in blood, huge blotches of blood on her face and arms and the bodice of her dress.

Where was she wounded? Where was she wounded?

Then he realised that the blood was not hers but the blood of the man whose hand he had severed, flailing over her like an obscene shower.

Her eyes were wide open, and the hand Gresham had grasped so tightly was pointed over his shoulder, behind him. A part of his brain found time to notice the rough, red marks all round her slim wrist, where he had manhandled her and held on with such force.

He turned, feeling as he did so that his every movement had been slowed down ten or twenty times, noting Mannion's mouth open ever so slowly in warning, suddenly inhabiting a world of total silence. There, almost on the other side of the theatre, was a warped figure in a black cloak, the hood thrown back to reveal a whitened and shrunken pate with a wig ludicrously hanging off to one side. He held a crossbow in his hand, the bolt resting in its groove and notched, the string cocked. Slowly, ever more slowly, Gresham saw the fumbling hands, hands behaving as if they could not feel the wood and iron, raise the crossbow and hold it rock steady.

He must have watched the whole fight. Organised it. Hidden the crossbow earlier. His insurance.

The finger tightened on the release. There was a twang. The figure threw the crossbow away. It tumbled to the floor, and the figure scurried out of The Globe.

A scream of agony tore its way from Gresham's heart to his throat, but he heard nothing. He saw the bolt leave the weapon, and with agonising, awful slowness compared to the speed of the bolt turned again to thrust Jane to the ground and himself in front of her. But his hand found nothing on which it could push. Jane had dropped to

141

the ground with a lightning reaction. With nothing to block his momentum, Gresham knew his body would coincide exactly with where Jane's body would have been, with exactly where the bolt was heading. With the very last of his strength he sought to twist in mid-air, to at least present his arm and rib cage to the bolt rather than his exposed back.

He was like a man doing a back-flip over a high bar, feet just off the ground, head flung back, chest arched upwards, when the bolt struck.

It pierced his doublet as if the satin was thin air, and ran across his rib-cage with such precision that the line of its passage was not marked with red swathe over the whole flesh but simply with reddened areas where the upwards thrust of his ribs had felt its passage. The bolt thwacked into the rear wall with massive force, embedding a third of its length into the soft timbers. Pinioned, Gresham hung by his doublet for a moment, suspended, face up to the sky. Light, sound, colour and heat returned to his life as by the click of fingers.

Mannion, in the last second of his mad rush towards his master, crashed, over the broken bench and tumbled on to his back.

'God's blood!' said Gresham, drawing his head up to look at the bolt that suspended him from the theatre wall.

A quiver of something that might have been release ran through Mannion's body. Picking himself up, but making no attempt to remove the pin that hung his master from the rear wall, he announced casually, but in a loud voice, 'I've told you what happens to people who hang around the theatre.'

The smooth silk of Gresham's fine doublet, any more than the linen of his shirt, offered no resistance to the steel of the crossbow bolt. Gresham dropped unceremoniously to the floor, in a tangle with both Mannion and the blood-stained Jane.

Suddenly Mannion's comment was the best joke ever made by anyone in the history of the world. Young Harry, a great wound on the side of his head already beginning to dry and blacken, started it with a thin, almost insane giggle. It spread through the other men, to Mannion, to Gresham and to Jane, so that they rocked and sobbed with laughter, making the very floor shake.

Their laughter did not last long. For many the pain was too keen to be overlaid by relief. One man was unconscious, another still only half conscious. Three others were coated in their own blood, groggy, confused, nursing wounds that made walking difficult. At least one had a broken arm. Others would find, in a few minutes, as the red heat of battle dissipated in their blood, that they had broken a finger or even a rib. Those that could stumbled to their feet, the wounded ones pathetically trying to smooth their dress while new red blood seeped through the blackened mess.

'Not bad,' said Mannion matter-of-factly, 'for beginners. Not bad at all.'

They stiffened with pride. Proud of what they had done. Proud of what they had prevented. Proud of their master, who had out-guessed their enemy from the start, who had thrust himself forward at perilous danger, who had risked his life first and in some strange way not commanded but rather asked them to risk their lives second, if that was their choice. And, if the truth be known, proud of their mistress. No screaming, no pouting, no fainting. A mistress who had become in a moment a soldier, one of them, obeying orders. Who could look at her and deny that she was a woman? Yet who could see her courage and deny that she was in every vital respect a man?

'Thank you,' said Gresham. They nodded. It was all that was needed. The talking had been done by their weapons, their bodies and their courage. 'We need to get young Harry home to some clean water and a bandage,' he said easily. 'And we needs remember that there could still yet be an enemy out there for us.'

That sobered them, the thought of the men they had fended off regrouping, waiting for them in the narrow streets outside.

The world had heard about the disturbance. There was excitement in the streets, women huddled in corners looking up quickly as they passed, pointing, gossiping. They put Harry in the centre of their group, with Jane, who saw no shame in helping to hold him up. The crowds, chattering, watching, curious, parted before them as they marched, heads held high, alert, towards the boatyard. They reached it without incident, followed by a crown of street urchins. Even they were silent for the most part, gripped by the stern, dark figure of Gresham and the startlingly blooded figure of Jane, who had only

144

been able to clean off a portion of the mess in the theatre.

'D'ye want a man or two to help you back over the river?' asked the surly owner of the boatyard, moved to interest for once.

'Do we need help?' asked Gresham. His men stiffened, looked offended. 'No, thank you. We don't need help.'

The wife of the owner rushed out, a dumpy little woman with three chins and rosy cheeks. She carried a jug of clean water and a surprisingly clean cloth. She was all flustered.

'My dear ... mistress... I just wondered if you might want to... I mean, I don't know what's happened, but...'

Jane gazed down silently on the head of the woman, who was becoming increasingly sure she had made a dreadful mistake with the great lady. Fancy calling her 'my dear'! Why, what was she...

Jane put her hands on the woman's shoulders. Surprised, the woman lifted her head. Jane planted a kiss firmly on her forehead.

'You're the kindest thing I've seen all day,' Jane said.

'Oh, my lady!' said the woman, blushing from her roots, overwhelmed. 'Do keep the jug and the cloth...' At that she rushed off back into the timber-framed house she occupied with her husband. A few moments later, Jane's face and hands at least were clean.

'Can you helm a boat as well as fight off an enemy?' Gresham asked Jane.

'I'd build the bloody boat myself if it got me home and into a bath!' she muttered, gathering up her skirts and grabbing the tiller, a huge tract of her mind still numb, anaesthetised by shock.

Only three of the men were fit to row. Mannion and Gresham looked at each other. Gresham pulled off his doublet. There was a film of blood on his shirt where the crossbow bolt had grazed his ribs and the collar he wore was torn. Mannion took up the place by his side, replacing young Harry and the other most seriously hurt man. The men grinned, amused by their master taking on their role.

Gresham turned to Mannion. 'Old man, whatever you do – don't breathe over me!' Mannion belched contentedly and settled to his oar. 'Now row!'

And they moved out of the wharf, limping in comparison with the speed they had made when they left the jetty at The House only a few short hours ago. They were clearly a grand boat, of the sort to attract attention anyway. The presence of someone who was clearly a gentleman at an oar, wounded men at the back of the boat and, most of all, a glorious beauty manning the helm, got them more attention on the crowded river than the Armada had when it first entered the Channel. There were whistles, hoots and then cheers from professionals running the ferries back and forth, which in turn attracted the attention of all the other traffic on the river. Before long, they had an admiring escort of small and some quite large boats, intrigued, following them to wherever they were going.

Someone from The House must have spotted them, and spotted that this was not a normal return. Figures began to gather on the jetty. More and more joined them, until it seemed that every occupant of the warren that was The House was gathering to welcome its lord and its mistress. A hush fell on the assembled crowd of servants, from the might of the steward to the lowliest of the kitchen boys, when they saw their mistress's bloodstained clothes, and wounded men in the bay of the boat. They counted the numbers. Had everyone come back? Then young Harry raised his head and managed a grin, and one of the other wounded waved a greeting. There was an almost explosive roar of relief as the gathered crowd realised that all their team had returned, and that even the wounded were walking. A huge rolling cheer rocked the jetty.

There seemed to be hundreds of hands reaching out to grab the prow of the boat and ground it. Jane, her lips pursed in concentration, was determined to make no mistake. The boat kissed the jetty as lightly and as delicately as a mother kisses her firstborn. She's about to burst into tears, thought Gresham. That first quiver. It's there. She's had enough. He rose to his feet, rocking the boat.

'Next time,' he said loudly, matter-of-factly, 'steer a little finer, will you? Otherwise, that was *quite* good. For a woman.'

She looked at him and stiffened. The tremor vanished. Three weeks of words passed between them in an instant. Gratitude. Annoyance. Anger. Amusement. Understanding. Fear. Pride. Worry. Total exhaustion. Gresham went to her, took her hand. He looked over to what must by now be

147

every resident of The House except, he dearly hoped, the gateman.

God, he was tired, he thought. As ever, there was the physical tiredness. But it was the mental exhaustion, the throbbing pain in his head, that was by far the worst. Yet he had to say something, didn't he? The whole house had gathered to welcome their master and mistress home. They would remember this for generations, tell each other stories into the small hours of the morning as the filched candles in the servants' hall guttered and died. He glanced at Jane. She nodded, imperceptibly. How not to sound pompous and vainglorious? How not to patronise these men and women, who had fought for him and shown every willingness to die for him. How to say the impossible?

'Thank you for your concern,' said Gresham, bloodstained, a thin line across his chest and on his arm where a glancing blow from a club had scathed his skin. Not for a moment did he realise what an extraordinarily violent, dark and powerful figure he cut.

The boat was bobbing under him, uneasy in the short, choppy waters of the jetty. He kept his feet easily.

'We went to the theatre, and a group of men liked us even less than the play. There were ... how many of them were there, young Harry?' asked Gresham theatrically, looking at the bloodied figure still slumped on the deck.

'Fifty!' came the clear reply, to a cheer from the others in the boat.

'So we defended ourselves against a hundred

148

men,' said Gresham seamlessly, to a roar of laughter from his assembled servants. 'And, of course, The House won.'

There was an uproar from the assembly. The reality of blood, and pain, and man's vicious inhumanity to man, excused by jokes and bravado. Unbidden, lines came into his head. Shakespeare. *King Leir*.

As flies to wanton boys are we to the gods.
They kill us for their sport.

He helped Jane out of the boat, and politely shook off the offers of help as he put both feet firmly back on dry land. They clapped them both as they alighted from the boat. Gresham turned, embarrassed, to his men in the boat, the ones who had done the real men's work. They were clapping him too. *They* were clapping *him?* Sweet Jesus, was there no justice in this world? He should be clapping them.

Jane was delivered into the hands of numerous women, with a clucking and fussing of vast proportion, and vanished up the jetty. For once, Gresham noted, she succumbed to it willingly. This was a woman who really wanted her hot bath. Young Harry was delivered into the arms of an equal number of women, though rather younger than those who had flocked to Jane, Gresham noted. Well, he was guaranteed a good night, one way or the other. The other wounded were ushered up the jetty, the hubbub of conversation diminishing with their progress.

Two men took the boat back to the boathouse,

bobbing their heads as they passed Gresham, a thousand questions in their minds which would never pass their lips. There was still a fair crowd left gathered on the jetty, gazing in awe at Gresham and Mannion. Gresham wanted to dismiss them, to walk back to The House with Mannion as he had walked with him after so many battles, fights and feuds.

Then, all of sudden, he saw what neither he nor Jane had noticed before. The nurse had brought out little Walter and Anna to watch the return of their parents. They had stood at the back, and not even Jane's huge sensitivity to the presence of her children had alerted her before she was whisked off. What on earth happened to children when they saw their parents come back blood-stained from a battle? Surely it was too early in their poor, innocent lives for them to realise that their parents, and the whole damned world, were mortal? And why the hell wasn't their mother here to sort this dreadful finale out? Women knew about these things! Men were ... men were there to do the fighting, not the explaining!

His son and his tiny daughter were standing either side of their nurse, hands in her hands. Both tiny figures gazed at Gresham with eyes as round as full moons.

'Well,' said Gresham, eyes locking on those of his children. It was, of course, entirely in his imagination that the other servants drew back to let him speak to the children. 'The truth is, some nasty men...' He felt, rather than saw, a flicker rumble through Mannion's body as he tried to stop the laughter inside him. 'Some nasty men ...

150

decided to be ... not nice to me and to ... Mummy.' Was Mannion about to spontaneously self-combust with hilarity? Or was it Gresham's imagination? 'Then some nice men...' If he didn't stop this now, Mannion would certainly die. 'Oh, bugger it!' said Gresham to his children. 'Some bastards tried to kill your mother and me. We won. They lost.'

There was a huge cheer from the servants.

'And I was wounded a bit, but not badly.'

Gresham's children were still looking at him as if he was the eighth wonder of the world.

'And the truth is, I'm really tired, and I wouldn't mind a helping hand from you both to get me back to the house and into a warm bed.'

The children ran to him instantly.

'It's all right, Father,' said Walter. 'We knew you needed to swear.'

'Are you really not hurt?' piped up little Anna.

'Look, little one,' said Gresham, picking her up and cradling her. He pointed to his chest. 'A scratch. No more than you do when you fall over a stony path. Less, probably.' He put her back down on the ground, hiding his pain as he did so.

Walter was trying to push his father's hand so far upwards to support him that it threatened to imbalance Gresham. Anna was content to hold his hand lightly, taking care to match her step with his so that she did not jar his arm. At the same time, she did not let go of Mannion, who was holding her other hand with a gentleness that belied his size.

'Jesus Christ!' said Gresham as they both collapsed inside the first doorway that offered itself

151

after the children had been detached from them. 'Can we go to bed?'

'No!' said Mannion, firmly. 'At least, not before we've washed and cleansed that wound across your chest.' Body-servants had, after all, a duty to the body of their master.

11

July, 1612
The House, The Strand, London

'To unmask falsehood, and bring truth to light'
SHAKESPEARE, *The Rape of Lucrece*

The shock had set in for Jane, as it always did, when it was no longer necessary for her to cope, to keep a good face in front of others.

She had tried to take up some needlework. It was a task she hated above all others, but a strange sense of duty drove her to try, believing it to be a proper accomplishment for a lady. She stabbed and hacked at the poor backing cloth, her stitching for all the world like the work of a mad doctor on an open wound. She sucked in her lips, muttering as the needle went where it wished. This morning her normally erratic results were self-evidently unspeakably bad.

Gresham watched her in silence. How extra-ordinary that a woman's body, the same size more or less as a man's, could achieve so much more. That slim body, perhaps a half inch shorter than his own, needing all the organs his body needed, had managed to grow and nurture two children, house, home and feed them within the confines of one flesh for nine months apiece. If so great a portion of her body was given over to

153

childbirth, wondered Gresham, how about the mind of a woman? Was the child to her mind in its life as it had been to her body in pregnancy? Would her love for him persist, or would it drain away silently into the love of her children? Men loved themselves, thought Gresham. So much so that many failed to see when love in others had died.

Jane spoke, eventually, as he had known she would. 'That was ... appalling,' she said, with a catch to her voice. She was white-faced, and the fingers of her left hand were trembling very slightly, Gresham noticed. It made the stitching even worse. 'To go to the play, and to be set upon by a bunch of murdering oafs... Is there nowhere safe?' She was clean, sweet-smelling and outrageously beautiful. In the privacy of the room, her black hair was loosely gathered above the nape of her neck, like a sweeping, swooping coil of ebony. The remnants of breakfast had been cleared, and she and Mannion were grouped round the table with Gresham.

They looked expectantly at Gresham. He had been distant all morning, not hostile but rather withdrawn. They knew the mood of old. His mind had gone deep, weighing up what was known and what was not known, trying to draw the map of where they were and where they should be. He got up and started to pace the room.

'Safe? It's not a word I can recognise. Not when the plague or an ague could rip any one of us out of life and into oblivion at the flip of a coin. At least in the theatre there was an enemy you could see, an enemy you could fight.'

'An enemy you could fight!' said Jane. 'An enemy gathered in your business! All I can do is run, not fight. All I can do is receive the hatred of the enemies you make.'

There was no answer Gresham could utter that would deny the truth of what she said. He stopped pacing for a moment and looked at her. 'I'm sorry,' he said. 'Truly sorry.'

'So am I,' she said, holding his eyes. 'Sorry for what happened. And sorry if I seem to blame you for the evil of others. And I never said thank you. For saving my life.'

The emotions that flickered across Gresham's brow were too complex for words, but she saw them all the same, and understood. Gresham's tone became businesslike.

'The man with the crossbow has to be this Cambridge bookseller Coke was so concerned about. The description fits too well. What's new is that he wants to kill us as well as sell some papers – and no, I don't know why. He could be working independently, or with Overbury. I humiliated Overbury. He was there at the theatre. Though he took no part in the fight.' Gresham was pacing again. 'For once it's not *why* that bothers me. It's *how!* There are a thousand ways to kill a man if that's what you really want. Slip a servant in and drop some poison into the man's wine...'

'That couldn't happen now. We take too much care over who we hire as servants,' Jane said. Years earlier Cecil had slipped a spy into Gresham's house.

'It's *less* likely to happen now,' corrected Gres-

155

ham. 'The minute you allow yourself to think it's impossible you're placing yourself at risk. Bribing a servant would still be the easy option for this bookseller, or for Overbury. Or there's a knife in your back while walking down a dark street, or a crossbow bolt from a deserted alley. Poison, knife, arrow, gun – if you want to kill someone, why do it in front of two thousand spectators at the theatre, for God's sake?'

'Go on,' said Jane. There was clearly more.

'And why try to kill you as well?' he said to her, swinging round to face her. 'You're hardly going to carry on the investigation after my death, are you? For all Overbury knows, you're as feather-brained as the rest of the women at Court.'

Jane forgot her depression for a moment and a smile tugged at the corners of her mouth. She mock-fluttered her eyelashes and swooned. 'My lord, as a Court lady I do not need a brain. What I need is–'

'But think seriously on it,' Gresham interrupted quickly. 'The theatre. That's what's worried me all along. It runs through this in a way we haven't got hold of. Right from the start it's not just been a set of letters from two male lovers, it's been manuscripts of *plays*. This bookseller ... he tells LongLankin he wants the students to put on a *play*. A man gets murdered because someone wants the manuscripts of two *plays*. They try to murder us in a *theatre*.'

'Bloody expensive way to go about it,' said Mannion. 'And risky. Never know what might happen with that many people around. And not exactly secret either.'

'Why does the theatre run through all this like a thick vein? We just don't know!' The tension came through in Gresham's voice, the way he still walked up and down the room.

'Well,' said Mannion carefully, putting down his tankard. 'Mebbe we do.'

Gresham and Jane looked at him, startled.

'Come on, old man. Don't keep us in suspense.'

'I've been thinking,' said Mannion.

'That must have hurt,' said Gresham with compassion. 'Have another drink to get over the pain, and mind you don't do it again.'

'Ssssh!' said Jane, irritated at his banter and intrigued. Mannion did have a brain. It was simply not the organ he found most use for. He also had, when he cared to use it, an outstanding memory for faces and people, as well as a capacity to make instant and lasting judgements.

'I reckon as how that bastard with the crossbow wasn't any bookseller, not leastways any one as I've ever seen. I think that bookseller was Christopher bloody Marlowe.'

There was a stunned silence.

'But Kit Marlowe died in 1602...' said Gresham, his mind spinning.

'We was *told* he died in 1602,' said Mannion. 'But then again, *we* told everyone he died in 1593, when we bloody well knew he hadn't. If he died once when it was convenient for him, but didn't really die, why shouldn't he do the whole trick again without our help?'

'Now I remember!' said Gresham, clapping his hand to his head. 'Cornelius Wagner!'

157

'Who's he when he's at home?' said Mannion.

'It's the name Cecil's spies gave to the "Cambridge bookseller". Coke told me when we met. Cornelius Wagner. Cornelius and Wagner are two characters in Marlowe's play, *Doctor Faustus*. Wagner is Faustus's servant. It all adds up...' Gresham's mind was racing. 'Are you certain it was Marlowe?'

'I spent time with him, didn't I? It was me who got him over to France,' Mannion replied.

'You faked Marlowe's death? Got him over to France? Alive? And now he wants to kill you? I don't know this story at all,' said Jane. She felt the great tidal wave of intrigue, of double- and treble-dealing, of plots, of deception, tugging at her, the tidal wave in which her husband had chosen to swim for most of his life. Or was it a whirlpool, sucking them to their deaths? Together with Gresham, Jane had been swept away by the magnificent verse of Marlowe's *Tamburlaine*, chilled by *Doctor Faustus*, horrified by *The Jew of Malta* and *Edward II*. 'Tell me.'

Gresham laughed. 'Did we get him over to France? Yes. Did we fake his death? No. That was Marlowe's idea.' He nodded towards Mannion, who pulled his tankard towards him and continued the tale.

'Marlowe'd got himself into trouble. Well, to be truthful, he was never out of it. 'Cept this time it was real trouble. He was a spy, for old Walsingham, spying on the Catholics. Leastways, meant to be spying on the Catholics, but with a nose for trouble that meant he ended up spying on everybody, including some very inconvenient people.

158

Like the Queen, f'example. When Walsingham died he started to work for Cecil.

'Always getting drunk, he were, always fighting, always shooting his mouth off. Bad thing, for a spy, that. Started to shoot his mouth off about Cecil being left-handed, so to speak.' Mannion used the slang term for describing a homosexual. 'And loads of other stuff no one could understand. Cecil's father, old Lord Burleigh, decided he were a risk too far and got him summoned to the Privy Council. After that, he'd have bin referred to the Tower, and probably died of some mysterious illness short after...'

'He never was a very good spy,' said Gresham. 'Too fiery, too intelligent, too much wanting to be the centre of attention.'

'Anyways, we gets to hear of it too, before Marlowe even. Sir Henry here, well, Marlowe's a bit of a hero for him, literary speaking.'

'I thought the man was a genius,' said Gresham simply. 'A pain in the neck, right enough, but a genius for all that. Burleigh and Cecil wanted him dead and even then I was pleased to do anything I could to put a stop to Cecil's plans. I thought in exchange I might get some real dirt on Burleigh, and on Cecil. And I really did want to stop them killing the man who had written *Doctor Faustus* and *Tamburlaine*. Think of it as my early patronage of the arts.'

'So what happened?' asked Jane.

'I warned him that if he went to the Privy Council hearing he'd never walk out of it alive or a free man. I arranged to spirit him over to France,' said Gresham, 'but that wasn't good enough for Marlowe. He had to fake his own death first, with the biggest crowd of villains in the country. We got to hear of that too late to stop it, but we reckoned those particular villains would take his money, do what he'd arranged and then kill him anyway. That way they could claim a second payment from the government. Mannion managed to tail him on to the brig we'd hired to get him over the Channel.'

Gresham looked to Mannion.

'As it was, two of the crew on the brig over to France tried to murder Marlowe in his sleep.'

'What did you do?' said Jane.

'I killed 'em,' said Mannion simply, slurping at his small beer. 'Anyways, I got him over to France. We know he took himself off to Spain after that – separate story. We heard he'd died or been killed in 1602. He always were a stupid bugger, excusing my language, mistress. It were no surprise to hear someone had topped him.'

'Are you sure it was him at The Globe yesterday?' said Gresham.

'Yes, I reckon. He's changed a lot. Shrunken, sort of. Lost his hair. So it took me time to spot him. But that's who it is. Marlowe. Back from the grave. Reckon he's got a dose of the pox. Did you see him with that crossbow?'

'I saw him fire it,' said Gresham.

'I saw him put his hand on the release,' said Mannion. 'I mean, he rested the bow on the woodwork, wedged it into his arm and then he put his hand on the release with his other hand, as if he couldn't really feel it. That's what they do with a bad dose of the pox. They can't feel much

160

in their hands or their feet. I know about these things.'

How Mannion had avoided a dose of the pox was a quite remarkable story of there being no natural justice in life. There was no doubt that his extra-curricular lifestyle brought him into contact with many who had not been so lucky.

'Well, well,' said Gresham. 'My old friend Kit Marlowe.'

'Why should he want revenge on you?' asked Jane, bemused. 'You helped him get away, didn't you?'

'I think I know,' said Gresham. 'Hold on here while I fetch something.'

Gresham left them in the breakfast parlour and moved through the corridors with a greeting, by name, to the servants who bobbed, curtseyed or doffed their caps to him. He went to his private study, at the centre of The House and guarded by its stoutest door. Lifting the extravagance of carpet that lay on the floor, he revealed the planking. He gave a sharp tap on the end of a join, indistinguishable from the others. The plank-end jumped up, and settled down a half inch or so higher than its neighbour. Gresham lifted it, revealing that it was hinged at its other end. The cavity exposed as the plank swung back had a dullish sheen to it. Gunmetal. There was a metal box beneath the floor, with its own lock. Gresham swung back the heavy door with a key from his golden keyring. No money lay there, as might be expected in a rich man's house, a rich man who had gone to the expense of constructing a special metal box hidden beneath the floor of the most secure room in his property. Nor were there deeds of land, or sureties, or any of the paperwork beloved of the lawyers. Rather, there were letters. Letters and papers. Of no apparent significance or value to the idle viewer. Gresham smiled inwardly as his eyes lit on some of the papers. Monarchies, kings and queens were compromised by those innocent-looking documents.

Men have to tell their secrets, to prove that they are men. Great men merely have to know great secrets, and tell no one.

Gresham found the two letters he had come for and closed his private store. Would it survive a fire? he thought. For a while, perhaps. It was gunmetal, after all. More likely, the survival of it and its contents would depend on him or one of his very few trusted servants making the gunmetal box their only priority in the case of a fire. Nothing was certain, Gresham thought, except death. The readiness is all. You cannot predict. You can only prepare.

He brought the two letters back into the room. Mannion had replenished his tankard, Gresham noted.

'Two letters,' he said to Jane, 'three months apart. Both from Marlowe. June and August 1602. Someone had just tried to kill him, he said. I hadn't saved him at all, he said. I'd set the whole thing up on Cecil's orders, so Cecil wouldn't be embarrassed by the revelations Marlowe would have made at any trial.'

'They weren't planning any trial!' said Mannion with a guffaw.

'No, but Marlowe'd obviously imagined one,

162

with himself playing the heroic role. He'd been meant to go to France, but went to Spain instead and sold himself as a spy to them. Worked with them for years, as I understand it. Then he fell out with them, and blamed me and Cecil for poisoning the Spanish against him.'

'Had you?' said Jane.

'God help us, no,' said Gresham. 'To be frank, I'd more or less forgotten about him until these letters came. He'd have been better off dying in The Tower, he said. There, you can read it. He was in poverty. He'd never had the recognition he deserved ... and more. And, of course, the accusation that it was Cecil and I who'd tried to have him killed.'

'Had you?' asked Jane again.

'I hadn't, of course not,' said Gresham, shrugging his shoulders. 'There was no need, no reason. He was just history as far as I was concerned. I suppose I hoped he'd write things abroad, under another name, set up theatres in Europe... I remember feeling quite shocked when we heard he had actually been killed, after he'd written to me. It was in September, I think. I also found something out later that convinced me Cecil had done it.'

'What was that?' asked an intrigued Jane.

'For a long while I don't think Cecil knew Marlowe was alive. He took over Walsingham's spy service but he never ran it properly. Preferred to work through ambassadors, official people. Well, the letters make it clear someone tried to murder Marlowe in 1602, in Spain. I think it was Cecil. I think that's when Cecil found out

Marlowe was alive, and who he was working for. It must have been the biggest shock of his life.'

'Why the biggest?' said Jane. 'We know he had quite a few shocks in his life, even before 1605.' She could not help smiling at the memory of the Gunpowder Plot, and the exact nature of the shock administered by Gresham to Cecil.

'Because in 1602, when it was clear Elizabeth was dying, when everyone thought Robert Cecil had chosen King James I as the new King of England, and when Robert Cecil himself was writing away to James and declaring himself his most loyal servant, all the while the bloody man was plotting with the Spanish to get the Spanish Infanta on the throne in place of James! He was riding both horses, wasn't he?

'Well, Cecil is fearful of the Queen finding out he's been writing to James in Scotland, and fearful of her *and* James finding out he's been trying to ride two horses and back Spain as well. Then, lo and behold, what does he discover? That Marlowe's been an agent for the Spanish for years! Marlowe, who hates him! Marlowe, who's privy to all the Spanish secrets – might even have seen some of his cursed letters. He must have ordered Marlowe knocked off as soon as he heard. Obviously Marlowe got away, if it was him you saw this afternoon...' Gresham glanced at Mannion, who nodded.

'Are you sure Cecil was riding both horses? Backing the King and the Infanta?' asked Jane. 'It's absolutely explosive if it's true. Elizabeth could have had him killed for it, and James could never have let him run the country for him.'

164

'Oh, I'm sure, right enough,' said Gresham with the grin of a devil on his face. 'You see, I've got two of his letters to the Spanish! I've held them as a bargaining counter for years. It's one of the main reasons Cecil didn't have me killed long ago.'

Jane's head was reeling. 'Are you telling me you could have proved Cecil a traitor since 1602? And I know you could have done it again in 1605 with the Gunpowder Plot? If you hated the man so much, why didn't you topple him?'

'You know why,' said Gresham. 'Power is a filthy business. It dirties all those who wield it. There's no room for a good man in government. We've had peace for years now, haven't we, over the land of this country at least? No babies killed, no villages razed to the ground, no women raped, no harvesting of all the best young men to die stupidly in battles no one understands. If the price we pay for that peace, that stability, is to have the anti-Christ on the throne, I'll take it. Cecil's evil, the fact he had no morals, the fact he would assassinate without thinking to keep the peace – we need someone like that as our ruler. And if he damned himself in the process, why should I care?'

'So you're saying Marlowe got away some'ow, and buggered off somewhere to lie low? When he knew people was trying to kill him?' said Mannion.

'Must have done. The Americas, perhaps? Or Russia? That's where I'd have gone. Wherever it was, it must have turned his brain. Not that it ever needed much turning. And now, all of a sudden, he turns up in England again,' said Gresham, 'and I bet I could dictate the letter he sends to Cecil. "I'm going to get my revenge on you at last," he says, "and on that arch-villain Gresham who helped you ruin my life."'

'Oh dear God!' said Jane. 'I see it now ... it's so simple.'

'Isn't it?' said Gresham.

Mannion, whose face was screwed up like a cow's, was clearly not finding it simple at all. Gresham carried on.

'Cecil sets me, his best agent, on to finding Marlowe, carefully not telling me it is Marlowe, of course, just to add a bit of spice to it. So I'm moving about with the highest possible profile, more or less guaranteeing that Marlowe's going to come screaming out of a side alley and try to kill me. If I kill Marlowe, which is the best option of all, then what a joke for Cecil from his grave. He's got his oldest and bitterest enemy to preserve his reputation, pure and unsullied, for all of history. That would appeal to Cecil's sense of humour. And if Marlowe kills me – the second best option – what a joke as well! Cecil's oldest enemy follows him to the grave with a helping hand from Cecil, and the killer is the person whose escape I arranged twenty years ago partly to spite him! Poetic justice and the wheel come full circle, isn't it, if Marlowe kills me?'

'Are you sure Cecil's *first* aim wasn't to get you killed by Marlowe? We only survived by luck. If you hadn't been prepared... What an evil man,' said Jane. 'What a horrible mind.'

'Brilliant mind,' said Gresham in appreciation.

'Almost as good as mine.'

'Well,' said Jane, 'at least we know why everyone's talking about a lost play by Marlowe. He must have written his masterpiece in all those years of exile.'

'And now one of his aims is to get it performed,' said Gresham. 'He's obviously been peddling it in the disguise of this bookseller.'

'But not got it performed yet,' said Jane.

'Any decent company's going to get itself laughed out of court if it claims a play's by Marlowe without concrete evidence. It'd take time and money to get one of the respectable companies to put it on. I doubt Marlowe's got a great deal of either.'

'It's almost pathetic,' said Jane, 'if he is trying to get the students to put it on. It's almost like a homecoming. Or beginning all over again.'

One of the greatest playwrights of all time reduced to having students put on his play? There was little sympathy for Marlowe in Gresham's heart. That commodity had been used up long ago.

'So where do the buggers' letters come in?' asked Mannion, direct as ever.

'Do you have an answer?' asked Gresham.

'How about this?' replied Mannion. He got up and put his mug down on the table. It was half full. It was almost unheard of for Mannion to put down a mug with drink still in it. 'You're Marlowe. You've got dirt on Cecil and you want to cause as much 'avoc as possible in as short a time as possible. Who do you go to?'

'The King?' suggested Jane.

'No!' said Mannion scornfully. 'Think on't, mistress! How does Marlowe get to the King? Goes up to 'is man on the door, does 'e? "Excuse me, Mr Gatekeeper. I'm a sodomite ex-spy and playwright who died in 1593 and who's been working for the Spanish ever since. Oh, and by the way, I died in 1602 as well. Anyway, I'm here and I've got the dirt on the King's right-hand man. So let me in, will you, to talk direct to His Majesty?"'

'Put like that,' said Jane, 'it doesn't sound that easy.'

'Marlowe's a spy, isn't he?' Mannion was pacing up and down now, his brain engaged. Did he realise how like his master he looked? 'He knows about real power. So who's the real power in England?'

'Carr. Robert Carr. The King's lover,' said Gresham, happy to feed Mannion, fascinated by what he was seeing.

'No, master! Not Carr! Carr's just the beautiful body! Who's the brain? Who's still trawling taverns and going to stews where gentlemen shouldn't be seen? Who's accessible to a runt like Marlowe?'

'Overbury,' breathed Gresham. 'Sir Thomas Overbury.' Someone had just opened a window in the darkness of his knowledge. 'It's about comfort. It's all about comfort.'

'What do you mean?' asked Jane, perplexed now.

'The King's tired, losing himself more and more in hunting and wine and beautiful young men, selling out to comfort.'

'There's men as can't take power,' said Mannion, speaking to Jane. 'We've seen 'em often enough in the wars. Men who get tired of decisions. First it's the wine. Takes the place of thinkin', blocks it all out. Then, if that don't work, beggin' your pardon, there's women.'

'But it's a young man in King James's life!' said Jane, unabashed.

'Yes,' said Gresham, 'and a brainless one at that! All James wants is comfort and freedom from strain, and all his lover wants is the same! Robert Carr can't make a decision to save his life, other than what doublet to wear – and I bet that takes all morning and most of the afternoon. So that's where Carr's friend comes into his own. Overbury. Sir Thomas Overbury. Able. Intelligent. Wanting nothing more than to take the King's decisions on his behalf. Wanting nothing more than his share of power.

'The King's lover, more perplexed and far less able to deal with matters of state than his master, breathes a sigh of relief when his friend offers to help. Overbury. Brash. Arrogant. Receiving at third-hand unopened papers of state. It is Sir Thomas Overbury who now wields part of the power that Cecil once held. Yet Overbury has no protection of office. Ordinary men still have access to him. As did Kit Marlowe.' Gresham was speaking quickly now, as if to preserve his view in words before it slipped from his grasp.

'Marlowe goes for Overbury. Tells him he can destroy Cecil. Overbury's flattered. What power! Takes him in. Pays for him to be lodged Out of harm's way. Talks to him. And then, one evening, Overbury lets slip the existence of these letters.

Too much drink, probably, fed him by Marlowe. Brags to Marlowe that Marlowe isn't the only one who has power over people.'

'"They could be your insurance policy, these letters!" Marlowe says to Overbury. "They could be your pension!"' It was Mannion now, picking up the baton. '"Think on it. Your friend Carr will lose his looks one day. There are enough pretty men in the Court, aren't there? And the King hates you. And his Queen. Let *me* have a look at these letters. I'm a spy, ain't I? I know about these things." So Overbury brings these letters along, to show off. Lets Marlowe hold them. Tells Marlowe where he keeps them. Puts them back somewhere Marlowe knows about.'

'So the next thing that happens,' Gresham said, 'is that the letters disappear. Marlowe's also gone. And Overbury's set up to be the biggest fool in the country. Carr will lose faith in him if it becomes known he's the reason the letters are in the hands of an enemy. James will kill him, or kick his creature Carr out, which'll be just as bad. So how does Overbury cover himself?'

'He reports the letters are stolen,' said Jane, realisation dawning on her face, 'but stolen from Carr, not from himself. And he reports it to Sir Edward Coke, the legal bastion of the kingdom. Knowing full well that Coke will run to Cecil, of course. Suddenly it's somebody else's problem. He's covered himself brilliantly. But ... why would Cecil care so much about Marlowe? He was dying, knew he was dying,' she continued. 'It seems an immense amount of effort to go to to get someone killed, when you won't be there to be disgraced. Why would Cecil bother.'

'*Reputation!*' said Gresham. 'More than any-thing else, he wanted his reputation not only to live on after him but to grow. Marlowe's the threat to that. I'm the other, knowing what I know. So set the two against each other. That way he can guarantee one threat at least's removed.'

'So Cecil wasn't really interested in getting the letters back?' said Jane. 'All he really wanted was for you to kill Marlowe and preserve his repu-tation as an honest broker and a loyal servant?' Something in her soul rebelled at the thought of Gresham being used merely as an unpaid assassin.

'Oh, I think Cecil would rather the letters were destroyed than not. He wouldn't wish more instability for the King he'd made his life's work out of. But they were just the lure to get me into the arena, draw me in. My getting the letters was always the secondary aim. The first was to force Marlowe to reveal himself to me, and for me to kill him.'

'Or for Marlowe to kill you. Why didn't Cecil tell you it was Marlowe? Why use this Cambridge bookseller thing?'

'Do you think I'd have taken on the job if I'd known straight away the real reason was to save Cecil's reputation for posterity, instead of the King's? I'd have laughed in Cecil's face.'

'Where do these plays come in?' added Jane. 'The manuscripts by Shakespeare? We can explain everything else, but not them.'

'God knows,' said Gresham, 'but haven't we

solved enough problems in one sitting? Marlowe wants to stir up as much trouble as possible, and get some play of his performed. Probably reveal himself, like a genie out of the bottle, on its first showing. Look at me, everyone. The late, the great Kit Marlowe – alive and well! What a show-stopper that'd be... And anyway, that's not what bothers me...' He had to stop and think for a moment before completing his sentence '...what bothers me is you.'

'Me? What've I done wrong?' asked Jane, rather plaintive.

'Nothing. You've done nothing wrong. Cecil gambled that Marlowe would risk showing him-self if it meant killing me. But haven't you spotted the really terrible thing?'

Jane looked nonplussed. Gresham stared at her. He had to tell her. For all the hurt, for all the pain, he had to tell her. If she was to protect herself she had to know.

'He didn't try to kill me. He tried to kill you, Jane.'

'But I don't–'

'I saw his eyes in the theatre,' said Gresham. 'They were looking at you, not me. The second bolt was aimed at you. And that first bolt, the one I felt go by me earlier. It hit the wall just where you'd been a second before. I was six or eight feet away.'

'*What have I done to deserve this?*' she cried out. 'I've never set out to hurt or destroy anyone *in my life.*'

'He's a sick man, Jane. Sick in his mind as well as his body. He was always unstable. Now he's fired up with years of festering revenge, and the pox. I think he's decided the best way to hurt me isn't to kill me, not yet at least. It's to kill my happiness. To kill you.'

The silence seemed to stretch on for an eternity. She had fought against the thought that she and Gresham were equal targets for whichever madman was hunting them down. The realisation that she was the target, the way of inflicting the most pain on those she loved, threatened to clutch at and cut the parts of her mind that moored her to sanity. *Where was the justice in this world?*

'Not here, not on this earth with us,' said Gresham. Jane had not realised she had spoken out loud.

'So what hope is there?' She turned her face, despairingly, towards his.

'The hope in our own strength,' he said intensely. 'Justice lies with how strong we are. Safety lies in how strong we are. Survival lies in how strong we are.'

'I feel very weak,' she said.

'We all feel weak sometimes,' said Gresham. 'The strong are those who fight the feelings and carry on living.'

'I'll try,' she said, feeling like a lost little girl.

'I know you will,' said Gresham simply.

'Are you sure?' It was a very small voice that Jane spoke in.

'That you're my happiness? Absolutely. That it's you he wants to kill, to hurt me? No, not absolutely. But it'd be wise to assume it, until we can prove otherwise. We both know you're my weak spot. You and me, we're both at war with Marlowe, and Overbury for all I know. You know what it means. We're under siege.'

Oh God, not again, thought Jane. No leaving any house without an armed escort, no going out at all unless it was totally unavoidable...

Mannion chose not to help Gresham, but to answer a different question. His mind had been working on it, clearly.

'That bastard Overbury wasn't behind the lot trying to do us in in the theatre.'

'Why not?' It was Jane who answered. 'He has reason enough to hate your master, and it's surely too much of a coincidence that he was there on the afternoon when it all happened.'

'He were surprised when he met us. You could see it in his eyes. And he only had a couple of men at best with him, and neither of those armed. He could have made a real difference in the fight, with a sword, but he cleared off. Are you telling me a bastard like that wouldn't want to watch and gloat if he'd gone to all that trouble?'

Gresham thought for a moment. 'You could be right,' he said, 'but it makes no difference if it's one man or two we've to guard against.'

He was pacing the room again, hand running unconsciously through the black mop of his hair. 'It's the mystery I want solved. The mystery isn't Sir Thomas Overbury or Sir Edward Coke, or even Christopher Marlowe. It's Shakespeare and these confounded manuscripts. We need to meet with Master Shakespeare. Urgently. All three of us.'

'I'm flattered,' said Jane, seeking to hide the

174

pain in her mind and the awful, threatening waves of paralysing fear. 'But why do you need me?'

'Firstly, to stop me killing him on sight. Secondly, to stop me being too rude to him, and thirdly, because you're a trained hand in dealing with drunken writers.' Keep it flippant, make light of pain. Ben Jonson, now masque-writer-in-chief to the King, had been a friend of Gresham and Jane's for years. Only the three people in the room and Jonson himself knew that Jane read Jonson's manuscripts in draft. He howled, swore and hurled things around the room when she made criticisms, and called her every name under the sun and several from below the moon. But he always made changes, Gresham noticed. In fact, he reckoned Jane had written nearly a quarter of Jonson's *Volpone, or The Fox.*

'It's a pity we can't call Ben in on this. He's a great pal of Master William's, or so he says.' It was Mannion. Jonson was touring Europe as tutor to Sir Walter Raleigh's son, one of Gresham's better ideas for a pairing.

'Well, yes,' said Jane, 'but there's a lot of jealousy as well. He's always trying to put Shakespeare down. Come to think of it, Ben's actually put me off meeting Shakespeare once or twice.'

'I think I must meet this genius,' said Gresham. 'Or rather, meet him again, with his new name. We'll need to be careful. He'll know I'm one of Raleigh's party, and if he thinks I'm after him he'll run. Mannion, send our people off to see if he's still in London. He was there at the play, doing a bit part, I saw him. Maybe he's scuttled back to Stratford, like they say he's doing more

175

and more now. Find out where he is, but do it quietly. And fix a time – a time very soon – for me to meet him with my mistress.'

12

September, 1612
Granville College and
King's College, Cambridge

'No place, indeed, should murder santuarise.'
SHAKESPEARE, *Hamlet*

The trail had gone cold.

It had happened before, often, in Gresham's life, but of all eventualities it was the one that left him most restless and ill at ease. He craved action. The combination of tension and inaction made him like a pent-up hound that turned to chew its own flesh in frustration. Shakespeare had apparently fled town immediately after the riot in The Globe. The men hired by Mannion had scoured London and then Stratford for a trace of him, but had found nothing. At least there had been no more attacks on Gresham or his family. That fact did nothing to relieve the tedium of living their lives under permanent guard.

At least the evening ahead might offer some excitement. Was Gresham becoming a creature of the night? he wondered as he put on his academic dress for the evening meal. Work started at dawn and finished at sunset for students as well as for farm labourers. The main meal of the day at Granville College was therefore at noon. Candles and lamps were expensive, servants need to be abed early if they were to be up before the dawn to light the fires, and students needed at all costs to be discouraged from treating night as day. It all argued for the main meal to be in the full and free glare of God's sunlight. Yet Gresham had instituted, and paid for, three feasts a year, to be held in the evening in the Hall his money had built.

Why go to the extra expense? It was not something Gresham could explain easily. The light flickering off the walls and the portraits hung against the panelling, its yellow contrasting with the roaring red of the huge fire blazing in the magnificent fireplace halfway along the left-hand wall, was magical to him. That light gave the evening dinners the air of a happy conspiracy, the flowing food and drink easing conversation and loosening inhibitions. He revelled in the sense of holding back nature, flinging a challenge of light and warmth and noise into the face of the all-encompassing darkness and silence of the night.

The Fellows all met in the Combination Room before the meal, the noise of the students gathering in the Hall filtering through even the thick oaken door. The room was a new development, the common rooms of the colleges hitherto being largely the local taverns. Alan Sidesmith, the ageless President of the college, stood and greeted the Fellows and their guests as they arrived. Gresham had never seen Alan without a drink in his hand, yet had never seen him drunk. Sidesmith had a guest of his own tonight.

'Be on your best behaviour, Sir Henry!' he warned Gresham with a twinkle in his eye. 'No less a person than the Bishop of Ely has asked to come to tonight's dinner.'

'Asked?' said Gresham.

'Indeed,' replied Sidesmith. 'He was preaching at Great St Mary's some weeks ago, and I went to listen, as one does. We were admiring the new tower. If I remember, his words were that if the college would see fit to invite him, he would see fit to accept. Oh, and by the way, he asked explicitly if you would be dining.'

The instinct for survival had placed tiny trip wires in Gresham's mind, trip wires that rang a jangle of bells inside his head when they were disturbed. Suddenly the noise was deafening, audible only to Gresham. One of the greatest theologians Cambridge had ever produced and the ex-Master of Pembroke Hall was entitled to invite himself for a dinner, wasn't he? And Gresham's dark reputation might be an added lure for a stately prelate, might it not? Whether or not he would appreciate the company of Gresham's guest was another matter. Bishop Lancelot Andrewes and Sir Edward Coke as bosom friends? Gresham rather doubted it. Yet such strange meetings were at the heart of college life – the clash of ideologies, the spur of debate and the strange conjoinings of people united only by their intelligence.

It had amused Gresham to invite Coke as his guest. It gave Gresham an edge, forced Coke to conform to the rituals of being an invitee. It was also time they met on home ground. Coke was a Trinity man, and Gresham guessed that curiosity about the torrent of novelty that was Granville College would override suspicion on Coke's part.

179

He also guessed that under the carapace that hid Coke's real feelings from the world lay the fierce, burning fascination with university felt by all men who had left it.

'Are your rooms to your satisfaction?' enquired Gresham solicitously as Coke sidled in to the Combination Room. Coke never walked, Gresham had noted. He either paraded or sidled. The rooms in question had been built to receive James I on his visit to Granville College.

'Quite satisfactory, thank you, Sir Henry,' replied Coke drily. His eyes flickered over Gresham's face, forever seeking advantage, weakness, a loophole. 'Fit for a king, even.' A sense of humour, noted Gresham. A very *limited* sense of humour, dry almost to despair, but a sense of humour nonetheless and therefore very interesting. Was Coke offering an olive branch? More likely it was poison ivy. Gresham motioned Coke aside and into one of the bay windows that flanked the room, unaware of the natural courtesy with which he treated one of his bitterest enemies.

'Let's make this a university night, if you agree. But there is business. It can be disposed of quickly, if you're willing,' said Gresham.

It was as if he were on holiday, Gresham thought, sensing the lightness in his own soul. The college did this to him. Its backbiting and its petty rivalries followed known and even agreed rules. The backbiting and petty rivalries of Court knew no rules, nor any limit on the damage they might cause. By comparison life in a Cambridge college was heaven on earth to the hell of the Court.

That hooded look came over Coke's eyes, and

he could not resist glancing over his shoulder, but he nodded. You would be no spy, thought Gresham. That look over your shoulder tells any interested party that you are worried about what we are going to discuss. It screams guilt to the careful watcher.

'Firstly, I know it's Marlowe who has possession of these papers.'

A tic started in Coke's left eye.

'He's already tried to kill me in the theatre incident you know about.'

Coke's face went red. Interesting. Most men went white when shocked with sudden news. Was the red the red of anger? Did Coke become angry when shocked, seeing everything as a personal attack?

'I've a host of men out searching for him, here and in London. He'll be found, eventually, though he's gone to ground.'

'How long before Marlowe is found?' Coke's voice was grating, sharp. He did not challenge the identification of Marlowe. It was as if his mind ticked an issue off, like a clerk with a list of household goods up for sale. Once ticked, however threatening or revelatory, it was gone, merely a piece of information.

So you knew, thought Gresham, who this Cambridge bookseller was, as did Cecil. Yet you did not think it important to tell me.

Coke's eyes were dark pinpricks. Gresham decided to answer his question.

'Tonight. Three months on. Who knows? Patience is crucial to this game we play, Sir Edward. Without it, the tension eats us up from within, burns our soul. And another concern who's gone to ground is Shakespeare. Vanished from London and from Stratford.'

'Shakespeare was always the lesser concern,' said Coke, a little too hurriedly. 'Could Marlowe have killed him?' Coke was uncertain, hiding it beneath a face that might now have been carved out of plaster. Clinical. That was the word. He was driven by huge self-esteem and vast pride, but at the point of contact with his conscious mind all that emotion, all that energy, became focused into something as hard and cold as steel. His own ambition. Does this man have the capacity to love another human being? thought Gresham.

'Marlowe's made one very theatrical attempt to kill him already. Equally, with that knowledge in mind, Shakespeare may have simply gone into hiding.'

The real cause of Old Ben's death had been known to very few people. One of them had been willing to talk to Gresham for a purse that could have doubled as ballast for a big ship by its weight.

'Your answer on Overbury?' Gresham asked. He had written to Coke detailing the bare outline of the attack, and been unequivocal in his demand. Find out if Overbury was behind the attack on Gresham and Jane.

Coke sighed. It was a theatrical gesture, but for the briefest of moments, his age – he was sixty – showed through the veneer of his face.

'As best as I can judge, Overbury knew nothing of the attack on you. He is an impossible man.' There was venom in Coke's voice. 'The only certainty about him is his arrogance. I base my

182

conclusion on the vehemence with which he expressed the wish that you and your kin had been slaughtered, while denying setting up the assault. If it had been his idea, he would have bragged about it.'

Coke had the capacity to be glaringly honest when he so chose. It was an excellent ploy, thought Gresham. The brief moments of sincerity served to validate the months of lies.

'We must join the assembly,' said Gresham. 'Before we do, tell me about the atmosphere in Court. Is the King troubled by the loss of these letters? Indeed, does he know the letters are lost?'

'The King? I have told him. After much agonising on my part. It seemed best,' said Coke.

Best? thought Gresham. The theft of the letters shows Carr and Overbury to be fools, it tells the King that Robert Cecil trusted Coke above all others and makes it clear that Coke is a man of discretion, not one to blab secrets to the whole world. *Best*, therefore, for Sir Edward Coke. 'He is troubled, certainly,' Coke carried on smoothly. 'The letters are, by the way, in his own hand, so I believe.' And therefore infinitely more damning and damaging. What prompted men to put things in writing? Or women, for that matter? It had killed Mary, Queen of Scots, and could have done the same for Elizabeth. 'Yet His Majesty ... seems more fickle by the moment.'

Fickle? Drunk, more likely, and settling in to an ever-increasing lassitude. Nor had he appointed a successor to Cecil, though it was believed to be only a matter of time before the job went to the beautiful Robert Carr. Which meant, of course, that the real power would be in the hands of Sir Thomas Overbury.

'We'll stay in touch,' said Gresham lightly. 'Now let me introduce you to the feuding clan I call my Fellowship...'

Whatever else the joint invitation to Coke and Andrewes had done it had certainly set the other Fellows alight. Granville College was entertaining the greatest theologian in the land, the man who many said had done far more than translate much of the Old Testament in the new King James Bible, and also dining the man held to be the greatest lawyer of the age. It was a coup.

They filed into the Hall, Alan Sidesmith leading with Andrewes by his side, the Fellows in pairs either with their guests or with each other. There was a rustle and scraping back of benches as the students, over a hundred now the college was expanding so rapidly, stood up and fell silent. It was early evening, and the golden light of the sun slanted through the high windows and gleamed off wood and silver. The candles and lamps were not yet lit, and would not be so for another hour or more. There were two high tables, to meet the number of guests. Unusually, there was no distinction among the lesser tables. Other colleges allowed money and influence to buy a place at high table, and had separate tables for pensioners, the students who paid for their education. The poor scholars, the sizars, held a third category of table, if they were lucky enough to be fed at all instead of serving their fellow students to pay their way. Gresham had pioneered a simple rule. Only those with a Cambridge or Oxford degree could sit at high table. So in Gresham's college on the night of a feast, sizars and pensioners sat together and ate the same food. He paid for outsiders to come and wait at table on these nights. Let the poor students be served for once or thrice a year. Their brains were no worse than their richer peers so let their stomachs be treated as the same. Gresham had appointed a new cook, the best in Cambridge, before he had appointed a new president. It was the main reason for the college's huge popularity.

There had been two exceptions to the rule that only those with a Cambridge or Oxford degree sat at high table: Queen Elizabeth I and King James I.

The gong was struck and a senior student rose to read the long Latin grace. At a normal dinner his peers would have tried to pinch him, or fallen into a spasm of coughing. On a feast night they let him be. The student had a deep bass voice. The sonority of the Latin grace rolled around the great Hall and up into its beautiful rafters, increasing the raw power of the language. The grace ended. The feast began.

For all that Gresham's money had saved Granville College from total collapse, his place on the Fellowship had started at the bottom. Now he was quite advanced, in the top third even of the Fellows gathered. Traditionally, a Fellow's guest sat on his right, the President's guest at his right at the top of the table. At Andrewes' request, Gresham and the President had exchanged guests. Sir Edward Coke sat by the side of Alan Sidesmith, surrounded by an adoring audience of sycophantic law Fellows. Andrewes sat to the right of Gresham, three or four seats from the top of the table. He let the theologians who surrounded Andrewes have their fill of him.

It was not until the candles had been lit and the flames were dancing over the faces of the guests that Gresham and Andrewes turned to each other, each confident that they had paid their social dues to those sitting within earshot. Andrewes had been witty, Gresham noted, in telling stories of how the forty-six members of the panel drawn together to write the King James Bible had undertaken their duties in very different ways, but not a note of malice had crept into his conversation.

'Well, Sir Henry,' said Andrewes at last, 'can you confirm the rumours I hear, and tell me whether or not it is in fact the anti-Christ by whose side I sit tonight?' There was a sparkle in his eyes, alongside a strange darkness, and a lightness of touch in his tone.

Gresham replied equally lightly. There was no offence in Andrewes' tone, and none taken. 'Before I answer, my lord Bishop, perhaps I could ask if I am indeed sitting next to the Saviour Himself, a man so pure as to be canonised before the formality of his death?'

Andrewes laughed out loud, a rich, gurgling noise of such deep humanity and happiness that it caught Gresham unawares.

'Why, Sir Henry,' said Andrewes, wiping his face with the linen napkin supplied to him. 'If I'm as far from the description you've heard of me, then I must guess you're as far from the description I've heard of you! Is it possible we're

186

both mere mortals, with all the sins and all the strengths associated with that kind?'

'On the other hand,' said Gresham idly, 'it's probably more fun playing at being Christ and anti-Christ. Now there's a dialogue to light up a high table.'

'If lighting up a high table is your pleasure, then so it would be.' There were few men who could hold their gaze with Henry Gresham. Andrewes was succeeding, with no sign of flinching. 'But it would only be play, wouldn't it? Like so much of the talk at these evenings, splendid though they are. We're both too intelligent to believe that we're God or Satan. I fear we'll hear neither of them speak tonight. Only alcohol, and good food ... and a fearsome headache for too many of us when dawn breaks!'

'My lord Bishop,' Gresham responded, 'if we're not here to play – with words, with our illusions, with our own self-importance – then why do we dine at high table?'

'Perhaps,' said Andrewes, 'to enquire after the truth?'

'Well,' said Gresham, 'that would be a rare thing in a Cambridge college, wouldn't it?'

'True,' said Andrewes, 'but I understand you're a man who sets precedents, rather than believing he should slavishly follow them.'

There was a moment's silence before Gresham answered. 'So, my lord Bishop,' he replied, 'would you care to set a precedent and tell the truth here tonight?'

'I'll do more than that,' responded the Bishop of Ely, 'I'll tell you a secret, Or rather, part of a secret. After all, there could be no safer place, here among all these people.'

Now you would have made a spy, thought Gresham, in a way that Coke never would. As the evening wore on the triple spell of good wine, good food and good company had worked their magic, loosening the tongues and heightening the sensitivities. Nowhere in the world were there more people talking and fewer people listening than at a Cambridge feast, except perhaps in a court of law. The deal to insert the serpent into Eden could have been concluded tonight, and no one would have heard.

'My lord,' said Gresham, a rare intensity in his tone. 'Tell me what you will, but I can guarantee you no secrecy in return. Be careful before you confide in such as me.'

'Ah,' replied Andrewes, lifting the goblet to his mouth but merely brushing his lips with the wine, 'but, you see, I come prepared. I've done my homework, Sir Henry. I've asked people their opinion of you.'

'And who have you asked, my lord Bishop?' asked Gresham, intrigued at the inner calm of the man.

'Not the courtiers, the politicians and the pre-lates, that's for sure. For them you're a strange and fearful creature, to be trusted as much as Beelzebub, a man rumoured to have had a strange hold over Robert Cecil, and even the King. A dark, explosive force, they see you as. A man who has killed, and who has ordered others to be killed. A man with a remarkable capacity to survive. And, of course, a man to be envied above

188

all others. Vast wealth, a stunningly beautiful wife, fine heirs, a good brain and a good body... My, my, Sir Henry, how you do provoke the sin of envy in others.'

'Thank you, my lord, for telling me who you've *not* asked. My question, if I may be so bold and impertinent as to repeat it, is who you did ask.'

'Your servants, Sir Henry,' replied Andrewes, taking a clear drink of his wine at last. Gresham stiffened. Andrewes noted it – a good spy indeed! – and put out his hand as if to calm him. 'Don't worry. They haven't let you down. The opposite, in fact. I always go to the servants when I want to find the quality of a man or a woman. Your servants are particularly good at telling those who question them nothing. Details of your whereabouts and your movements? Details of your security arrangements? The layout of your houses? I doubt most of them would give up those secrets even under torture. But, you see, a servant doesn't feel bound by any vow of secrecy when it comes to telling how proud they are to serve their master, or their mistress. And even if they don't say it, they make it clear in the language their bodies speak whether or not they would die for you.'

Gresham, embarrassed, interjected, 'All men give up their secrets under torture, if the torturer is skilled in his trade. All too often servants are not given the choice of whether or not to die for their master.' Why was this man in danger of forcing him on to the back foot?

'Well,' said Andrewes, 'your servants trust you, and your mistress. They do rather more, actually.

189

They love you both. But forgive me for being an old cynic, if you will. I rate the trust on a higher level than the love.'

The hubbub around them was increasing. There was a sheen of sweat over most of the faces, and fingers were being pointed and tables thumped as points were made.

'You were summoned by Robert Cecil, I believe, for a very last meeting?' Andrewes continued. 'I also believe that at that meeting the loss of certain papers was discussed, and a rather unholy alliance forged between you and your declared enemy, Sir Edward Coke, for the retrieval of those papers.'

Good God! thought Gresham. Had Cecil posted a broadsheet around London detailing their meeting? And, what was it to do with an East Anglian bishop, a master of sixteen languages? Gresham revealed nothing of his inner turmoil. Instead, he consciously relaxed every muscle in his body.

'I thought men of God were committed to the ultimate truth, my lord. I didn't realise how skilled they were at fiction. You have no proof of your version of events.'

That hit home for some reason. Tiny muscles contracted along Andrewes' face and neck. Tension. A shock. Gresham filed it away.

'Well,' said Andrewes, recovering quickly, 'let's stick to truth. Very many of those papers you've been set after have no relevance to me.'

'And no capacity to harm you?' Gresham asked.

'Neither relevance, nor harm,' said Andrewes. 'Politics I despise. I'll do what I have to with courts and with kings. They exist, as does a final hill on a long and wearisome journey, or the need to pay the shopkeeper before acquiring the food. They exist, and as such need to be met. But they're not existence. Existence is about the soul. The spirit. That which places us above the animals. There's little to be learned about that in courts, or in converse with kings.'

'So what is it that you fear in these papers that I might have been set on to find?'

'You know Sir Francis Bacon, I believe?'

Another change of course, another shock for Gresham. He showed none of it either in his body or his voice.

'We've met.'

'Sir Francis and your guest tonight, Sir Edward Coke, are locked in battle for royal favour and for the legal dominance of England. You appear to be in alliance with Sir Edward.'

Appearances can be deceptive, thought Gresham, without intending to speak it. Andrewes continued.

'Not unreasonably, Sir Francis opposed my coming here tonight. Gently, of course. Unlike you, he doesn't deal in force.' Ouch, thought Gresham. A hit, a palpable hit. 'He thought no purpose would be served by my confiding in you. He even thought it could be tantamount to suicide for us both. He said that you answered to your own masters, and that they were different masters to those I serve, and to those he served. Not better, nor worse. Just different. Are they that different, Sir Henry?'

'How can I know,' answered Gresham simply,

'until I know you, and Sir Francis, and who your masters are, far better than I do now?'

'A fair point,' Andrewes sighed. 'So let me tell you my half truth. The papers you most need to find are between a monarch and his ... friend.'

'And do you condemn such friendships? You, a bishop of the Church of England?'

That stopped Andrewes in his tracks, Gresham was pleased to note.

'That depends,' Andrewes replied at length.

'Are bishops allowed to depend?'

'Probably not,' said the Bishop of Ely, 'but this one is contrary. At least in being so he is true to the habits of a lifetime, if not to the doctrine of the Church.'

'Contrary? But God's will is clear. It is definite. At least, it's so in the eyes and ears and heart of every bishop I've ever talked to.'

'Perhaps this bishop is aware of the difference between being God's representative on earth and being God himself!' snapped Andrewes. 'As for my condemnation, I condemn lust. I find it far harder to condemn love.'

'The difference?' asked Gresham, intrigued.

'Lust? It satisfies the needs of our bodies. Love? It satisfies the needs of our souls. The body dies, and shrinks through appalling and sickening putrefaction after death. It is fallible and rotten. The soul lives on.'

'So if a man finds solace for his soul in a relationship with another man, and the bodily relationship is merely a passage to that meeting of souls, then he is free from sin?'

Why was the silence between these two men so

separate from the noise which surrounded them? How had they managed to create their own private globe of communication amid so much letting down of barriers?

'I ... I...' For once in his life, Bishop Lancelot Andrewes was lost for words. Sir Henry Gresham spoke for him.

'You've offered secrets to me. Now let me really surprise you. Let me offer a secret, a hugely damaging secret, to you. I offer it in the full knowledge that you can give me no vow of secrecy in return.'

Now the shock was on Andrewes' face. Of all things, this was not what he had expected. The burning intensity in Gresham's face and voice was frightening. Such intensity did not convince or heal. It burned an inexorable mark into the recipient.

'I once loved a man. And, yes, for one night, and one night only, that love ceased to become spiritual and became physical. And later that same young man was charged *with my sin*. I was the leader. I was the instigator. I was the master. I pleaded to be the victim. And as they ... executed him, I sobbed out loud to be the one who was blamed. And as–'

Even Gresham was forced to pause.

'And as they did ... unspeakable things to him on the way to his death...'

Was it true? Were there tears in the eyes of Sir Henry Gresham, that famous dark force against whom there was no resistance?

'He cursed me for the suffering I had brought upon his poor body and his poor soul. And so he died, in hatred of me. So tell me, Bishop Lancelot Andrewes, *is there forgiveness in the Church of England for men like me?*'

'No,' said the Bishop simply. 'No forgiveness. Not from the Church. But from another poor mortal such as me, yes. Forgiveness. And pain for your pain. And, if you would believe me, understanding. And one more thing. The screams a dying man gives out in his agony are not the truth. I do not hold that Christ in his agony believed that his Father had forsaken him. Yet he asked if this was so. If you remember the dying moments of your friend, you remember him as his enemies wanted him to become. Remember him rather as the man you loved. As he, I believe, will be remembering you, in his new place of rest.'

There was no absolution that could cleanse Gresham's soul, no alchemy to heal his wound. He had thrown his bitterness and his story at the Bishop as a weapon, to unseat the man and see whether the calm he radiated was genuine or merely a front. In return, for the first time in twenty years, something had crossed the air between them that touched Gresham. For the first time, something approaching a sense of peace started to seep in to that most damaged part of Gresham's brain.

'Well,' said Gresham, snapping back to life and his normal sense, 'you have my secret. Are you still willing to tell me yours?'

'More than I ever was,' Andrewes responded, his face retaining a smile of intense compassion, 'but I'm still bound by secrecy. I can – no, I will – only tell you half a tale.'

'It will like be more meaningful than many that are being exchanged around us.' With a faint nod Gresham pointed to the man opposite, who, in gales of laughter, was telling the story of the student whose illicit emptying of his piss-pot always seemed to hit the same servant, and the servant's novel revenge.

'If you find these letters, you will have a choice,' said Andrewes. 'You can hand them over to Sir Edward, who will use them to promote himself with the King. You could hand them to Sir Francis Bacon, who will do likewise. I suppose you could hand them back to Sir Thomas Overbury, were it not for the fact that he would lose them again to the next flatterer who came his way. You could even try to use them yourself, for your own advantage. Or you could hand them to me.'

'To you, my lord Bishop? You said you had no interest in politics?'

'Precisely. That's why I would destroy them. Their revelation serves no purpose other than to unsettle the state. Their use is only for personal ambition. They were better never to have been written. Once written, they are better burned.'

'Why could I not burn them, if I find them?'

'Because your reputation is such that no one would believe you'd done so. Me they will believe.'

'Forgive me, my lord,' said Gresham, 'but you've no cause to love the King. He gave Canterbury to that pliant fool Abbot when you were the obvious choice. We have a king who's said in public that he doesn't give a turd for religion. How do I know – in the mythical state where I have these letters –

that you wouldn't use them for your revenge?'

'You don't know,' said Lancelot Andrewes. 'You'd have to trust me. As I've trusted you by this request. You see, Sir Francis Bacon, with whom I am involved in this for other reasons, doesn't know that I've made this request. He thinks I'm seeing you on a different matter.'

'Is there a different matter?' asked Gresham.

'Yes,' said Andrewes. 'With these letters are other ... papers. I won't tell you of their nature. I will tell you that they hold great potential to damage me, and Sir Francis Bacon. You know Bacon's hand? Here's an example of mine...' Andrewes reached into his purse and brought out a folded half sheet of paper. It held notes for an old sermon, Gresham saw, in a clear, flowing style. 'You'll recognise any papers that concern Bacon and myself. They'll be in our respective hands. I ask you simply to destroy them, immediately. Not even give them to me, or to Bacon. Destroy them.'

'And you will trust me to my word, when you've just told me that the world won't do so?'

'I will trust *you*, Sir Henry Gresham. I've no power over whether you trust me.'

Love letters again? thought Gresham. Did Andrewes, this most saintly of men, have a past to regret? Had he and Bacon even been in dalliance? Bacon made no secret of his fondness for young men. He filled his household with them, and allowed them to milk his estate for all it was worth, to the vicious amusement of Court circles.

'You may trust me, my lord Bishop,' said Gresham levelly, looking full into Andrewes' eyes.

'Yes,' said Andrewes, 'I think I may.'

Gresham was not drunk, but he knew his head would show that he had drunk the next morning. He eased off his gown in his college rooms, sensing his loneliness. Jane was safely tucked up in The Merchant's House, well-guarded. Mannion had seen Gresham into college, then signed himself off for a night roistering in Cambridge. Even he believed Gresham safe behind the locked gates of college.

He reacted to the noise almost before he consciously heard it, a sixth sense forcing him to swing round and grab his sword silently from its sheath. The third floorboard up on the staircase had been deliberately rough-sawn so that it squeaked when trodden on. It had squeaked now, after midnight, when all of college should be in bed and no one walking up the staircase that led only to Gresham's room.

He had not closed the outer door to his rooms, and the inner door was simply on its latch, not bolted nor barred. There was a sound of heavy breathing from outside, a rustle of clothing and then a click as the latch lifted and the door opened slowly.

Gresham waited until it was half open, and then kicked it back on itself as hard as he was able. The door shot back, met flesh and bone, and whoever it was creeping up on Gresham was flung back down the stairs with a wail of pain, protest and shock. Gresham ran out of the room, to see what mess, living or dead, waited for him.

It was LongLankin. A tumbled, head-over-heels and half-conscious LongLankin. But judging by the language, definitely alive.

'What d'yer fuckin' do dat for, yer pox-blasted twat!' he mumbled reproachfully, feeling gently for his loose teeth and a nose that looked broken. He drank the ale that Gresham had found for him with a shaking hand.

'What did you go creeping around college for in the dead of night?' asked Gresham malevolently, with a total lack of contrition.

'To find you, o' course. To tell you 'bout that man, that bookseller.'

'The bookseller?' Gresham felt a shock go through his system.

'Yeah, 'im with the play. E's in town tonight. E's got a room down a back street.'

It appeared LongLankin had been making his way home after a night of intellectual enquiry, and taken a turn down a back alley to relieve himself. Standing to do the job he had noted a light on in the downstairs room, its window curtained over. He had wondered if it was a whore setting up business on her own, and had gone to peer through the thin gap in the curtains. There he had seen the strange figure of the so-called bookseller, and come running to tell Gresham.

'How did you get into college?' asked Gresham. Doors were bolted and barred, a porter on duty.

'Never you mind,' said LongLankin truculently. Well, Gresham did mind, and tomorrow there would be a review of security. Moving as fast as the man would allow him, Gresham asked for a clear set of instructions for finding the house and then bundled LongLankin out to the porter's lodge with some money for his pains. He had with him a dark cloak with hood, his sword and dagger, and a lantern, its shutters closed for the moment so that no light escaped from it. Nodding to the startled porter, paid extra so as not to question Gresham's comings or goings, Gresham turned left out of the gatehouse, passing St John's on his right, turning again past the darkened bulk of Trinity College, dominated by its Clock Tower and the Great Gatehouse, heading towards the old Trumpington Gate.

It was a bad night for stalking, with a cloudless sky and the fullest possible moon. This was poor housing now, earth-floored and stinking. The house was there right enough, the light still burning in the room as LongLankin had described.

Was it wise to be out here on his own, when men had already been mustered to kill him, in a street of hovels where the proceeds of his cloak alone would feed a family for a month? How sure was he of LongLankin? What if the man, a vagabond and a vagrant, had been set up to lure Gresham out from behind his stone walls and the protection of his men? Gresham had rushed off on LongLankin's word with hardly a thought. The chill of the night and the funereal, harsh white light of the moon were giving him second thoughts. He grinned sharply to himself. Was he more frightened of nameless men waiting to ambush him in the dark, or the reaction of Jane and Mannion to his foolhardy casting of caution to the winds? He had been careful for too long! He felt the pulse of excitement again in his veins, and picked up his pace, still moving silently through the deserted, moonlit street.

A noise from the end of the alley. Gresham pressed himself back into the wall of the mean house he was standing by. The building had shifted at some time in the past, as if a giant had pushed it forward, so the already steep overhang of the roof was doubled, creating a pool of darkness from the moon's glare.

It was only one man. He was heavily built, lumbering rather than walking, making noise enough for an army. He stopped at the door of Marlowe's house and knocked, a peculiar tap-tap-tap that was obviously a code. The light moved from the curtained room and spilled out under the cheap, warped wood of the doorway. It opened to reveal a short, hooded figure.

Marlowe.

Something tightened across Gresham's heart as he saw the figure he had last seen firing a crossbow bolt at Jane. Hold back! Clamp down on the emotion, use head, not heart. Revenge would come. A greater need now was information.

Marlowe muttered something at the man. All these years on, and still that same odd, high-pitched voice. As Gresham watched he managed to reduce the lantern's outpouring to a mere sliver of light, and handed it to the man, motioning him to start off. Marlowe was dressed for the night, boots and heavy, black cloak. He used that same high-prancing step.

At this late hour in the dark, close streets, anything live scuttled and scurried rather than walked, unless it was the drunk singing softly as he staggered solemnly round and round in a circle, thinking all the while he was headed home. Gresham kept his distance, moving crab-like from house to house as he followed the two men. They were moving to the centre of town, Gresham saw, past Bene't Church and on to King's.

The chapel was even more magnificent bathed in the stark moonlight. It rose over Cambridge like a blessing, soaring yet monolithic, so simple yet so infinitely complex.

King's College Chapel? Why was Marlowe headed there? It was long past midnight – there were no services. The strange couple made their way to the west end and its door. Locked, surely, at this time of night? If they had a key then Gresham had no hope of following them inside, presuming Marlowe would lock the door behind him. No. No key. The door simply opened and swallowed the two men, closing softly behind them. So someone had been bribed to keep the door open. Cheaper and far less risky than letting a stranger have a key.

Gresham flitted over the ground to the door. He could hear nothing through its thick, ironed oak. Gently, ever so gently, he lifted the huge handle. It was smooth, easy: grease. The mechanism had been greased beforehand. He could smell it.

He paused for a second, the great door ready to swing open. His senses were screaming signals to his brain. Did a man ever feel so alive as when he risked his life on one throw of the dice? In battle, perhaps, or in the moment of sexual relief. If he went in it was to face two men who knew where

201

they were going and what they were doing. He was far from any help or assistance. If he died here, it would be unseen and unexplained, a mystery to keep the high table talking and the taverns full for six months or so, and then to be forgotten, just another of the strange legends of Cambridge. The spy who was found dead in King's College Chapel. Was he to be like Marlowe, an enigma whose death history would argue over for ever?

He took three, careful, deep breaths. With infinite gentleness and in one single fluid movement he entered the chapel. Its walls were not walls at all, but windows, bursting out in colour in the daylight, now an eerie patchwork in the intensity of the moon. The windows rose to the intricate, soaring passion of the fan vaulting, visible now only as the merest variation in light and shade in the blackness of the roof. A rare cloud passed over the face of the moon, and a blanket of total darkness swept up the chapel like a threatening high tide. Gresham stood just inside the door. So gently had he slipped into the building that the air had hardly moved around him. He stood, poised, waiting, in total silence, listening. Waiting for the blow, the sudden indrawn hiss and snap of breath so many men took before a sudden action.

Nothing. Silence. Wait. Yes, there it was. The tiniest scrabbling noise, soft in itself and coming as if through a door or other barrier. There, in the corner. The narrow doorway that led up to the roof through one of the corner turrets. He eased across the stone floor, sword in hand, just another silent shadow. The doorway up into the turret was ajar. The slightest of sounds made it clear that Marlowe and his hired help were scrabbling up the narrow, circular staircase. One of them must have kicked a piece of loose rubble. It skittered down the stone steps, each noise as it landed as loud as a gong in the prevailing darkness and silence. The noise startled Marlowe and his companion. They halted. Silence. A brief whispered conversation and they started off again, both panting and heaving with effort. Unfit, thought Gresham. Dying, in Marlowe's case, from a rot within. Dying for the third time.

Gresham eased himself on to the first of the steps. They were smooth, cold. The soft leather of his fine shoes kissed the stone and made no noise. There were long, thin, slit windows up the side of the tower, more like those built for archers in a castle than those built for a church. Gresham's night vision was perfect now, and the harsh moonlight shafting in from the thin windows was just enough to allow him to discern the pattern of the steps. No tricks here, Gresham thought grimly. In some of the places he had fought the builders had put in a straight run of ten or twelve steps of uniform size and then put in a step with two or three extra inches of height or depth. The effect on attackers hurtling up them was catastrophic, catching them out and sending them tumbling time after time.

He was coming to the first exit now, the one that would lead off into the gap between the top of the magnificent fan vaulting that formed the ceiling of the chapel and its lead and timber roof. The small door led to a stone corridor that ran the whole side length of the chapel. It had windows, and pools of moonlight interspersed with black holes of dark. To the right was a passage up on to the top of the vaulting. For all its fine and delicate tracery, hanging suspended as if floating, the magnificent, unprecedented fan vaulting was built of the heaviest stone, each of the central corbels that seemed to draw the delicate strips of stone together weighing over a ton. A man could easily walk along the centre of the vaulting, which rose up in a quarter circle from both sides, without a tremor. In effect, the two halves of the stone roof met in the middle, leaned against each other and supported their vast weight, passing it down to the buttresses on the side walls.

Light! Not the petrified light of the moon but a lantern, flickering a third of the way along the side of the vault. Marlowe was muttering, cursing. His man was reaching clumsily into the area behind where the great roof beams nestled snugly on to the outer wall. Behind each beam was a cavity, perhaps a foot or eighteen inches deep, a perfect masonry box without a lid. The man grunted and brought out a package which looked for all the world like an oiled, canvas satchel.

The papers. The papers which seemed to have haunted him and so many others for so long. It had to be them.

What a magnificent place to hide documents. The space between the roof and the vaulting was dry as tinder, ventilated by the wind that drove through the end windows. There would be no mould or decay, though God knows there was enough dust. Each of the vast, arching roof beams formed in effect an alcove, several in number. Who would think to look behind the timbers, reach down and fumble for a package in the hidden cavities that lay there?

Marlowe and his man were less than halfway along the roof space. Their lantern stood at a tilt on the curving stone of the vaulting. Silently, Gresham reached out for the random, rusty nails embedded in the great timbers. He prayed for no clink of metal, hung his darkened lantern over the largest and sturdiest nail. Then, in one swift movement, he flicked open all four shutters of the lantern with a twist of the wheel that operated the mechanism and stepped behind the nearest beam, his back to the door that led out again into the tower.

The shock was dramatic. The extra light speared through the darkness at the end of the chamber. Marlowe gave a sharp cry and whirled round, losing his footing and falling with a curse to the floor. His man said nothing, but let out an animal grunt and came charging, instinctively aggressive, towards the source of the light. He dragged from his belt a cudgel, a club of hardened wood that some men would have found too heavy to lift, never mind swing. In confined spaces it was a good weapon. Gresham had seen one snap the fine blade of a sword in half, before being driven down to crack wide open the swordsman's skull. Marlowe looked up, saw the man and his satchel charging down the length of the vaulting, and tried to cry out to stop him. It was no use. Marlowe was part-winded. Even if his strangled noise had been heard, the brute of a man had the wind behind him and would not be stopped. As he reached the lantern, looking wildly round him, Gresham rose like an avenging nemesis out of the side wall and grabbed the strap of the satchel. The man's headlong rush was stopped sharp by the pressure of the canvas around his neck. His feet skittered out from under him, and as he hit the floor Gresham gave a savage, downward jerk of his arms. The hulk made a noise between a gurgle and a cry, and lay silent. His mouth lay open, and Gresham saw that the man had no tongue. That was why his noises had been so animal. Had he killed him with the blow? No. He was still breathing. Damn!

Gresham sensed rather than saw or heard the movement from further up the roof and instinctively swung back behind the beam, There was a flicker of silver and the knife – an Italian throwing knife, Gresham had time to note – swished by like liquid metal to embed itself, quivering slightly, into the next beam along.

Marlowe was standing now, fumbling for a second knife, eyes blazing hatred. It was not clear if he recognised Gresham. Without stopping to think, Gresham reached up to the rear beam, dragged the still-trembling knife from deep in the old wood and hurled it back to its owner.

It was a bad throw, taken in too much haste. Instead of heading for the centre of the rib cage, it veered to the right. Marlowe was holding the second knife now, hand and arm upraised, ready to throw. His own returned knife sank into his wrist, just below the hand. Marlowe was flung backwards, the second knife flying out of his grasp and landing with a clang on the centre of the vaulting, from where it rolled down to the side. His scream was more animal than human, a tearing, wrenching noise that opened the doors of hell. He crashed to the ground, looking in appalled horror at his own knife embedded in his arm, the blood starting to seep down to soak invisibly into his black cloak. With a last, croaking cry, he passed out.

Or had he?

There was red in Gresham's eyes. The overwhelming, overriding urge to survive had him in its wildest grip. He must kill the brute with no tongue. He must kill Marlowe. *Now*, while both were defenceless. *Now*, before they could rise up on either side of him.

He had his sword raised over the throat of the brute nearest him, choosing him first.

Then he stopped.

Fool! Was he an animal to be dominated by a blood lust? He needed Marlowe alive, needed him to tell him the truth, needed that truth to plot Gresham's own survival through the tangled paths of Coke, Bacon, Overbury, Andrewes, King James and the ghost of Robert Cecil.

With all his force Gresham kicked the huge man in the stomach. He hardly moved. Satisfied, Gresham ripped the man's tunic further apart at the neck along the stitching and dragged it half down over his unresisting body, pinioning his arms to his side. Then, for good measure, he took the flapping arms of the tunic and tied them across the man's back in a fierce knot, making an impromptu straitjacket.

Eyes on Marlowe's prone figure, he crept forward. His every sense was on sword edge. There was no need to test Marlowe's unconsciousness. The knife through his arm would have him screaming if he were conscious. Noting distastefully the blood that lay around the body – it would not be a fair gift to Jane to pick up a dose of the clap from this man's bodily fluid and pass it on to her – he picked up Marlowe's booted foot, noting the stench of the man as he did so, and dragged him, head bouncing off the floor, to join his servant. He took a leather studded belt off the servant and used it to bind Marlowe's feet together. That left Marlowe with one arm free. He would not be using the other to unpick any belt or rope, not with his own knife embedded in it. Time! Time! This was all taking far too long! He would have to bind Marlowe with his own doublet, then hope to carry him unseen through the streets. The other servant had better be imprisoned too, which meant Mannion and others coming back up here, all before dawn. Time! Why was there never enough time?

Time stopped. Motion stopped. The world froze.

A noise.

A noise of hasty breath and a footfall. Faint. Very faint. A flickering shadow of a noise, as of the softest of feet making the quietest possible haste along the corridor alongside the vaulting.

He *had* no more time.

Was the man on the roof, waiting? Or was the noise him fleeing the violence below? It made sense to have him on the roof at the start. Send someone in ahead – someone to unlock the door even – to scout out the ground. Mount to the roof, wait there in silence. Hang the tiniest of lights from the parapet – no one to notice it at that time of night – to show the coast was clear. Whoever it was may have left his post to greet Marlowe when he saw him scuttling across the green. That would explain why the watcher had not seen Gresham, following on and skirting the edge, a minute or two later.

So was he on the roof? Or waiting in the corridor outside? Damn! With enough lanterns lit to guide an armada, Gresham had lost his night vision. If he doused both the lanterns now the listener would have the advantage. There was no alternative. He chopped the light, then crouched back against the wall, having first placed Marlowe's lamp across the entry a man would have to walk over if he entered the vault.

Silence. Not even a breath of wind. Harsh moonlight cutting through the end window. Even the upward side of the vaulting was beautiful, though only a handful of men would ever see it.

Gresham rose to his feet and moved carefully out into the corridor, then up a few flights of the tower's circular staircase and on to the roof. Inch by inch, he crept upwards. His sword he extended at full length ahead of him. Anyone lunging down would be pierced before they could reach him. The coward's way, an old sergeant had laughed at him in the Lowland Wars. Three weeks later the man was dead, killed storming a tower. Not the coward's way. The survivor's way.

The door was open at the top. Gresham could

see an arch of the night sky outlined at the stair's head. Quandary. Was there room behind it for a man to hide, to plunge the door into his face as he had done with LongLankin? He moved up on to the last step. The slightest breath of night air touched his face. He had not noticed his thin sheen of sweat. He took two or three deep, silent breaths. Then, gathering himself up into a ball of muscle, he hurled himself through the opening. As he landed over the threshhold, out in the open now, his foot caught in the clumsy wooden duckboards that ran alongside the roof. He fell, still gripping his sword, with an almighty clatter.

He rolled forward, freed his sword. Silence. Nothing. He lifted his eyes to the line of the roof.

Nothing.

The thin rooftop passageway in which he lay was faced to his left with ornate stonework, shoulder high, the parapet wall of King's College Chapel. To his right, the roof rose steeply to its ridge. The moonlight showed there was no one in sight. Yet the further along the channel the eye went, the more the shadows merged into each other.

Where would Gresham have hidden?

Suddenly he knew the answer. It was a terrible risk. He knew what he would have to do to find his enemy. It would hinge on a moment of balance, a reaction a split-second early.

But life was risk. It was not the fear that mattered. All people felt fear. It was the ability to conquer it.

The roof ladder, laid flat on the roof itself, was a clumsy thing, roughly fashioned out of unseasoned timber, leading up to the ridge. Its

210

partner would lie on the other side. To crawl up it or to stand on its bottom rung and walk up? He stood.

The ladder was rock firm, surprisingly so. As he walked up the roof, ever so carefully, measuring each step, his sword arm upraised, his other arm flung out preposterously for balance, he sensed rather than saw how high he was. Something dropped in the pit of his stomach as he imagined his height above ground. With each careful step he took, the ridge line of the roof dropped one notch towards him. Agonisingly slowly, the top line of the roof came to his head height. Next step and his eyes were above it. Next step and his shoulders...

The man had lain himself flat on the other side of the roof, by the side of the ladder. As Gresham's head appeared shadowed against the moonlit sky, the man leaned slightly down on his left shoulder and slashed his sword arm from the right side of his body through the area occupied by Gresham's head and neck.

He had acted too early! One more step up the ladder and the whole bulk of Gresham's upper body would have been there to meet the blow. As it was, a normal man would have flung his head back as the flicker of a blade headed for his eyes, thereby probably unbalancing himself and falling backwards off the roof. Instead Gresham leaned forward and parried the blow with his own sword, inches from his cheek. He held the other's blade, slammed his wrist down to a rasp of steel and waited for the hilt to engage with the hilt of the other sword. A fierce, vicious twist. The other's sword flew through the air, over the ornate stone-work. It must have fallen on earth. There was no noise. The man was spreadeagled below Gresham now, struggling for a knife, a hand clutching the timber of the roof ladder. Pitilessly, Gresham brought his blade back, selected his spot and plunged it through the neck of his assailant.

Kill or be killed. This man was no innocent. He had made his choice, taken his chance. And he had lost. A spasm passed through the prone body, the hand gripped even tighter to the ladder for a moment, and then let go. His body slid down the smooth surface of the roof, tumbling into the narrow passageway at its foot.

Gresham looked around. A ghostly mist, some fifteen or twenty feet high, shrouded Cambridge, the moonlight picking out its every curl and fold, Housetops and church spires poked out from the enchanted smoke, glinting with moisture. The throbbing in his head began, the throbbing he knew would develop into an agonising pain, the pain he knew came with the killing and the fear.

He walked down the opposite roof ladder. To his surprise, he found the man still alive. Dying, certainly, blood pouring uncontrollably from his neck, but still living. With an agonised last puls-ing of muscles, the man turned his head towards Gresham, the blood thickening and spurting as it streamed from the wound.

Gresham stopped, as if struck by a blow.

It was Heaton. Nicholas Heaton. Cecil's mes-senger. The man who had been so confident of serving the King. And who was dying, covered in blood, an accomplice to Marlowe, *wearing the livery of the King!*

'What does your master have to do with this man Marlowe?' hissed Gresham, hauling Heaton up to face level, dagger pressed against his chest. Heaton's eyes were glazed, blinking. With a superhuman heave Gresham hoisted him on top of the ornamental stonework that fringed the wall, hanging him over it, facing the terrible drop to the ground. His thick blood fell before him, showing the way, leaking from his torn neck.

'Will you tell me now?'

But Nicholas Heaton was dead, carrying whatever secrets he held with him. There was much here for Gresham to think on.

Minutes later, and with a final heave, Gresham pushed at the body. It slid, about to fall to the ground, but hung for a second by the tunic, ludicrously, off a cone of carved stone. Then, with a ripping and tearing of cloth, it slid over the edge. What was it he had said to Heaton all that time ago, at their last meeting?

Take care. Those who rise to greater heights have far further to fall.

Marlowe had gone. The servant still lay there, comatose. The belt, severed with stabbing rasps of a knife that Gresham must have missed, lay at his feet.

Well, if Marlowe was in league with King James, killing him might have been a murder too far, until Gresham could ascertain the nature of their link. Much more here to provoke thought.

Clutching his satchel, Gresham finally left the chapel. One servant would be found pulped on the ground the next morning. The other would

213

probably still be in the roof. Did King James hold enough power to keep what had happened secret? Or would Cambridge be buzzing tomorrow with strange murders and men falling off college roofs?

Gresham, the pain growing in his head, decided he didn't care either way. He had a satchel to open.

13

September, 1612
The Merchant's House, Trumpington

'There is no fear in love; but perfect love casteth
out fear.'
                              THE KING JAMES BIBLE

'How could you leave the college with no guard?
On your own?' Jane was incandescent. He had
never seen fury like it. To her, a vision of him
slumped like a broken doll at the foot of the
college, the sheer madness of his going out to
meet Marlowe, felt like a betrayal of their love.
'Do you think your wife and children want to live
without you? Are we so little to you that you can
throw basic caution to the wind? How would you
have spoken to me if I'd run off into the night
with your children, on the word of a drunken
informer, because in the final count excitement
mattered more to me than my love!'

She was right. That made him even more angry.
Mannion was no help. He had said nothing about
Gresham rushing off into the night, but he
looked mournful and reproachful, like a vast cow
that had not been milked or a dog whose owner
had suddenly ceased to walk or feed it.

The letters, the damned, cursed letters, had
been there in Marlowe's satchel, in lascivious

detail, the hand presumably that of the King himself.

'Well? Will you give the letters to your Bishop, as he asked?' said Jane. Was her anger subsiding, or did she merely have it under her control?

'Probably. Possibly. I'll think on it.' He was trying to show his hurt at her failure to understand why he had had to go out into the darkness and confront Marlowe. *So often there was only the one chance!*

Why are men such *children?* thought Jane. If a child's tantrum is ignored it loses its power. So she would ignore his tantrum. With a massive effort she reined in her anger.

'Are the other papers useful?' He had shown them to her so she was in a position to make her own judgement. By asking him for his thoughts she placed herself below him. Well, God had made the first mistake in creating women second. Who was she to deny God? Except that by a subtle use of her second place she might still lead this damned fool of a man into thinking he had made the right decision on his own.

Useful? They were two play manuscripts. Both, apparently, the text of *Hamlet, Prince of Denmark*, but in two different hands. Neither bore even a passing resemblance to the hand of Bacon, or of Andrewes. Gresham's interest had waned.

'No. Not useful,' he had confided. 'Confusing. Yet Marlowe kept these papers alongside those that damn the King of all England and Scotland as a lusting sodomite. They must have some value I don't know of. I need to meet Shakespeare. In some way I don't understand, he's a key

216

to the sub-plot of this whole business.'

'He's renting rooms in the old Dominican Priory, at Blackfriars.' It was Mannion. 'And he's back there. I heard, yesterday. Just after you'd gone into your feast. There's talk he's trying to buy them. Quite the little property magnate, our Master Shakespeare. You know he's been buying up half of Stratford?'

Gresham didn't know.

'There's too much we don't know,' Jane and Mannion noted the use of the conciliatory 'we'. Perhaps the storm was over. 'What I do know is that I want to meet Master William Shakespeare again.'

14

September, 1612
The Dominican Priory,
Blackfriars, London

'For now we see through a glass, darkly ... now I know in part; but then shall I know even as also I am known.'
THE KING JAMES BIBLE

The Priory was a warren of a building. Shakespeare was renting rooms over the east gate. They had left The House by a back entrance, disguised as masons in rough jerkins and with hammer, mallet and chisel carried around their belts. It was a good disguise. A hammer was a handy weapon. Strapped across his back, hidden under the jerkin in a special harness made of the finest Spanish leather, Gresham had strapped a sword, with a dagger positioned just above each ankle. He had not bothered to ask what weapons Mannion deemed suitable for the outing.

Jane was dressed as a housewife. It was always a worry how to disguise her. Even the worst clothes did little to hide the bloom and leanness of her figure, and the high cheekbones, sparkling eyes and lift to the chin made her a beauty however much soot was rubbed into her face.

Gresham and Mannion followed immediately

behind Jane. Two of their men were stationed in front, two at either side and two to the rear. It was easier to train men to kill than to train them to accompany and guard their master and mistress without seeming to do so. It required intense concentration, as well as the ability to appear nonchalant when every nerve was straining.

Blackfriars was down The Strand and along Fleet Street, then over the stench of human and animal sludge that had once been the Fleet river. There was not one London, but several. A man who fitted into the hectic bustle of Fleet Street would be out of place among the weavers and cobblers of St Giles in Cripplegate, or the whores of Cheapside. Masons, however, went everywhere there was stone to chip, carve and repair.

The noise and bustle was immense. Everywhere the dust rose and clogged nostrils, put little icicles into eyes and caused the well-bred to walk with a handkerchief across their faces. Everywhere there were people trying to sell things, shouting out the value of their wares. Everywhere was the incessant building that seemed to be going on across all of London. The wooden scaffolding jutted out into the streets, where wagons, coaches and horses vied for what little space there was. Its own people filled its medieval walkways to overflowing, yet there was always more. London's teeming thousands needed feeding, and with every month that went by the city seemed to suck in more and more farm carts.

Mannion went to check with his look-out, who had alerted him that Shakespeare had been seen entering his rooms an hour earlier. 'He's still there,' said Mannion.

The gatekeeper was an old man, half asleep after his dinner. He woke to full consciousness with a start as Mannion banged on the half open door to his tiny lodge.

'We're 'ere to see Master Shakespeare. Master William Shakespeare. Some'at about some stone work he needs doin' up.'

'What you got that there with you for?' enquired the gateman, leering at Jane. She had rubbed her eyes hard and placed fresh spring water in them a few moments ago, blinking it out and over her cheeks. She looked as if she had been crying hard.

'Why, that hussy!' said Mannion, with feeling. 'If you'd a' seen where I had to drag 'er out from, you'd know why she ain't getting out my sight 'til I get her home! It's a trial in times like these, bein' a father and with no mother alive to keep her in order, I tell you!'

'Goin' to spank her, are you, when you gets 'er 'ome?' said the gateman, licking his lips and grinning like an aged satyr at Jane. 'Thrash her, are you? With a belt, an' all?'

Mannion was nearly knocked off his stride. His glance caught Gresham, who was frantically trying to contain the laughter threatening to explode inside him.

'Oh, sir, he will, an' that!' Jane's accent was an excellent imitation of Middlesex, ''e's so cruel to me, he is, so cruel ... he beats me, he does, somethin' rotten.' She let her voice drain off into a pathetic snivel,

Good God, thought Gresham. Who needs to pay to go to the theatre? Let's just hope she doesn't start to strip off and show him her bruises...

'Ay, right then, up you go. Good luck to you. No time for these actors, me. Satan's chapel, that's what these theatres are. Satan's chapel.' The old man subsided into grumbling, though not without his gaze lingering lovingly on Jane's rear as they walked up the stairs.

They knocked on the heavy panelled door that Mannion had already established was Shakespeare's. There was silence. They knocked again, louder. A faint scrabbling could be heard from within. Gresham and Mannion exchanged a brief look, stepped back and in perfect unison drove with their feet at the place on the door that held the lock. It sprung open with a mighty crash.

When Gresham had first met him, Shakespeare, or William Hall, had been nondescript – medium height, medium build, medium everything. It was no bad thing for a spy to pass unnoticed. Even now, kneeling on the floor, hands raised in supplication, he was entirely forgettable. A bald pate with brown hair straggling on the side, a middle-aged paunch, the archetypal ageing prosperous merchant. How could the mind that wrote his plays be housed in a body of such drab normality?

Shakespeare had almost finished opening a hidden door in the heavy panels of the far wall as they burst in, an expression of sheer panic across his face. 'There's nothing I can do!' he shrieked now. 'I can't please you all! I don't have the papers!'

The gateman would be here any moment, calling out the watch. Jane stepped forward, knelt down beside the distraught man.

'Please,' she said quietly, 'we're here to help you. Not to harm you. Believe me. And send the gateman away when he comes.'

Gresham's heart went out to her. Most of the men he had worked with would not have recognised the danger the gateman posed without being told. Hardly any of them would have had the initiative to do something about it. Surely enough, clumping, urgent footsteps could be heard on the stairs outside.

Shakespeare looked into the most startling pair of dark eyes he had ever seen, housed in a face of such handsome proportions that it was guaranteed to take any man's breath away. 'No harm?' he asked pathetically. 'No threats?'

'No harm,' said Jane calmly. 'No threats.'

Shakespeare got up. 'It's all right, Ben,' he called out as the wheezing figure of the old man rounded the stairhead. 'Just a misunderstanding. These are ... friends of mine.'

Ben looked suspiciously at the group.

'Well, I 'ope as 'ow they're better "friends" than some of those others you've 'ad comin' round 'ere these times. You sure? You don't need no 'elp?'

'I'm sure. Thank you. I'm sure.'

Ben left the way he had come, grumbling. Interesting, Gresham thought. The old man cared for Shakespeare, in his way. Servants – and particularly grizzled, perverted, cantankerous and liver-frazzled servants like Ben – cared for a very few

222

people. Shakespeare must have something to command a residue of affection.

Shakespeare forced himself to look at Mannion. He is frightened he has made the wrong call, thought Gresham. This is a very scared man. Mannion saw the scrutiny coming. He stepped back, raised his arms, palms outwards. No weapons. No threat. It was a universal language.

The beating pulse in Shakespeare's neck began to subside. His doublet was of rich satin and velvet, copiously slashed. 'Do you close doors, as well as smash them to pieces?' he asked Mannion. Good, thought Gresham. There's wit there, at least, and a quick recovery. Gresham looked at the man's eyes. They were hooded, dark, as if a shutter was permanently closed over them. Normally Gresham gained a feeling for a person within minutes of their first meeting. Was there some strange smell, some ghostly aura invisible to the eye that passed between people? With Shakespeare he felt nothing. No sense of personality, no feel at all for what lay behind the exterior.

It was time for Shakespeare to know to whom he should talk.

'He does what I tell him,' said Gresham, 'usually. But he's no good unless he can smash something, sleep with it, eat it or drink it.'

'Then all he can do with me is the first. I doubt I'm his type in bed, and about the only thing no one's threatened to do to me recently is eat or drink me. God knows, they've tried everything else.' That wit again, with more than a note of tired resignation in Shakespeare's voice. He got up with Jane's assistance, and allowed her to help

223

him to a chair. It was an expensive item, Gresham noted. Seasoned oak, with a high back and arms. A chair Robert Cecil would have been proud of. A rich man's chair. Even better, thought Gresham. The more a man had to lose, the more pressure could be brought to bear on him.

Shakespeare's beard and moustache were reasonably full, without being luxuriant. He wore a fashionably starched yellow collar, with two laces hanging down from it. Thickish nose, eyes quite wide-set. A drinker, Gresham thought – what actor wasn't? – with the veins just starting to go in the nose and cheeks. And those hands, with long, bony fingers. Why on earth did someone his age wear the earring in his left ear? It was the mark of a young dandy, not an ageing actor.

'So would you mind explaining why two ... masons ... need to smash down my door to see me?' Shakespeare reached for the goblet on the paper-strewn table. Jane, long practised with Ben Jonson, had the jug pouring the wine before he realised what was happening. He took a huge swig of the fluid.

He is outwardly quite relaxed, thought Gresham, but there was the faintest, most distant something in the air. Mannion looked at Gresham. Yes, they had both sensed as much as smelled it. Human fear. The smell both of them knew so well.

'May we sit down?' asked Gresham politely. There was another beautiful high-backed chair to match the one Shakespeare was seated on, and four or five stools.

'Be my guest,' said their host, his eyes not managing to stay on Gresham but flickering between him, Mannion and Jane.

'My name is Henry Gresham.'

'Sir Henry Gresham. I know your name,' said Shakespeare. 'I remember you from a past it seems I'm not going to be allowed to forget. My name is William Shakespeare now. Not William Hall. And how is Sir Walter?'

'Imprisoned, having lost most of his estates. Locked up on a false charge laid by a scum of a man with no morals except his own best interest. And he's still very angry. As indeed am I.' The menace in Gresham's voice was palpable. Shakespeare had begun to relax, but Gresham's speech caused him to bolt upright.

'You promised no violence!'

'Nor will I deliver any. Not yet,' replied an icy Gresham. Shakespeare blinked, and spoke again.

'You come to the theatre. You're the one they attacked in the riot at The Globe. All the company have done since is talk about you. You work for the King, don't you? Has the King ordered you to kill me?' The tension crackled out in Shakespeare's voice. It was nondescript, a slight trace of Stratford, country-boy burr, not un-attractive. The accent of rural England.

Now why on earth would a playmaker think the King of all England and Scotland would be bothered enough to have him killed?

'No one's ordered me to kill you,' said Gresham.

'Then what do you want?' asked Shakespeare. His voice was like footsteps treading on ice, fearful that it might give way at any moment.

'To talk to you,' said Gresham. 'And, please, if you could manage to spare some of that wine for my body servant here, it would stop his gaze boring into the back of my head like someone turning a screw.'

'Would you mind, Lady Gresham?' said Shakespeare, inviting her to fill a tankard for Mannion. He slurped away at it, happily.

A ladies' man, Master Shakespeare, thought Gresham, noting the brilliance of the artificial smile he flung at Jane. Full of contrasts. The wild smile of the actor, the drinker, the philanderer, the man with every mask at his disposal but no mask to call his own. The signs of dissipated living, the veins about to burst out. Yet at the same time the prosperity, the room with its fine chair, the fine hangings on the wall, the expensive goblet, all signs of worldly, rather than artistic, success. And hardly any books, just one chest with two or three volumes and some desultory papers! No pen, no paper! And no stains of ink on those long, bony fingers.

There was silence. Shakespeare looked away under the scrutiny of Gresham's gaze. 'What is it you want to talk about?' he finally asked.

'I was invited to investigate the loss of certain papers by Lord Cecil of unlamented memory, Sir Edward Coke and, I suppose, Sir Thomas Overbury.' At which name had Shakespeare started? He was trembling so much it was difficult to see. 'I now know much more than I did. I know, for example, that Kit Marlowe is back here in England and hell-bent on a killing spree.'

Shakespeare's hand gave a spasmodic jerk. His

goblet flew off the table and rolled across the floor. There! That had made a crack in the wall! Shakespeare was not fat, at least not grossly so, but there were too many layers of softness over the bones that smoothed out his features. His gut wobbled as he jerked. A good few evenings in the tavern were stored there, thought Gresham.

'What I don't know is where a set of manuscripts relating to the work of Master William Shakespeare fit into this very complicated figure. And I would very much like you to tell me.'

'Will you kill me? Torture me?' Shakespeare's voice was plaintive now, almost as if he had been through this conversation before. Was it acting? Was it real? Or had this man lost the ability to distinguish between fiction and reality?

'If it appears you've betrayed me, or placed myself and my family at risk, I'll have no compunction in doing both. If you tell me the truth, then I'll do neither.' There was a certainty in Gresham's voice that was unanswerable. Jane remembered the spy of Cecil's infiltrated into their household years ago, held over a stinking pit that led to a deep, stone-walled chamber full of water, a chamber from which there was no escape. He had told the truth, eventually. They had then carefully broken his legs, as a reminder. No one betrays Henry Gresham. Jane shuddered at the memory. How was it possible to know so much and yet so little about a man?

'How simple life must seem as a spy!' barked Shakespeare. Another part, another role for the actor to play. The superior, angry man. Yet not played well, Gresham noted. He stopped short of

227

making a true impact, like a punch pulled at the last minute. Shakespeare looked fully at Gresham now, into his eyes. 'You'll not torture and kill me if I tell you the truth, or so you say. Yet there are others who'll most certainly do both if I tell you what I know.'

This man, thought Gresham, is about to break up. He flings different personalities at me, each one less convincing, each one more fragile, each one less revealing of the man within. Whatever is happening to him, it has gone too far for him to be able to cope. Any moment now his heart will stop, or something will crack inside that bald pate. He is caught between a rock and a hard place.

'Is it Marlowe who's threatening you?' asked Gresham gently.

'Threatening me? He's tried to kill me once – and on stage! Good God! Some people really do take the theatre too seriously! If only it were that simple!' Shakespeare had slumped back in his chair and started to cry, a wailing, keening noise, racking sobs near lifting his plump body off the seat, his head held in his hands.

Gresham made a decision. 'Jane,' he said to his mistress. 'Would you please be nice to Master Shakespeare for a while, and talk about how bad you think some of Ben Jonson's writing is? You, Mannion, take Master Shakespeare's wine into a corner, after you've given him some of his own drink, and if he tries to run, kill him.' Gresham smiled at Shakespeare. 'I can't stand the smell of that bread through the window any more. We could all do with a bite to eat. I'll be back in a while.'

Gresham remembered the moment of communication with Andrewes, the single, fleeting meeting of minds in a strange communion. There would be no such meeting with this man. Every signal skittered off the face of his personality, tumbling, falling, never hooking in to anything permanent.

Gresham went down the stairs and greeted his men, who drew themselves up as he made his exit. He took four of them with him, leaving the others to guard the gatehouse. First stop was the bakery, where the soft, pungent aroma of freshly baking bread was taunting passers-by with its promise. Then rough-cut country cheese and butter from a farm wagon, and fresh smoked meats from a stall. Then to the tavern, a respectable-enough looking place, to explore the wine on offer. They haggled and, whistling, Gresham took his wine, picked up his men and went back to the gatehouse.

Jane was seated by Shakespeare on a stool, prattling away as if she had known him all her life. A storm of light flashed from her eyes as he entered, warning him off.

'And while I thought *Volpone* and *The Alchemist* were brilliant – and I told him so – I thought *Sejanus* was awful. Told him that, too, and he threw a chair out of the window. Fortunately, it was open...'

Underneath it all, her heart is bursting with worry – for me, for herself, for her children, thought Gresham. She hates the world I live in, and lives in it simply for me. Not so long ago she was fighting for her life and manning a boat like an Amazon. Now she's sitting here, chattering

229

away as if she is a stage-struck girl hardly out of swaddling clothes. In a minute she'll tell me something I was too stupid to spot, and, God willing, by the time the night's over she'll have been a bed-mate for me and a true mother to her children. How many minds did God give this girl?

'I didn't think *Sejanus* was that bad...' said Shakespeare generously. Then he stopped. His eye had been caught by Gresham laying out a simple supper, two bottles of wine still under his arm. He was humming a tune to himself as he did so, Tom Campion's 'My Sweetest Lesbia'. The change from avenging fiend to table servant had startled Shakespeare. It had been meant to.

'But tell me about your plays, Master Shakespeare,' said Jane. 'I mean, I know he wants me to calm you down and soften you up so that you'll let out more information than you want to...' Shakespeare's eyes opened even wider. Well, thought Gresham, there's nothing like a dose of the truth to make things work. He had tried the tough way and lost. Let Jane do her worst. 'But I really, really do like your plays. And so, by the way, does he. More than that, in fact. He loves what you write almost as much as he hates the man who writes them.'

Why was this line of conversation seeming to make the man panic again? Gresham thought.

'I think you must be an amazing person, to write those comedies and then move on to histories and tragedies. If it was anyone else, they'd have stayed with one style, like Jonson has, and made it their speciality. Your plays – you seem to

230

do each style better than anyone else and then move on! It's extraordinary.'

'Yes, isn't it?' said Shakespeare distractedly, as if he was trying to pass a large and sharp stone from his bottom. 'Actually, I prefer to talk about my poems, you know. The plays are how I earn my keep. The poems are where I feel I can write...' He wanted to talk about his *Rape of Lucrece*.

He babbled on, genuinely happier now he was off the subject of plays.

Gresham moved around the table. Shakespeare had only been renting these rooms for a month or so, Mannion had said. An old Dominican Priory, with more bolt holes and secret passages than a Catholic household, Gresham guessed. The water was only a few paces away, down St Andrew's Hill to Puddle Wharf. Had he moved here so he could run when danger threatened? If you looked carefully you could see where the door in the panelling opened up, but the carpentry was superb and it could only be seen as a door if one knew where to examine. There were no bookcases, Gresham saw with surprise, no sign of a library. Not even copies of his own plays, those that had been published. Only three books. *Venus and Adonis. The Rape of Lucrece.* His poems. And there were his sonnets, of course. Brilliant. Gresham, who had published his own sonnets under a false name, had felt the sharp sting of envy when he had read Shakespeare's work, always the sign of real power in another writer. It was a pirate edition, with the famous acknowledgement to 'Mr W.H.' as the 'only begetter' of the sonnets. In any event, the book was there, stuffed carelessly along with the others, in a chest with its lid open, a chest stuffed otherwise with printed pamphlets and broadsheets. One of them caught Gresham's eye. It had been torn out of something. *To our English Terence, Mr Will. Shakespeare.*

Terence. The classical author.

Light exploded in Gresham's head. *Of course! The explanation! It had to be! What a fool he had been!*

'I'm sorry, Master Shakespeare,' Gresham said charmingly. None of the revelation in his mind showed. Shakespeare had paused in his explanation of *Venus and Adonis* to Gresham's own Venus. 'I really should have asked if you wanted to eat before I set your table. May I ask you to sit and sup of this very humble fare?'

Humble it might have been, but the way Shakespeare attacked the food after his initial hesitation confirmed what Gresham had thought. Master Shakespeare, who looked as if he had the capacity to be a good trencherman, had been feeding as well as drinking out of the bottle in recent weeks.

The wine was good. Not excellent, but good. Gresham treated himself to two glasses. Shakespeare had adapted with some ease to his attackers becoming his dinner guests. Actors, thought Gresham, do not live by any known codes. They are outsiders, perhaps even outcasts. They make their own rules. Shakespeare had insisted on moving to the next room – Mannion had moved casually to the door to make sure another priest's escape route was not being utilised – and bringing

232

back four exquisite glasses, clearly Venetian. In Mannion's paw the vessel looked like a new-born babe in the hands of a devil. Just pray he doesn't smash it, thought Gresham. And that Shakespeare doesn't drop one, as he had dropped the goblet, when I tell him what I now know.

There are moments when humanity thinks history is made, when a great battle is fought or a mighty coronation observed. Yet there are other moments, hidden in the warp and weave of everyday conversation, masquerading as normality, that change lives and sometimes even the world. Moments which expose or hide a truth for ever more, that write a new version of human history. Moments based on the chance of a particular pamphlet lying at the top of a pile, and the chance of a particular man seeing it there at a particular moment when two glasses of wine had been drunk just ever so slightly too fast.

Gresham let Shakespeare finish his meal. He would need all the strength he could muster. He waited until the man, garrulous by now, was telling Jane about his plans for a new sonnet sequence. It was as if the room shivered before him. It was an extraordinary sensation, one he had never experienced. He had dealt with kings and queens! He had held their fate in his hands! He had kept secrets the world would have shuddered for! So why now, with the plump and drunk figure of a nobody in front of him, did he feel that something inexplicably important for the future was taking place in this room? He shook his head to rid it of this nonsense. He must have drunk more wine than he had thought.

Then, in a pause while the actor reached for yet another glass, Gresham spoke.

'You didn't write your plays, did you, Master Shakespeare? You wrote your poems, I'm sure, but your plays – the work you've become famous for – *you didn't write them, did you?*'

Shakespeare looked at Gresham with an expression of such appalled horror that for a moment Gresham felt the most intense and cutting pity for the wreck of a man in front of him. Was he going to throw up the first food he had eaten in days? Or would he make it to speech first?

'I ... how could you? Are you some devil incarnate?' There, it was out. And it was the truth, Gresham noted. If it were otherwise, the man would have denied it in his shock.

'No, no devil, as far as I know,' said Gresham. 'But I observe, and I listen. Manuscripts of plays are stolen, manuscripts presumably in the handwriting of their author. There's panic in the corridors of power. With the Catholics banished to hell for ever more after the gunpowder plot, there's a new power in the land. The Puritans. They get their Bible. They rail against the corruption of King and Court. And they hate the theatre above all else! They call it Satan's chapel, and the actors the spawn of Lucifer.'

'So?' said Shakespeare violently, rallying. 'We've endured their vilification for years. And not just them. We're vilified by the people who use us most, just like a whore! What of it?' There was a pathetic *braggadocio* to the man. Or perhaps a trace of real courage. Would Gresham have been happy to fight alongside this man? he wondered.

Strangely, against all reason, perhaps he might have been. Providing, of course, he had been able to pour a bottle of wine down him first. Dismissing the thought, he bored in to Shakespeare.

'What if the very powers of the land, the Establishment, its aristocracy and nobility, have succumbed to the new power of the theatre? What if, instead of wanting their thoughts and dreams and the wild imaginings read out in private to a closed group of adoring Court ladies and fawning men, they want them played before thousands, night after night? What if they have found themselves lured into writing plays? Plays they cannot own up to, of course. Heaven forbid that the ruling classes should stoop so low as to write a play! Yet suppose their idle brains have found amusement in so doing? What easier than to find a cipher, a nameless man of the theatre, to give his name to their offerings? What if they chose a feeble poet, a man who had proved his ability for deceit in his life as a spy, and an actor of at best limited ability, to put his name to their work?'

'What if they have?' mumbled Shakespeare, seeming to see the end of the world in the bottom of an empty wine glass.

'Well then,' said Gresham, 'what if some mischief-maker decides to expose these idle aristocrats? Expose them to the Puritans. Expose them to the people as too cowardly to own up to their own words. Expose them as liars. Expose them as deceivers. *Expose them to ridicule!*'

'And what if they do?' Shakespeare had looked up from his glass now. He gazed into Gresham's eyes, but did not see them. He was looking into a void, an abyss of hopelessness that not even Gresham's greatest depression had plunged him in to.

'What if they do?' continued Gresham remorselessly. 'Well, we know our rulers are liars. Machiavelli told us why they have to be. Yet look at the response when Machiavelli dared to tell people the truth. He was consigned to hell. *We must not know that our rulers tell lies!* But if they do want to expose the truth,' Gresham carried on remorselessly, 'then two separate forces will work on the source of the lie. On you, Master William Shakespeare. The supposed author of these plays. The man who in reality takes the manuscripts, tidies them up a bit for theatre and puts them out as his work – all for a healthy fee, of course! There'll be the force of those who desperately want their foray into the theatre kept a secret. Then there's the other party, the ones who want their genius acknowledged, who want to take the glory of their writing for themselves.'

Shakespeare's head jerked up at that. So at least one person wanted their anonymity removed, wanted to claim the credit for the play they had laundered through Shakespeare's name.

'What a mess you're in, Master William Shakespeare! One party will try to keep your secret by having you killed. The other party will try everything to keep you alive and pressure you into telling the truth. And the manuscripts, the original manuscripts of the many and varied plays by William Shakespeare, will be in the handwriting of the original authors, for all that one or two may have trusted the writing to a treasured clerk.'

236

Shakespeare's head shot up. A hit! Which of Shakespeare's wealthy clients had sent his manuscript in by a clerk's hand, and not his own?

'No wonder you're being torn apart,' said Jane. 'You poor, poor man. You just can't win, can you?'

'How did you guess?' asked Shakespeare, looking bleakly at Gresham.

'The pamphlet. There, in the chest. *"To our English Terence, Mr Will. Shakes-speare."* Terence. Wasn't he the impoverished Roman writer who agreed to publish under his own name works that Roman noblemen had written but for one reason or another didn't care to acknowledge? Congratulations. Ben Jonson would be proud of you. For all your lack of classical learning, you've acted in a true classical tradition.'

'You think you know it all, don't you?' Shakespeare had gone beyond despair, into a region Gresham did not recognise.

'No,' said Gresham truthfully. 'I never think I know it all. I like to find out enough to survive.'

An agony of thought passed over Shakespeare's raddled face. Finally, he came to a decision. 'I was a nobody! I was struggling in the company. I can't act, you know. I'm hopeless! They were going to get rid of me, a poor country boy with no talent except a way with poems. Poems never filled a house. Then this manuscript arrived. A complete play! Addressed to me, with a covering letter and a promise of money if I did what I was told. I knew it was Marlowe, from the writing, the words, the way he used language ... so I took it. And I gave it my name. I told Hemminge and Condell. My friends, no one else. They thought it

237

was a gold mine. The others in the company, the ones who wanted to get rid of me, looked at me with new respect. "It's good, Will," they said, patronising me, when I produced the first script under my name. "We'll put it on, for a trial, you understand. See how it goes down. See if it works." And it meant I could stop working for Cecil. Say goodbye to William Hall. Be William Shakespeare only.'

'Poor old Marlowe, not wanting to be dead at all,' said Gresham. 'And most of all not wanting to be a dead dramatist.' He stopped for a moment. 'So what went wrong with the system?'

'I don't know!' said Shakespeare. His hands were running over his bald pate, as if the hair was still there. 'Marlowe's plays stopped, ten, maybe twelve years ago. They just stopped. Until now. When he came back. Mad. Diseased. Barking.'

'Any others know?'

'All the bloody world and their grandma for all I care!' exploded Shakespeare. 'Lots of people have suspicions. Jonson does, I know. As for anyone else who knows for certain, well, you're the spy. You tell me!'

'But it didn't end with Marlowe, did it?' said Gresham, relentless. Shakespeare rocked back, hit hard. 'I knew Marlowe. I know the works he wrote under his own name. I know the plays you've written. My favourites?' Gresham was pacing around the room. *Hamlet. King Leir*. Marlowe could never have written those! Marlowe's heroes never pause to worry about what other people think. Hamlet's crippled because he can think of nothing else. Leir's damned because he never listens until it's

238

too late! *Who else writes plays with your name on them?'*

'Oxford,' whispered Shakespeare, seeming to draw into himself as a penis will shrink and shrivel with intense cold.

'WHO?' said Gresham with intense rudeness.

'EDWARD DE VERE!' Shakespeare shouted back. 'The fucking Earl of fucking Oxford! There were lots of people who wanted to write plays back then. People who didn't dare to have it known.'

'The one who couldn't forget the fart?' said Mannion, who had been listening, engrossed, to the developing conversation.

'What?' said Gresham.

'Oxford. De Vere. The one who couldn't forget the fart.' Mannion gave a guffaw of laughter. Edward de Vere, the Earl of Oxford, had been a fierce patron of the players. He had equipped and served on-board a ship for the Armada. Then he had farted. Before his Queen. In full assembly. He had run from the Court before a word could be said and exiled himself to Europe for years. There he had developed a fondness for the most extravagant Italian style of dress. On his return, he had presented himself before his Queen in all his finery. Whatever else she may have possessed, Queen Elizabeth had a raucous sense of humour. Faced with this extraordinary vision of Italian fashion, she had received his supplications of loyalty with regal splendour. Then she had reduced the Court to fits of suppressed laughter by her next statement.

'My lord, I had forgot the fart.'

239

De Vere could not now forget it. He had fled the Court a second time, permanently humiliated. He had died of the plague in 1604.

'*So who were these others?*' asked Gresham in a sibilant hiss.

If Shakespeare had made himself any smaller he would have vanished. 'Don't ask me any more!' he pleaded. 'You've a horde of men to protect you, against Marlowe and the rest of them! I've no one!'

'*Who else?*'

'Rutland.' It was said in a very, very small voice.

'*Who?*'

'Rutland. Roger. Roger Manners. Fifth Earl of Rutland. He died, in May. Just after your lord and master Robert Cecil! There! You've got it now, haven't you? Marlowe. Oxford. Rutland.'

'Marlowe. Oxford. Rutland,' said Gresham thoughtfully. 'What do they want of you?'

'Marlowe wants it shouted from the rooftops that he wrote my plays. All of them. Not just the handful he sent in a manuscript for. And he wants me to get The King's Men to perform his play, *The Fall of Lucifer*. He's tried to kill me once. Oxford and Rutland's heirs, they demand I keep silent. They don't want their illustrious parents damned by association with the theatre, don't want them seen as cheap conspirators. They've threatened me. Serious threats. Men with knives. I'm dead if I tell the truth, as Marlowe demands. I'm dead if I hide the truth, as the others want me to do.'

There were tears in Shakespeare's eyes, Gresham noted. There would have to be. He was an actor, after all.

'Marlowe. Oxford. Rutland. Are they the only ones whose plays you put your name to?'

'Isn't that enough?' Shakespeare shot back. 'How many more do you want?'

'One of the people you name is as mad as a hatter and likely to drop down dead of the pox at any moment. I can hardly be in ignorance of him. One tends to remember anyone who's tried to skewer your wife on a crossbow bolt. The other two are dead.'

'So?'

'So I think you're only telling me the names of the people I can't talk to.'

Stalemate. Whatever Shakespeare was hiding, even his very visible fear of Gresham was not bringing it out.

'And you remained a spy, didn't you? Long enough to infiltrate the Bye Plot and place Sir Walter Raleigh in the dock?'

Shakespeare flushed. Yet he also fought back. 'I was seduced into the whole wretched business when I was too young to know better – as perhaps were you! It was exciting, wasn't it, when we were young? You were working for the greatest in the land, there was money in your pocket and you travelled as a king's messenger. And you, and Sir Walter Raleigh, greatly overestimate my part in his downfall. Sir Walter's always been his own worst enemy. Challenge him to be silent and you've a guarantee that he'll shout out loud.'

The problem was, Gresham thought, he was not far off the mark. Raleigh, one of the very few people Gresham had ever considered a hero, was

241

too large for life. 'Your reward for Raleigh, and for acting as a front to other authors, was to have your company made The King's Men?' asked Gresham.

'Much more due to the latter than the former. My lord Cecil was amused to have a spy in the camp of a company of actors.'

Yes, I can see that, thought Gresham. The actors, the common players, despised of the Church, anarchic, a potential hot-bed of sedition and revolution and riot – and all the time, one of Cecil's men in a pivotal position in their midst. It would have amused Cecil, all the more so for the fact that no one would know.

'And if he was to have a spy in a company of actors, then of course it had to be the greatest, the best company of actors. Which meant we had to cease to be The Lord Chamberlain's Men and become The King's Men. And yes, Hemminge, Condell and Burbage, they knew I was the reason. I told them. Though I didn't tell them why.'

'So William Shakespeare's plays aren't William Shakespeare's plays at all.' It was Jane, breaking a long silence. She was too old for there to be tears in her eyes. Yet the tears were there in her voice. 'Those plays that seemed so magical to me, they were nothing more than the playthings of noblemen too cowardly to admit their art, noblemen playing at writing plays, posturing beneath an adopted disguise. Well, my thanks to you, Master William Shakespeare. I used to think there was artistry and beauty and magic in the world of the theatre, even when it was stripped away from the world I actually lived in. Now I

242

find it's just the same as everywhere else, just a little more dressed over. Thank you for educating me. Now I know there's no art. No magic. Only self-interest. How silly of me to need a reminder.'

She stood up and left the room, passing through the door to Shakespeare's sitting room, there presumably to commune with her own ghosts.

There were tears in Shakespeare's eyes, Gresham saw. One actually dribbled over his eyelid and fell down his cheek. It was a truism Gresham had heard countless times that a man could not counterfeit tears. His age respected emotion, not as something womanly in a man, but as a sign of genuine feeling. How good an actor was William Shakespeare? Gresham thought. Were his tears the burning mark of truth? Whatever the answer to that, Shakespeare was clearly a man who was down and out. Which, of course, was exactly the time for someone more ruthless to hit him twice as hard.

'How many plays did Sir Francis Bacon and Bishop Lancelot Andrewes write under your name?'

It had to be that! To hell with love letters! It wasn't those that Andrewes had asked him to destroy if he found them! It was plays! Bacon was too clever ever to put down in writing his love for another man. Andrewes would sooner burn his balls off with an altar candle than succumb to carnal temptation, if Gresham was any judge. But both men were prime candidates for the play-writing urge. They had fearsome intellects, the willingness to dare to be wise and the desire

243

to try their hand at this new art form while knowing that their station and ambitions forbade them from so doing.

Gresham had never seen a man reduce in size before his eyes. Shakespeare seemed to wilt and shrink as he spoke his words. 'How much do you know?'

Gresham could have driven home then, taken all the advantage possible from his inspirational guesswork. Instead, remarkably, he decided to be merciful. Was it because the infinite compassion of Lancelot Andrewes had touched him to his soul? Or because he had seen his wife bid farewell to magic? Or was it because, all of a sudden, he was tired of the world, its double and treble deceptions?

'Far less than you might imagine,' he confided to Shakespeare. 'Yet I'd be willing to bet that Bacon and Andrewes were two of the men who submitted to your play-writing factory. Bacon wishes to be Attorney General. Andrewes wishes to be Archbishop of Canterbury. Neither would be helped in their ambitions by the realisation among the general public that they'd also wished to be stars at The Globe. Yet they're both writers of some brilliance. Both have minds that are incredibly active. Catch them at the right time and I doubt either could resist the chance to try their hand at this whole new world of plays. Like lambs to the slaughter, I imagine they were.'

'I...' Gresham had a sense that something had slipped in Shakespeare's mind, that at long last the truth was going to emerge. He waited, hardly daring to breathe.

There was a ferocious clatter of hooves outside and shouted orders. Jane came in almost immediately. Soldiers rushed up the stairs – the King's soldiers. Gresham's men would have been powerless. Their leader was Sir William Wade, the gruff Keeper of The Tower.

'Sir Henry. I am bidden by the King to bring you to his presence.'

'To Whitehall?' enquired Gresham mildly.

'No,' said Wade. 'To the Tower of London.'

Gresham would have expected a look of exultation on Shakespeare's face as they were led out. His victors vanquished. Instead, all he caught was a look of infinite sadness. William Shakespeare and Henry Gresham had stared into the same abyss, and were doing so even now.

15

September, 1612
The Tower of London

'Come, let's away to prison;
We two alone will sing like birds i' the cage'
SHAKESPEARE, *King Lear*

Damnation. This was bad.

'And is my wife also to be blessed with the privilege of meeting His Royal Highness?' asked Gresham.

'My instructions are that if she is with you, then yes, she also must ... she also is invited.'

Jane had retained most of her colour. The eyes were at their darkest. He alone could read the tension in her body.

'My lady, we have the honour of an audience with the King. Shall we proceed?'

They left the house and entered the carriage Wade had brought along with him, watched by a small and silent crowd. Why were two masons and a housewife being whisked off to king's arrest?

The Tower was a royal residence right enough, but no king or queen had lived there for years. It was bleak, forbidding and not infrequently stinking, and its main use was as a royal prison. It had a dreadful reputation, a building erected to sym-

246

bolise raw power where hundreds more had died within its walls than had been executed on its green, and even more than that had screamed under its torture. The summons to The Tower was a signal. A signal of extreme disfavour.

God knew how Mannion had managed to be allowed to ride in the coach along with his master and mistress.

'He's trying to frighten us.' Gresham spoke tersely to Jane.

'It's worked,' said Jane, shivering inside her cloak. 'And there's me,' she said with a wry smile, 'with not a thing to wear.'

'Stay calm. Let me think.'

There was no point feeling fear at moments such as these. It was simply a diversion and a distraction. Nor was there time for tears or for talk. Focus. *Focus*. Become as hard as the stone of The Tower, as slippery as the eels in the river. On his ability to handle this situation rested his own fate, and that of Jane, his children and Mannion.

The bulk of The Tower and its grim curtain walls squatted over the Thames. First was the drawbridge leading over the moat, which was coated with scum and full of noisome lumps that did not bear close examination. The heavy wheels rattled over the wooden planking; they heard shouted instructions. A sharp left turn, the carriage groaning, under the Lion Tower, across the moat again and over the second drawbridge. The two round, squat forms of the Middle Tower stood in their way. More shouted instructions, a rattling as of chains, and the coach lurched forward again. Yet another drawbridge, and then the taller, round form of the Byward Tower. Under its rusting portcullis. Into the prison, with three vast towers and their gates blocking the route to freedom. At least they had not stopped even earlier and been put in a boat to be taken to The Tower through Traitors' Gate. Gresham's heart sank as it always did when he entered this desperate place, even on the weekly visits he made to see Raleigh. This time his wife was alongside him. Stop it! Don't divert! Don't weaken!

They were not to be sent pell-mell into some dripping, foul dungeon. James had hurriedly made a room in the White Tower available. It smelled of damp and decay, and there were bruised lumps on the wall where plaster had fallen off. The marks of the servant's brush were still on the floor. There was a vast fireplace in the echoing room, unlit, and one large window high in the wall. An ancient oaken table had obviously been retrieved from somewhere, behind which James had ranged seats. In front of the table were two poor stools. The judge facing the accused.

'The wisest fool in Christendom' an ambassador had called James. Son of Mary, Queen of Scots, he had been in his mother's womb when a group of Scottish nobles had murdered her lover, Rizzio, with cold steel in front of her. It was said he had a horror of naked blades from birth. Of no great natural beauty or form, his tongue was too large for his mouth and he was prone to slobbering as a result. He rarely washed, and seemed not to notice the filth that accumulated on the fine clothes he wore. Addicted to fresh fruit, his bouts of diarrhoea were legendary among those who had to clean his linen. Sweet wines were his other addiction. Few had seen him really drunk; even fewer had ever met him cold sober. Increasingly driving the late Robert Cecil, his Chief Secretary, to despair, James had spent more and more money as his reign progressed, perhaps a reaction to the poor, cold country of his birth and its famous poverty. And then there was his obvious lack of interest in women, and his attachment to young men.

Yet he must never be underestimated, Gresham reminded himself now. The King could order his and Jane's death immediately. This man had survived as King of Scotland, a country that ate its monarchs like others ate meat. While James was increasingly handing power to Parliament and the Puritans by his indolence and inaction there was no hint of rebellion in the country. James was a writer and an intellect of no small merit. Like any king, he only enjoyed debates he was guaranteed to win, but the sharpness of his mind – when he cared to use it – had always been clear. King James I had an instinct for survival.

But so did Henry Gresham. And he had no doubt that it was his survival that formed the agenda for today's meeting.

James did not stand as Gresham and Jane were ushered in through the creaking door, and Mannion forced to stand by the back wall by the armed guards. Deliberate rudeness? Indolence? Or simply the Scottish informality James was renowned for, when it suited him? He had the pair of them at an immediate disadvantage, of course. Gresham was dressed as a mason, Jane as a housewife. The guards had taken the weapons from both men. Their disguise, and the weight of their personal armoury, made it clear they were up to some dissembling, devious purpose. It was extraordinary also how poor clothes stripped away a man's – and a woman's – self-respect. Well, Gresham had the power to imagine himself dressed in a king's ransom of clothing if he so wished. *He must not let it affect him!* It was also crucial to know how drunk James was. Gresham blotted all else out for the moment, even the other figures seated by the King.

The glass of wine was there, of course, easily to hand. Yet the hand was not quivering, and the eyes – small, hard – seemed steady enough. Oiled, then, but thinking. Well in control.

Gresham let his eyes move to the others at the table. Dear God. On one side was the popinjay Robert Carr, Viscount Rochester. On the other was Sir Edward Coke. Was this to be his tribunal? Was his vision of hell, to be in a court chaired by Sir Edward, now a reality? If so, he and Jane were dead. But give nothing away.

Gresham walked to a position just in front of the two stools. He bowed deeply to the King. The other two he ignored. He sensed the curtsey from Jane by his side. He was so proud of her. No tears, no wailing. She felt the fear, of course. Yet she had the mark of real courage. Feel the fear and conquer it.

'Sir Henry ... and Lady Gresham...' The accent was already quite thick. Under pressure, or when the drink was truly in him, James retreated to a thick Scottish burr. The 'Sir' had almost been

'Sair'. *Pressure or drink?*

James waved a hand, carelessly. 'Or *is* it Sir Henry and Lady Gresham? Or two stonemasons and a housewife?'

There were titters from Coke and Carr, *Sycophantic idiots!* Gresham calmed himself.

'I believe we follow in a tradition set by Your Majesty's illustrious forbears,' said Gresham, bowing to the King. 'Previous monarchs of this country have changed their garb and wandered unannounced through their realm as though they were mere subjects...' *Or they had in folklore, at least. Most of them in reality wouldn't have lasted two seconds in a real bar room brawl.* 'It is sometimes good for those of lesser worth, such as my wife and myself, to emulate the actions of our superiors, and by doing so learn from them.'

You clever bastard, thought Gresham. And, no doubt, thought King James. Yet it was good at this stage to not show too much fear.

James paused for thought. Carr, Gresham had time to note, was gazing vacantly out of the window. There was a long pause.

'Would you care to take a seat?'

'We thank Your Majesty for his courtesy,' said Gresham. A seat in front of a monarch was a privilege. Courtiers spent most of their time standing. Yet the delay in asking them to sit had made it clear just what a privilege was being offered. Neutral. Neutral. Nothing yet on which to base a ploy. Listen. Look. Learn. Personally Gresham would have preferred to stand. He sat.

'Perhaps ye may be wondering why I summoned you here, rather to your surprise I should not wonder? I do apologise, of course, for any disruption to your plans.' The 'of course' rendered the apology meaningless. The threat was clear, unequivocal. It breathed out from the evil stone and brick that surrounded them. No one was brought to The Tower for their pleasure. 'I'm sure I may have dragged ye away from more important things.' The accent again. 'Ye' rather than 'you'. Had it been 'more', or was it 'mair'?

'There can be no more important things than Your Majesty's pleasure,' replied Gresham. *God, why do I hate this sycophancy so much?* 'We are more than pleased to serve Your Majesty, and count it a privilege to be in Your Majesty's presence at any time.'

'Aye,' said the King, 'you do that well, Sir Henry, well indeed.' Was there the slightest hint of a smile beneath the bearded face? If so, it vanished almost immediately. 'Yet the reason for my ordering this meeting is a good deal more important than the exchange of Court pleasantries, however well ye may do them. There's shite on the velvet of your reputation, Sir Henry. I fear you may be working against me, sir!' James's coarseness was legendary. In the popular eye it was one reason why he had felt uneasy at appointing the clean-mouthed Andrewes as Archbishop of Canterbury.

Time for a hard stab.

'I am mortified to hear so, Your Majesty. Yet I will say to you now, sire, with your permission, that I have never in my life knowingly stood against any crowned monarch, or sought to dispute the right of any monarch to govern and to rule. I believe the health of the nation lies in the health of the monarch. I have been willing in times past to put my own life down as my bargaining counter to support that belief.'

Well, thought Gresham, that's almost the truth. I actually believe better the devil you know, and better any devil than the devil of rebellion. I've seen where that leads.

There was a dignity and power to Gresham's simple statement that carried its own weight of meaning. There was a prolonged silence. James reached out and took a lingering sip of his wine. Then he looked, pointedly, at Sir Edward Coke.

Coke was the accuser! That look told Gresham his true enemy!

Coke also knew that he was on trial. Yet there was the flush of achievement in his face. He had manoeuvred Gresham onto his own choice of battleground. This was a court hearing. Coke was the prosecutor. Gresham and his impossibly beautiful wife the accused. But there was no jury here to call the prosecutor to order. Merely a half-sodden monarch, whose single word could mean that this man and his wife never left The Tower.

'Yet you would not deny, Sir Henry,' asked Coke in his most silky voice, 'that you were instructed by the late Lord Salisbury to find and return certain ... papers. Papers that were of importance to His Majesty? And that you were instructed by the same good lord to work with myself in pursuit of that aim?'

Carr was gazing, his mouth half-open, at Coke. The distaste he felt for the wrinkled lawyer was clear. Did Carr have any brain at all?

It was an old lawyer's trick. Start reasonable. Ask questions to which there was only one, positive answer. Establish thereby one's desire as a prosecutor to be fair to the witness. And then screw him. Therefore, it was necessary for Sir Henry Gresham to stop the process somehow.

First of all, he looked to the King, his eyebrow slightly raised. Do I have your authority to answer this man? the eyebrow said. After all, in a room where the King of England (and Scotland, in this case) sits there is only one authority. Before speaking to a lesser authority, one should obtain the permission of the higher authority.

There was an almost imperceptible nod from James. Yet he would have noted the courtesy.

'I fear I would deny that, Sir Edward.'

Coke looked as if he had swallowed a prune stone. This was not according to the plan.

'It is possible that for you a summons from Robert Cecil was a new occurrence. I regret that for me, and indeed latterly for my wife, it was no such thing.' Gresham turned to James, speaking as if in confidence. 'Cecil used me as an agent in Your Majesty's interests on numerous occasions. Such summonses usually came late at night, latterly in the form of one Nicholas Heaton.' The air froze for a moment. 'These calls were peremptory and always involved me risking my life. For some reason, it always seemed to be my life and never Cecil's. I grew accustomed to accepting the challenges, but not without noting with whom lay the danger.'

It was there! Something that was unequivocally

a smile, albeit briefly, had passed over James's face.

'But you cannot deny that you were summoned, and that you were given instructions?' Coke bored in, only half-realising that he had given away most of his game plan. He was harsh, aggressive. This should have come later. Somehow Gresham had managed to jump the hearing forward.

'But of course.' Gresham was now all sweet reason. Yet he should have been nervous, on edge, and Coke the voice of calm. 'Of course I was summoned, as in countless times past. And, as in countless times past, I went. I went, Your Majesty,' and as Gresham spoke he turned again to the King, 'to meet Robert Cecil, your Chief Secretary. To my surprise, I found the meeting was with Robert Cecil and with Sir Edward Coke. And later, after he had beaten up a servant and tried to attack me, with Sir Thomas Overbury.'

'Ye met Overbury? And he was violent?' James had let his head sink into his vast ruff, but now he straightened up. Had Coke been stupid enough not to tell the King of Overbury's presence? Yes, by the look on his face! Before Coke could interject, Carr jumped, in.

'Your Majesty,' he said, 'this slander against Sir Thomas is unfair, without Sir Thomas here to prove it false. Might I ask to summon him...'

'No, sir, you may not.' The King cut off his favourite with a sharpness Gresham had never seen before. That tightening across James's brow – James tolerated Overbury because he loved Carr, and Overbury made it so that the one had to come with the other. Yet even James was not insensitive to the awfulness of the man. 'And did it surprise you, Sir Henry? To find Sir Edward there?' It was the King who spoke, to Coke's obvious annoyance. Coke had raised his hand to respond as well.

'Yes, Your Majesty,' replied Gresham candidly. 'And horrified me.'

Was he prepared to take the greatest gamble of his life? A gamble that would risk not only his own life, but the lives of those he loved? One throw of the dice to decide it all?

He threw the dice.

'You see, Your Majesty,' he explained carefully, 'I despise Sir Edward.'

Robert Carr sucked in his breath so hard as to make it ricochet in the half-empty chamber;

'I do so,' Gresham flung into the silence that followed his bomb blast, 'because I believe he helped betray the man I see both as my early patron and hero, Sir Walter Raleigh.'

There was a gasp from Carr. Walter Raleigh, locked up for years now on the King's orders after a show trial led by Coke. Walter Raleigh, his estate at Sherborne ripped from him and given to Carr. To protest his case before the King and to claim an allegiance to Raleigh was to appear before God and declare a pact with Satan. Double jeopardy. Was Gresham intent on suicide? An expression of glee crossed Coke's face. An expression of distaste flickered on James's brow. Before it could take seat, Gresham spoke on.

'I beg your forgiveness, Your Majesty, for my feelings towards that man. I know that in speaking of my belief in him I risk forfeiting my own life, and that of my wife and children. I know you believe he has done you grievous wrong.'

King James loathed Raleigh, saw him as the last of the great Elizabethans and one of the greatest threats to the monarch who had succeeded Elizabeth. Gresham's friendship with Raleigh was widely known. Coke had hoped to introduce it perhaps two-thirds of the way through the interrogation, and use it to damn Gresham. However, it seemed Gresham was going to use it to damn himself.

'And do you challenge that he is a threat to me? Do you challenge that he has sought to do me grievous wrong?' King James leaned forward as he spoke, aggressive, almost violent in his tone.

'I know you believe him to be so. I know you have the power to make that belief a lasting judgement. I would plead with you, as others have pleaded with you, to review that judgement, though at a different time and hopefully in a different place. Yet I give you my word that at no time have I or will I ever conspire against Your Majesty, or use my friendship with Sir Walter to do so.'

'Words are fine things,' said the King after a pause. It was impossible to judge his feelings from his face. 'Sir Edward here for one deals with them very finely. But words are not always the truth, are they, Sir Henry?'

'That certainly is true,' replied Gresham, feeling his way, 'but I would ask Your Majesty to consider one thing.'

'Which is?'

'Sir Walter Raleigh saved my life. I am indebted

257

to him. It would have been easy for me to cut off from him when Your Majesty's disfavour became clear, to dissemble, to lie about my feelings in order to worm my way into Your Majesty's favour. To become a fawning courtier. As so many have sought to do.' He turned pointedly to Coke, who had the decency to flush. 'My loyalties are worn on the outside of my body, for all to see. They are to Your Majesty, to my friend and to my wife and children.' Though in reverse order, as it happens, thought Gresham, bearing in mind that it would not be tactful to tell that particular truth at this particular moment. 'I suppose I am asking Your Majesty to see my declared love for Sir Walter as proof of something else. I am no dissembler. I am no liar. I am no threat. It may well be that I am a devil of sorts. At least I am the devil that is known.'

'Well, you have my eldest son and my heir on your side, Sir Henry, that much is true...' Prince Henry visited Raleigh, talked to him. Some said he viewed Raleigh as more of a father than James, admired him far more. It would not necessarily be of any help to Gresham. Indeed, it was rumoured that Prince Henry's affection for Raleigh increased his father's wrath against him.

'But yet...' King James's face lit up. Gresham had seen it do so once before, when he had paraded bishops and clergymen before him for a debate, and for a few brief moments the matter had gone beyond its tedious script and a real dialogue had taken place. It had been between James and Andrewes, Gresham now remembered. '...this is the issue Sir Edward brings to

258

me! He does believe you are a threat, Sir Henry. A most serious threat.'

Gresham felt the dryness in his throat, the tension rising in his neck.

'How might that be so, sire?'

Sir Edward leaned forward, eager to state his authority and his case. James waved him into silence, to an apoplectic response all the more fearsome for the fact that Coke could not vocalise it. Was he going to blow up? thought Gresham. It seemed Coke's fate to be told to shut up in Gresham's presence, either by the late Robert Cecil or by the King.

'I have a man called Marlowe in my care, Sir Henry. A dead man already, who from the wound in his arm is lucky not to have been killed twice over.'

Damn! How had Marlowe of all people gained sanctuary from the King?

'I understand that you were instrumental in "arranging" the death of this man many years ago. Testimony that despite your words, Sir Henry, there is much that you do and have done that is not worn on the outside, and about which the truth is not known.'

'Certainly, sire, I helped arrange for his escape. The fake death was Marlowe's idea. He never could distinguish between high drama and reality.'

'More importantly, I understand that this man had papers of mine that I wished to regain possession of. Sir Edward acted as my agent in this matter. You may speak now, Sir Edward.'

Coke needed no second bidding. Gresham

259

could see he was straining to stand up, desperate to pace the courtroom. 'This man Marlowe approached me after you, Sir Henry, failed in your attempts to track him down.'

So that was how Marlowe had broken through into the King's hearing. He had gone directly to Coke this time, as he had gone to Overbury before.

'With His Majesty's permission, we arranged for the return of the papers. I even sent one of His Majesty's servants with Marlowe to supervise the collection of this material, hidden, I believe, in a strange place...'

Gresham could sense what was coming.

'Nicholas Heaton was the servant. He seemed suitable for these ... underhand dealings, as he had gained experience under his former master. And lo and behold, what is the outcome?'

Coke was now well in his stride, declaiming, almost roaring. Gresham had seen the mood and the delivery once before, at Raleigh's trial. Its presence now, triumphalist as it was, did not bode well.

'We find that after weeks of apparent ignorance about this man Marlowe, the man whose false death you orchestrated all those years ago, all of a sudden you are there at the very time and in the very place these papers are being retrieved! An extraordinary coincidence, is it not? We find these papers are taken off Marlowe – stolen from him – *by you*. Marlowe is grievously injured – *by you*. His servant is crippled – *by you*. And Nicholas Heaton ends up a bloodied lump at the foot of King's College Chapel – murdered, we must assume, *by you!*'

Put like that, thought Gresham, it did not sound as if he had a terribly strong case for the defence.

Coke was in his element. 'Do you view it as your right to murder the King's servants? And why, when you are so contrite about posing no threat to His Majesty, do you continue to hold papers that you know could be damaging to him?'

'Your Majesty,' said Gresham. 'I do not believe it is my right to murder your servants.'

Though I would like to ask why it is that they seem to consider they have a right to murder me.

A few precious seconds to think. Some things at least were clearer now. Marlowe had some other hold over James. He had used it to strike a bargain – money? His life? Even a performance of his play? Heaton had been sent along as his minder. With the King's backing it became clear why the route into King's College Chapel that night had been so effortless, why so many doors that should have been locked had been opened. Gresham wondered whether the intended finale for the evening would not have been the death of Marlowe anyway.

'The story is a simple one,' Gresham said. Well, probably it was. The problem was that he had not yet written it. Gresham looked again to the King.

'Your Majesty, Sir Edward is correct in that I had failed to trace Marlowe. He despises me, by the way. I was instrumental in getting him over to France, but for whatever reason things went wrong for him after that and I became an object of his hatred. He attempted to murder me and my wife at The Globe theatre. By means of several vagabonds and a crossbow bolt. I'd even greater desire than Sir Edward to find Marlowe. He was a personal threat to me and my dearest, as well as to my ruler.'

James was clearly interested now. He had not sipped at the wine for minutes, was leaning forward with his head cupped in his hands, his eyes fixed on Gresham. James had enjoyed interrogating witches in the past, Gresham remembered, and had seen himself as a skilled cross-examiner. Unfortunately the witches had ended up being burned alive.

'Your Majesty, on the night in question I was visited by a drunken sot who is one of my Cambridge informers. LongLankin by name. He'd seen Marlowe in a house. LongLankin, and the college porter who saw me eject him after midnight, will confirm what happened. They're both simple men, not able to deceive. I set off to see if Marlowe was still there.'

'*Alone*, Sir Henry? Set off alone at night when by your own admission you knew you faced attempts on your life? Can we believe–?' Coke's tone expressed total disbelief.

So, to Gresham's intense surprise at her interruption, did Jane's. 'Yes, Your Majesty, we can believe! Hard though I found it to believe, and hard though I sought to make my husband's life when I heard of his crass idiocy!' Jane, silent until now, had risen to her feet, her head still bowed in deference to her King, her every muscle tense, her eyes flashing. 'A *lawyer*' – what a world of scorn there was in her voice – 'would have waited for other people to act, would have considered his position, hidden behind someone else, sat back, weighed the odds. A normal, sensible man would have waited for help, called out to servants! A normal, sensible man would have stopped to think! Yet my husband is neither normal nor sensible. He is a fool, Your Majesty, a fool who cannot resist the excitement of action and who throws caution to the wind if by haste he can speed up the resolution of an incident. I sometimes think he is in a hurry to meet his own death, and has been since the day he was born.'

'And you still love him?' James's voice was flat, without emotion.

'Your Majesty, I have no option,' she said simply. James looked at her for a moment, with the dark, dead eyes of a fish. He nodded to her, not without courtesy. She bowed her head and retreated to her seat.

'Carry on, Sir Henry.'

'Your Majesty, I followed Marlowe and his servant to the chapel. Followed them in. Saw the servant take a satchel out from behind the beams in the space between the vaulting and the roof. I knocked out the servant and took the satchel from him. Marlowe threw a knife at me. I threw that same knife back, hit him in the arm. I had partly tied them both up, intending to remove them to a place of safe-keeping, when I heard a noise from the roof. I went up. Whoever it was tried to knock me off the ridge. I killed him, after he had tried to kill me. Only then did I realise it was Heaton.'

'Why did you hurl him off the roof?' It was

Coke, trying to wind himself up again.

'He still had breath and some blood in him after I pierced his neck with my sword. I hung him over the parapet to try and extract information from him. Why was he there? Who'd sent him? Why had he tried to kill me? He was the King's servant. It seemed wise to know...' Gresham turned and gave a low bow to the King '...if I was indeed to have my murder sanctioned by Your Royal Highness. He died before he could speak, and slipped off the parapet. When I got back to the vaults, Marlowe had gone.'

'And if your actions were so innocent to the King's interests, why have you not returned these letters to me or to His Majesty?' Coke was almost screaming.

'Because the satchel was empty.'

There was a horrified pause.

'*Empty?*' It was Coke.

'And wad you be guid enough...' the accent was as thick as sour cream now '...to tell your King why you think it might have been so?'

'There is only one explanation,' Gresham replied. He said no more. The tension mounted with the silence.

'Go on!' said Coke.

'Nicholas Heaton. I guess he removed the actual papers some time beforehand.'

'Preposterous!' exploded Coke. 'Your evidence?'

'It is reasonable to suppose that Marlowe had told Heaton roughly where the papers were hidden. He would have to have done so, for Heaton to arrange for the relevant doors to be left unlocked. Yet there are very many bays behind the

264

beams, any one of which might have held the papers. You have to reach over a top layer of bricks to feel inside the bays. There is years of dust and bird droppings on top. Do you still have Heaton's clothes? If you do, you will notice that the bottom half of the sleeves on his tunic are soiled with just such dirt, and part torn. I noticed it immediately. I think Heaton had searched several of the bays before he found the one with the papers in it. He took them out before Marlowe arrived.'

'Why would one of the King's servants do such a thing?' asked Coke, floundering.

'You are innocent in the ways of espionage, Sir Edward, for all your skill in a court of law!' Gresham was scathing. 'The charitable reason was that Heaton did not trust Marlowe, was expecting some surprise or other. Far more likely is that Heaton intended to use the papers for his own advantage. It is my guess that he would have killed Marlowe and his servant, perhaps coming back to you and saying the papers were not there. More likely, you'd never have seen him again. He would've sold the papers to the highest bidder and vanished overseas with the proceeds.'

'Is this not disloyalty beyond belief?' Coke spluttered.

'Think, Sir Edward.' Gresham was lecturing now. 'For years the man had bullied and chased for Robert Cecil, dealing with the lowest of low life and, no doubt, taking bribes as a matter of course. Important and loyal enough to be granted a new job, surely, but with none of the access to that master that guaranteed him so much favour with his first employer. A servant's wages, Sir Edward? Compared with the value of those papers, and a life in the sun where he would never have to call another man master?

'Your Majesty, I do not have those papers,' continued Gresham, his eyes meeting those of King James directly and without flinching. 'I never did. I do have the satchel in which they were contained. No doubt you are searching my homes now. You'll find nothing, except the satchel. My people in Cambridge will confirm what I have said. And if you send a messenger up into the vault of King's College Chapel, ask him to check how many of the bays behind the roof beams have had their layer of dirt and dust recently disturbed. See if Heaton's tunic has been kept, and examine it. Or ask of those who stripped him before his burial.'

'So you did nothing, Sir Henry,' mused the King, 'because you thought it might be myself who wished to dispose of you? Are you willing to call a king a murderer then?' The silkiness of James's tone did nothing to diminish its menace.

'I would be most loath to do so, Your Majesty. Yet Your Majesty will understand me if I say that where there are plots, a wise man considers that all things might be true until they are proved false.' James had survived the Bye and the Gunpowder plots to kill him, as well as an attempt to blow him up in Scotland. 'I will suggest, with the greatest respect, that despite Sir Edward's attempt to have me beheaded, you've more need of my services than ever. Sir Edward is a great lawyer. He's a babe in swaddling clothes when it comes to darker matters. Those letters are still around. I will find them. I will return them to their author. If I am so permitted by Your Majesty.'

James sat back in his chair, reached for his wine and took a long, appreciative slurp. 'Well, well,' he said with a sigh. 'Who would have thought such a day could provide such entertainment.' He looked at Gresham. 'I am inclined to take you at your word. In every respect. As you have guessed, your houses are being searched at this very time. I will indeed send to Cambridge. I will send a trusted man into these vaults of which you speak. I will see if Master Heaton's clothing has been retained. In the meantime, I think a chamber can be found here for you, your wife and your man there. One with a real fire, perhaps.'

'I am thankful to Your Gracious Majesty for his hospitality,' bowed Gresham.

'One more thing,' said James, rising to leave. 'There will be guards posted at your door. For your own protection, of course. And to ensure that your close proximity to your good friend Sir Walter does not encourage you to visit him, or he to visit you.'

Gresham, Jane and Mannion bowed deeply as the King left the dank chamber. Coke waited behind.

'You–' Gresham rounded on him, cutting him short with the sheer compressed ferocity of his voice. 'You have tried to lose me my life, Sir Edward. You were unwise to make even more of an enemy of me.'

Guards came, politely enough, to march them off. Jane turned to Gresham, her eyes close to desperation. 'How could you...' she began. He

267

knew what she wanted to say. How could you give all those hostages to fortune – the torn tunic, the scruffed brickwork, denying you have the letters when they will turn our houses over and find even your most secret of hiding places...

He placed a finger to his lips and tried to force a world of words into his gaze. The guards would have been told to listen out for just such a conversation, and one misplaced word could cost them their lives. In their new rooms there would most likely be a hole in the wall or roof with a man or two listening for the duration of their imprisonment.

All this he tried to tell her, and more, silently. To tell her that, before pushing the body to the ground, he had rubbed the tunic arms of the dead Nicholas Heaton across the stonework and the bird shit on the roof until they were stained and one arm torn. That, for good measure, he had torn off a tiny strip from one of the letters, with a single, harmless word on it in the King's hand, and stuffed it into the pocket of the dead man's tunic. To tell her that he had descended from the roof and back into the vaults, his every nerve straining for sounds of more visitors, and carefully reached over and disturbed the dirt in every single bay in the vaults, filling his nose with dust and making his throat like sandpaper. To tell her that the secret hiding places in The Merchant's House and The House were now covered with a thick layer of sand, as if they had tried to soundproof the floors of both buildings, and that the mechanism that swung up the plank had been removed, the plank nailed to the joist just like any other. There were two other hiding places in both houses, full of trifles, designed to be found in just such a search. To find the truly secret places they would have to rip up every floorboard in both houses, and dig deep into the sand. He wanted to tell her, without words, that even if they did, both gunmetal boxes were empty. The papers were where King James could never find them. All this, he wanted to tell her, he had done just in case. That he was above all a professional, and it was because he did such things that he had lived longer than any other. To tell her that he had taken extra care to prepare his alibi this time, because he knew it was her life he was playing with as well as his own. To tell her that they were secure. To tell her that he had mentioned none of the precautions he had taken because if she did not know she could not tell others of them, even by accident.

She looked, and she looked, and she looked into his eyes. And then, the guards noticed, something almost like, a smile came over her face. She held out her hand. Sir Henry Gresham, Lady Gresham and his manservant walked together into captivity in the Tower of London, smiling.

16

7th November, 1612
The Tower of London

'And the king was much moved, and went up to the chamber over the gate, and wept: and as he went, thus he said, "O my son Absalom, my son, my son Absalom! Would God I had died for thee, O Absalom, my son, my son!"'

KING JAMES BIBLE

However much they built up the fires, the chill of The Tower entered into their bones. Winter had come to London late but with a vengeance; a cold, dripping winter rather than a fierce, freezing winter.

'How much longer?' Even though they were outside, in a brief respite from the cheerless rain, Jane half-whispered the question to Gresham. Sir William Wade, increasingly out of love with his job and his employer, had allowed them full use of his private garden. 'What a world for our children,' Jane spoke in her low voice. 'No mother, no father, a sense of dread hanging over them every bit as real as the sentence hanging over us.'

Gresham's own spies – James's court leaked information and gossip like a boat on the rocks – told him that the alibis had been proven. Heaton's tunic, too expensive to throw away, had been kept.

The scrap of letter had been found, and taken as proof that Heaton had in fact had the documents in his pocket. The searches of The House and The Merchant's House had been savage, and had led in the case of The House to a pitched battle between the soldiers undertaking the search and the servants. The servants had won, Gresham had been privately delighted to note, but someone had had the sense to call on Gresham to declare peace. He had been taken with Jane in a closed carriage to The House, where they had calmed their men down and told them to co-operate completely. They had shuddered at the ripped-up panelling and floorboards, but Jane had been stalwart in the face of Gresham's rising anger.

'Money can mend wood. Be thankful it's not more important things they've damaged.'

They had not found the gunmetal cabinet, Gresham noted, though they had found and ransacked one of the false hiding places behind a fireplace.

'How long?' Gresham answered. 'Who knows? There's no case to answer against us. I suspect the King no longer sees us as a threat. Yet he'll have Carr acting as a mouthpiece for Overbury, and arguing for us to be kept here for ever. And Coke will hardly want me on the loose.'

'Are you saying we're here for ever?' asked Jane, a plaintive note creeping into her voice. It cut to Gresham's heart, but he did no more than squeeze the warm hand that held his.

'No. I don't think so. I really don't think so, as distinct from simply telling you what you want to hear. James is indolent, above all. He takes the

271

easy route. With Carr and Coke biting at his heels, it's easier to keep me here than to release me. It does no harm to James, and it makes a point to anyone who cares to listen that no one is above the King's law. He'll release me eventually. What a pity there isn't a crisis to provoke him into needing me.' He turned to Jane, eyes laughing despite the pallor of incarceration. 'Perhaps I ought to threaten him with those letters!'

'Sssh!' she exclaimed, horrified. The fact that her husband still held damning letters from the King to his lover, and had flatly denied doing so to the King, was the stuff of her nightmares.

She did not have to be in The Tower at all, of course. Queen Anna was a featherbrained bar-maid who was as far away from Jane in appearance and personality as two human beings could ever be. Yet, from a distance, the two had struck up a perfectly serviceable relationship in which both women actually seemed to quite like each other. Gresham had questioned the relationship.

'Imagine being married to a wet frog!' was all Jane had said. There was a language that passed between women that Gresham did not understand.

Queen Anna had interceded with the King, on one of the rare times they actually met, and spoke to each other nowadays. She had swept into Gresham's rooms in The Tower, nodded dismiss-ively to Gresham and removed Jane to an adjoin-ing room. Half an hour later they had returned.

'You are very blessed,' Queen Anna had announced regally, 'with your wife.'

'As indeed is the King,' Gresham had bowed

272

low, 'with his consort and mother of his children.'

The two women had looked at each other and shrugged. Queen Anna swept out again.

The results of the meeting were immediately clear. Jane no longer had to remain in The Tower and was free to return to either of her homes. Equally, it was decreed, should she wish to move her children in with herself and her husband, accommodation would be found. She had compromised, staying in The House from Monday evening to Fridays, joining Gresham for the weekends. She had drawn the line at introducing her children to The Tower. Its air was frequently foul and always dank, the rooms cheerless and damp, and the atmosphere of the place was one of pain, suffering and tenor.

'They're too young for this,' she had declared. 'When we have to, we'll cope, as Raleigh's family have coped. Until we have to, let the children have their freedom. Even without their parents.' Yet she missed her babes on her Saturdays and Sundays with Gresham, missed them desperately. Gresham heard her sobbing in the small hours when she thought he was asleep.

'How reassuring,' Gresham had said, 'that you assume periodic sojourns in The Tower are doomed to be our lot.'

'I know who I married,' she replied dryly. There had been a near disagreement over the children's nurse on the Saturdays and Sundays when Jane was ministering to her master.

'Mannion?' Gresham had exclaimed. '*Mannion!* My young children lose their mother two days out of seven to *Mannion?* If fish drank like

273

him there'd be no water left in the oceans. His manners make a pig look respectable. Given half a chance, he spends every evening in the stews. He's a threat to anything on two legs, and for all I know anything on four! Whilst I'm languishing in The Tower, my children are being brought up by an ageing lecher with a drink problem and no education.'

'Who brought you up?' Jane asked simply.

Gresham rocked back on his heels, thought for a moment, and grinned. 'Mannion,' he replied, remembering his loveless childhood and the rough affection that Mannion had lavished on him.

'Well,' said Jane, 'don't deny your children the same opportunities.'

There were times when this woman really annoyed him.

For all that, he wished she were there when a bedraggled King James of all England and Scotland walked unannounced into his chambers that evening.

Gresham had heard the news. Setting up a decent information system had been almost his first priority when he had been consigned to The Tower. Sixth November, 1612. Prince Henry, the eldest son of King James I, heir to the thrones of England and Scotland, had died. The most brilliant, the most perfect and the most promising heir England had had in many a year. Handsome, intelligent and with a charismatic flair that lingered long after he had left a room and its inhabitants. A young man with a sense of occasion, but also with a sense of justice. A man in love with martial arts. A prude, some said, blessed with too great a sense of his own righteousness. A boy obsessed with warfare said others. A king for all seasons said the majority. A real king at last. For many of James's subjects, surveying the decadence and expense of his Court, it was easy enough to tolerate King James when the prospect of King Henry lay on the horizon.

And now Henry was dead. Dead of a flux and a fever, despite the best efforts of every London doctor.

Gresham had heard of the illness, and of the death, and his heart had sank. Prince Henry was a future king for whom spies would be willing to die. Now all that was left was Charles. Weak, vacillating, desirous to please Charles. What would the future hold for England under King Charles I?

King James stumbled into his rooms long after the bell signalling the closing up of The Tower. There was a clattering outside, muttered words, scurrying feet. Then James walked in through the door, unannounced. He did not knock, Gresham noted.

There was more than the usual filth on the extravagant clothing of England's king. The jewels around his neck and sewn into his garments would have fed a city for months. More extraordinary were the marks of tears down his cheeks. His doublet was unlaced. He sat down in Jane's chair. Gresham had spent a lifetime training his mouth not to drop – had he not done so, it would have dented the floor. And, by the by, his eyebrows would have become permanently entangled in his hairline.

'Drink!' the King of England roared to someone outside the room. There was a hurried scuffling and a terrified footman brought in a wooden tray with five bottles on it. Wine of the most tremendous value. With two extraordinarily beautiful goblets of pure gold.

'Open!' said the drunken King. 'No! Not for us both. That bottle' – he pointed firmly to one pillar of dark glass – 'for me. The other bottle, that one *there*, for Sir Henry. For him alone.'

The King turned to Gresham. '*In vino veritas*, Sir Henry Gresham. You'll drink that bottle there as fast as you can. And when you've drunk your fill, we'll talk. Man to man. Drunken man to drunken man. Drunken father to drunken father.' It was then the tears started to fall. Huge globules of water forming in the King's eyes and dropping from them down his cheeks, as if every liquid he had ever drunk was turned to tears.

And so it was that the strangest drinking session in English or Scottish history began and ended, in a set of rooms in the Tower of London in the late evening, with the King of England present and a prisoner his drinking companion.

Gresham took the bottle his monarch had gestured to and poured himself a full measure. He brought it to his lips. The wine was Rhenish – powerful, potent, intoxicating. He drank it in one single gasp. The King looked on, nodded approvingly and motioned to continue.

In the space of a few minutes, Gresham sank a bottle of wine from the King's cellar.

He had always had an extraordinarily good head for wine. Would it hold up tonight? The

276

excitement, the unexpectedness, the sheer maniac improbability of the evening began to take hold of him.

'And now we'll bide our time awhile,' the King stated, sipping at his own goblet, the tears still flowing. He wanted Gresham drunk before they talked. As drunk as he was. Or even drunker. 'You!' the King yelled to the servant again. 'That other bottle! There! Open it for my guest. You'll keep drinking, Sir Henry, if you please. Not whole bottles. But keep drinking.'

James and his son had been in frequent disagreement, Gresham reminded himself. Prince Henry had been polite, prurient and careful with money. The young man, only recently named Prince of Wales, had made no secret of the extent to which he disagreed with his father's lifestyle. Perhaps for this reason, Queen Anna had preferred her next son, Charles.

Yet the drinking contest had to be entered in to. James had not asked him to drink a whole bottle of wine, he had commanded it. First the lancing of thirst, then the tremors of excitement. Then the power of alcohol, the growing self-belief. Then the vainglory, the assumption that anything was possible. Then the tiredness, the overwhelming urge to sleep. Then the loss of consciousness. And then the payment, in pain and sickness, for the days to follow. Gresham knew all these. James thought he was the first person to have ensured truth with drink. Well he would, wouldn't he? Roman spies had used the trick as a matter of course. Roman spies, and spies for King James I of England and Scotland, had learned ways to cope. There was no point in denying the physical power of the alcohol. The trick was in learning to keep a part of the mind separate from it all.

'D'ye think they murdered my son, Sir Henry?' asked the King when there had been enough time for the bottle of wine to sink in.

The room was spinning slightly, and Gresham's brain seemed to have become so divorced from his speech centres and muscles. A chasm opened up in his mind, a dread, dark abyss that had nothing to do with the drink. Suppose the search for the papers had been nothing but a diversion to put me off the scent? To stop the country's best agent discovering or acting on a plot to murder the heir to the throne?

What had Cecil said? That on no account could the country be allowed to displace one king for another, however promising the heir? Could Cecil have masterminded the whole thing from the grave, removing from the scene the only rightful alternative to King James I? He had tried to sidetrack Gresham once before, attempted to send him off on a wild goose chase to take his mind away from more important things.

Gresham had to answer. He started to put his brain back in gear by clearing his throat, pushing through the vapours of alcohol to re-engage, and then halted. He had to sound as if he was part-drunk. It was his guarantee of honesty to the King.

'Your Majesshty,' slurred Gresham, 'it's ... it's a terrible thing.' The tears formed in his eyes then. He had let the image of young Walter and Anna come into his head, or the drink had forced it there. 'But ... but ... yes, it may be possible.'

The King gave a cry like none Gresham had ever heard. It was a call of pure agony, of a man into whose brain a white-hot knife-blade had entered, a knife-blade of recrimination and blame. Yet James, with his morbid fear of death, had fled to the countryside to avoid comforting his son on his deathbed. Queen Anna had locked herself up in Denmark House. *How much had he loved his son?*

'But sire...' Gresham spoke quickly. 'We learn in our trade that what *might* be is not always the same as what *is*. I shay... I say that a king's son may always be murdered, in Scotland as well as in England. But yet it need not be so. God knows, life is cheap enough.' Seven out of ten babies might die within months of being born, and even if a boy or girl made it to maturity, childbirth, the plague and a host of other illnesses still carried on taking their dreadful toll.

James was sitting back in his chair, eyes glazed, clutching his wine as a baby might clutch a bottle. 'I took scant care of him, my brave lad, scant care...' It was as if he was talking to himself. The accent was broad, pronounced. 'Too much love isnae any help to a future king. I had none of it, none of it, when I was a wean, It made me careful, it made me canny. He didna' need me.'

'Perhaps not,' dared Gresham, 'but I've no doubt he loved you.' The room had started to swirl now. He focused, hard. The room was *not* moving. It *was* still. It was only the drink. It slowed down, and the sickness that had started in his stomach abated. Why let it? He forced himself

279

to go to the side of the room, picked up the chamber pot and vomited into it. The liquid burned his throat and tongue.

'Well, Sir Henry, the problem is this.' James's eyes were hard, bright. He had ignored Gresham's retching into the pot. The drunken man who had screamed in mental agony a few seconds ago was gone. 'I can no longer help Prince Henry.' The tears were still there. 'And all of a sudden I am short of people to whom I can turn. You see, if they have killed my son ... then the next step is for them to kill me.'

Was that it? Was James's cry of agony for his son? Or was it for fear of his own life?

'Why so, sire?'

'To get the weakling Charles on the throne, so they can manipulate and dominate with all the more ease.'

'They?' Gresham left out any formal mode of address, always dangerous with a king or a queen. James appeared not to notice.

'All those who seek to deny a king his pleasures in hunting, or his few close friendships.' A maudlin, self-pitying tone was creeping in now. 'Or perhaps those who are friends of my few close acquaintances, and fear the loss of their influence if a man starts to listen to his son.'

There! That was it! James had more or less said what he feared. That Overbury might have acted to remove Prince Henry, fearful that the young Prince might one day find his semi-estranged father in a receptive mood and could damn Carr and Overbury as a package that could not be split. Was there real agony in James at the loss of

280

his son? Possibly. But, as always with this complex man, there was the overriding sense of survival. Of self-interest.

Would Sir Thomas Overbury have so much evil in him as to murder the heir to the throne of England?

'Now tell me, Sir Henry, am I right in my fears? And do take a drink. You'll find it guid wine.'

The room was quite stable now, Gresham noted appreciatively, giving only the occasional lurch. 'I think Sir Robert Cecil would have appreciated your fears. As for the friend of a friend, he is capable of almost anything. Almost anything. But of this? I simply do not know. Yet, sire, if this man had done this terrible thing ... it would pose no threat to your security.'

'How do you mean, man?'

Gresham was thinking himself now, his brain working on the problem, his own fear that he had been duped cutting through the alcoholic fog. 'The only reason for taking the life of the Prince would be to keep you on the throne, secure in your friendships. If there were those who wished harm to your son then, the damage done, there is every reason for them to keep you alive and well. You become the key to their continued success.'

How could this man maintain his relationship with Robert Carr while knowing that Carr's friend might have killed his son? How could Henry Gresham be playing with his own life, talking thus freely to the King?

'I think you speak with the voice of Machiavelli, Sir Henry. That Machiavelli of whom you have some knowledge,' said James in a low voice.

Again, it was impossible to gauge his mood.

'Machiavelli spoke in the true voice of courts and those who seek power,' said Gresham. And in the true voice of kings and rulers, but perhaps I'd better not say that.

'And your friend, Sir Edward Coke? Would he do this to me? Take away my son and heir?' James was not looking at Gresham but into the ashes of the fire, untended now since his arrival.

Humans plan and plot and train for their future, yet forever delude themselves into thinking that they have control over their destiny. The moments that define our lives, the moment that can affect the future of millions of people, are often hidden from sight, tiny triggers that are pulled without a noise or a sign that a threshold has been crossed, a decision taken and the future changed, for better or for worse. Gresham responded instinctively and without hesitation to the King's question. It took him only a moment to respond.

'No, he would not. If the death of your son was through anything other than natural causes then Sir Edward would have no part in it.'

'Yet he is the man who is responsible for your stay in these surroundings, the hurt to your beautiful wife, the fear in the hearts of your two children that they may never see their father again. He is the man you hold responsible for locking away your greatest friend, your saviour, your hero.'

'He is all those things, Your Majesty. Yet if I am any judge of men, he is not a murderer of the heir to the throne. For one, he is too scared. For another, though he has sold out to ambition long ago, he has lived with himself by believing that he works for and within the law. For a third, he has no advantage to gain from such a death.'

'And could the man you call Robert Cecil have planned this action, from his grave, and be reaching out to punish me even now?'

This man was no fool! Again, Gresham responded instantly.

'I had thought, for a brief moment, that it might be so. He talked about it once, indirectly. At our last meeting. He said that however great the heir to the throne, he must never be allowed to replace the King in case the people came to believe they had the power to choose a monarch. I cannot tell you what happened in Cecil's mind. My instinct, despite an appalled moment when you first spoke and I wondered if I had been misled, is no. This would be too unsubtle for Cecil.'

'Did you feel the axe brush across your neck just now?' asked the King. A cold breath ran through the drink-heated fires of Gresham's brain.

'I have felt the axe resting on my neck for most of my life, Your Majesty. The answer to your question, since you have come here in search of honesty, is no, I did not.'

'Then you should have done, Sir Henry. You are not the expert reader of men that you think you are!' There was almost an air of triumphalism in James's manner and tone. 'You see, had you sought to damn Sir Edward or my dead Chief Secretary, and to exact your private revenge on the back of my grief and loss, I would have despised you and believed that not only do you read Machiavelli but that you are him. And you

283

would have died, by axe or by poison. But died, beyond doubt.'

And do you think you could sneak poison past my defences, even in this, your holding-house for the damned? thought Gresham. Kill me you might well have done. Yet you would have had to have done it by the axe and in the open air, where a man could at least breathe a deep breath at his final moment and not face a dingy reckoning in a darkened room.

The two men sat in silence. Gresham had no idea how long it lasted. Finally, James spoke. 'You tell me the truth, I believe, Sir Henry Gresham.' There was moodiness, self-pity in his tone. 'And there are few such men around me. You will work for me now. Not Sir Edward Coke, nor for ... others. You are a free man, Sir Henry. You may leave. There are two conditions to your freedom. You will accept my commission to ascertain the truth of my son's death. You will tell me that truth. And should that truth need action, you will act on my behalf to make that action take place.'

Gresham jumped up and bowed deeply. James too stood up, unsteadily. He looked at the gold goblet in his hand and raised it to drain the dregs.

'You might care to know that a certain man in my care and custody ... a man with a sore knife wound in his arm ... escaped that custody three days ago. He had agreed to make certain other papers available to me. Not the letters you know of, Sir Henry. Other papers.'

'Would these "other papers" be connected to the theatre, Your Majesty?' That flicker again in his eyes, of amusement or pain, it was difficult to say. James looked at the door. It was firmly shut, the servants out of earshot.

'Aye, that they would.' He poured another dollop of wine into the golden goblet and drank it back in one huge swig. 'The second condition is this. You will meet, tomorrow night, in my Palace of Whitehall with two men who must needs speak with you. They will tell you of the second task I have set you. 'Tis better it come from them. Six o'clock, Sir Henry. Ye'll have had good time by then to take your wife in your arms, aye, and do more than hold her, I'll be bound.'

The King's lewdness, his fascination for other people's sexuality, was notorious. He gazed lugubriously at the pure gold in his hand, empty now, and weighted it. Then, unexpectedly, he tossed it to Gresham. Calling in a servant, he nodded at the man, who bowed deeply to Gresham and gave him a folded warrant.

'There, a present to your fine wife. The pair of them, this goblet and the one you are holding. Though I do not doubt it is the paper she will value more than the gold.'

With that, James stumbled out of the room, calling for his servants. Back, no doubt, to Whitehall, and a confused Court and a wailing wife and current beyond current of intrigue, suspicion and gossip. The environment, in fact, in which kings live all their lives.

As well as a pre-written warrant for his release, Gresham wondered, had James also brought along a warrant for his death?

17

11th November, 1612
The House, London

'Fortune is merry,
And in this mood will give us anything.'
SHAKESPEARE, *Julius Caesar*

Gresham went straight from The Tower, taking King James at his word. It was locked for the night, but the King's warrant was sufficient, with much grumbling, to have three huge doors squeakily unbolted and raspingly drawn back. Horses were summoned, hooves clattering on the greasy cobbles, and with two of the servants the King had allowed him Gresham rode through the gateway. He tensed as the final shadow of the Lion Tower fell over him, waiting for the call back, the clash of arms. Nothing came.

He was free.

He had already banished Mannion, worried about Jane and her safety at The House and feeling infinitely more relaxed knowing that Mannion was guarding her. He sent no messenger ahead, and it was in the pitch dark that he raced past the darkened bulk of St Paul's and up the length of The Strand. He pulled up the poor, panting beast that was all The Tower had been able to provide, hurled its reins to a startled doorkeeper and rushed into The House.

Jane was sitting in her parlour, the private room Gresham hardly ever entered. Even now he did not cross its threshold, but simply flung open the door. She turned, startled, towards him. She had been crying, he saw. She would do that – cry at night, when the children and the servants would neither see nor hear. Except Mannion, whose bed was positioned by the outside of the door. It was a campaign mattress, Gresham noted: rough canvas stuffed with straw.

He noted the expression of alarm and terror in her eyes and cursed himself for not putting himself into her mind.

'No,' he said, cutting in to her worst thoughts and disarming them. 'I've not broken out of The Tower, nor started a rebellion, nor come here three horse-lengths ahead of the executioner. Which would you like first? Two fine gold goblets that the King has gifted you – or his warrant freeing his good and noble servant Sir Henry Gresham from any taint of treachery?' He held the goblets out in one hand, the warrant in the other.

She looked for a brief moment, and then crashed into him with such force that goblets and warrant went flying and he, caught unawares, was cannoned into the back wall, pinned there.

'Are you really, truly free?' she said, stepping back to look at him, hardly able to breathe, her colour up in her face.

'As free as we've ever been. Which means, free until some monarch decides to lock us up, or a syphilitic maniac tries to kill us, or–'

'Do shut up,' she said, taking his face and hold-

287

ing it, looking into his eyes as though they were a marvellous, undiscovered country, 'and talk sense, for once.'

Mannion had stepped smartly aside as his master and mistress had rocketed from doorway to back wall. Ever practical, he had managed to catch both gold goblets as they went flying, and looked at them appreciatively before setting them down carefully on the floor on the tiny ante-room. Casually, he picked up the warrant from the King and read it, assuming that the pair of them would be cooing and doving for hours and not need him there at all. In fact, he was already making to leave the room when his eye was caught by some wording on the paper.

Mannion could read, very fluently. He just preferred people to think he was illiterate, believing reading to be rather foppish and unmanly. This time, whatever it was that had caught his eye made his face light up with a grin that was almost evil,

'Forgive me for interrupting, Your Lordship,' he said loudly, doing just that. 'But I thought I'd better check with His Lordship if His Lordship required my poor and humble services any more before I leave His Lordship and Her Ladyship–'

'What on earth are you prattling on about?' Gresham asked, confused. Jane addressed Gresham as 'my lord', a familiar title between women and men, but one the House of Lords had no trace of.

'You should read what the King writes for you,' said Mannion, grinning even more widely. 'Read it through to the end, I mean. According to this,

288

you're not only a free man, you're also very shortly to be Henry Gresham, First Baron Granville. Congratulations, my lord.'

Gresham looked nonplussed. 'But two hours ago I was locked up in The Tower... I don't understand...'

'I think,' said Jane, the light dancing in her eyes, 'that the King has decided to trust you at last.'

18

13th November, 1612
Whitehall Palace, London

'All the world's a stage,
And all the men and women merely players.'
            SHAKESPEARE, *As You Like It*

If there was insanity in the world, it all met and focused on the Palace of Whitehall. With so many candles, lamps and lanterns blazing fruitlessly into the cold November night, it was as if the Palace was on fire, lit from within, a funeral pyre to the finances of the monarch. So many were fed each day and night at the King's expense that a scurrilous broadsheet had christened it the Hospital of Whitehall. Even the servants seemed to have servants at Whitehall, yet it took ten minutes to find one servile enough to take their horses.

Gresham and Mannion were ushered through endless corridors. The two younger servants that had accompanied Sir Henry gazed open-eyed at the bacchanalia around them. What stories they would tell on their return! Even at that time, just before six in the evening, they passed two or three men clearly drunk, slumped in corners. A woman, clearly gentry, ran out of a door, giggling uncontrollably. One breast was out of her gown,

290

the other bursting against its rich material, one gasp away from freedom. She ran into Mannion. Rebounding, she arched eyebrows at him, giggled again and ran off.

Interesting, thought Gresham. The King had made available to them the private dining room Robert Cecil had long employed at Whitehall, with the huge length of table and finely carved oak chairs that Cecil had used to intimidate his guests. But it would not be Cecil who revealed himself as the door swung open – it was Bacon, and Andrewes.

Both men rose as Gresham and Mannion entered, and both extended their hands. 'Congratulations on your release, my lord,' said Sir Francis Bacon, with what appeared to be a genuine smile on his face.

'Congratulations on your honour,' said Bishop Lancelot Andrewes. He appeared genuinely pleased that Sir Henry Gresham was now First Baron Granville.

Andrewes and Bacon were seated on either side of the head of the table. Bacon, seemingly more at ease in the royal palace, pointed to Gresham's place. At the head of the table. It was the seat Cecil had squatted in, radiating malevolence on so many evenings. Bacon had arguably the best brain in the kingdom. Andrewes was the only bishop Gresham had ever respected.

'I think not, Sir Francis,' Gresham said, 'with your permission. The seat at the head of this particular table is tainted for me. This evening is one where I'd hope to be treated as a third – an exact third – among equals.'

With that, he sat alongside Andrewes. It allowed him the better view of Bacon's face. Of the two, Bacon would reveal his real thoughts and feelings far more vibrantly than Andrewes. Bacon smiled, and called out. His own servant was there, Gresham noticed, the grumpy, complaining old man Gresham had always associated with Bacon. Andrewes had no servant with him.

Those who ushered in the food were strangers to both hosts, looking around with interest as they brought in steaming dishes. Expecting to be asked to wait on the three men, they were surprised, and rather offended, when they were waved away.

'I suggest we dine and talk at the same time,' said Bacon, ever courteous. 'There's much to cover. Will your man agree with mine to serve us?'

Gresham looked at Mannion, who nodded.

'I would like the truth,' said Gresham. 'I've been shot at with a crossbow, been subject to a mass assault, nearly died in two separate parts of holy ground and been locked up in The Tower. Normal enough, you understand,' he reached out to put some fish on his plate. 'But it's always nice to know why it is you're being assaulted, killed or locked up. What are these "theatrical papers" about which there's been so much fuss?'

'There are three sets of them, to be precise,' said Bacon, sipping appreciatively at his wine. His servant fussed over him, offering him dish after dish. They were all cold, Gresham noted. After his master, the old man took the dishes with a show of deference and offered them to Andrewes. Following that, he looked with scorn on Gresham, and dumped the dishes within his arms' reach.

I hope to God Bacon doesn't ask me to sink a whole bottle before he will talk to me, thought Gresham. His prayer was answered.

'The first of these "theatrical papers" is a complete script of a play. A rather bad play, to tell the truth. Well, actually, if we are telling the truth, an execrable play. Publicly deemed to have been written, among others, by one William Shakespeare. *All Is True,* or *Henry VIII* as it is sometimes known. Written, as it happens, by King James I. Incidentally, Shakespeare had even less of a hand in it than normal. It was so dire that when he got it he had a fair copy made and sent it off to Fletcher, to see if he could make anything of it. He couldn't.'

Well now, thought Gresham. The King had tried his hand at a play for the common players. That would be news. Very powerful news.

'Also in this batch of papers are two plays, again both thought to have been written by Shakespeare: *A Midsummer Night's Dream,* as I believe the older one has come to be called, and *The Tempest.* Both about magic. Both actually written by my lord the Bishop of Ely, Lancelot Andrewes.'

Bacon nodded to his companion, who waved a tired, sad hand back at him.

'Finally, these "theatrical papers" also include manuscripts of *Love's Labours Lost* and *The Merry Wives of Windsor.* Written, in part at least, by myself. With a little help from my friends.'

Bacon sat back and transferred some meat into his mouth, before turning to Gresham again. 'It wouldn't be good for the author and prime mover of King James's fine new Bible to be seen as combining that part of his career with writing for actors and the public theatre, my lord.'

Something of a shock went through Gresham's system at the still-unfamiliar mode of address.

'Nor would it be a good thing for it to be shown that such an eminent member of the clergy wrote a play dealing with a man whose ruling power is based on magic. Any more than it would be good for the country's leading lawyer to be known as a play-maker, an associate of theatrical scum.'

Bacon and Andrewes gazed at Gresham.

'As for the King,' continued Bacon, 'God knows what laughter would be provoked were it known he had secretly penned a work for the theatre. Particularly work as bad as his play appears to be.'

It was revenge, Gresham thought. Divine revenge for his asking Shakespeare to cope with so much new information in so little time. Picking one single item of debris from the maelstrom hurling around his brain, he asked one question.

'I can understand easily enough why you, Sir Francis, would try your hand at a play. A new medium. One with immense power to inflame the heart, the mind and the imagination. But why would the King write a play? And, my lord Bishop, aren't there sermons enough without your feeling the urge to write words for actors to make a meal of?"

'There are three answers for three different authors. I won't presume to speak for the second. As for the third, he's here and able to explain for himself. I can speak a little for the first.'

Bacon was picking at his food. A log fell in the

hearth, and a cloud of fiery, red sparks shot up the vast chimney, for a moment giving Bacon's face a hellish tinge.

'Cecil started it. He saw how the theatre could inflame the popular heart and mind. Yet, as was always his way, instead of seeking to destroy it, he sought instead to control it. He was young then, in his father's shadow, a part cripple. He found out – God knows how – what few others knew, that this man Shakespeare was simply a front for Marlowe. Set up by Marlowe on his own, in the first instance. A country bumpkin who was a poet of sorts – a man with enough of a way with words not to be wholly unconvincing, but poor enough to be bought and to stay malleable. *Richard II* was Marlowe's. Along with *Julius Caesar*, and most of the plays that had a reigning monarch killed on stage. Marlowe liked to see monarchs die.'

'And you, Sir Francis? Your mind unable to resist the urge to write in this new manner, this writing that could reach three thousand souls at a sitting–'

'Ha! What power was there! It was shortly after Marlowe's supposed first death. A performance of *Richard III*, I believe, one of Marlowe's first offerings from the grave. It was a private showing. We entertained the actors afterwards. I fell to talking with this man Shakespeare. The wine flowed. We both had too much, I suspect. Did I ask him if a man such as myself might try his hand at a play? Or did he suggest to me that for a consideration – hefty consideration – such an opportunity might present itself? To be frank, I simply can't remember. And in any event, it matters little. A group of us emerged – myself, Rutland, Oxford, Derby. And did we have fun!' An expression of almost boyish enthusiasm filled Bacon's face.

'They were heady days, weren't they?' said Gresham, remembering the wild, mad and bad 1590s when everything had seemed possible.

'Heady indeed. We all thought we were destined to be the Queen's chief minister. We were all conspirators, vowed to secrecy in case our various political ambitions were threatened by involvement with the theatre. Yet in our heart of hearts, I believe we all looked forward to a moment when we would reveal our authorship, when we could bask in the notoriety and fame like adolescents allowed to walk up the aisle at their own funeral.'

'And Cecil spoiled it?' asked Gresham.

'How did you guess?' answered Bacon. 'He found out about the group, as he'd found out about Marlowe. Very gently, he started to blackmail us.'

'How so?' asked Gresham, intrigued. 'He'd no need of money, and while those you mention had power and wealth enough – you, Oxford and the rest – you weren't the prime shakers and movers of your day, with respect.'

'No, but we were all public figures, and Cecil loved to have hold over anyone in public life, or anyone who might become important.'

How true, Gresham thought. He had battled for years against the secret knowledge Cecil held on him.

'But it was more than that, if I may speak?'

replied Andrewes. 'I was one of those early recruits, though only for one play initially, before good sense took hold of me again, and before I succumbed once more in dotage. In the last three years or so of the old century, Cecil began to build his true power base. There was no direct heir to Elizabeth, no issue from her loins. A king from Scotland, from our own nobility, from Spain or even from France – all these had huge potential for civil unrest, for disobedience, for civil war. So Cecil began to force members of the group to write plays that would reinforce the absolute authority of kings.'

'Which created one or two rather lovely problems in its own right,' said Bacon. '*Henry IV* was meant to show the triumph of monarchy over the Lord of Misrule. But the great unwashed decided they preferred the Lord of Misrule in the form of Falstaff! Cecil was livid!'

Gresham thought briefly. 'I can see why you, my lord Bishop, a bright, intelligent man with a skill in and love of words, and a need to speak to an audience as you do so well in your sermons – I can see why you were tempted to experiment. But why in God's name would the King of England want to write a play?'

Bacon answered. 'Because he believes himself a writer and an intellectual, and because he cannot bear to think that he's not more skilful than others. And because Robert Carr suggested it to him, before the King or Carr knew about the convenient service Shakespeare provided for others. Andrewes here picked up wind of it and panicked, inasmuch as my lord Bishop knows the meaning of the word. He persuaded James out of publishing a play under his own name and told him of the service Shakespeare offered.'

'In doing so, I had to reveal my own involvement in the whole business.'

'James's reaction?'

'Initially amusement, rising to apoplectic anger. He is more proud of his Bible, believing that it will be his spiritual monument to future generations, than of anything else except his hunting skills. He persuaded himself that if it were known I had written for the actors it would devalue the whole work. Indeed, the King took steps to reduce my involvement dramatically as far as the public awareness went. I was – I am – the final editor of the King James Bible. The credit will go to another, for all history in probability.'

'And it lost you the Archbishopric of Canterbury?' asked Gresham.

'Indeed,' said Andrewes. 'A fair reward for youthful vanity. The King made it clear that he viewed the existence of this play as a sword of Damocles hanging over me were I to gain Canterbury. Or was he told so by Carr and Overbury? I don't know which.'

'And Marlowe?'

'He came to the King – via Coke – wounded. He said he knew the whereabouts of the manuscripts in the King's hand and in mine. In exchange for money and a free passage back to Europe, he guaranteed to provide them. James threatened to torture him. Marlowe laughed in his face. Asked if the King knew what pain he was in already. Laughed and said how much he would welcome death. Threatened, I believe, that if he, Marlowe, were to die then the manuscripts would be released anyway.' It was Andrewes speaking. Interesting to note, thought Gresham, that it was Andrewes who still had the ear of the King, not Bacon.

'And the King agreed?'

'Yes,' said Andrewes, 'but for the wrong reasons. He has a morbid fear of death, as you know. He fled to the countryside when Prince Henry was dying. It's likely he won't be at the funeral. In some way Marlowe made himself a symbol of death for James. A symbol of his own death.'

'So where do we stand now?' said Gresham.

'Marlowe's gone off, God knows where,' said Bacon. 'The man may be mad, but his capacity to vanish at will is exceptionally sane. Shakespeare hasn't been seen since Wade grabbed you and your wife from his apartments. The letters between James and Carr still haven't been found...' The eyes of both Bacon and Andrewes swivelled round to focus on Gresham. He met their combined gaze, unflinching, that infuriating half-smile on his lips. 'A group of people could be exposed at any minute as having written plays claimed by someone else. Some of those who wrote Shakespeare's plays want it kept secret, and will be seriously damaged if the truth comes out. There are others who want nothing more than for their genius to be recognised. It is, to be frank, a total mess...'

'And,' said Gresham, 'the rumours are already starting that Prince Henry was poisoned, a point to which I have to make an answer to the King.'

That brought silence.

'Was he poisoned?' Gresham looked straight at Bacon.

'I don't know,' he replied simply, after a few moments. 'But I doubt it. The only possible reason would be if Overbury felt Henry was threatening Carr's position, and hence Overbury's power. Yet there was no sign of it. James didn't listen to Henry. He thought his son was a prig, and Henry considered his father decadent.'

'So who are the *coterie* who wrote Shakespeare's plays for him?' asked Gresham.

Bacon and Andrewes exchanged glances.

'Do you really want to know?' said Bacon. 'You may find yourself hurt by the knowledge, mentally as well as physically.'

With a sinking feeling in his stomach, Gresham felt he could guess what was coming. 'Tell me,' he said. 'I need the truth.'

'Well,' said Bacon, 'myself and Andrewes here, obviously. The King. The Earls of Oxford, Rutland and Derby, in differing measures – and remember that sometimes two or even three of us worked on the same idea. Marlowe. And the Dowager Countess of Pembroke, who, by the way, is ruffling the most feathers by insisting that her authorship of two plays – *As You Like It* and *Twelfth Night* – is acknowledged.'

'Her son, the present Pembroke, knows the actors. Correction. He's besotted by them. He knows the truth and he hates his mother. He's keeping her silent by threatening to take all her money away from her. He tells Shakespeare it's to help him, but it isn't. It's because he can't bear

300

the thought of his mother being seen as good at anything,' said Andrewes, with feeling. Pembrokeiana, as she was known, had made a favourite of Andrewes, a situation from which few men emerged alive.

'And there is one more,' said Bacon.

Gresham knew what was coming. He had felt it in his bones. 'Sir Walter Raleigh,' he said flatly.

'Yes,' said Bacon.

His saviour and his hero. The man Gresham had named his eldest son after. The man he had visited, supported and sustained all these years past while he was imprisoned in that very same Tower Gresham had so recently left. The man who had seen fit to keep this a secret from his younger friend. The man who had chosen to do so despite knowing that Gresham's life was at risk from the moment he became entangled in the thorns and briars of these damned plays and their authorship.

As they rode back to The House, their escort all around them, Mannion was clearly troubled. He spat down on to the roadside and turned his head to Gresham.

'He didn't give you your freedom, those goblets or a baronetcy for nothing. He's going to want results. And sooner rather than later.'

'I know,' said Gresham. 'I work it out as seven separate issues.'

'Well,' said Mannion, 'I can see most of them. First, decide what to do with those letters. I agree with Her Ladyship.' He used the word without irony. 'Pretend you've found them. Get rid of them, and tell the King. Or, better, give them

301

back to him. Then, second, sort out whether Prince popped 'is clogs from God or from that bastard Overbury. Third, give Marlowe his third and final departure from this earth.'

'Four, five and six are just as easy,' said Gresham. 'Find Shakespeare, neutralise Overbury and locate these manuscripts.'

'Fair enough,' said Mannion. 'What's number seven?'

"See Raleigh, and ask why he never told me this conspiracy with Shakespeare was going on.'

'I can help you on the first six,' said Mannion. 'I can't help you with the seventh.'

No, thought Gresham, no one else can do that. The anger started to rise within him.

'And you've left out Poke,' said Mannion. 'Not like you to let someone get away with it, especially when they've had you locked up for weeks.'

'Oh,' said Gresham, a sudden, fierce grin on his face, 'I've got plans for Sir Edward.'

19

21st November, 1612
Dr Simon Forman's House,
Lambeth, London

'If you poison us, do we not die?'
SHAKESPEARE, *The Merchant of Venice*

It was a lovely house that Dr Simon Forman had
rented in Lambeth, close to the river and with an
orchard so luxuriant as to be able to supply a
shop. On this cold, crisp morning the frost hung
on every branch and twig and the breath steamed
out of men's mouths. The orchard was a white
hanging garden, a fantasy world of stillness and
frozen beauty. Gresham would miss Simon
Forman, self-proclaimed doctor, astrologer and
dealer in secrets. For most of his life he had been
courted by rich and poor alike for his medical
skills, while being hounded near to death by the
Establishment who considered him both a quack
and an evil magician. Gresham had never made
use of Forman's skills as an astrologer. On
countless occasions he had needed his services as
a doctor, and adviser on poisons.

Poor old Forman had died in September, taken
by a fit while rowing alone across the Thames.
According to his widow, Anne, Forman had pre-
dicted his own death a week beforehand. Well, if

it pleased her to believe it, it did no harm, Gresham thought.

The days after Forman's death had seen a flurry of coaches and servingmen queuing at the widow's door, asking for papers and any letters their distinguished mistresses had sent to Forman. The rush had now subsided, and today's visitor was a quiet, bearded, thoughtful figure. Dr Napier was from Buckinghamshire and had been a close friend and an apprentice of Forman's for years. He was at the Lambeth house now to collect his inheritance – all of Forman's medical books and manuscripts and the details of his famous cures. It had taken Dr Napier a week already to see what he wished to remove back to Linford and what he felt could be destroyed. He was not a man accustomed to moving quickly. He was a man whose medical judgement Gresham trusted implicitly and, knowing that the heir to his old friend was in the Lambeth house, he had asked to meet him.

'Congratulations, my lord, on your recent honour,' Napier said ponderously, but genuinely enough. The King's proclamation had been almost instant, unusually so for such an indolent man. The formalities would wait.

'I think it more a payment in advance than payment for services rendered, Dr Napier,' replied Gresham with a grin, 'and in order to earn my fine title I need a medical opinion.'

'You may have it, such as my skills are,' replied Napier, privately flattered and not enough of a deceiver to hide it nearly as well as he thought.

'I will not dance around the edge, Dr Napier,'

said Gresham. Enough secrets had passed before Napier's eyes, and not one of them leaked, for Gresham to be sure in him. 'I need to know if Prince Henry's death was from natural causes, or from poison.'

Napier's face blanched a little, but he maintained professional composure. 'I know only what the gossip says about His Highness's illness.'

'I have detailed the course of the illness here in this paper,' said Gresham, handing the document over to Napier. 'In summary, it is this. The Prince first became ill in the spring. Low spirits, weight loss and what he called a giddiness and a lumpishness in his forehead. He tried to drive out the illness by hard exercise and a spartan diet, to no effect. Increasing tiredness, headache, and by autumn severe bouts of fever and diarrhoea. His stool light yellow, like pea soup. Bleeding from the nose. He collapsed. Eyes couldn't endure light, lips started to turn black, complained of incredible dryness in his mouth. Convulsions, fits, serious pain. The rest you know.'

Napier made a noise that sounded something like 'Hmmph!' and sat down to read the papers, which included all the treatments given to the Prince. 'Idiots!' he exclaimed a short while later. 'Complete idiots!'

'Why so?' enquired Gresham. 'It's said they asked every leading doctor in the land for advice.'

'It's a great pity that the only one who could have helped them died in September,' responded Napier gruffly. 'The idiots shaved his head and put the warm bodies of pigeons to it, as if that ever did anything except give a poor servant a

305

good dinner of pigeon pie shortly afterwards. Oh, and look here at this...' Napier flicked the paper he was reading with disgust. 'A unicorn's horn with stag bone and pearl...'

'Sounds impressive to me,' said Gresham.

'*Sounds* impressive is correct,' snapped Napier, 'but that's all it is. The unicorn is a mythical beast. Even if it weren't – and it is! – the chance of grinding up some chalk and selling it at a king's ransom to the King's idiot doctors is a business proposition very few of London's apothecaries could resist. Pah! Unicorn horn? You might as well prescribe the devil's pizzle!'

Gresham nearly asked if the good doctor had a store of that, but decided that for all his evident qualities, a sense of humour was not Napier's strong point.

It took the doctor over an hour to read through the papers. Seated by a blazing fire, a companionable cup of warmed ale in his hand, Gresham felt more relaxed than he had done in months. Mannion sat with him, while the four servants he had brought as bodyguards rested in the kitchen, where the noise suggested they were getting on well with two of the maids.

The pressures on Gresham were huge and the stakes high. But at least now he had direction, certainty and clear targets. The game was on, and he had an idea of the rules as well as the desired outcome.

Napier rose three times to consult books that were part packed away, and once to peer closely at a sheet of papers in Forman's cramped hand. Finally he came back to the fireside and sat down.

'My conclusion,' said Napier ponderously and with great assumed dignity, 'is this.' He paused to gain greater effect. 'You should understand that I did not have the chance to examine the patient myself, and that therefore at least an element of my conclusion must be conjecture.' He paused.

'And that conclusion is?' asked Gresham, hiding his impatience. All men have their hour, and need it.

'The symptoms are those of a specific fever. Even if that were not the case, the manner of the illness's growth and maturation argues against poison. The majority of poisons affect the digestion and stomach. Few of the known ones first affect the head, and indeed that is reported as being one of the hardest areas for a poison to reach. The illness developed over a long period when, according to these records, the Prince underwent several changes of diet, and periods of hardly eating at all. It would have been nigh-impossible for a poisoner to sustain an effective dosage over such a period of time.'

'So you believe the Prince was not poisoned?'

'No. On the contrary. I believe he was poisoned.'

Gresham felt a bolt pass through his body. 'How so?'

'I suspect the Prince was poisoned by drinking water. This fever of which I speak is often linked to foul water. The Prince was an abstemious man. I have no doubt he would order liquid drawn only from the finest well. Yet all it needs is for a servant to confuse two pails, or indeed for the servant who draws the water to be ill himself, or for the servant to save time by going to the nearest rather than the purest source. Or perhaps the servant left his master's water by a privy. Dr Forman was most insistent that on no occasion should water be drunk. Small ale is the least that should be permitted.'

'Well,' said Gresham, 'at least the Prince's father is safe from this fever.'

'How so?' enquired Napier. Gresham had forgotten the absence of a sense of humour.

'His Royal Highness is not renowned for drinking water,' said Gresham.

He endured the lecture on the problems created by excessive consumption of wines, thanked Dr Napier profusely and left Lambeth.

Gresham and Mannion sat in the rear of the boat as they were rowed home across the river.

'It costs a fortune, you know, every time you do this,' grumbled Mannion.

'It's a fortune I have. And we have to find Marlowe and Shakespeare.'

Gresham had ordered every contact, agent and informer they knew in London to locate them.

'They're both of them good at disappearing, that's all I can say,' said Mannion. It was a difficult time to trace someone; the winter weather was making travel difficult. In addition, it was as near certain as could be that neither Marlowe nor Shakespeare were in London, where wagging tongues were far more numerous, and there was no sign of Shakespeare in Stratford, the only other easy possibility for his whereabouts.

'What do you reckon Marlowe's game is? And Shakespeare's?' asked Mannion.

'Shakespeare's easier,' said Gresham, resisting the temptation to drag his finger in the water as they rowed smoothly in mid-stream. 'He's got himself into a mess he can't get out of, so he's just bolted, like a frightened rabbit. Marlowe may have had an idea where these manuscripts – the one's in the writers' original hand, the ones that prove authorship – were, but Shakespeare must have moved them by now. He's the only one who knows their hiding place, unless Marlowe, or the King, or you and I torture it out of him. He's terrified that one of us will get to him.'

'Why doesn't he just burn the lot?'

'Who'd believe him? The risk then is that we'd all torture him to death, believing he knew where they were, and he'd have nothing to buy us off with.'

'And Marlowe?'

'He's harder. He wants the truth about the plays he wrote under Shakespeare's name acknowledged. He wants his new play performed. And he wants revenge. All before he dies of the pox. Most of all he needs those manuscripts to prove his authorship. His problem is that the minute he raises his head he's a dead man. He's not just got me on his tail, he's on the run from the King. I think he's probably hunting Shakespeare as hard as we are. *We need those manuscripts*. And Shakespeare's the only one who knows where they are.'

'Be a laugh, wouldn't it,' said Mannion, picking his teeth again, 'if he had gone and destroyed them? If we're all charging around for something that don't exist?'

309

'Hilarious,' said Gresham. 'Positively side-split-
ting.' Yet the thought had occurred to him. Life
was fond of such great jokes as that.

20

November–15th December, 1612
Cambridge

'Thou unnecessary letter!'
SHAKESPEARE, *King Lear*

The King would not return to London, not for his son's funeral, nor for his new Baron. He hated London anyway, and now it was tainted with the death of his son. So it was that twenty-four chaplains, Prince Henry's pages, his gentlemen, his solicitor, his counsel-at-law, his groom porter, the grooms of the privy chamber and the bed chamber, his sewers, carvers, cup-bearers, his secretary, his treasurers and the Comptroller of his Household, his Master of Horse, distinguished nobles, friends, ambassadors from all Europe, four thousand mourners, servants, gentry and noblemen, took four hours to wind their way from St James's Palace to Westminster Abbey for the most ornate funeral service anyone could remember. Prince Charles, now heir to the throne, was chief mourner. Of his mother and father there was no sign.

Nonetheless, it was vital for Gresham's plan to have Coke, Bacon and Andrewes there with him when he met the King. Gresham's messengers took on new horses. The final agreed meeting

311

ground was ironic. Granville College, Cambridge. Near to James's favoured hunting grounds at Royston and Newmarket. Fitted out with rooms built for a king.

They held another feast, of course, but it was a strange, subdued affair, the students hardly daring to speak in the presence of the black-garbed and black-faced King of England. Even the Fellows were quiet, respectful. James drank heavily, but remained taciturn, the wine failing to lift his mood. It was, the announcement had said, a 'private visit'. As if the King of England, with his hundreds of retainers and the noise and bustle of a whole household, could ever go anywhere privately.

They met after the meal in the Combination Room, the five of them. King James, Gresham, Bacon, Coke and Andrewes. And Mannion, of course, slipping in behind them all. It was the same room Gresham had had built for the Fellows of the college. The fire was blazing to impossible proportions. The fine, oaken table, designed to hold the whole Fellowship with space to spare, had a high-backed chair made into a throne by the adornment on its back of the royal arms. The other chairs along that side had been removed. On the opposite side were four lesser chairs. A beautifully decorated silver jug sat by the King's throne, full of the King's favourite sweet wine. By it sat a golden goblet. One of the goblets James had given to Gresham in The Tower. Gresham had thought about the symbolism. The servants to their King are as silver to gold. What the King has given he can just as quickly take away.

312

Gresham bowed James to his seat, and motioned the others to go to their allocated places opposite him. Coke was fuming, angry and uncertain.

Gresham retreated to the opposite side of the table from James and motioned Mannion forward. He handed Gresham a bound package, which he opened. Inside it, written on fine paper, were two letters. Gresham brought the letters out and showed them to James. The letters from the King to his lover. The explicit, detailed letters.

'Your Majesty,' said Gresham, 'three days ago my servant here' – he nodded in the direction of Mannion, who bowed his head to the King – 'heard that these letters had been, so to speak, placed on the open market. I assume that Nicholas Heaton released them, expecting to profit from his treachery. The new owner saw no reason in Heaton's death to postpone a sale. I sent my servant to purchase these letters.'

'And did he pay good coin for them?' asked James, staring at his own handwriting in the flickering light from the great fire and the candles.

'He paid in a different way, Your Majesty,' said Gresham. 'The owner paid with his life. Your Majesty, these are the letters, are they not? The letters Your Highness wrote? It is only Your Majesty who can confirm them for what they are!'

Gresham thrust the letters towards James. He let his eyes run down them but made no offer to take them. It was as if he felt distaste at touching them.

'They are the letters,' said the King, his lip lifting. 'I thank you for doing at least what others seem unable to do.' He did not look at Coke, but

313

Coke squirmed. 'You may leave them on the table.'

Gresham threw the letters on to the wooden surface. 'Might I make a suggestion, Your Majesty?' Gresham asked.

James did not agree, but neither did he deny the request.

'Some time ago now, the Bishop of Ely asked if he could be given these letters. Were they to be found.'

James looked up at that, with a sharp snap of his head.

'The letters are dangerous. The Bishop asked that he be given them, I do believe, so that he might destroy them. Because if such a man as he stated he had destroyed them, then he would be believed. While, I regret to say, a man such as myself might not be so believed. These letters are a threat, Your Majesty.' Something approaching a pleading tone was there in Gresham's voice. 'As their finder, might I ask in all humility that the Bishop be allowed his request? To burn these letters? Here, in the fire in this hearth.'

James had still not touched the letters. He looked at Gresham, and then to Andrewes, who gazed levelly back at him. He nodded. No words. Just a nod.

Andrewes bowed his head, stood up and took the letters. He did not look at the writing. He walked slowly over to the great hearth. He held each page near the fire until it caught alight, let it burn almost through and only then cast it into the fire. No unburnt scraps would float up through the chimney to land on Cambridge's streets.

'It is finished,' said the Bishop. 'Thanks be to God.'

'You set me another task, Your Majesty,' said Gresham, standing beside his still unoccupied chair. There was a pause. 'It is my belief that your son died of natural causes.' James's mouth dropped open at that, and he took the golden goblet and emptied it. It was Mannion who came up and refilled it, as silent as night. 'I have written for you here the opinion of several leading doctors.' He drew more papers out of his pocket. 'One of the opinions is from the apprentice to Simon Forman. No man knew more about poison than Forman, who died recently. His apprentice believes there is no poison suitable to these symptoms. The fever of which Prince Henry died has a known progress. Moreover, events in the Prince's life prior to his tragic loss would have made it nigh on impossible for a poisoner to do his work. There is no one who might have contemplated such a deed who would reap benefit from it sufficient to justify the appalling risk. It is my belief that no human caused your son's death. Rather, it was God who called him.'

'I thank you, Baron Granville,' said James. 'You have resolved yet another problem. And do these three wise men here' – the King motioned to Bacon, Andrewes and Coke – 'agree with your conclusion?'

Bacon glanced at all three, and made to speak, but it was Coke who got in first. 'I agree with Gresham on nothing.'

James raised an eyebrow. Bacon started and Andrewes remained still. 'Except, Your Majesty,

315

on this.'

Four bodies relaxed, three of them noticeably.

'My third task from Your Majesty remains to be achieved,' continued Gresham. 'The play scripts relating to yourself. Marlowe is still at loose, Shakespeare also gone to ground. They will be found. When they are, so will any other papers in Your Majesty's hand. They will also be destroyed, Your Highness. I give you my word.'

'Why were ye so insistent on these three others being gathered here tonight?' enquired the King, eyes resting on the ashes of the letters to his lover. He rose and went over to the fire. Taking the iron poker that sat by its side, he poked at the ashes until they were dust, caught by the heat and sent swimming madly up the chimney.

As the King had risen, so had Andrewes, Bacon and Coke. They stood by the table like naughty schoolboys told to stand in class.

'There has been much bad advice, Your Majesty, in these matters in which I have become involved,' said Gresham, standing by the other three and turning towards the King. James was backed by the fire now, the hellish red flames silhouetting him. 'Much bad advice, deceit, intrigue and lobbying for position.' Neither Bacon nor Coke shifted. 'It is better for me, and for Your Majesty, if any resolution I might bring to your dealings is done if not in public, then at least in front of a sworn audience. So there is no misunderstanding.' He paused to let the meaning of his words sink in. 'I was put on to these letters by Sir Edward. I resolve the issue in front of Sir Edward. I was put on to this play by Bishop

Andrewes and Sir Francis. I hope to resolve the issue in front of them. If such can be allowed, as my fancy if nothing more, then I believe there will be no room for deceit, intrigue or jockeying for position.'

'Ha!' said the King. 'You would have done well in Scotland, I think. You have a mind for it. Would you take a peerage from me now from the land of my birth, on condition that you reside there and be my agent in sorting out that troubled country's deceits and intrigues?'

'Your Majesty,' replied Gresham, 'allow me first to sort out the deceits and intrigues of which I know here in England.'

'Yet you ask for these issues to be resolved in front of those who set you on to them in the first instance,' said the King. There was a small stool by the side of the fire, left in the hurried clearing of the room. James took himself to it, sat down. Half his face and body were lit by the flickering flames, half in darkness. An emblem for this man, thought Gresham. James motioned impatiently for the others to sit. They did so, turning their chairs towards the King. Gresham remained standing. 'There was another person present when you were first "set on" to these issues by Sir Edward. Sir Thomas Overbury. You did not call for him to be here tonight...'

'Your Majesty,' said Gresham, 'you have a rare jury here tonight.' He pointed to Andrewes, Bacon and Coke. 'A saint, a sinner and a solicitor. And myself.'

'Come, come,' said James, chuckling. He flicked his hand and as if by magic the golden goblet full of wine appeared in his hand. Mannion had been waiting for the signal and was the only one to understand it. '"Myself" is hardly enough to describe you. "A saint, a sinner and a solicitor", eh? Well, what word do you use of yourself, Baron Granville?'

'A dangerous word to use in front of a king who has shown his power so recently to the person in question. But if commanded, as I have been, I would add a fourth word. A saint, a sinner, a solicitor and a survivor. Which, Your Majesty, might perhaps make two of that latter kind present here tonight.'

The fire crackled in the grate and a log collapsed down, throwing up a series of sparks.

'Be warned, Henry Gresham.' The King spoke in level tones, looking directly at Gresham. 'You push things to their limit. And sometimes the survivor survives only at terrible cost to himself.'

'I know,' said Gresham simply. He let the silence work, then spoke again. 'I despise Sir Edward as much as he despises me. He was wrong when he said he agreed with me on nothing except one thing. There are two things on which we, as sworn enemies, agree.'

'And what is the second?' asked the King.

'It relates to the subject of your first question. Sir Thomas Overbury. You have a Privy Council, Your Majesty. On it sit the highest in the land.' And Robert Carr, thought Gresham scathingly. 'Yet will you accept the advice of this, your extraordinary private council, tonight?'

'I will hear it,' said the King. 'For this once.'

'We are united in one thing, other than loyalty to

Your Highness,' said Gresham. 'We think it a wonderful thing for those in Your Majesty's court to have experience of serving Your Majesty abroad. Thus does a man prove himself. Sir Thomas Overbury is ripe for advancement. Yet he lacks something in the skills of diplomacy.' Something like a snort escaped from Coke. Bacon merely smiled, as if at a huge joke. 'A wise king might well seek to school such a man in these skills, as well as bind him even further in loyalty to His Majesty. What better answer than to appoint him as ambassador for His Majesty. Ambassador to a foreign country. A very far distant foreign country.'

There was silence from the fireplace. It was followed by another deep chuckle. 'You have another work in my hand that you must find, do you not, Baron Granville?'

'I do, Your Majesty.'

'Then find it,' said the King, with a sharpness that stung the air. 'Reward my largesse, as so few seem to do. And be my hawk, Baron Granville, as Cecil was my beagle.' The King had often referred familiarly to Cecil as his 'little beagle'. 'As for the rest, I have heard. I am a king, beset by more quandaries than ever a mere mortal conceived of. Yet still I listen.'

He stood, and the others stood with him.

'My saint.' His gaze lingered on Andrewes. 'The problem with sainthood is the trials those who receive it have to endure in order to earn it. They become too good, too divorced from the politics of power. My sinner? Well, all of those here are that.' He gazed at Bacon. 'Sin can be forgiven, if the quality of service merits the forgiveness. My solicitor? Well, there are two of those, are there not?' His gaze flicked between Bacon and Coke. 'And my survivor?' He looked directly at Gresham. 'There is a bond between those whose gospel it is to survive. And a special bond between those who believe that mere survival is not enough, and that to survive with honour is all that matters. Do you wish that bond to be cemented, Henry Gresham, First Baron Granville? I doubt it. Your survival has always been linked to your independence. Yet if my hawk is to return to my gloved hand, it needs to know I am its master. Perhaps the best way is to ensure that our survival is linked.' He paused for a moment. 'Thank you,' he said. His eyes were on Gresham. 'We will reconvene, I hope. My private council. When the business is concluded.'

He swept out of the room. The fears of those present were represented by the depth of the bows they offered to the departing monarch.

Later that night, Gresham lay with Jane. The house was silent, the flames dying in the hearth, the light that of one single candle.

'So the letters are destroyed...' She breathed, feeling easy in her mind for the first time in months. She lay with her head on his chest, arm flung over him, unconsciously seeming both to clutch and protect. She was naked. He could feel her breast pressing against his side, and the first signs of arousal.

'Well ... sort of,' replied Gresham, shifting his body.

'Sort of? Sort of? What do you mean "sort of?"'

The alarm was clear in her voice and the stiffening of her body.

'Well, the King and two of the country's leading lawyers saw them burned by one of its most respected bishops,' said Gresham meekly, fearing the storm to come.

'But?' said Jane.

'That's why the meeting took so long. I needed to slow the timing for the work to be done properly. It was so important for James not to hold the letters close, which is why we needed to meet in the Combination Room after nightfall. The light in there is always bad.'

'Why did you need bad light?' asked Jane darkly.

'The letters that were burned were forgeries. Brilliant forgeries, I might add. I doubt the King would have seen them for what they were even in broad daylight, but I wanted to lessen the risk.'

'But why burn forged letters?' asked Jane, confused now beyond all belief.

'So that I can retain the originals, merely as a bargaining counter, should the King decide to set his hounds upon his hawk. One never knows when such things might become useful.'

Was there no end to the lengths this man would go? Exasperated, Jane rolled on to her stomach and hit her pillow. Unwittingly it revealed more of the length of her body to her husband.

'Are they safe?'

You are not, he thought, looking at the sweep of her back and the tantalising hint of what lay beneath. Out loud, he said, 'They're safe. Where they can never be found, and where they'll be destroyed instantly if any hand other than my own turns the key.'

'Isn't this betraying the King? The King who's ennobled you, given you his trust?'

'I'll serve the King better than any,' said Gresham, 'and I'll give him my total loyalty. I'll risk my life in his affairs, if needs be. But what one must never do with kings or queens is give them your trust. Never. Not to them or to anyone, as it happens, if you wish to live. The only person to hold complete trust is oneself. His Majesty knows that of me, as I know it of him.'

'And do I have your complete trust? Am I the breaking of the golden rule? Or is there a part of you that's withheld from me?'

He swung round to face her, eyes taking in the glorious curve of her body. 'I intend to prove conclusively in a moment that I withhold no part of me from you,' he said, grinning. 'And the answer to your question, damn you, is yes. I've weakened myself in the way I swore I would never do. By allowing you into my heart. Now, enough of this prattling! Will you allow me to weaken myself a little more?'

She shivered as his hands began to move. 'Well,' she said, gazing at him with the innocence of a child and her eyes half closed, 'I don't suppose it'll do me very great harm.'

21

December 1612–13th February, 1613
The River Thames

'the story of my life,
From year to year, the battles, sieges, fortunes,
...moving accident by flood and field,
hair-breadth 'scapes...'

SHAKESPEARE, *Othello*

As Gresham had long ago ceased to believe in Christ, the feast of his birth meant precious little to him. Yet he enjoyed the entertainments laid on for his two households, seeing them not merely as a duty but as a way of thanking his servants. The excitement in the faces of Walter and Anna was something new for him. Unconsciously, he began to enjoy the twelve days of Christmas through the eyes, ears and stomachs of his children.

Destroy the King's letters. Done, to all intents and purposes. *Determine the manner of Prince Henry's death.* Done. *Neutralise Overbury.* Not quite done, but well on the way, Gresham thought. The King's response to his idea regarding Overbury suggested the ambassadorship would flower and flourish in its own good time.

Find Marlowe. Not done, and the man still a very real threat to Gresham and his family. *Find Shakespeare.* Not done, and a key to the manuscripts. *Destroy the manuscripts*. Not done. There was too much left undone, Gresham raged inwardly. Including his plucking up the courage to meet Sir Walter, he added to himself.

Yet there was something else troubling him. Beneath all this was the feeling that somehow and in some way that he did not understand, he was missing a vital clue, failing to see a piece of the puzzle that was yet there, waiting to be stared in the face. The nagging fear grew like a headache. However much he shook his head, he could not stop the growing pain.

The King seemed unperturbed, delighted that the Court could come out of mourning in time for the Christmas celebrations. One of them included a performance of *The Tempest* by William Shakespeare. Or, more accurately, by Bishop Lancelot Andrewes of Ely. Gresham hoped it might flush out either Marlowe or Shakespeare. He was disappointed. Gresham attended as few of the other celebrations as he could decently manage, but Jane still needed two new gowns to meet the minimum obligations placed upon them.

'Is that a dress or merely a pelmet?' asked Gresham puritanically, noting how low the neckline on Jane's fabulous gown had plunged.

'My lord,' said Jane, 'it is a positive curtain wall in comparison with most of those you'll see tonight.' It was true. Daring though it was to Gresham, his wife's neckline still covered her breasts, more than could be said for many of the flimsily dressed women giggling and shrieking their increasingly drunken way through the evening.

The festivities at Court were even more extravagant than usual. The Elector Palatine had come over to England to be betrothed to the Princess Elizabeth in November, but the death of Prince Henry had forced a postponement. Elaborate entertainments were laid on for his extended stay, which it now seemed would last until the wedding in February.

December passed and January crawled on. There was increasing excitement at Court about the impending wedding, and an increasing dread in Gresham's heart as silence greeted his every enquiry as to the whereabouts of Marlowe and Shakespeare. The strain was greater on Jane, he knew, never knowing as she walked in the garden of The Merchant's House whether or not a madman with a crossbow was hiding in the over-shadowing woods, for all the extra men they had hired to police them.

'Perhaps he's dead, after all,' said Jane one morning, as the rain poured down and blotted out the view from her window. 'Perhaps he killed Shakespeare, and then died of the pox himself...'

Gresham desperately wanted to reassure her, to agree with her. Yet he knew that to do so might allow her to relax her guard.

'It's possible, but we daren't assume it's so,' said Gresham, hating himself.

'I'm only guessin' as to how far gone he is with the pox,' said Mannion. 'But I've seen worse than him live a year or more.'

Jane could not conceal her excitement at the festivities laid on for the royal wedding. Outwardly she scorned Court and its ladies, inwardly becoming as excited as a maid-in-waiting when a great event beckoned. The climax, the evening before the wedding, was to build a replica of the fort and town of Algiers on the south bank of the Thames at Lambeth, and stage a mock sea battle and storming of the town. Well over five hundred watermen and a thousand musketeers from the local militia had been pressed into providing this spectacle, and Rochester and Chatham stripped of every longboat, pinnace and barge that could have mock masts strapped to it and bear at least one cannon.

There was the usual chaos at the Palace the day before the wedding. The old efficiency of Elizabeth's Court was a long-gone memory; James's household was run on excess and confusion, The Chapel Royal at Whitehall was relatively small, which to Gresham's common sense argued for moving the wedding to somewhere larger. Instead, attendance at the ceremony had been limited to barons and above, but in order for others to see the couple they would be sent on a circuitous route to the chapel prior to the wedding. To his intense chagrin, Gresham had been summoned to a rehearsal.

'You can guarantee the bloody King and his wife won't be at any bloody rehearsal!' he muttered, climbing into Court clothes. He had decided that Mannion could act Jane's part, to the immense amusement of the household, and spare her the need to kick her heels for hours in the shambles he knew they would find at the Palace of Whitehall. He would see her that evening, at the great naval battle, with the children. Their excitement had filled The House for days

326

at the news they were allowed to watch.

So it was that Jane was left to her own devices on February thirteenth. Managing a household as vast as that of The House was second nature to her. She had become involved in its running as a young girl, when as a ward of Henry Gresham she had first entered its gloomy, almost derelict walls. It had been sadly neglected then, its servants corrupt, its fabric wasting. Gresham had had no wife, and The House to him had been no more than the extravagance of the father he had hardly known. Jane realised that in gifting to the man who was now her husband the best and most efficiently run household in London, she was in some way trying to pay back the man who had rescued her from rural squalor and given her his heart and mind as well as his body.

It was long after noon. Jane was humming happily to herself, checking the preserves in the vast larder, reassured that they would see The House well through into spring, when the messenger came. Young Tom was the grandson of Old Tom, who had for years been Gresham's Master of Horse. Increasingly, the servants in Gresham's household had a family lineage less illustrious in heraldic terms than those of nobles but nearly as long. Young Tom, as he would probably be known even if he lived to his sixties, had served only a year, and was at the gangling stage between boy and man. He was panting with exertion.

'Please, mistress. Master says as 'ow you're needed at the Palace as they've had to change all the plans, and please would you bring the little master and mistress along as well. Use the coach, he says, as it's safer, and for reason that all the landings at the Palace are clogged with boats for the fight tonight, and please you...' He said all this in one breath, having had little enough left to work with after his run home. Jane laughed, thanked him and felt only a mild twinge of annoyance. It was typical of the Palace to change plans at the last minute, or to have none at all. It was also increasingly the fashion to show off one's children at high-born weddings, using them almost as accessories, dressing them like little puppets in the high fashion of the day. Well, thought Jane, they could have her children if they wanted them, but young Walter would turn out in a very plain doublet and little breeches and Anna in a simple dress with no farthingales, and not a jewel in sight on either of them.

Jane felt a slight stir of unease when she bustled the children into the courtyard to enter the great coach and saw not John, who usually drove them, but his underling Nicholas. Nicholas too came from long-standing stock, men who had served the Greshams for years, but she had never been driven by him before, and the cargo, with her children on board, was precious. It would not have helped her unease had she heard that John had failed to return from the tavern last night, unprecedented in his long service. It would have been reported to Mannion that morning, had he not rode off so early with his master. No one had thought to report it to Jane.

'Can you manage us all in safety now, young Nicholas?' she called up to him, part in jest, as she clambered into the coach. He was white-faced, she saw, but put it down to nerves at his first full outing with his mistress and her children. He made no reply except to wave his whip reassuringly in her direction.

They assembled in the yard, as Gresham had instructed. Two riders in front, two riders each side and two at the rear, and a man with a charged pistol sitting beside Nicholas. The great gates were opened, and the whole magnificent *entourage* swept out into The Strand. The two lead horsemen, knowing they were heading to Whitehall, turned their mounts to the left.

With a cry, Nicholas cracked his whip and turned the lumbering coach right. Pedestrians turned in horror to see the huge vehicle with its fine horses bearing down upon them, gathering speed with every minute, and leaped to safety.

Jane felt a massive lurch and knew instinctively that they had turned the wrong way. Oh God! she thought. Nicholas has seen an enemy and driven the coach away from him.

The two lead horsemen failed to realise that the coach had not followed them. By the time they reined in, it had vanished from sight. Looking hopelessly at each other, and cursing themselves for their certainty that things would go as they had planned and expected, they yanked on the reins and reversed their path. Mannion's advice was ringing in their ears. *Always expect the unexpected!* They had been strutting ahead of the coach, clearing the way, full of their glory at serving the First Baron Granville. They knew the depth of their mistake, and in their stomachs hung the awful fear that tomorrow they would be dismissed in ignominy with no reference. Their panic lost them even more of their judgement. They drove their horses not back down The Strand but to the gates of The House.

'There! There!' shouted Nicholas meanwhile to the armed man by his side on the careering coach, his arm outstretched. The man gaped at him, looked in the direction indicated. The next thing he knew a tremendous kick landed in his side, and he was flung from the vehicle. He fell directly under the hooves of one of the escorting horsemen on the left-hand side. Reducing him to a bloody lump, the horse stumbled and fell, one leg at least broken, its rider hurled from his mount into a crunching, bloody collision with the earth. The horse lay there, twitching. Its rider lay still.

The five remaining escorts were confused beyond belief. Had a devil taken hold of Nicholas? Had the horses bolted on him? Had he seen an enemy they had missed?

Their confusion was not to last much longer. Heading into the City and its warren of streets, Nicholas hauled the coach by sheer brute force to the right, down a noisome alley leading to the river. He knew the odds, had known them all along. He could commit the horses, now in panic and frothing, to the hole that formed the alley. After that, it was their instinct for survival that decided life or death. The horses chose life. They drove themselves neatly between the poor houses on either side, as neatly as a cork in a bottle.

The escorting horsemen were caught unawares

by the coach's sharp turn to the right. The two on the inside reined back savagely as the coach threatened to squash them between its great bulk and the wall. Their horses stumbled, catching the sense of panic. The one remaining escort on the outside overshot completely. The two behind had time to rein in. Their mounts ground to a halt and reared in panic, but the riders controlled them and dug their spurs hard into their sides, driving them after the form of the coach. It was then that the men hidden in the alley dragged up the two ropes they had firmly stationed on either side. One at the height of a horse's head. The other at the height of its rider's head. Both horses caught sight of the first rope, instinctively dropped their heads and, at their speed, stumbled on their forelegs into a tumbling fall. Their riders were flung forward, still holding the reins. One caught the second rope full in his rib cage, the other on his Adam's apple.

Instantly the two men had fallen, a farm cart trundled across the alleyway. Its driver cut the traces, the horse bolting away. From nowhere four men appeared, cudgels in their hands.

The three remaining horsemen of the escort regrouped. None lacked courage. All felt a bitter sense of recrimination. They had failed their master and his mistress, delivered her and her children up to God knew what evil. Without a word being exchanged, they drew back on the reins and flung their horses forward at the barrier, trying to leap it in one bound and follow their mistress. The sickening thud of the crossbow bolts hit man and horse alike, the screams of the dying horses easily drowning the rattle and gurgle of the dead men.

One horse tumbled so hard that it careered into the farm cart, breaking a wheel and skewing it aside. The gap through to the alley had been opened at last. Yet there were none of Gresham's men to take advantage of it.

Except one.

Young Tom had delivered his message, then taken time to regain his breath. He was used to the comments of the maids and other girls, but he knew what he would get if he appeared among them breathless and sweating. He had caused a stir, right enough, by his message. He could see the coach being made ready. He considered going to the kitchen to claim his bread and cheese for lunch. He'd done his bit, hadn't he? And then a thought struck him, fiercer even than the pangs of his hunger. What about the horses? The man who had come from his master had said he would find a boy to look after the horses. But he'd been a rough sort of fellow, and what if he'd simply not bothered to find someone? Those horses had been his charge.

Tom ran out then, thoughts of bread and cheese banished, to see if he could beg his mistress to let him ride on top of the grand coach, so as to get back to the horses. But it was too late, the great coach was rolling out of the yard as he got there. What was there to do?

Be damned to bread and cheese! he thought. What matters is those horses. He ran after the coach. It was going the wrong way! Heart pumping, sweat pouring again, he chased after it.

He saw Nicholas, one of his heroes, point wildly with his arm, saw him kick his armed escort off the coach. He saw the carnage wreaked by the fallen body among the escort. From even further away, his limbs at full stretch, his breath threatening to tear his lungs apart, he saw the sharp, manic turn of the coach into the alleyway. And then, his ribs rising and falling as if there was no oxygen left in the world, he saw and heard the sickening noise of the crossbow bolts thudding into flesh. Saw and heard the death of men who had chafed him, helped him, guided him, men he had looked up to as the bastion of all knowledge in this world.

There was a gap. Between the farm cart and the entry to the alley. A gap rammed home by a horse still in spasms and a rider who lay totally still. Had the men with crossbows melted away like the men with cudgels? Or were they still there?

Well, the still very young but soon to be much older Young Tom thought – if thought is what happens in a man's brain at these moments – good men have died today. I will be in fine company if I join them. He ran for the gap.

No sudden blow in his side. No yells and cries. He was through. He ran on, the narrow houses blotting out the sun. Despair. No sign of his mistress. How long could this winding alley run? Hope. The coach. Halted.

They were edging on the river. There were four, five men dragging his mistress from the coach. She fell out, drew herself up, seemed to be speaking. Seemed to be reaching to raise her skirt. One of the men flung out at her, knocked her back to the ground. She lay there, in the dust, motionless. The little girl was screaming. The boy just stood there, looking at the man who had struck his mother. There was a hurried conversation between the men, orders issued. Two of them picked up the body of his mistress, the others threatening the children to move in the same direction.

There was a boat by the rough jetty that abutted the alley. A longshoreman's boat, a cumbersome, single-masted thing designed to carry small cargo but needing four men to row it. The meat and drink of London's river traffic. They bundled the captives on board. The boat was unnamed, or, if it ever had been named, its emblem had fallen off through neglect. The men hauled oars out, prepared to row, the fitful wind giving them no help. As they did so, a figure flitted out from one of the poor lodgings that fronted the river. He was a small, dwarfed man with a strange, prancing high-step and a ludicrous wig. He stopped for a moment to give instructions to one of the men. That same man nodded, touched his forelock and hurried off back up the alley. Young Tom shrank into the wall as he passed by. He need not have bothered. The man had more important things on his mind than a young servingman.

An agony of indecision hit Young Tom. *What was he to do?* He had coin enough in his pocket to hail a waterman and follow the boat on her course through the Thames. Yet even if he knew where she landed, what use could he be, a mere apprentice? Far better, surely, to take what he knew and run with it to his master at Whitehall.

Young Tom was growing up by the minute. Let God decide, he thought. I will stand by this derelict jetty and raise my hand and cry *'Westward Ho!'* If a boat takes me to follow, so be it. If I am ignored, then will I rush to my master.

The first boat he hailed answered, and drew in to the jetty. He showed his coin first, as one did if one was of his status. 'Follow that boat ahead,' he ordered with far more conviction than he felt.

Would God or his master decide if he had made the right decision?

Ahead of him, Tom could see the men on the boat arguing. They gagged the little ones – the boy had been shouting, to try and attract attention Tom noted with approval – and bundled the two of them and their mother down into the forward hold. She was gagged too, his mistress, Tom's sharp eyes saw. Pray God they didn't suffocate her...

An overwhelming, burning sense of excitement came over Marlowe. Patience was hard for a dying man but he had grasped it as his only path to success. Vengeance, he thought, was a dish best savoured red-hot. He was about to enjoy the taste.

The boat was rocking up and down in a river that was frantically busy with the preparations for tonight's mock battle. This vessel was decked, with hatches cut into the planking to access the hold. The focs'le, at the bow and where the anchor chain was kept, was unusually large. A single lantern swung there, showing crude, straw-filled mattresses that had been nailed to the floor and halfway up the rough-timbered side of the hull. Set into the planking were three iron ring bolts, each with a short chain through them. At the end of each chain was an iron neck collar. Splinters of wood, lighter than the surrounding areas, showed where the ring bolts had only recently been screwed home.

Lady Gresham had been flung on the rough straw mattress, half-soaked through with river water. Her mouth was gagged, her hands tied behind her back with twine, her feet similarly imprisoned. The great, clumsy and half-rusted neck chain clasped her, rough against the smooth length of her skin. She was conscious now, eyes flickering wildly about the dim room. Her children had been similarly secured to the great ring bolts. The girl was crying quietly; the boy too, but trying desperately not to.

'Welcome to my royal barge, Lady Gresham,' said Marlowe. 'It is a pleasure to meet you, at long last.'

Jane shook her head back and forth, trying to speak through the filthy cloth rammed into her mouth.

'Take off the gag, Your Ladyship? I think not, really I do.' He was enjoying this more than he could ever have imagined, the old sense of power flowing through him. He felt the swelling in his groin. 'You see, you might shriek and draw attention to this poor and humble boat. I hope these precautions–' he motioned to the canvas sacking – 'will make this little patch of heaven almost soundproof, but why take an extra risk? You might cry out now, Lady Jane. You will certainly want to cry out, I hope, in a moment or so. *I want you to feel everything—*' he leaned his loathsome face close to Jane's. The teeth had almost all gone, and what were left were blackened and decayed – 'but the noise I make will be sufficient.'

Those huge dark eyes pleaded with him. There was a shout from on deck and the boat lurched. The rowers muttered curses and one shouted abuse at another craft that had come too close.

'What am I going to do?' asked Marlowe. 'Is that the question you would ask, were you free to do so?' The hold stank of fish and tar, and creaked with every sharp movement of the boat. 'Take my revenge. My revenge for your husband, who pretended that he wanted to help me, and who all the time intended to sell me into slavery as a spy for Cecil!'

He ignored the frantic shaking of Jane's head. Her hands were heaving on the twine so hard that blood was flowing from her wrists; a sharp, bright red against the pure white linen tracery on the dark of her gown.

Marlowe noted her breasts, their proud swell under her gown; the sculptured, chiselled perfection of her face. Very carefully, he leaned forward and delicately lifted the hem of her dress, strewn around her ankles, until it rested just over her knees. The slim, stockinged legs, pressed sideways down on the rough deck, were smooth yet muscled like an athlete. They were trembling, Marlowe noted with pleasure. He yanked the dress upwards, hearing it tear. Those delicious legs were now revealed in all their length, tapering into her hips.

'Yes, Lady Jane, proud Lady Jane, beautiful

Lady Jane. I intend to rape you. There is a long history, you know, of conquerors expressing their power over the conquered by using their women.' Even through the cruel gagging some sound managed to emerge, a strangled cry of ... hopelessness? Of anger? She was bucking and writhing against her bonds. Good, thought Marlowe. It would make it better when he had her. 'Your children? Oh, I would not rape them. But I think it will be good for them to watch their mother meeting her real master, don't you? And, oh, just one more thing. I have the pox. A dreadful shame. Yet in my temporary distressed state, the best gift I can find to give to you and your dear husband.'

She kicked then, as hard as she could with both legs tied together. Marlowe was expecting it, had moved to her side, forcing her to twist even more of her body. Yet still she caught a glancing blow to his wrist. It was bandaged, seeping a yellow and green pus. He screamed, and bent double, holding his wrist to his side. When he finally gazed up, it was with a look of pure and sustained evil that Jane nor no other human had expected to see this side of hell. It was to haunt her for the rest of her life.

He stumbled towards her, grabbed her with surprising strength, and flipped her over on to her stomach. The neck collar caught and held her cruelly. Half strangled, she was kicking with her legs, flailing, but there was a great weight on her back. He cut the bonds tying her legs together and hit the back of her legs hard, forcing them apart. Using a knife, he slit her undergarments.

338

She was exposed, defenceless. Marlowe was gasping now, sweat on his face, lips drawn back, hands tearing at his own breeches.

There was a crash so great as to topple him over, and a series of yells, footfalls on the deck. The boat lurched and lurched again. High, imperious voices were speaking to the rowers.

'By the King's command!' a voice was roaring. 'We're ten boats short from Chatham and the King has need of this vessel! Shut your mouth! You'll get paid for your pains!'

There was a thud, more yells, feet hitting the deck. His ruffians had decided to make a fight of it. With an obscenity, Marlowe bound himself up, grabbed Jane's legs and tied them again, and went to the hatch.

The fight was taking place at the rear of the boat. Marlowe slipped out on to the deck and snapped the padlock shut over the hatch before he was seen. His men were losing the fight, outnumbered. The leader of the King's men was a serjeant-at-arms. The Palace must be desperate indeed if a man of such standing was sent out to scour the river for extra craft. Then, to his horror, the serjeant-at-arms called out, 'Hey! You there! Ain't you that Cornelius Wagner?'

In the hope that Marlowe might be lured into attending *The Tempest*, a full description of him, under the name he had chosen, had been circulated to all the Court.

Marlowe took one look around him and leaped into the river. Other boats had gathered as the King's boat had smashed up alongside. There were catcalls, whistles, shouts of support for the defenders. No one believed the owner of a boat so commandeered would ever see a penny this side of Armageddon. There was no love lost between the King's men and those who worked the river. Rough hands hauled Marlowe out of the water almost as soon as he landed in it.

The serjeant-at-arms wasted no time. Who cared about a man who had jumped overboard and been rescued? They were desperately short of craft for the King's display and desperately short of time to prepare the craft they had. As if in answer to his prayers, a sudden wind got up after the fitful spasms they had had all day. He roared at his men to unfold the primitive sail, put four of his best rowers on the oars and set off to find more vessels. The river had emptied around him as word spread.

In the forward hold Jane and her two children lay half-crippled with the chains around them, eyes staring, the cloth cutting terribly into their mouths. An agonised grunt was the only noise they could manage. Jane had wriggled and squirmed so that her dress had fallen over the triangle between her legs, covering her shame from her children.

Young Tom had seen the encounter and his heart had lifted. He had yelled and screamed at the men in the distance but to no avail. He was too far away. Frantic, Young Tom saw the sail drop, bellow and fill with wind, and the boat holding his mistress turn upstream to join the gathering masses at Lambeth. With the wind in its favour, it picked up speed and was soon lost in the mess of traffic on the river.

It was late afternoon and nothing of any significance had been achieved at the Palace of Whitehall except further chaos. Gresham had resigned himself and was reading a book, seated on the stone wall of a colonnade, when he sensed a bad smell.

It was Sir Thomas Overbury. There was a flushed look on his face, one of almost eager excitement.

'Good day, Gresham,' he said, halting before him, chin out.

Gresham said nothing, did not move from his stone seat, and gazed coolly back at Overbury. Overbury flushed, He seemed intent on walking away, but changed his mind.

'Look to your wife, Gresham!' he snarled.

A chill struck Gresham's heart.

He stood up and Overbury sneered at him, turning away. He walked straight into the bulk of Mannion, who had appeared silently from nowhere. Again Overbury appeared to be about to say something, but without warning he leaped from between Gresham and Mannion on to the balustrade of the stone archway, vaulted it and sped off across the grass. There had been something in his eyes. Triumphalist. Vindictive. Vicious.

Both men ran to the gatehouse without a word, to where their horses were. As they reached the place they heard a young man's voice, screaming. 'Let me in! Let me in! I must see my master!'

It was Young Tom, exhausted, frantic with fear and worry. Gresham reached for him, took him from between the two guards, nodding to them.

Betrayal! Tom poured out his story. *Never place*

341

your complete trust in anyone! The coach driver had served Gresham's family for over ten years, and his father before him.

Jane and his children were locked in the bow of a boat commandeered for this evening's mock battle. The boat could be one of hundreds on the river, hurriedly rigged now to look like galleasses, galleons, carricks and argosies, their appearance changed even further.

'Send to The House,' Gresham ordered. 'I want every boat and every man on the river. Tell them to break through the booms if they have to.' The battle area was protected by booms upstream and downstream. 'Stop at every boat, check if the forehatch is open and its contents known. Explain there's been a kidnap.'

What if Marlowe had followed the boat, re-boarded it? What had he done to Jane before he had been forced to leave?

Men were flocking past them now to take their seats in the specially rigged stands from which the battle would be watched. Night was beginning to settle and torches were being lit.

'Master,' said Mannion. 'They're using real cannon, some of them live-shotted. Some of the boats are being blown up.'

'You, Young Tom, any other of our men – go down to the shore, grab a vessel each, somehow, anyhow. Start to check the boats. We know the size, roughly. We know it had only one real mast. It must shorten the odds. *Go!*'

It took a lifetime for Gresham to find Sir Robert Mansell, the Treasurer of the Admiralty and the man in charge of the evening. He was sweating profusely, despite the cold. He was flustered, angry.

'No, damn you, no!' he was roaring at a group of men. 'We must have more Venetians! More Venetians, I tell you! The men will just have to change sides, whatever they've rehearsed!' The river was in chaos. Several of the watermen were drunk, a payment in advance having been given to many to draw them out in the first place. There was powder everywhere. Some of the barrels were open-topped and perilously, near to torches. Brass cannons had been hurriedly lashed to the decks of the vessels, many of which were dangerously overloaded with guns, extra masts, mock rigging and armed militia men.

Mansell's plan was for the invading forces to set forth from the Whitehall bank to be met in mid-stream by the vessels of the defenders. After a battle at sea, the attacking vessels, with the majority of the militia on board, would land on the Lambeth side and storm the fort. At the climax a whole section of the fort would explode, and defenders would put out from the breach for a last pitched battle before the attackers won home.

'My lord! You must cancel the battle!' cried Gresham. 'My wife and children are on board one of these vessels! Kidnapped by an enemy of the King!'

Wild-eyed, Mansell looked at Gresham. 'Stop it? Stop it? My lord, it's already started – can't you see?' There was a flare of smoke and a thin rumble crossed the river. The first cannon had been fired. Speckles of light began to flower from the walls of the mock fortress opposite. Muskets

343

– though what idiot would fire a musket when no men had yet landed on the shore was beyond Gresham.

'There must be some way you can call back the boats!' insisted Gresham, shouting to make himself heard above the increasing noise.

'My lord, I tell you – I can do nothing to control this ... this ... chaos!' Mansell flung out his arms, embracing the anarchy around him. There was a crash and a scream and a newly rigged spar on one of the largest boats tore from its temporary mast, burying two men beneath it in a tangle of rope and canvas. The sail caught fire from the tub kept for lighting the cannon fuse and the crackle of flames was added to the noise as men rushed with canvas buckets to douse it. Gresham had to hold on to Mansell's arm as he went to turn away. 'If it is as you say, my lord, then there is every chance those who commandeered the boat will have found her,' Mansell continued, eyes already looking beyond Gresham. 'Half the boats commandeered never made it to Whitehall. Even if she is in one of the boats, the ones to be blown up have been in preparation for weeks. There's barriers round them. And the live shot, God help us! Only in a few guns, and those aimed at the lower section of the fort!'

He rushed off and was soon lost in the mêlee.

Gresham was ice cold. The time for recrimination would come later. All he could do now was focus his terror on action. Splitting his forces had been the only way. They had to achieve maximum cover of the Thames. He ran down to the river bank. He would seize a boat. If needs be, he would search every vessel before the night was out.

The battle was not going well. The wind had sunk again to virtually nothing, and what little there was was in the face of the boats on the north bank, driving them back to shore when they sought to set out. The overloaded boats were setting out and, with no wind to aid them, being swept downstream too fast. The smaller boats on the far side were milling around with no enemy to fight. When a boat did make it to halfway across the river, five or ten of the defenders surrounded it. Embarrassed at what in a military battle would have been a sinking, the attacking boats then retreated. There was much popping of muskets and the increasing blast of badly loaded cannons. To the spectators in the stands, including the King and Queen, it was increasingly boring.

For those on the river it was hell on earth. A sailor ran across a deck as one of his companions set off the vessel's only cannon. With no ball to stopper and focus its force, the burning powder sprayed the sailor's face and sides. The skin was ripped off him like a chef boning a fish, and with a scream he was hurled, his tunic burning, over the bow and into the river. Elsewhere, an excited boy ran to place another charge of powder into the smoking mouth of a ship's gun, forgetting to sponge out the barrel first. A fragment of still-burning powder caught the new supply as the boy spooned it down. The boy watched in disbelief as the exploding roar shot the ramrod out of the barrel, taking his hand with it. The gun captain was also unprepared for the involuntary ignition. He was standing behind the gun, which snapped back at him with the recoil, crushing his legs and pinning him against the mast. His scream drew the other crewmen to him. With no man at the helm, the boat veered out of its path, following the current. It crashed into another vessel, the splintering shock sending men over-board. Very few sailors could swim.

Jane felt as if she would never breathe properly again. She had bitten down on the rough gag in her mouth so many times and dampened it with her saliva that it had at least thinned. Yet it made no difference – she could not cry out. The boat had clearly caught a good wind, had turned, leaned over and beat up the Thames to wherever it was heading, the thuck! thuck! thuck! of its bow driving into the waves. Jane eased herself over on to her back, her mind remembering the feel of the diseased hands spreading her legs. Pushing upright with all her might, she leaned against the side planking. Damn! Her head, as hard as she could push upwards, still rested half against the straw-filled canvas nailed to the wall. She had wondered if bloodying her body against the wood would have attracted the attention of those sailing the boat. She looked at her children. Their terrified eyes looked back at her. She winked at them, denying the despair in her own heart. It's all right. Mother is here with you. The man has gone. Someone will come and rescue us.
     They did not believe her.

There were yells from the deck, and a lurching, forward motion as the sail was dropped and the boat brought round.

Jane struggled with all her might to get noise out of her mouth. The children, seeing her, tried the same. All that emerged were strangled, gurgled noises, easily absorbed by the straw, the timbers and the oiled canvas.

Footfalls on deck. Silence. The men had left. A lurching yaw to the right. Someone had hooked a rope on to their vessel. Movement, far less forceful than when they had been under sail. Silence on their own deck. Towed. They were being towed.

More shouts. As from afar. Cessation of motion. Footfalls on deck, brief. They were being moored to something, somewhere. Quick jerking movements of the boat. They were in quiet water, but water disturbed by other vessels. Heavy, heavy thuds on the deck aft of them. Strange noises, distorted, as of voices far away.

Jane knew what celebrations had been planned for that night, the celebrations she and her children should have witnessed from the stands at Whitehall. They had been commandeered for the great mock naval battle. Some man hired by the King had saved her from rape, saved her from being spoilt evermore for the man she loved. Perhaps a crew would come on board, find them, release them. Her heart soared. Yet she prayed to God the thumps she had heard on the deck had not been gunpowder.

And then, the lantern hung on the swinging hook so long ago began to flicker and die. Oh

347

God, she thought. Within seconds the cabin was in total darkness. No sight now. No feeling in her numbed hands and legs. Only the sharp rocking motion of the clumsy boat on the short waves.

Above her, on the deck, the five squat barrels sat. From each a fuse led, joining together at deck level and running as a strand through a scupper on the side, hanging a foot and a half on the outside below deck level. A rough nail secured the fuse to the planking. An easy height for a man in a small boat to drive alongside, stand up and light the fuse, and get away before the powder exploded.

Gresham pushed through the increasing chaos to the waterline. More and more of the attacking boats were trying to set out. Many were simply swung downstream. A number, their rowers reduced to frantic exertion, were crawling towards the opposite bank. Every now and again a crew gave up and the boat shot off with the current.

A young man was roundly cursing five others. It looked as if they had set out, been swept downstream, rowed all the way up to Whitehall once more, and now he wanted them to start again. Gresham went up to him.

'I need to beg the greatest favour of my life from you,' Gresham said simply. 'Can I at least know the name of the person I'm asking?'

The young man gazed at the figure in front of him. Tall. Dressed in black, every fold breathing money. The most unsettling eyes the young man had ever seen. Soft leather shoes muddied to destruction. A courtier, all right. But something else.

'I'm called Walter,' the young man stated, equally simply.

'I'm called Henry Gresham,' he said, every particle in his body shrieking out for him to speed this up.

I bet you're not, thought Walter. I bet you're an earl of something like that, dressed as you are. But the man had given him his name.

'Pleased to meet you, Henry Gresham,' he said, offering his hand. Now he'd done it. Call an earl by his real name and it was your head bobbing along in the river the next morning. 'My full name is Walter Andrews.'

The first name of his son, thought Gresham. The second name – spelling apart – the only Bishop he had met and respected. Was it an omen? Henry Gresham did not believe in superstition. Yet his heart lifted. 'Pleased to meet you, Walter Andrews,' said Gresham as they shook hands solemnly. To business. 'My wife and my children have been kidnapped. Two of them. A boy and a girl. They're on one of the boats out there in this ... mess.' As if to echo his words, there was a blast and a column of flame, followed by screams. 'Will you take me out on to the river and check all the boats...?'

Gresham had learned his self-control early. Learned to bear the taunt of 'bastard!', to bear the scorn of others, learned that to show what you feel is the ultimate weakness. Yet he had based that philosophy on a lonely, appalling self-ishness. He had never allowed for the fact that one reasonably large person in his life, and two rather smaller people, would breach the route to

349

his heart. So, for only the second time in his life, his emotion overrode his control. Disgusted and hating himself, he felt the hot tears burst up uncontrollably in his eyes and fall, burning, down his cheeks. 'Will you help me find my wife?'

Walter turned to his men. They were gawping at the scene in front of them. They had heard it all.

'Well,' said Walter, 'as for me, it's the first time someone's asked me to do anything useful all evening. As for these bastards–' he turned to his men – 'they're in revolt. Played out. Knackered. I don't suppose for a minute they'll agree to give up their sweat...' He turned to look at them.

'Bastards!' they called out in unison, with a strange happiness.

'We won't do it for fuckin' you, Walter Andrews!' said the oldest of them, rising to his feet.

Gresham's heart sank.

'But we'll do it for fuckin' 'im!' he shouted. 'Show us the way to your wife, master! We're the men for it!' There was raucous cheering, a rush to put the oars in the water.

'They're not exactly easy,' explained Walter. 'In fact, they're fuckin' impossible. But they're good when they do get it together.'

Gresham grinned at him, the fire of war in his blood. He grabbed Walter's hand. 'One-masted, biggish, a hatch for'ard and a much bigger one aft. Taken late in the day, so presumably with minimal decoration, fake masts and the like.'

'We'll find 'er,' said Walter Andrews, 'if she's there to be found.' His eyes were looking for a way through the crowded waterway. His hand was raised, waiting to drop and signal for his oarsmen to bite the oars into the water. Suddenly he saw the opening, dropped his hand. They careered through three boats, rigged as galliasses, whose rigging had become inextricably entangled.

'Where d'you want to start?' asked Walter Andrews.

'Where the danger is,' answered Gresham flatly.

It was clear even to Sir Robert Mansell that the promised battle was not going to happen. It was rumoured that the King and Queen were about to leave the stands, bored by a few small boats firing cannon and muskets with blank shot. James would be more than bored, thought Sir Robert, if he knew what this failed extravaganza had cost him. He had one ace up his sleeve. Half of the fortress of Algiers was primed to explode at the climax of the battle, its wood and plaster walls impregnated with barrels of powder set to ignite with the lighting of one fuse. Just before the walls collapsed, three of the attacking boats were meant to explode as if hit by shore batteries. The powder set in the 'walls' and that in the three boats was not normal gunpowder. Those responsible for the fireworks had been allowed at it. The boats would go up with a fiery blue flame, sending rockets into the sky. The explosion of the fortress would be predominantly red and yellow.

Well, the mock battle was over, with all that did for his standing and his reputation. Current, wind and tide had meant that the two opposing fleets had never been properly able to meet. Not to mention the shamefully drunken crew, and the gross incompetence of the Court. Yet all was not quite lost...

To hell with it, he decided. They would only dismantle the fortress the next day were it not blown up. What had he to lose? His reputation was gone already, yet might be restored by this last throw. *If only he could manage the fortress to be blown up before His Majesty left the stands!* He hurried to give his orders. One of his lieutenants, the most trusty, was there. Six fresh oarsmen were in his boat. The twisted rope that would ignite the fuses was smouldering happily in its barrel. He sent them off to the three boats moored on the Lambeth side.

'There's three boats on the Lambeth side – primed with powder! Set to be blown up before the walls of the fortress fall apart!' Walter yelled to Gresham above the sounds of musketry, cannon and men being maimed.

'What of it?' yelled Gresham back.

'One of them ran into a stone jetty. Holed itself badly. My men tell me they were desperate. Word spreads on the waterfront. They set out to commandeer another boat. With one of the King's men on board.'

'So?' yelled Gresham.

'Look over there.' Walter pointed to the Lambeth shore. The Algerian fort was lit by what seemed hundreds, thousands of torches. In front of it, darkened and anchored, lay three other boats. Two of them were rigged as Venetian galliasses, double-anchored, a rude disguise over their plain origin as London riverboats. The third had no such disguise. Bobbing on only one anchor, it was single-masted. The barrels of powder, bound together by strong rope, were silhouetted against the light.

Hope flared in Gresham's heart. He nodded. Walter turned the tiller sharp over and yelled at his men. Already working hard, they redoubled their efforts.

Another boat shot ahead of them, for all their efforts. There was someone who looked like an official in its prow. As it crossed the halfway mark in the river, Turkish boats swarmed towards it, the fitful wind at their backs. The livened official stood in the prow, shouting at them.

'Back off! Back off! Make way! Make way! On the King's business! Make way!'

Walter stood at the prow of his boat, hurling a gesture to Gresham to stand by him. 'Back off! Back off! Make way! Make way! On the King's business! Make way!' he echoed, pointing to the man dressed so clearly as a nobleman standing beside him.

The Turkish boats hesitated, backed off. Let them both through.

The King's boat shot towards the first mock galliass moored upstream. It made sense, work down the stream. The furthermost would have the longest fuse.

With a nod, Gresham directed Walter towards that furthermost boat downstream, the darkened vessel with no extra mast to hide its humdrum origins and only the five barrels of powder on its deck to show its purpose.

The current had eased now, wind and tide turning far too late to be of any real use. Walter still felt the need to heave a grapnel over on to the other boat, its claws digging deep into its wood. His boat slewed round, smashed against the hull of the other with a jarring crash.

There was a guard too on the middle galliass. He jumped up from his perch on deck, yelling at them, misunderstanding, warning them off the boat packed with powder.

Gresham leaped on board regardless, the ceremonial sword he had worn all day in his hand. There! A hatch for the main hold, beneath his feet almost. A smaller hatch forward.

The King's boat, on the orders of Sir Robert Mansell, reached the first of the ornately rigged galliasses. There was one man on board, keeping guard. Curtly, the steward ordered him into his own boat. He took the corded twine, smouldering redly at its edge, and applied it to the fuse, which was hanging over the side of the boat, at a convenient height for a standing man to ignite it. Thank God something had gone right tonight, as his own red-ended yarn ignited the spluttering fuse. On, he ordered, on to the second boat. Before they were blown to hell and beyond by this one. The men needed no encouragement.

There was a padlock oven the forward hold, Gresham saw. All he had was his sword. He punched it through the hasp of the lock, wrenched it upwards. With a sharp 'Snap!' the blade broke off. With a despairing glance he turned behind him. Walter was there with something between an iron hammer and a chisel. He wasted no time going for the padlock. Instead he chopped, savagely, at the wood securing the hasps. One side

354

sprang free.

Darkness. A stink of fish, tar and lamp oil hit Gresham from Out of the hold. And something else. The smell of people breathing.

'A light!' Gresham yelled, beside himself. 'Give me a light!' Walter looked nonplussed for a moment, then yelled to his men. Something spluttered, and a thin, poor lantern was handed to Gresham, its flame already guttering. He half jumped down the ladder into the hold. In the dim light he saw his wife and his two children. Gagged. Eyes open wide. Necks held in cruel iron collars. Hands and feet bound.

He felt for the knot to Jane's gag, lost patience and grasped the dagger at his belt, ramming it into the stiff cloth behind her smooth neck. The gag came away and she fell forward, heaving, sucking in breath. Her hands cut into his body, holding him so hard that it was as if she was drowning. She turned her head, vomiting into the corner. He cut through the bonds around her wrists and legs, seeing the blood that stained the lace on the arms of her dress. The collar, the cruel iron collar, was still around her neck. He yelled to Walter, who smashed at the wood around the ring bolt. Gresham pushed Jane away with all the gentleness his enraged body could muster, moved to the children, ripped the cruel binding off Anna and then Walter.

The thud of the explosion hit them before the vast, eyeball-scarring intensity of its flame. The first boat had exploded, those who had fired it unaware that the King had left his seat in the stands. A sheet of fire vented its way to the stars, a moment of blue and white brilliance turning night into day. Yet the King's boat, shielded from the blast by its next target, had already made its way to the second moored galliass. The guard on its deck was screaming at them. The captain of the boat ignored him. His vessel crashed into the side of the second galliass, the fuse directly opposite. He lit it, and it spluttered into life. Then he heard for the first time what the guard was screaming.

'She's shifted! She's shifted! The anchor's gone!'

Christ Almighty! Instead of the two anchors, fore and aft, that had meant to secure the boat, there was only one, and that had clearly lost its footing in the bed of the Thames and was dragging. Only a few ropes kept the vessel from careering down the Thames to explode in the midst of God knew what collection of other boats and people. Cursing, the captain turned to hack the fuse off, but as he did so three or four short sharp waves flung his boat upwards. He fell forward, into the gap that had suddenly opened up between the two craft. The next wave pushed his boat back in again. His head exploded like a squeezed orange as it was pressed between the two hulls. The men on the boat saw the fuse well alight and backed off, the guard hurling himself into their boat, threatening to capsize it. With a final, bucking scrape the second galliass lifted over the ropes holding it against the current and swept downstream.

The ring bolt came away from the hacked woodwork. Jane was free now, yet it would need a locksmith to take the collar off her neck, and she had to stumble to her feet holding the chain and heavy ring bolt in her hand. Gresham hacked at the bolt securing Walter and, with a final, tearing sense of relief, saw it come out of the planking. He picked up little Anna, already free, silent and shivering now, in his arms, his hand under the harsh collar, the chains wrapped around his arm. Jane tried to pick up Walter, but Walter the boatman stepped into the crowded area and took him off her. They made their way on deck. Walter's men were waiting in their craft, arms open to draw the children and the woman into their boat.

From out of the dark a wildly rigged shape bore down on them as if from nowhere – the second galliass, out of control. Its bow swept Walter's boat aside, pushed it away as if it were paper. The stout timbers held, but the boat was pushed upwards, first hurling its men into the water and then capsizing. It floated forlornly for a few seconds, its crew hanging grimly on to it, and then began to move downstream.

The second galliass was crashing down the side of Gresham's boat when suddenly it snapped to a halt, dead in the water, bucking and yawling. Its dragging anchor chain had snagged on the ropes. Horrified, Gresham saw the fuse on the second galliass now hard by his side, fizzling to only a few yards away from the powder barrels.

There was a high-pitched yell from the other side of the boat. Gresham ran and looked out. In the darkness, lit by the strange flames of the mock battle, was a tiny rowing boat, a grizzled waterman at the oars, Young Tom in its bow.

'The other boat's about to blow! Here – take the children!' Gresham cried.

Tom grabbed a spare oar, dug it into the water and his boat careered to the side of Gresham's vessel. Walter the boatman was desperate to see if his men were still alive and his craft afloat, but he handed the boy Walter down to Tom as Gresham handed over Anna. Gresham turned to yell to Walter that there was a lit fuse on the second galliass, but the man had gone, a clean dive into the dark river to swim towards his capsized boat, still just visible in the murk, and the shouts of his men.

Gresham looked down into Young Tom's boat. It was dangerously low in the water. It might take one more, if they were lucky. Two and it would sink. 'Go!' he said to Jane, shrieking at her. She looked at him. Did he feel a squeeze on his hand or was it imagination? The little boat sank deeper, took water in over the side but righted itself as Jane tumbled more or less on top her children. Gresham took one glance back at the fuse. It was almost at the powder. He could just make it, perhaps...

There was a cry from the boat. Anna's chain had snagged on something. Young Tom and Jane were hanging on to it, taking the whole weight of the boat, or else Anna would have been dragged overboard, her neck broken with the impact.

Damn! Gresham followed the line of the chain in the darkness, saw it snagged on a rusty nail. With a superhuman heave he released it. The rowing boat swept away, off into the darkness. He

358

turned. The fuse was two, three inches out of the powder. Time for him to do a deep, clean dive, hopefully be underwater when the explosion went off.

He turned to the water and did not see the line of fire jump two inches and bury itself in the heart of the powder. He felt an almighty blow in his back, something tearing at his arm, and the breath was punched out of him as if he had been hit by God's hand. His body, not under his control now, was hurled forward out over the face of the Thames, his arms outflung as if in a mock crucifixion. In the extended, terrible moment before his body hit the water, Gresham knew that he was losing consciousness; knew that something had hit and hurt him badly, though as yet there was no pain; knew finally that this was his time to die. As the waters closed over his head, his last vision was of Mannion screaming at him. Strange, he thought, in that moment of strange near-clarity that comes to dying men. I thought it would have been Jane. Then it was over.

The rest was silence.

22

Late February to March, 1613
The House, The Strand, London

'Tired with all these, for restful death I cry'
SHAKESPEARE, 'Sonnet 66'

He was in hell, he knew. The agonising, burning, searing pain was as anticipated and more, the perpetual agony of the incessant heat to be expected. But why was it so dark? Surely Lucifer would want his prisoners to see the flames as well as feel them? And why were there sometimes these voices, flittering in and out of his brain, never so close as to be understood? And the tiny, fragmentary moments of great peace, when a cooling balm seemed to come over him? It was strange. Well, he had eternity to understand it...

There had been two explosions, though Gresham had felt only one. The first as the powder on the second galliass was ignited by the fuse, the second as Gresham's boat blew up in sympathy. The blast had mostly been directed upwards – the engineers had secured iron panels around the barrels so that the explosion made a fiery plume up into the sky. It had still nearly swamped Jane's tiny boat, and for a few seconds she could see herself and her children being dragged down to the bottom of the Thames by the weight of the

360

chains and the neck collars. Then there had been a thump alongside, willing hands reaching down to help them. The House. A boat from The House. The largest boat, sturdy, able to survive almost anything, full of men, angry men, their men.

Mannion had been in the second boat. For a brief moment he saw his master silhouetted, arms outflung, against the impossible light of the powder. He had ducked as the surprisingly weak blast passed over them, wrenching the boat around and leaving them deaf but otherwise unharmed. He had seen the body, face down in the water, the cloth ripped off its back, blood across the white of the flesh. As he came to within yards of it, urging the men on and on, it, sank. Mannion dived cleanly into the water, into the pitch black, down and down and down. His hand flailing in front of him caught hold of something. Hair. His master's hair. He kicked upwards with huge force, arms now around Gresham's chest.

They thought he was dead. A huge, jagged splinter of wood had struck him in the arm, just above the elbow, and hung there. A leg was broken. *He was not breathing!* Mannion flung himself on Gresham's chest and pushed down with all his might three times. He turned his master over, hung his head from the edge of the decking, thumping at his back. One minute. Two minutes. Nothing. An awful, hacking retching suddenly came from Gresham's throat and his body convulsed, arching upwards in a spasm so powerful that it threatened to tip him over the side. Mannion waited for the vomit and foul water to

361

dribble from Gresham's mouth, pushed down on his rib cage, waited, and then placed his mouth firmly over Gresham's. He removed his lips from the cold flesh of his master, repeated it. With another shuddering, heaving spasm, Gresham sucked in his own breath. Mannion cradled him until they reached the shore.

They sat by his bedside. His breathing was slight, feathery, threatening to stop at any moment. He was in a deep coma, showing no sign of consciousness. The first doctors shook their heads, retreated into a corner and muttered, and then suggested intensive bleeding.

He had been covered in blood when they had brought him back home. A part of Jane rebelled, not least against the thought of the cruel little knives piercing her husband's flesh. God had put as much blood in him as he needed, and he had lost pints of it. Why did he need to lose more? Mannion took her aside.

'Look, mistress,' he said. 'I ain't no surgeon. But your master and me, we seen a lot of injuries on campaign, never mind the ones he's 'ad. He never did like bleedings, I can tell you for sure. He refused when he had a fever once, wouldn't be doing with it. We saw lots of people bled on campaign. Bled on purpose, that is. Didn't see any of 'em get any better for it, and saw a lot get worse.'

Dare she take the risk? No, she muttered firmly to the doctors, you will not bleed him. You will let him be.

It took an age for Dr Napier to come to them, for all that Jane knew he had come as quickly as he could. Gresham was weaker now, his face hollow. The gaping wound where they had taken out the huge splinter was angry and red, seeming not to heal, threatening at any time to break out into the gangrene that they knew would lose him his arm or more likely kill him.

Napier spent an hour by Gresham's bedside. He demanded the fire be built up to chimney-threatening proportions, then closed all the windows and doors, increasing the heat. Only then did he take the clothes off the bed and strip Gresham down to his bare flesh.

'Have him washed, while we're at it,' said Napier, 'from top to toe. Warm water, and soap.'

He came back to Jane and Mannion. 'There is one thing you must understand. I believe you are a strong woman, from what you endured on the river. Sometimes when a man is in water and does not breathe for a period of time, strange things happen in the brain. The life of the person, his character, his individuality, seems to leave him, the brain carrying on only the basic functions of the body. I cannot guarantee this is not the case with your husband. It may not be so. Yet you must prepare.'

'Is that all?' asked Jane bleakly.

'No, far from it. First, there is this.' He produced two boxes, each containing a paste, one white and one brown. 'Exactly *this* much of each paste must be placed on his tongue every night at nine. He must be watched to see he does not spit it out or the material drop from his mouth. In time it will dissolve. It is essential that the dosage is regular and that it is taken without a single exception.'

'Unicorn's horn?' asked Mannion hopefully, who liked his medicines exotic.

'No,' said Napier scathingly. 'The first is made of a mould that grows in very wet conditions on the bark of a certain tree. The other is a compound of roots and herbs.'

'Mandrake root?' asked Mannion, unrelenting. The mandrake was said to grow where a man had spilled his seed on the ground, and it was also said that it screamed when it was picked. Napier did not deign to answer. Instead he gave other instructions. Gresham must be kept warm, but given a cooling bath every hour. At all times someone must try and force beef broth through his lips. 'Most of it he will reject, some will stay. Place a small amount of fine wheat bread in his mouth. Watch him in case he chokes, but keep it there and let it dissolve. Also honey and sweetmeats. Any wholesome food that will dissolve in his mouth, anything, will help.'

Napier turned again, ponderous, slow. 'I believe he thought himself dead. Death has not called him yet, but it will do so if he waits long enough at its door. His mind has withdrawn. It is at a level we mere mortals cannot reach, somewhere near to Hades. Smell is a potent sense, a most potent sense. And sound. What smells does he respond to?'

'My perfume,' said Jane, looking down, flushing.

'Fresh bread, and bacon well done on the spit,' said Mannion instantly. 'A really good wine...'

'Music,' said Jane. 'He loves music.'

'Then sprinkle your perfume on his pillow at all

times,' said Napier, 'and have music in the room – some half hour of playing, and then some half hour of silence. Bring your fresh bread in here, fry your bacon. And pray.'

'He does not believe in God,' said Jane, a terrible admission that could have brought a terrible punishment. Yet she trusted this cumbersome, pedantic man.

'No, but God might believe in him,' smiled Napier. He took a deep breath. 'I will stay, if I may, Your Ladyship, for the duration of his illness.'

And so the vigil commenced, Jane at Gresham's bedside until her head was dropping on the counterpane with fatigue, then a few hours of blessed sleep while Mannion took over, then the bedside again. They brought the children to see him, on Napier's advice.

'Children are more robust than anyone imagines,' he said. 'This is a world they do not understand, and from that lack of understanding comes fear. The more they are shown, within reason, the less they fear. The less they fear, the stronger they become.'

Had they been asked to understand too much? wondered Jane, the horror of that closed hold coming on her again. 'Was that man a bastard?' Walter had asked, remembering their father's outburst by the river side. 'What is rape?' queried a thoughtful Anna. Neither child seemed outwardly much hurt by what had happened, though neither wished to talk about it. Jane asked the servants to enquire gently, but they said nothing. And then Anna woke up screaming one night after such questioning, and Jane ordered it to cease. Scars can be covered up on the flesh, and covered up on the mind, but they never go away, she thought sadly. On her or her children's minds.

The vigil went on. The paste provided by Napier seemed to do something to lessen the angry redness of the wound. The broken leg was mending, a clean break. Yet still he lay there, breathing lightly, eyes closed, expressionless.

The chief beneficiary was Mannion. He had assembled nothing less than a small kitchen in front of Gresham's bed, cheerfully bringing the bacon to sizzle on the hearth and the newly baked bread to fill the room, and the wine for Gresham to smell which had, after all, to be drunk once it had been opened. Gigantuan snores were emanating from the corner where he had fallen asleep. Jane, for whom his company had become as natural as that of the sky or the walls around her, did not wake and move him.

'It is the small hours of the morning that are the danger time,' Napier had said to her. 'You must, if you can, be by his bedside at these times. You must talk to him. It will be hard, but you must talk.'

It was a half hour past two. London and The House were silent. The candles gave enough light to see by, softened the room. The servant would come any minute now with fresh coal to build up the fire. Mannion would wake with a huge grunt in an hour or so, see he had fallen asleep in the room and apologise. She would brush it aside, perhaps go and throw cold water over her face, see if sleep would come for a few hours. Then The House would slowly come to life as its people stirred and started their lives again, yet for Gresham that daily rebirth would have no meaning, and for it he would have no ears or eyes. Just lie there, breathing ever so gently.

And so she talked to Gresham. She talked of the doings of The House: the silly servant who had poured sugar instead of salt into the beef pie and the anger of the chef; that Young Tom's father and mother were both taken by an ague that looked to see them off this world and Young Tom was torn between going to see them and staying to wait out his master's vigil. And talked of how there seemed to be a dearth of good, fresh meat in the city, and the milk had come in sour yesterday, the farmer swearing it had come straight from the cow and an old woman had given the bad eye to his beasts, so she had.

And when she ran out of tittle-tattle, she told him of their children. How little Anna had asked her what rape was, and how she had tried to answer without spoiling the innocence of her little girl, and how Anna had known, as Anna always did, that she was not being told the truth but had said nothing more, choosing instead to spare her mother on an instinct that ran deeper than anything else.

She talked then of her love for him. How, as a beaten and starved little girl, this man had ridden into her village, thin and emaciated, with the trappings of a lord on his back and horse and that strange man-mountain riding beside him. How could a man so rich be so thin, and look so unhappy? she had thought. How could a man be more glamorous? He had talked to her, by the pond, and then her stepfather had come out and whipped her and he ... he had broken his arm. And there had been a massive row and she, Jane, had found herself riding out of the village she hated with all her heart, seated on the saddle of the man-mountain's horse. And she had screamed and screamed and screamed until even these great men had listened, screamed that *he* had saved her and she was going to ride on *his* horse and no one else's, and so with an expression of disdain Gresham had plonked her on his saddle and they had ridden in triumph to London. How from the moment she had first seen him, her knight in grubby armour, she had decided that there would be only one man in her life. She had spurned the endless advances of other men, and even the servant boys, her contempt withering their pathetic desire even as it blossomed. She was not for them, nor for any other man. She had organised his house for him, put it straight, become his housekeeper without his knowing. And then, one evening, she had forced him to look at her as a woman.

And because she was lonely, appallingly lonely, and more terrified than she had ever been in her life of losing the man who gave meaning to her existence, she talked of that terror, the lurching, rattling moments in the coach when she had clasped the children desperately to herself, being flung from side to side and terrified that she would be hurled out on to the road. The awful silence as the coach had ground to a halt and she had been hauled roughly out, reaching down in a paroxysm of anger and fear for the knife she carried strapped to her inside leg and feeling the blow to the side of her head. She talked of the utter horrors of waking, devils beating at the side of her face, to find herself trussed and chained by the neck like a slave girl. The appalling feeling of helplessness in the face of this bloated monstrosity. The anger and the bitter recrimination ... why had she not spotted something was wrong? Gresham would have seen something was wrong! She was just a weak, stupid woman, in her element checking the supply of preserves and feeble as a child when real business was in hand. And then the sickening, stomach- and brain-churning realisation that this foul, evil thing intended to have her, in front of her children, and there was nothing she could do! Without realising it, her hand tightened on Gresham's as she gazed into the fire and recreated her own hell. Could she have been born to be penetrated by this satyr? Well, many a woman had endured worse and stayed silent – *but her children would know and have seen her so violated!* The syphilis! The pox! To live on for a few more years in the face of her husband, diseased? And then the answer had come to her. *She could bite off her tongue!* And her mouth had been open at its widest, ready to clamp down hard and without hesitation, when the other boat had hit.

She was panting now, breathing heavily, her hand still clutching Gresham's.

His hand tugged at hers.

She looked down, disbelieving. His hand,

gently, was squeezing hers.

She leaned over him. His eyes were closed still. Two, three huge tears dropped from her eyes and fell on his lids.

'Warm,' he said. 'Warm.'

An eye opened, blinked in her tears, and shut again. Hurriedly, she brought the cloth by her side to his eyes and wiped them. He was speaking, croaking, a half-whisper. She leaned forward, her ears nearly pressing his lips.

'I should ... have been there,' he was trying to say. 'I should have been there.' Then, something else, stronger this time. Both his eyes were open. 'You must never die on me. Never...'

She screamed her happiness, screamed it out for the whole house to hear, screamed it so that Mannion leaped up as if the whole Spanish army was in his tent and The House under attack.

'If he comes back, you must hold on to him. Do not let him slip back into oblivion...' Dr Napier had said.

Her grip threatened to kill him all over again. Crying, babbling, calling out, she made him keep those eyes open, made him speak, made him live.

It was easier being dead, thought Gresham. Much calmer. Much quieter. Yet perhaps, after all, this was better. He smiled into the eyes of his wife.

23

Late March–27th June, 1613
London

'I am as true as truth's simplicity,
And simpler than the infancy of truth.'
SHAKESPEARE, *Troilus and Cressida*

There was so much to do. Yet it would be months
before Gresham was physically able to do it. He
lay there, fretting, in his bed, knowing that the leg
must be kept still at all costs in its wooden splint,
knowing that on his calm depended his ability to
walk again without a limp. He ordered weights,
used them until his breath tore at his throat,
building his upper body strength.

The arm had healed beyond his belief. There
was an angry scar there, for sure, to join the
others on his body, but he felt no lessening in his
control, no weakening.

They had lost five men in all from the coach,
and one disabled for life. John, the coachman,
found in a back alley with his head broken open,
a blow that should have killed him and was probably designed to do so. Two of the men had been
on the river and at The Globe when they had
beaten off the attackers. Gresham felt their loss
like brothers. Scars mend, but never quite heal.
People die, and are never quite replaced. Young

Tom he promoted to deputy coach driver. No conquering general surveyed his army with more pride than Young Tom surveyed the coach on the first morning he drove it out in all its glory. It was an ugly, cumbersome thing, but for Young Tom there was nothing more beautiful in the world. There were pistols, loaded and ready, on the coach whenever it set out, and four blunderbusses loaded with nails. Walter the boatman and three of his crew were working for Gresham now.

They had found Nicholas. With something approaching despair, Gresham and Mannion had known that Marlowe would slip again into anonymity. Walsingham's spies had received a training in the field that was second to none. Yet Nicholas was easier meat, a bought servant.

He told them everything, without torture. The thin face and bloated body of the man who had come up to him in the tavern. The bag of gold, more money than he could have hoped to earn in a lifetime. The moment when he had decided to betray a lifetime of service.

Weeks ago, there would have been no argument. An implacable Gresham would have killed Nicholas himself without thought. Instead, stuffed in his bed, he looked to his wife as Nicholas sobbed and screamed before them. She gazed at the face of the man who had betrayed her and her children, driven them to what would have been more than her death, her eternal shame, but for a chance holing of a boat and a random meeting on the river.

'Let him go,' she said quietly, 'and never let him come within a mile of my family again.'

Too much death, too much suffering. It would have been easy to have him killed.

Mannion dragged him to the gateway of The House. He looked at the traitor in front of him, itching to do justice. Nicholas gibbered and shrieked, convinced he was going to die. I would like to take the gold you were paid, thought Mannion, and heat it until the coins melt all into one. And then pour it into your mouth. Instead, he looked at the pathetic thing in front of him.

'If you're seen or heard of in London, in Cambridge, or within a hundred miles of my master and my mistress, you'll die,' he said flatly. 'And if I catch sight or sound of you ever again you're dead, as you deserve to be now.' He paused. 'Well,' he said, 'you came into this world with nothing. That's how you'll leave.' He turned to the men he had stationed by the gatehouse. Laughing, jeering, they came over and none too gently stripped Nicholas of all his clothes.

'She said I shouldn't kill you,' said Mannion, 'so I won't.' He smashed his huge fist straight into Nicholas's mouth and nose. There was an explosion of bone, teeth and flesh and Nicholas was flung to the ground in the dirt of the yard. Staggeringly, he was still conscious, more the pity for him. The branding iron, in the shape of a straight 'T' for traitor, was ready. Mannion plunged it down on to Nicholas's forehead. He screamed and bucked under the pain.

'Now, Master Nicholas,' said Mannion, 'go out and face the world as you've made it for yourself.'

Four men grabbed an arm and a leg each and like a sack of flour the naked and branded

Nicholas was hurled into The Strand, the gate closed on him.

They contemplated kidnapping Overbury, in the long discussions Mannion held with Gresham by his bedside when Jane was not there. Kidnapping and killing him. In one sense it would have been easy enough. He was no great noble, no great lord surrounded by guards and walls and stout, locked gates. Yet this was no vanishing of a simple man, another body face down in the Thames, another unexplained disappearance. Robert Carr would scream, the country would scream and the King, for all they knew, might scream in sympathy with his bed-mate.

In the event, it was made easier for them. Overbury's closest servant, the chamberlain to his household, proved willing enough to talk. A man had come, he said, demanding to see his master, late at night. He had seen him before, had let him in several times for drinking sessions with his master. A strange figure, with a small head and a bloated body and a high-prancing step. He had papers his master would pay a king's ransom for, the man had said imperiously. Almost against his better judgement, knowing the violence of his master, the chamberlain had let him in. Overbury had drawn his sword at the sight of the man, buffeted him and pinned him against the wall. 'Thief!' he had screamed. 'Betrayer of my trust!' 'No,' the man had replied, calm despite the sword pinned to his throat, 'perpetrator of your sweet revenge!' There was a moment when he thought his master would have pierced the man's neck.

Then Overbury dropped the sword. Ordered the chamberlain to leave, peremptory. Scuttling to the embrasure that should have been bricked in when the new building was made but somehow had never been done, the chamberlain sat and listened. Revenge. That was the theme. Overbury had been beaten, humiliated by this man Gresham, had he not? He, the speaker, had the most foolproof plan for revenge, a revenge that Gresham could never scrub from his body or his brain had he access to all the waters of Lethe. All it needed was gold to bribe servants and to hire men and boats. And in return, as well as the most beautiful spoiling revenge, there were papers! Papers that could be most damaging to the King, to his bishops and his ministers! Papers Overbury could use. Papers in exchange for the letters the man had stolen. And then, as the details of the plan to despoil this Gresham's wife had emerged in the strange, high-pitched voice of the man, a mixture of terror and fascination had overwhelmed the chamberlain, huddled behind the embrasure. He was primed to tell, hating his master, fearing the man who had visited him, out of his depth.

Revenge was enacted in another place. In April, a grinning Mannion came to tell Gresham that Sir Thomas Overbury had been required to undertake an embassy to Russia. Refusing the offer, the King had consigned him to The Tower, and was showing no signs of intending to release him. The two men's laughter shook the house.

Gresham had thought it fit to tell the King of the night on the river. At first, buttressed up in his bed and with the quill feeling strange in his hand, he had been tempted to get a secretary to write the note. Then he had rebelled against his own weakness and persisted. Four lines into his carefully penned manuscript he had crumpled the paper into a ball and hurled it from him. Then he had settled again, taken new paper, recharged the quill. He told the story simply; his wife's kidnap, Marlowe's plan, the frantic evening when His Majesty had been dismissing the evening's events as a damp squib and men had been dying on the river beneath him. He made no mention of Overbury.

He had thought there would be no response, had written simply to explain his own inaction, pinned to a bed with a leg in timber. The King's messenger caught him by surprise, arriving in a blare of trumpets. The messenger was obsequious, emphasised the gift was to Lady Jane Gresham. They opened it together. A jewel, a ruby of immense size and beauty. Set in a simple gold ring, the more to show off its extravagance.

'It's worth a thousand ... two thousand pounds!' Jane gasped. The note with it was on the finest possible paper. 'For your pains', it read, with a simple 'J' scrawled at the bottom.

'Wet frog?' asked Gresham dryly.

'*Rich* wet frog!' said Jane in delight, pushing the jewel on to her finger.

Then came the morning that he walked for the first time. They took the wood off his pale, shrunken leg. It was strange to feel the air breathing against the flesh after so long. He sat up and tried to swing his leg off the bed. It did not move.

He ordered it, more firmly this time. It obeyed.

Jane looked at him. Mannion looked at him. Dr Napier, the long-suffering, pedantic, marvellous Dr Napier, looked at him.

He stood up. Carefully, it was true; painfully, even. Yet he stood, on both his legs, and remained standing.

They clapped him, and he grinned back at them.

But still no sign of Shakespeare, and Marlowe lurking out there in the shadows. Jane felt a sickness to the pit of her stomach at the thought of him. The security measures they were now forced to take were more and more burdensome, the toll of so many seemingly endless nights and days sitting by Gresham's bedside mounting up. At times she felt like screaming with frustration.

Perhaps it was this frustration, the pent-up energy of a mind without enough to do, that turned the final key and made clear what had been muddied for so long.

Gresham needed to sleep less and less during the day, but in payment for the strenuous exercise he insisted on undertaking to rebuild the strength in his leg Dr Napier made him rest for an hour at noon. Jane sat by the window. She had gone for her copy of Shakespeare's *Venus and Adonis*.

'It's beautiful,' she said. 'What a pity they never really let him write his own plays.'

It was as if she was gazing into a full-length mirror when all of a sudden the whole length of it shattered, as at one single blow, and the world dissolved. And she was left staring at the truth.

'Quick! Quick!' She rushed to her feet, so

urgent as to grab Gresham by the arm. 'The papers you took from Marlowe! The writings that were with the King's letters! Where are they? I must have them, now!'

'Are you mad?' he asked, grumbling, his thoughts disturbed. 'Bits of a play in two different hands, two hands we cannot recognise. That's all they are!'

'But don't you see? They were important enough for Marlowe to put them in the pouch! Get them for me, please! Now!'

He swung his feet off the bed, noting with satisfaction the strength in his legs and through his whole body. When he came back, minutes later, she had been to the library and was clutching a dusty volume.

'You're lucky,' he said. 'Most of my papers are still hidden elsewhere from when it seemed we were going to be searched. I've only brought back a few papers, and those the ones that seemed likely to do the least damage. Here they are, for all they're worth.'

He handed her the sheets of paper, watched as she sat back in her chair, eyes devouring the handwritten manuscripts. She delved into the book she had brought, scrambled through the pages until she found the passage she wanted.

'Yes!' she breathed, 'yes! Can't you see it?'

'See what?' asked Gresham, now totally confused.

'Do you remember *Hamlet*?' she said. 'We've seen it several times, here and in Cambridge. Do you remember?'

'You know I remember it. We've talked often

enough.' Lines from Hamlet had stuck and resonated in Gresham's mind. *'The readiness is all. The rest is silence.'*

'Do you remember that speech about death?'

'Of course I do. *"The undiscovered country from whose bourn no traveller returns".'*

'Then look at this.' Her excitement was so great she nearly dropped the book as she thrust it into Gresham's hand. It was titled *Hamlet,* and claimed the play had been shown at Oxford and at Cambridge.

'There!' she said, her finger pointing. 'Read!'

He read.

To be or not to be. I, there's the point,
To Die, or sleep, is that all? I, all.
No, to sleep, to dream, I marry there it goes...

He looked up at her, laughing. '"Ay, marry, there it goes!" This is gibberish. It's comic! This isn't the speech we heard...'

'Read on!' she said. Reluctantly, he let his eyes return to the page.

For in that dream of death, when we awake,
And borne before an everlasting Judge,
From whence no passenger ever returned,
The undiscovered country, at whose sight
The happy smile, and the accursed damn'd.
But for this the joyful hope of this,
Who's bear the scorns and flattery of the world,
Scorned by the right rich, the rich cursed of the poor?

'What is this book?' he asked, looking at it distastefully.

'Published in 1603,' said Jane. 'Now look at this...' She thrust one of Marlowe's papers into his hands. The speech, that same speech, commenced just over halfway down, in a florid hand.

'It's the same,' said Gresham. 'Word for word. I still don't understand...'

'Now read this.' Jane thrust the second of Marlowe's papers into his hands. 'There! Read it!'

To be, or not to be – that is the question;
Whether 'tis nobler in the mind to suffer
The slings and arrows of outrageous fortune,
Or to take arms against a sea of troubles,
And by opposing end them? To die, to sleep –
No more; and by a sleep to say we end
The heart-ache and the thousand natural shocks
That flesh is heir to. 'Tis a consummation
Devoutly to be wished. To die, to sleep;
To sleep, perchance to dream. Ay, there's the rub;
For in that sleep of death what dreams might
come...

'Magnificent,' he breathed. The words reverberating in his head were even more powerful now than they had been from the mouth of Burbage. He looked down the page for the lines he needed:

Who would these fardels bear,
To grunt and sweat under a weary life,
But that the dread of something after death –
The undiscovered country, from whose bourn
No traveller returns – puzzles the will...

Had the man who had written this been where Gresham had been? Had he also so nearly crossed the divide between life and death? Whoever had written these lines had been everywhere men go, and to places men could only dream of, thought Gresham.

'*Don't you see it!*' asked Jane. 'We've assumed that Bacon and Marlowe and Oxford and all those others sent plays to Shakespeare and he just fiddled around with them for a bit – got them dressed up for the stage and stuck his name on them. But what if the scripts they sent in were rubbish? What if they were awful? What if Shakespeare has this ... talent, this ... knack of taking other people's work and making something beautiful out of it?'

Gresham was thunderstruck.

'*What if Shakespeare was the real genius behind the plays all along?*'

Something massively simple fell into place inside Gresham's mind. 'So there's this bumpkin from Stratford, this front man for half the nobles in England, this man who can't write anything worthwhile from scratch but has this skill when other people seed his brain ... the skill to create amazing, incredible language, probably something he never realised he had until other people's manuscripts landed on his desk ... and he starts adding bits and improving on the original, small bits at first, almost despite himself, and then the bits he writes get the crowd cheering so he does it more and more...'

'And the nobles can't do anything about it

381

without breaking cover, or revealing that what they write is rubbish. Or they pretend to each other that it's what they wrote in the first place because they love to bask in the glory...'

'What a truly wonderful, god-awful, inspirational, appalling mess!' said Gresham, unsure as to whether to laugh or cry. 'So what are these papers?'

'I bet the one with the real speech on it is Shakespeare's writing. And if you want me to guess, I'll lay odds on the dire version being in the Earl of Oxford's hand.'

'Why him?' asked Gresham.

'You remember when you went out to get the food when we were in Shakespeare's rooms? I was pumping him about the plays all the time, and he was giving nothing away. But I asked him about *Hamlet*, because it was your favourite play, and all he would say was that the Earl of Oxford hated the way it was performed. Then he looked shifty and backed off, and I didn't think anything about it because he was looking so shifty all the time. I bet the other paper is Oxford's writing. And I bet something else too – that Oxford published that book on the bed!'

'Why so?'

'He died in 1604, remember? Been ill for long before that. Everyone says he was a strange man at the end, half mad. Mad enough to think his version was the real one, the better one. Mad enough to publish it too, particularly when he felt he was dying.'

'The Earl of Oxford's last will and testament, you mean?' said Gresham. 'If he wanted to be remembered by that he must have been mad!'

'Perhaps it helped kill him, poor man,' mused Jane. 'The book was a disaster. That's why I could pick it up so cheaply at St Paul's. I wonder if Oxford waited for it to be hailed as a masterpiece, and then died when it was laughed off the bookstalls?'

'He died of the plague,' said Gresham. 'In Hackney. Don't you remember? There was a scandal about it. Apparently he left no will, and his son forgot to put up a memorial to him.'

'So if there was a will, bequeathing his manuscripts...'

'It's gone now,' said Gresham. 'Buried by the heir who wanted nothing to do with it all. It's a brilliant theory. But we need a copy of something in Shakespeare's handwriting to prove it.'

But they found something better than that.

There was a crash on the door and Mannion appeared, throwing something in front of him. It was a drenched Shakespeare, shivering to his bones, dripping foul water all over the floor. He was dressed as a housewife, his beard and moustache gone but the stubble on his lips ludicrously at odds with the lace around his neck and the full-flowing gown.

'Look what I found crawling out of the woodwork!' said Mannion proudly. 'Thought I'd just go and check up on our man outside The Globe, the one keepin' an eye on things. Lo and behold, this woman comes out of the play. 'Cept no woman I've ever met walks like that. So I goes up to him or her, curious, and the rest's history. Very fetching, he was, in his little bonnet. Got swept away, that did, in the river.'

'*You great fat fool! You total idiot!*' This was another new Shakespeare, standing eye to eye with Mannion, his rage seeming to run through his every fibre. For the first time in his life, Gresham saw someone actually physically shaking with rage. '*I was coming to see your master!*'

Even Mannion was stunned by the intensity of the stupidly dressed man in front of him. What an extraordinary figure Shakespeare was, thought Gresham. He must have kept this rage in check for the boat journey over to The House and then unleashed it just now as he was thrust into the room. Could this man store moods, like others stored food, and bring them out of his emotional pantry on demand?

Shakespeare turned to Gresham. '*It's all over!*' He was calming down, but like a boulder that has tumbled down a huge scarp and is now on more level ground, his range still had momentum and power.

'*What* is all over?' asked Gresham, beginning to feel his own anger rise within him. If this damned man had had the decency to be either an artist or a fraud then perhaps lives would have been saved, the sum total of human terror reduced if only by a little. Yet he had to be both a supreme artist and a fraud, complicating things beyond belief.

'Marlowe. Your friend Marlowe.'

Gresham felt rather than saw the tide of revulsion, the gasp of fear from Jane at the mention of the dread name.

'He went to Burbage, Hemminge and Condell.

My friends! My friends who at the clink of coin and sight of a manuscript were willing to betray me!'

The tears were of anger, not self-pity. Gresham motioned Shakespeare to sit down, Mannion to bring wine. Shakespeare looked for a moment, then sat, suddenly deflating like a stuck bladder.

'How to betray you?' asked Gresham quietly.

'They told him where the manuscripts were kept. The original manuscripts. In the handwriting of the King, Andrewes, Bacon, Oxford, Derby, Rutland, Raleigh–' there was the tiniest of flickers across Gresham's face – 'the Countess of Pembroke, you name it ... and, of course, Christopher Marlowe. They knew, the three of them. Always have known. Encouraged me in the fraud...'

'And did they know that most of the original manuscripts were hugely enhanced when you put your hand to them? Did they know that the ideas came from others but that the real genius came from you, Master William Shakespeare? Did they know that most of these plays would be just another afternoon's entertainment if it weren't for the poetry you have in your soul?' Gresham's voice cut like a saw.

Shakespeare had wine in his hand now. It was forgotten. Two, three huge tears formed in his eyes, rolled down his muddy cheeks, carving a little wobbling path of white in the brown. 'They knew. And they were prepared to sell me out. My friends. My lifetime friends. That was the deal, you see. Marlowe would get all the manuscripts, after giving Burbage, Hemminge and Condell a great lump of money. There'd be a performance, a big one. And then Marlowe would appear. It's what he's always wanted, don't you understand? The biggest dramatic moment of his, of anyone's, life. Christopher Marlowe, the great Christopher Marlowe, the founder of the Elizabethan stage, the master of the blank verse line ... and not dead after all! Here, alive, on stage. His great enemy Cecil vanquished by death.'

Something cold and still had entered Gresham's mind, speeding his thoughts as a sledge with razor-sharp edges cuts through snow, silent, powerful and vicious.

'And after he appears like a Jack-in-the-Box, and the audience is gasping with wonder and amazement,' said Gresham, 'then he makes his second announcement. That while they, his loyal public, thought he was dead, he was dead only in name. His writing continued, almost to the present day. They know the plays of William Shakespeare? Did they really think that such plays could be written by a poor country boy from Stratford with no education? No! He, Christopher Marlowe, in the long, long years of his exile, had used Shakespeare as other noble minds had used Terence thousands of years ago.' Gresham had risen to his feet now. He stood in the centre of the room and flung his arms wide in the manner of the great Burbage in a great tragic lead. 'I AM MARLOWE AND I AM ALIVE! I AM SHAKESPEARE, AND HAVE LIVED ALONGSIDE YOU IN THIS THEATRE AS HIM FOR TWENTY YEARS PAST! MY ENEMIES ARE DEAD! THE MASTER HAS RETURNED!'

There was silence in the room.

'My God,' said Mannion, 'wouldn't the little bastard love that? Wouldn't he really, really love that?'

Jane was struggling to overcome her revulsion, desperately seeking to prove to herself that she could think logically about Marlowe. 'But wouldn't the other authors complain? Claim the credit?'

'Don't you see?' said Shakespeare, almost in desperation now. 'He's cleverer than all of us. Many of the authors don't want to be revealed. They'll stay silent. Someone like the Countess of Pembroke will be laughed out of Court if she claims authorship – a woman, for heaven's sake, able to write like that? What a joke! Either that, or it will herald a very different attitude to women, for life. And without the manuscripts, and with half the original authors dead, where's the proof? If Hemminge, Condell and Burbage are prepared to betray me – and they are – then he claims my plays as easily as a hawk cuts out of the sky and catches a newly born rabbit.'

'Are you sure they will betray you?' asked Gresham. This time he got up and poured a new measure of wine into the goblet of his old enemy.

'Yes. They've been different, strange with me recently, but that's not how I know. They did the deal with Marlowe in The Globe, over a meal they had brought in. They forgot the servant who served them the meal. Said enough to make him suspicious. He came to me. "Sorry, Master Shake-speare," he said. "Very sorry to intrude. But it sounds to me as if Masters Burbage and Condell and Hemminge are going to let someone else take the credit for all those plays what you wrote. And that ain't right..." Pathetic little man,' said Shakespeare with a sad and bitter laugh. 'His sense of justice was outraged by what he heard so he listened at the door. Didn't know it was Marlowe, of course.'

'Do servants often talk to you?' asked Gresham, remembering the grumpy old man at the Dominican Priory.

'All the time, actually,' said Shakespeare, rather wistfully. 'Don't know why. They always have. Remember that speech in *King Leir?* About poor wretches who bide the pelting of the pitiless storm?'

Gresham nodded his head.

'That came from the same man who warned me about Burbage and the rest of them. He came in drenched one day. Said as how wretches like him had no defence against the rain. Pitiless it was, he said.'

'And from that you wrote what you did?'

Shakespeare looked surprised, his grief forgotten. He also looked confused. 'Why ... of course I did. I mean, he virtually wrote it for me, didn't he?'

'No, he didn't actually,' said Gresham, looking at Shakespeare with new eyes. 'He gave you the raw material. Very raw material. God – if he exists, which I very much doubt – gave you the poetry.'

There was a long silence.

'Well, that's it, isn't it?' Shakespeare had changed again. He was now the Stratford grain merchant, rather plump, needing to go about his business because time waits for no man. 'I suppose he'll leave me alone at last once he's made his grand declaration and claimed my work as his own. No one will listen to plain old William Shakespeare, uneducated old William Shakespeare.' He turned to Jane. 'Do you know, I shouldn't wonder if he claims my sonnets. And my *Venus and Adonis*. And *The Rape of Lucrece*. Why shouldn't he? He's got all the rest...'

And then he broke down into uncontrollable tears, the sobs racking his body as if each one was an arrow sinking into his flesh. Gresham did not stop Jane from going to him, putting her arms around him. She was holding him like a baby, rocking him back and forth. She was someone who knew what it was to have the products of one's imagination for ever claimed by someone else. She liked Ben Jonson, loved him in her own way. Yet what did it cost her to know that so much of his *Volpone* was her own work?

Gresham's voice came like a sudden cloudburst damping summer fire. 'I think if anyone has the credit for your writing, Master Shakespeare, it should be you. I will see it is so.'

Shakespeare looked up. He wanted to laugh out loud, yet something stopped him from doing so. Something implacable, quite fearsome in nature.

'Where are the manuscripts stored?' asked Gresham very quietly.

Stunned, Shakespeare told him. 'They're all in the thatch of the Lord's Gallery. I hid them there after Marlowe raided the bookkeeper's room. I gambled he'd never think of my taking them back to The Globe.'

'Do you have a separate copy of all the plays? A fair copy? Kept somewhere else? Not in The Globe, I mean.'

'Yes, for almost all of them,' said Shakespeare.

'And when is the performance they're putting on to allow Marlowe to reveal himself?'

'Two days from now. *All Is True*,' said Shakespeare. 'The actors call it *Henry VIII*. It doesn't matter what you call it. It's the play written by the King. It's dreadful. But it's got lots of spectacle, lots of show. They decided it's the one that would drag the most people in.'

'Do you trust me to restore to you what Marlowe and the others are threatening to rob you of? The right to your work?' asked Gresham.

Shakespeare looked at the man who had been his sworn enemy, his tormentor, and had now offered to be his friend. 'Quite frankly, I don't,' said Master William Shakespeare. 'I doubt the devil himself could do it.'

Sir Thomas Overbury sat slumped on his bed in the Tower of London. The other prisoner sat opposite, on a chair Overbury had arranged to be carried over from his apartments. He was a poor figure, his fellow prisoner. Someone Overbury would not have paused to spit at only a few weeks before.

'I was right to refuse the King!' Overbury said bitterly. The other prisoner nodded, taking a gulp of the putrid wine that was all Overbury had managed to get into The Tower. 'Me! To go as ambassador to some godforsaken frozen hole! Oh, I know what they all wanted. The plan's clear as day. Get me posted overseas and then, with my brains gone from the scene, get rid of Robert Carr.' Overbury lurched to his feet, taking a swig of his own wine. 'My friend Carr wouldn't last weeks in the ... cess-pit of the Court once I was safely posted overseas!'

'You were offered an ambassadorship? By the King?' asked Overbury's companion, who had damned the King without ever actually seeing him, and might well die without seeing him too. He was not sure whether to laugh at Overbury or bow before him.

'I refused it! Of course! Who is the King to tell me what to do?'

The other prisoner blanched at that. He knew who the King was. The person in whose name he had been arrested. The person in whose name he would most likely be tortured, executed or left rotting in this place. A trace of fear swept into his mind. Was this person, this Sir Thomas Overbury, a wise man to drink with?

'This imprisonment won't last! It was necessary. The King has to do it, for the form's sake! Carr will wheedle and charm James into releasing me soon enough.' Overbury was pacing the narrow room now. 'And then there'll be revenge for those who put me in this stinking pile of stone. Carr needs me. *The King needs me!*'

This man *is* mad, the other prisoner thought. He put his cheap cup down and started to edge towards the door.

'Damn this imprisonment!' Overbury raged, hardly noticing the other man. The Court was a whirlpool of intrigue, current and cross-current, and here he was with his vessel swept into a backwater, land-locked with no oars and no sail. *The inaction was intolerable!*

A few miles away, Henry Gresham felt a quiet satisfaction at the way Overbury had been neutralised. Yet even he did not realise that when one man causes a prey to stop alive in its tracks, he opens up a route for others to give it the death blow.

24

29th June, 1613
The Globe Theatre

'the great globe itself,
Yea, all which it inherit, shall dissolve
And, like this insubstantial pageant faded,
Leave not a rack behind.'
                    SHAKESPEARE, *The Tempest*

'Ready for the big day?' John Hemminge grinned at Henry Condell.

'Are you sure this is ... the right thing?' Condell answered.

'Look,' said Hemminge patiently, as if explaining to a child, 'we're actors, aren't we? We deal in *drama*. Kit Marlowe was a legend in his lifetime – for what he wrote, what he did and for who he was. There's been God knows what rumours about his death ever since it was meant to have happened. This revelation that the great Kit Marlowe didn't die in 1593, that we've been watching his work for twenty years – this is going to be the greatest defeat of death since Jesus! It's the most dramatic moment of our lives. Of anyone who's alive now! Remember poor old Will's speech in *Henry* V? About all those who would rue the day they weren't there at Agincourt? What will people give to have been there on the day when Kit Marlowe revealed himself at The Globe? In front of The King's Men, with The King's Men putting on his cursed play a day later! Henry...' Hemminge moved over to Condell, put his arm around his shoulders. 'Sometimes history asks you a question, and you have to say yes.'

Condell thought for a moment. 'But it's not the truth!' he said. 'You know what those scripts Marlowe sent in were like – *Richard II*, *Richard III*, *Julius Caesar*. Oh, I know they had good bits – but most of them were raving, ranting gibberish! We know it was Will who turned them into plays that the likes of us could perform. Is it right to ditch Will in favour of a man who was nothing but trouble in his first incarnation, and who seems to have brought nothing but trouble in his second? We're denying our friend his inheritance, John. We're taking Will's art away from him.'

'Art!' Hemminge snorted. 'Sod art! What are we players to do with *art*? We're to do with whatever gets them flocking over the river to see us perform. I know we fancy ourselves. We don't put on bear-baiting or cock-fighting after a play,' and he started a mincing walk, affecting a high-pitched voice, 'not like some of those other *low-brow* theatres. But we would, if it meant the difference between living like gentlemen or starving, wouldn't we? Would you starve for art? Would you?'

'Probably not,' said Condell with a long sigh, 'but if I was a king negotiating a treaty, I'd rather do it with Will Shakespeare than Kit Marlowe.'

'Forget it!' said Hemminge. 'We'll make it worth Will's while in money, and it's not as if he doesn't have enough of it already.'

'But I still worry–'

'Don't! He's claimed the credit all his life for stuff other people sent him. Now someone else wants a share. It's poetic justice. He's got his property and his business in Stratford. Not bad for a terrible actor. Don't worry about it! We'll be drinking with him and having a laugh about it in six months' time!'

Condell doubted that but did not show it. He had a part to play in the performance that was even now limbering up. His mind would not be on the show, he knew. It would be on the revelation that would follow it, at the point where the audience might have been expecting a jig. Christopher Marlowe. Killed in a bar-room brawl twenty years ago at the peak of his dramatic powers. Yet not dead. Alive, here in The Globe. And managing to talk to his audience these twenty years past as if from the grave. Dammit, they had to make Marlowe do a sequel to *Doctor Faustus*, before he really did die. Only a matter of time, and short time at that, given the look of him. It had to be a sell out.

Thank God Marlowe had come to them! Hemminge thought exultantly. What if he had gone to The Rose, or even The Red Bull? The mere thought made him grind his teeth. The Globe it was. As it should be. As it had always been.

'When's he turning up?' Condell asked aloud. He and Burbage had left the negotiations to Hemminge.

'He didn't – wouldn't – say,' answered Hemminge, rather distractedly. 'All I know is that he's going to make his appearance from the Lord's Gallery when we've finished the show. He's written ten lines for Burbage to say. Then he'll appear.'

The stage area was covered by a thrusting thatched roof, the underside of which had a painted canopy. Just above it was the turret, from which the cannons were fired for special effects and the flag hoisted and the trumpets blown to mark the start of a show. Sheltered by the roof, immediately under its protection, was the Lord's Gallery. Highly privileged members of the audience, who were willing to pay an extremely privileged price, could watch the play from there, on occasion having to share it with the musicians. For tonight's performance the musicians had been banished to the side of the stage, and no tickets sold to the Lord's Gallery. That would be Marlowe's platform, the podium from which he would return to life and reinvent it.

Hemminge and Condell disengaged, returned to the throng of actors ready and excited to present *All Is True* to a nearly full house.

For how many years had Christopher Marlowe been invisible? All those years of hiding, twenty in all, from the fact of which he was most proud: *he was Christopher Marlowe.* Twenty years of fearing above all to be recognised, of cultivating invisibility. And now this truly poetic opportunity to come back to life once and for all.

He would not enter for the start of the play. That would be too obvious, there could be too many people looking for him. One great moment, his liaison with Lady Jane Gresham and her children, had been spoiled by his being recognised. This time he would wait until the play had commenced, wait for its first great ceremonial moment and then slip in up the deserted stairs to the Lord's Gallery, hooded and cloaked. The knife he had with him was razor sharp. It would cut as a hot knife through butter into the hardened canvas that upheld the thatch in the Lord's Gallery. From out of the incision would tumble the manuscripts of that charlatan Shakespeare's plays, like a surgeon cutting out babies from a woman's flesh. The original manuscripts. He would pick up one or two. His *Richard III* for sure, his *Richard II* by choice, written so long ago in a faraway land, his version so greatly preferable to the one the upstart Shakespeare had chosen to write, with all his 'changes' and his 'improvements'. He would wait then for the end of *All Is True*. The great Burbage would make his announcement – instead of an epilogue for *All Is True* he would read the ten lines that Marlowe had penned and changed and corrected over twenty years of dreaming of this moment. Then he, Christopher Marlowe, would reveal himself. And when the double shock was over, he would announce that The Globe would be presenting tomorrow the first ever performance of his new masterpiece: *The Fall of Lucifer*.

It was a desert outside of The Globe ten minutes after *All Is True* had started. The hawkers had gone their way and only a few hopefuls guarding horses stood outside the whitewashed walls. He slipped in through the back gate, the

397

attendant forewarned and granting him a brief nod. The stairs challenged him. How to climb such stairs when feet did not feel the bite of wood on flesh? The ferocious determination of his anger took him over. Ludicrously, stupidly, he raised each foot high and plotted with his eyes its course as it landed on firm surface.

He was in the Lord's Gallery. The bulge of the thatch was restrained by canvas strung underneath it. He put his own manuscript down, his *Fall of Lucifer*, took out the knife, slashed at the canvas. It hung, sliced, then spewed out two, three rolled papers, each tied with an innocuous ribbon. It was a truly Caesarian birth, except there was no blood on the papers.

On the main stage, Prologue came on, gloriously overdressed, to wolf-whistles from the Pit. There was a curtain drawn across the façade of the Lord's Gallery, blunting and dimming the words spoken beneath.

'*I come no more to make you laugh...*' Prologue pronounced.

'More's the pity!' came the cry from a wag in the Pit, and the audience roared.

...things now
That bear a mighty and a serious brow,
Sad, high, and working, full of state and woe,
Such noble scenes as draw the eye to flow,
We now present...

More and more manuscripts came tumbling from the thatch where they had been hidden. Marlowe crouched on the floor, fumbling, opening, reading.

They were due a great moment on stage. The cue came. The boy playing Anne Boleyn said pipingly, '*You cannot show me...*' and Lord Sandys replied, '*I told your grace they would talk anon...*' On cue, the trumpets sounded, the drums rolled and there were two cracks of thunder from above, shaking the building. Two brass cannon had been placed in the turret, loaded with blank shot, making a terrifying noise.

'Christ Almighty!' said the armourer in charge of the cannon. He had loaded the weak charge of powder that morning, in preparation, and had then gone off for his beer and cheese in the tavern. He knew from the sound of the discharge that something was wrong. Somehow the cannon had been double-shotted. From the mouth of both cannons flew a flaming wadge of powder, still half-burned, followed by two or three sheets of burning wadding that the armourer knew he had never placed in the barrels. It all landed on the thatch on either side of the roof, smoulder-ing. The armourer turned for the buckets of water and sand they kept up there if ever a chamber was to be fired. Damn and blast! They were gone. Where the hell were they?

The thatch took light almost immediately. In the first moments there was more heat than smoke, the only sign of the fire the shimmering heat haze immediately above it. Then, when the fire penetrated the surface layer to the slightly less sun-drained straw, there was a tell-tale, deceptively gentle wisp of smoke.

The audience ignored it, their attention drawn

by the noise of powder, drums and trumpets, oblivious to the fact that a fire had been set in the roof that already no man could put out. Or rather, two separate fires, one on either side of the stage, racing through the thatch to meet in the area above the Lord's Gallery.

A part of Marlowe's mind heard the growing panic as both word and sight of the fire spread among the crowd. Yet it was not that which stopped his hungry examination of the manuscripts he had torn from the roof. It was a noise. There was someone here in the room with him. Hemminge? Condell? He turned with an ingratiating smile on his face. It froze where it lay.

'Good afternoon,' said Henry Gresham casually. 'We've met before, haven't we? And, of course, you know my wife.'

Henry Condell pushed a disconsolate toe into a small pile of the still-smouldering ashes that were all that was left of The Globe. His Globe. They had hoped that 29th June would go down in history: the day that Christopher Marlowe returned from the grave. Well, his wish had been granted. It would go down in history, that was for sure: the day that The Globe burned down. God knew where Marlowe had got to. No one had seen him enter the theatre. Well, he could whistle for Will's precious manuscripts. They had gone up in smoke together with the theatre. Will would be relieved, at least. Marlowe would want his money back, of course, that ludicrous amount of money, and his bloody play performed.

Condell felt a slight lightening of his spirit.

They could still fulfil that part of the bargain, couldn't they? They still had Blackfriars. All right, it was smaller, indoors, but it was a theatre, wasn't it? And they were still the best company of actors in the country, weren't they? All they needed was the script. Marlowe – and he was half beginning to doubt he had been who he said he was – had been due to bring it yesterday. Still, if he'd lived twenty years after his death, a couple of days probably didn't mean too much to him. When he turned up with the manuscript, they'd do a deal. He could have his comeback at Blackfriars, couldn't he?

Condell's eye caught a lump, something blackish, sticking out of the ashes. His nose curled as he advanced and caught an overripe stench. There must have been birds nesting in the thatch to produce that smell of burned flesh. Thank God no one had died in the fire, only birds. It had caught in the roof and the Lord's Gallery had gone first, but the actors had known to evacuate and Marlowe's gold had paid for the gallery to be empty. One man's clothes had caught fire as he ran from the theatre, but another customer had had the wit to put the fire out with bottled ale.

Condell took the stick he had with him and poked at the lump. Half of it had melted with the fierce heat of the fire but the rest was clear enough. An iron neck collar, with a section of chain leading off it. Where on earth had they used that as a prop? *Tamburlaine*, with all its prisoners? Strange he couldn't remember. It must have dropped from the turret or from the Lord's Gallery. A pity The Globe hadn't been built of iron, he thought. If it had, more of it might have survived.

Well, he consoled himself, at least it was an accident. No one, not even Marlowe and certainly not Will Shakespeare, was mad enough to burn down The Globe to make a point.

EPILOGUE

The Cambridge University Library
Cambridge, England
12th August, 2013

'Our revels now are ended.'
SHAKESPEARE, The Tempest

They closed the library at 7.00 p.m. in the long summer vacation. It was irritating because he could only come in August, and the extra two or three hours it remained open in term time would have been a godsend. His old college helped with accommodation, of course, but could do little about food. It was still an expensive luxury, his three weeks intensive research in Cambridge, taken at the expense of his new young wife and even newer children.

The library still had half an hour to go before its official closing time, but the thought police started the campaign to get rid of readers long before that. The litany of announcements stating that books could no longer be borrowed seemed to start at 5.30 p.m. and rise to a positive crescendo by 6.00 p.m. After 6.30, all the library staff, usually so helpful, seemed to start coughing in unison while making busier and busier packing-up noises.

All in all, a strong feeling that his presence was

403

no longer welcome. One box to go of the eight boxes he had ordered that morning of papers pertaining to the life and works of Lancelot Andrewes, sometime Bishop of Ely and Winchester. He wondered if he would ever get this thesis written, with the demands of a parish that seemed to occupy most of Lancashire now being matched by the demands of two young children, and the crucifying worries about money. He was skimping the material, glossing over papers that in the first flush of academic youth he would have pored over for a whole morning.

He had actually started to stand up, on his way to taking the box back to the desk, when something made him stop.

Its catalogue designation stated that it contained unpublished papers relating to sermons penned by the late bishop. Unpromising material, essentially. Lancelot Andrewes had written clearly, fluently and with a commendable sense of discipline. Papers he had discarded as being worth little were likely to be just that, minor memorabilia of no use to someone trying to research the features of a great life. But the new preservation techniques they had applied to these papers were quite extraordinary. The injection process – or was it more properly a process of osmosis? – protected the manuscripts from heat and light depradation, but also meant they could lie on top of each other and be handled by greasy fingers, all the while with an invisible barrier between them and the handler. It also preserved their natural colour. Which was why his attention was drawn to the box. A corner of paper protruded from it. Its colour was different to all the others he had been looking at. More eighteenth-century than seventeenth. He sat back down again, heavily, more tired and dispirited than he cared to admit. Why not untie the box? If at the end of the day he could tell the library they had misfiled a bit of paper, at least he would have achieved something.

It was a folder, he saw, the clumsy eighteenth-century version of a modern wallet file. It had been catalogued with the GRESH prefix. Any historian from the late sixteenth-century onwards knew that was the code for the Gresham family. This was obviously something dating from the first serious attempt to catalogue the vast Gresham papers, started around the 1780s but which sadly showed huge goodwill but little academic rigour. This particular folder had clearly been part of the Gresham collection, but at some stage had been transferred to the Andrewes papers. Interesting, he thought, his brain starting to engage again. A librarian walked heavily past him, sighing. He decided to ignore it. He opened the wallet.

There! The familiar look and feel of the paper Andrewes liked to use, flowing writing in the hand he had now come to see after three years of research as almost the same as his own. Then one final clutch of papers in a different hand, different paper. That could wait. He turned over the first document in Andrewes's hand.

The code! Andrewes had used a simple code for some of his letters, normally when in correspondence with his friend Francis Bacon and he

405

had the need to say something vaguely scurrilous about a clergyman or courtier of their mutual acquaintance. A clever eighteenth-century librarian had spotted the code and who it belonged to, without having the key to translate it. With the marvellous freedom they had had in those days, the librarian had transferred the papers from GRESH to ANDREWE in the hope that someone else would make sense of them.

Despite this effort, it was probably nothing; just more gossip. Yet something made him take the table from his own file and convert the code to English. There was a heading, first of all. A librarian stopped by his work station and noisily began to gather up books, papers and boxes. He ignored him.

To My Lord Henry Gresham, First Baron Granville and Friend to My Heart
I am dying, my friend, and will shortly find if the Maker in whom I believe with all my heart and soul will pass good judgement on my life...

He could hardly believe what he was reading! The undiscovered last will and testament of the great man himself. Written to one of the most notorious figures of the age. A librarian could have exploded by his side and he would not have noticed. His eyes flickered from the original to the key, his hand starting to shake uncontrollably as it grasped the cheap biro and transcribed the code on to the thin, cheap-ruled A4 paper, far, far too slowly for the pressure of his mind.

...you preserved my reputation, and perhaps even my soul, when by your action you took my plays from me and gave them instead to William Shakespeare. I now concede what I found it hard to concede before. They were always his, for all that my vanity sought to persuade me that they are mine...

William Shakespeare? He ran the code again. Shakespeare. William Shakespeare. *Plays?* Plays written by the man credited with a great part of the King James Bible? He was set to move on, translate more, but his eye was caught by the bottom paper in the box. Different, cheaper paper. A closer hand. Paper was expensive in those days. All except bishops and the mightiest of lords wrote close and hard together on such a valuable commodity.

Most Gracious and Honoured Lord,
The honour done to me by the trust of your most recent package knows no bounds, as my admiration of the skill you bring to this most noble art knows no bounds. For this humble spinner of words to offer more than thanks is in itself an insult. It is therefore in a spirit of submission, regard and humility that I seek to question as I do, in the belief that even the noblest of building needs the humble mason to see to its design. It is in this spirit that I ask first of all if to call this work The Magic of Man *is sufficient testimony to its true brilliance and worth, where a proper description of its power is that it unleashes a* tempest *of thought and a* tempest *of wonders into the mind of its audience...*

The letter was *five* pages long. As he moved to continue the translation, his hand skewed the other sheets up, revealing the last page. The signature.

William Shakespeare.

For a moment, the world stopped. Then, slowly, colour, light and sound returned to it, though it was as if the pounding of his heart would never cease.

A librarian was standing by his side. 'I'm sorry, sir, but we're closing now. If I could ask you...'

He looked up at the man and pointed to the end sheet. He gathered up the five sheets as if they were the souls of his two children, held them up as an offering to the librarian.

'A letter,' he said simply. 'A five-page letter *by William Shakespeare.* Hitherto Unknown,' he added.

The librarian looked at him. Something in the moment had caught him, caught them both. Suddenly the librarian felt, knew even, that this was a moment that would be replayed time after time after time, replayed for as long as there were humans who cared about art.

'Not a will, or a legal document, or something about his second-best bed,' he said to the librarian. 'A five-page letter. A letter which seems to go into intimate detail about the authorship of Shakespeare's plays. A letter,' he added for good measure, 'which was found in the archive material of The Cambridge University Library.'

'A letter by ... Shakespeare?' said the librarian in a reverential tone.

'Do you think,' he said, plucking up his courage, 'that just this once you could ask someone if the library could stay open a little longer?'

He saw little of what the future held for him as he proffered the five pages that had lain unseen for so long up to the lowly library employee. The fame, the notoriety, the divorce, the resentment of his children, the abuse and, finally, in his old age, the post as Chaplain of Granville College, where he spent most of the day and night in his rooms, followed by the whispers of the tourists on the rare days when he faced the college quad.

Yet even then his heart told him something. Every book written about Shakespeare, or with even a passing reference to him, redundant now. Every film, every play and every parody – redundant now. The huge, vast and magnificent edifice of Shakespearian scholarship, its pontificating secular bishops, demolished, empty and meaningless. A hundred thousand voices who had sneered at their opponents over four hundred years that of course Shakespeare was, had to be, the only author of his plays, redundant now. A hundred thousand voices who had joined together in societies, campaigned, lobbied and sometimes sneered that of course Shakespeare could not have been the author of the plays credited to him, that they were written by Oxford, Marlowe, Rutland, Derby, all redundant now.

The huge, vast, multi-million dollar industry of Shakespeare, that world-wide industry, all redundant now.

My God, he thought, even then, before more than a tiny portion of the truth settled in his brain. The God in whom he believed every bit as much as Bishop Lancelot Andrewes. What have I done?

HISTORICAL NOTES

The first complete edition of Shakespeare's plays was published in 1623, edited by Shakespeare's old friends John Hemminge and Henry Condell. Both men commented, in what is now known as the First Folio on the speed and ease with which Shakespeare wrote, evidenced by the fact that the copies on which they had based their text had so few corrections or blots on them. Debate over whether or not the man we know as William Shakespeare could have written the world's greatest plays has raged ever since. In this book, I have quoted from the Alexander edition of Shakespeare's *Complete Works*, Collins, London, 1975.

Lancelot Andrewes (1555–1626) had been made Bishop of Ely in 1609. He was a leading figure in the writing of the King James Bible and widely recognised for his wit, his command of English and his mastery of numerous other languages. Widely expected to become the Archbishop of Canterbury, he missed his chance and was appointed Bishop of Winchester in 1619. Throughout his career he refused to comment on political issues of the day.

Francis Bacon, First Baron Verulam and Viscount St Alban (1561–1626) supported King James in his view as to the absolute power of the monarchy. He was appointed Attorney-General in 1613 and Lord Chancellor in 1618. He flattered the then-favourite Buckingham, but was impeached partly because of his link with Buckingham in 1621, sent to The Tower and fined £40,000. Released after a few days, he retired in disgrace and devoted the remainder of his life to writing. He was the first great scientific philosopher in England, and reported to be the most intelligent man of his age.

Robert Carr, Earl of Somerset (1586–1645) lost favour to the new favourite, George Villiers, later Duke of Buckingham, around 1615. He and his wife (he married the infamous Frances Howard, Countess of Essex, in December 1613) stood trial for the murder of Sir Thomas Overbury and were convicted and imprisoned in The Tower until 1621. Carr lived in retirement in the country until his death in 1645.

Sir Edward Coke (1552–1634) was moved sideways in 1613 and Sir Francis Bacon appointed Attorney-General. Contemporary rumour related that one reason for his falling into disfavour concerned certain letters between King James I and Robert Carr. Though coming back into favour at later times in James's reign, Coke became something of a thorn in the side of royalty, seeking to limit in law the power of the king. Aligning himself more and more with the

Parliamentary cause, he was instrumental in drafting the Petition of Rights in 1628.

King James I (b. 1566) lived until 1625, and was succeeded by his second son, Charles.

Sir Thomas Overbury (1581–1613) died of poison in The Tower of London in September, 1613, while being there on the orders of the King.

William Shakespeare (1554–1616) died in April 1616 in Stratford, where he seems to have been remembered as a grain dealer. His death took place shortly after Sir Walter Raleigh was released from The Tower of London in March 1616. For information regarding the controversy over the authorship of Shakespeare's plays, and his possible role as a spy, see the Author's Note on page 15 of this book.

The publishers hope that this book has given you enjoyable reading. Large Print Books are especially designed to be as easy to see and hold as possible. If you wish a complete list of our books please ask at your local library or write directly to:

Magna Large Print Books
Magna House, Long Preston,
Skipton, North Yorkshire.
BD23 4ND

This Large Print Book for the partially sighted, who cannot read normal print, is published under the auspices of

THE ULVERSCROFT FOUNDATION